THE WOLF KING

LAUREN PALPHREYMAN

Cover Design by: Damonza

Copy Edit by: Rachel Rowlands

ISBN: 9798853931916

Contact the author:
www.LaurenPalphreyman.com

Chapter One

Dog fights are barbaric.

They say the fighters in the ring revel in violence. They say the wolf inside them is always looking for a release. Even on nights like tonight when the moon is not full and they look like men.

And don't they deserve violence for what they have done to our lands?

Yet how many will die? And for what?

I shift on the wooden chair, tugging at the high collar of my gown, then pushing an errant strand of red hair out of my face. It's hot in here. Too hot. Claustrophobic.

When I stepped out of the carriage two days ago, the rugged landscape of the Borderlands called to something deep inside of me—even though I have never been this far north before.

Thinking of what lies beyond these stone walls makes me want to rip off this dress, and escape this castle. I want to tear through the untamed grass and feel the wild dandelions between my toes. I want to smell the pine trees, and hear the wind howling through the mountains.

Instead, I take a sip of water, and clasp my hands tightly in my lap. I try not to flinch at the crack of bone that resounds through the Great Hall as one of the males is thrown across the floor. Blood splatters the flagstones by my silk slippers.

Lord Sebastian, sitting on the other side of my father, looks at me, something cruel and hungry in his gaze as he observes my discomfort.

I wonder if he's thinking about tomorrow night, our wedding night.

The thought makes me feel even sicker than the fight.

"Your daughter doesn't approve, Your Highness," he says to my father, only partially misreading the distaste that must be showing on my face.

"She is a woman," my father replies simply.

I bristle. Of course that is all my father sees when he looks at me.

It doesn't matter how many lords I have sweet-talked on his behalf, or how many balls I have attended to serve as a pretty distraction while he makes his plans for the war.

It doesn't matter that I agreed to this marriage to strengthen his kingdom.

"Of course." Sebastian nods, leaning back in his seat as though he doesn't notice the crown atop my father's neat white hair. "These creatures are unpleasant to behold for those of the fairer sex. Though surely she gains enjoyment from them killing one another. The wolf clans have ravaged our lands for centuries. They murder, and brutalize, and steal. To any woman traveling alone, unlucky enough to encounter one, they bring about fates even worse than death." He arches an eyebrow. "If you know what I mean."

"I do," says my father.

Sebastian sips his ale. "Though, I suppose your women do not encounter many Wolves down south—thanks to my armies guarding the border."

"An honorable duty in service of our great kingdom." My father doesn't deign to look at the lord. "And one that comes with its rewards."

"Oh, indeed." Sebastian's eyes darken.

I try not to recoil. I will my body to be a statue, a vessel for the soul within. I allow my mind to glide across those wild mountains, even though I can never go there myself. Even though I will always be a prisoner to castle walls, and a woman's body.

A prisoner. Or a prize. That is all I have ever been. I will be both when I am wed to the lord in exchange for his continued allegiance to my father.

"If she has some sentiment for the creatures, however—"

"She does not."

"Still, she should know that not only is this beastly aggression in their nature, there is glory in fighting, too," says Sebastian. "People throughout the Borderlands learn the names of the top fighters. And those who win their matches tonight will be moved to the more spacious kennels and fed a good supper. Concubines will tend to them too, to help them release their wolf in different ways." He drums his fingers against his cup. "As distasteful as that may be."

"Indeed," says my father.

I watch the muscular, shirtless forms in the ring, snarling and bloody. There is certainly cause to be wary around

Wolves. And yet, as I look at the murderous eyes of the crowd, the coin passing hands, and the way my father's lip quirks as one of the warriors is pummeled to the ground, I wonder if all men are monsters deep down.

I glance at my betrothed. He isn't muscular, or rugged, or nearly as tall as the monsters in the ring. His dark hair is tied neatly at the nape of his neck, not wild like those north of the border wear theirs.

But there is something cruel in the angles of his face, and the way his dark eyes keep running up and down my body. I have been around monsters my whole life, and I can recognize the one that lurks beneath his pale skin.

I think I would prefer someone who looked like a monster to one who was adept at hiding it.

One of the Wolves tears out the other's throat. He grins, and crimson spills down his chin. Nausea rises within me but Lord Sebastian merely smiles and claps as though he is watching a theatrical performance.

"Good show, good show." He clicks his fingers at a couple of stewards. "Escort him to the kennels and clean this up. Then bring the next ones in."

The stewards balk at the task at hand, but lead the bloody wolf away as the Great Hall echoes with noise. People exchange coin, make new bets, and refill their cups.

I can't stop looking at the body though.

It's so still. It looks so heavy. It makes my body feel heavy, too. Perhaps he was a monster. Perhaps he had a wolf beneath his skin that came out when the moon was full. Right now, he just looks like a man. A dead man. A man who will never run through those howling mountains again.

Two stewards cross the hall, grab his arms, and drag him across the stone floor as though he is a piece of meat.

I take a sip of water to steady my trembling hands. At my side, Lord Sebastian and my father enter into a conversation about army numbers on the northern border.

I'm putting my beaker back down on the table when silence falls. It is followed by an excited murmur as two more males—two more Wolves—enter the ring.

My attention is first taken by the one in front. He is young. Too young for this kind of violence, wolf or not. He must be sixteen at most—four years my junior. His coppery hair sticks up in tufts as if he's been frantically running his hands through it. There is fear and sadness etched into his expression, yet his jaw is set. It's as if he knows there is no hope and has resigned himself to his fate. Something in that expression feels familiar. It fills me with anger that I don't dare to summon for my own situation.

When I turn my gaze to his opponent, I see why he knows that hope is lost.

"It took five men to bring the big one in," Lord Sebastian tells my father. "He killed three of them. He doesn't talk much, but we think he's one of the alphas—possibly from the Highfell Clan. Quite a specimen, isn't he?"

The larger male is the epitome of the wild and rugged mountains where he must have come from. He is tall, with a strong jawline, and his muscular body looks like it is carved from rock. His unkempt hair is dirty-blond, almost the color of straw, and it's shorn closely to his head at the sides in a style I have never seen in the south. He stands, still and expressionless, and the crowd howls and screeches like the wind around him.

"Indeed." My father runs a hand over his neat white beard. "And what was he doing this far south?"

"Who knows with these creatures."

The alpha looks at me. And those eyes. . . they're the dark green of the forest, and they brim with hatred. No one has looked at me like that before. My mouth dries as we stare at one another.

And yet, my soul stirs.

"It won't be much of a fight," my father says, as if he is discussing the weather, not the fates of two living beings.

"No." Sebastian smiles cruelly. "We thought we'd break him in tonight. We have something a little more exciting planned for him at the celebrations tomorrow night."

The alpha stares at me, his jawline hard. He is still as stone, but there is violence in his eyes. I will myself to be that statue again, to be that vessel for my soul, and I look right back at him even though my heartbeat skitters.

"Well," says Sebastian, clicking his fingers at the Wolves in manner that could be deemed brave or foolish if it weren't for the armed guards standing around the ring. "Begin."

A muscle feathers in the alpha's jaw.

Nausea rises in me as the young man's face drains of color. He's going to die, and everyone—he, the alpha, the crowd— knows it. He doesn't break eye contact with the man who towers before him.

He is brave, then.

Courage, I will him, remembering that my mother said the same to me once. *Have courage, little one.*

The alpha's big fist clenches at his side. It could be my imagination, but I think the younger opponent dips his head—as if in submission.

A growl vibrates in the alpha's throat, and in it I feel the ripple of hatred and rage that he is about to unleash. It claims me too. Hatred so thick and bitter I can taste it. Hatred at this towering giant for what he is about to do.

He roars—loud and wild—a war cry that ricochets off the stone walls of the hall.

The fight is over in minutes. It is bloody, and violent, and I hear the crack of bone at some point, along with howls of pain from the younger man. The alpha holds him down on the ground, a hand curled around his neck.

He raises a fist to deal the death blow—pausing with it in mid-air as if savoring the kill.

The young one looks into my eyes rather than at the monster on top of him.

And I cannot bear it.

This is not right.

"Stop!" I jump to my feet.

The alpha stills. The crowd quiets. Sebastian looks at me, eyes narrowed, while a muscle tightens in my father's jaw.

My heart is pounding in my chest.

Yet I do not sit back down.

"This is not sport." I force my voice to sound steady, even though my knees are shaking. "This is murder."

The air in the hall thickens. The crowd turn their anger, their bloodlust, from the Wolves to me. The alpha's shoulders rise and fall, hard.

My breathing quickens. I shouldn't have said anything. I am a woman. A statue. It is not my place.

Yet I do not sit down.

"Putting down an animal is hardly murder," says Sebastian, a bite to his tone. "Or does my betrothed have a thing for beasts? Do you know that they take their women like dogs? I have heard that some women—"

"That's enough." My father's command rumbles across the hall.

Sebastian dips his head to the king. "I did not mean to offend, Your Highness."

"Aurora is tired. She will excuse herself and go to bed," says my father.

I have disappointed him, and shame heats my cheeks.

But I don't move.

Neither does the alpha. His arm is still raised, his gaze trained on his victim as he awaits the conclusion of our conversation. The boy's wide eyes hold mine. Tears and blood stain his cheeks.

"Let him live." My mouth is as dry as bone.

Sebastian is barely containing his rage. He clearly does not like to be challenged in front of his people. "What use is he to me alive, my love?"

"He is young. Fit. Put him to work in the stables." I want to disappear, but I force myself to look at him, to smile. "A wedding gift to me, my lord."

Sebastian appears to consider. He stands and takes my hands; his fingers are cold and curl around mine like a vice. I push down the disgust that is rising inside me at his touch. He smiles back.

"Very well, my love. A wedding gift." He leans close, bringing his lips to my ear. "You know, if you have a fondness for these creatures, and wish to be taken like a common mutt, that can be arranged tomorrow night after the ceremony. Who knows, perhaps I will throw you into the kennels afterward.

Perhaps I will even let this alpha have a go with you, seeing as you have denied him his kill."

Every muscle in my body hardens as the monster I knew was lurking inside him makes his presence known to me.

He releases me and turns to his people.

"The fight is over," he says, and the monster slips back beneath his skin. "A gift to my betrothed, who is as gentle-hearted as she is beautiful."

The muscles in the alpha's shoulders are knotted and hard. Hot, raw anger radiates from him. It's as if the wolf inside him is furious that he doesn't get to kill someone.

He drops his arm to his side.

I'm breathing fast. My dress is too tight and the air too hot.

The alpha stands and turns away from the crowd. He lets a couple of guards cuff him.

"Put them back in their kennels," says Sebastian. "The winner can go to the nicer ones. It's only fair, and he will need his rest for what we have planned for tomorrow. Put the loser back with the rest. If he survives the night, we will find a job for him as my betrothed wishes. These creatures prey on the weak, though, so I doubt there will be much left of him by morning."

A couple of armed guards lead the alpha away through the oak doors at the end of the hall, while a steward hurries forward to drag his opponent off the floor.

"My betrothed—like many women from the south—hasn't the stomach for this sport, and why should she when she is such a beautiful flower? She will be taking her leave now, before the next fight. She needs to prepare for tomorrow night."

His eyes harden, and my heart thuds frantically against the cage I keep it in. I dip my head regardless, and, steadying my trembling hands, I curtesy.

Without a backward glance, I hurry across the ring. I try to ignore how my skirts trail in the blood as I head through the doors.

Just ahead, the two fighters from the ring are being escorted away.

The alpha is almost at the end of the corridor. Behind him, the young wolf is drooping over the shoulder of the steward, his breathing ragged. He is not in good shape. If someone does not tend to his wounds he won't be working in the stables any time soon. And if what Sebastian says is true—about Wolves preying on the weak. . .

"Wait!" I internally curse the shake in my voice. I should not be afraid. This is to be my home.

The alpha stills, and the torchlight from the corridor flickers across his hard profile. Though he's twenty feet or so away from me, his body heat washes over me. His scent does, too—sweat and blood and the mountains. My heart races, but I turn my attention to the injured boy.

"Take the young one to the nice. . . *kennel*." The inhuman word catches in my throat.

I know these men are not human—even though they look it. I know that, being from the south, I've not had to face constant attacks from the Wolves like the north have. Perhaps if I had, I wouldn't judge. The way the alpha fought in the ring proves the Wolves have little mercy within them.

Still, it feels wrong.

Ahead, the muscles in the alpha's arms tense. He looks as if he's going to turn around.

But then the guards push him through the next set of doors and he's escorted away.

I let loose a breath.

The steward who is propping up the boy turns to me, his thick eyebrows knitting together. "The lord said—"

"I am to be your lady, and I'm the daughter of your king." I stand straighter.

I have played pretend all of my life. I have smiled when my heart was breaking, I have laughed when I have been disgusted. I have swallowed my rage when a lord has been handsy with me on the dancefloor at a ball.

I can play the part of the formidable lady of this castle.

I raise my chin. "Put him in the nice kennels, and make sure he has a decent supper."

I skirt past the two of them, and make my way through the labyrinth of stone corridors to my chambers in the northern wing.

There are a couple of handmaids waiting for me, and I allow them to dress me for bed in a long-sleeved white nightdress that reaches my ankles. I dismiss them, walking past the four-poster bed to stare out of the window at the rugged mountains in the north. The sky is lit by a crescent moon.

A growing restlessness writhes inside me as the trees sway in the distance and the wind batters the walls of the stone castle. What I said to the steward was true. Tomorrow I will be the lady of this castle. Yet I have no power.

I never have.

I have no power to take my leave of this place—to breathe in the scent of heather and fern, to bathe in bubbling brooks, or drink in local taverns. I have no power to speak to whom I choose, or form friendships, or to fall in love.

And I have no power to save the young wolf who will surely meet his end—if not tonight, then tomorrow, when he is deemed not fit to work and put back into the bad kennels.

I grit my teeth, then I grab a cloak from my wardrobe and throw it on.

Powerless as I am, I cannot do nothing.

The memory of my mother's voice chases away the fear.

They will make you feel as if you have no choice, she told me before she died. *But there is always a choice. Have courage, little one.*

Perhaps I have the power to do one small thing before I am wed to the lord and left here to rot. Even if getting caught could mean losing my life.

Even if it may put me in close proximity to that monstrous alpha.

I put up my hood to hide my recognizable red hair. Then I grab a satchel, and slip out of my room.

I am going to the kennels.

Chapter Two

The castle is quiet, most of its inhabitants sleeping or at the dog fight, so I reach the staircase leading down to the kennels undetected.

As I walk onward, the air gets colder and damper. It's as if I am heading into the jaws of a great beast—the darkness below a hungry mouth waiting to swallow me.

When I'm faced with the two guards flanking the heavy iron door at the bottom, I adjust my hood to make sure my hair is hidden. I pray to the Sun Goddess that they do not recognize me. Beneath my cloak, the weight of my satchel is heavy against my thigh. It's full of the items I stole from the apothecary—fabric for bandages, alcohol, willow bark, and water. Items that reveal my intent to help the enemy.

"Alright, love?" says one of the guards. "What are you doing down here?"

I still my nerves. I remember what Sebastian said about how the Wolves are rewarded for their wins.

"I've been sent from the brothel," I say, making my voice sound as husky as I can.

The guard who spoke snickers and opens the door. He passes me a key.

"It's silver," he says as I take it. "Burns if it comes in contact with their skin. But if they try anything, give us a knock and we'll come put them down."

The other guard looks at me with disgust when I slip inside. I am disgusted too. Disgusted at the thought of a woman coming down here and providing such a. . . service to these creatures. Disgusted that he believed I am one of those women.

When they lock me in, I am faced with a long corridor—a damp stone wall adorned with flickering torches on one side, and tall iron bars on the other.

The air is musky with mildew and sweat and blood, and my breath mists in front of my face. There is no one within the cell on my right, but ahead, I can hear a man snarling something under his breath, followed by whimpers.

Pulling my cloak close to me, I make my way down the corridor.

Someone growls from the shadows on my right and I hurry on to the next cell, where the wolf who won the fight that took place before the alpha's is leaning against the bars, a grin on his bloody face. As I pass the next cell, a male with dark tangled hair walks alongside me.

"Hello, sweetheart. I've got something in here for you." He grabs his crotch through his green kilt. "Do you want to come see?"

I look away, quickening my pace. I reach the final two cells.

The alpha is sitting against the wall with his arms resting on his raised knees. He's snarling something through the bars at the shuddering form huddled on the floor in the middle of the final cell. My jaw sets. Hasn't he tormented the boy enough?

He shuts up as I approach and I feel his full attention on me as, hands shaking, I slip the key into the lock.

"You shouldn't be here, Princess," says the alpha as the lock clicks and I slip into the cell. His voice is as gruff as gravel and it's thick with the accent of those north of the border.

My face is concealed by my hood, so I don't know if he has recognized me by some other means. Perhaps that is what he calls all women.

I kneel on the straw by the young wolf, then shrug off my cloak so I can access my supplies.

The male in the green kilt whistles as my nightgown is revealed. A low growl reverberates in the alpha's throat, and he quietens.

I ignore them both as I slip off the satchel.

I am no stranger to healing—my mother was ill for a lot of my childhood, and she often had bruises and scrapes. But this young male looks particularly bad. His face is bloody, and he's writhing in pain.

"Shh." I push the coppery hair off his sticky forehead. "It's okay. What's hurting? Tell me what's wrong."

I feel the alpha's eyes on me. "I dislocated his arm," he says.

"Be quiet," I snap.

I wet a rag, and start to wipe the blood from the young male's face. Surprisingly, the bruising beneath it is not as bad as I expected. The cut across his eyebrow looks like it has already healed, and his nose is crooked, but barely swollen.

"Bring him over here so I can deal with him."

The boy winces.

I turn to glare at the alpha. "Haven't you done enough?"

He stands up and leans against the bars between the two cells, dangling his big arms through the gaps. It's cold in here, and even though he is dressed in nothing but a kilt, his body heat washes over me.

My pulse quickens. If he stretched, he could almost touch my hair. His expression gives nothing away as he watches me.

"You're brave to come here," he says.

On my knees and in my nightgown, he seems even more imposing than he did when he was causing havoc in the ring. Even with the bars between us.

My jaw sets. "I've faced worse monsters than you."

I'm not sure if it's a trick of the torchlight flickering across his face, but I think the corner of his lip twitches.

"Bring the lad to me," he says. "And let's see how brave you really are."

I turn away from him, and lift my leather flask to the boy's mouth. He takes a small sip of water before grimacing and laying his head back on the dirt. He's clutching one of his arms, and it looks red and swollen. I run my hand softly over his elbow and he groans. If I bandage it up tightly before it starts to heal, and create a sling, it might help. First, I pull the willow bark from my satchel.

"For the pain," I say.

"They said you were a beauty, but I didn't know you were a redhead," says the alpha.

"What has that got to do with anything?"

"Not a hair color you tend to see south of the border. Perhaps you have ancestors in the Northlands."

"I don't."

I put the willow bark in the boy's mouth and he chews, looking up at me with bloodshot eyes.

"My people say those with red hair have fire in their souls," says the alpha.

I glare over my shoulder. My mouth dries at the intensity in his gaze, and I swallow. "I don't."

"Hm."

I turn back to the shuddering boy.

"Stop your whining," says the alpha.

Something wild and angry grows inside me, and before I can tame it, I find myself on my feet, whirling to face him.

"How dare you speak to him." At my full height, my eyes align with his shoulders and I have to tilt back my head to glare up at him. "Look at him. He's just a boy. . . and you. . . you did that to him. You're a bully. And a monster. And a bloody horrible *brute*."

This time, I'm sure the corner of his lip quirks. "No fire in your soul, huh?"

"He's just a child. And you were going to kill him. Are you pleased with yourself? Have you no shame?"

All the humor drains from his face and his expression darkens. "It was your *betrothed* that put me in that ring."

"So you bear no accountability for your actions? Is that what you're saying?"

A low growl reverberates in his throat. "I had no choice."

"There is always a choice," I snarl back. "It may not be an easy choice. But it is a choice nonetheless."

His breathing is hard, and he swallows—as if pushing down whatever emotion my words have provoked. "What would you know about choices, *Princess*?"

"Enough."

He drags his teeth over his bottom lip. "I wonder if you'll be so brave when there are no bars to separate us."

"There will always be bars to separate us."

"Will there?"

My heartbeat quickens at his tone—at the implication in it—and from the curl of his lips I wonder if he can hear it.

He turns his attention to the boy as though he is done with me. "Get over here," he snarls.

"No," the boy whimpers.

"Stop being such a bloody great wuss."

"I told you to leave him alone," I snap.

"And I told him to get over here." The alpha's eyes narrow on the boy. "And it's the second time he's disobeyed me in just as many days."

"Why on earth would he obey you?"

He sighs as though I've asked the most exasperating question in the world. "What is he wearing?"

"What?"

He nods at the boy, and I look down at him—at his pale slender chest, then the red tartan kilt he wears.

"And what am I wearing?" he asks.

I turn back to the alpha, noting his kilt, made from red tartan. My gaze inadvertently drops to his calves, which are as thick as tree trunks. I swallow hard.

"They're the same, aye?" he says.

"So?"

"So! You destroy our lands, steal from us, do your experiments on us, kill us, imprison us, and still you don't know a damn thing about us." He shakes his head, and sighs. "We're from the same clan. He's one of mine. The wee shite's called Ryan." He glares at the boy. "And if he doesn't get his arse over here, then he won't be coming with me when I leave."

"I. . . Why would he. . ." I frown. "What do you mean, when you leave?" I fold my arms and look pointedly at the cell he is confined within. "I hardly think you're going anywhere anytime soon."

He shifts, folding his corded forearms through the bars. "No?"

"No."

"Why do you think I'm here, Princess?" He looks pointedly around his dank cell. "For the accommodation?"

"You're here because you're an enemy of the kingdom. And you're a prisoner. And a wolf. And," I add, somewhat shrilly, unsure of why he's getting under my skin so much, "because you killed three men and almost killed this poor boy."

He shrugs a big shoulder. "Be that as it may, I don't plan on staying for long."

I grit my teeth, my breathing faster than it should be. I don't know what is wrong with me. I am a master of my emotions. I have been all of my life. I have pushed them down far enough that most of the time, I forget they are even there.

Why is this prisoner—this *wolf*—provoking this wildness inside me? "So, what? You actually think you're going to escape?"

"Aye."

"If you're so certain, why on earth would you tell me? That's not very smart, is it?"

"What are you going to do, Princess? Tell your *betrothed*?" He shakes his head. "I don't think so. Because that would mean telling him you came down here. And I don't think you'll want him to know about that, will you?"

My blood turns cold and the alpha smiles wickedly.

"Now *you* have a choice, Princess. Bring the lad to me so I can fix his arm, then you can make him a sling. Or leave him here to suffer."

"That's. . . that's why you want him to come to you?"

"His shoulder is dislocated." He points at the whimpering form on the ground. His hand is close enough that I feel a waft of air at the movement. "Look at how his arm is jutting out at that angle. If I don't fix pop it back into the joint, he'll lose use of it until he can see a healer up north. And that'll slow me down. Bring him to me so I can fix it. And be quick about it."

He speaks like a man who is used to people doing as he tells them. Yet he is in no position to be barking orders at me.

"You were going to kill him," I say.

"And you stopped me. And now I'm going to save him. But only if you do as I say."

I furrow my brow. "If this is a trick to. . . to try and get the key from me or something, you should know that it's silver, and there are armed guards outside anyway."

"Aye, I figured as much. It's no trick. And I don't need you to get me out of the *kennels*."

He says the word with the same distaste as I did earlier.

I look into his eyes, almost evergreen in the darkness. Again, I feel that strange tug on my soul. And for some strange reason I believe him.

I sigh and, as if sensing my submission to his will, he inclines his head. "Bring the lad to me."

I take a deep breath, then I crouch down. "Ryan," I say softly. "You need to get up so we can help you."

He groans. "I don't want to."

"You have a choice," I tell him. "But if you choose not to get up, you'll likely die."

"I wish I'd never come here." He glares over my shoulder.

"Aye, I wish you hadn't too," says the alpha darkly. "But here you are. So stop acting like an insolent pup and do as you're told."

Ryan's sharp jaw sets, and he looks as if he's about to throw a temper tantrum. But then he sits and I see the alpha is right. His shoulder is swollen, and his arm is out of place. It must hurt.

I help him up, and he drags his feet across the dirty floor as I lead him across the cell.

"Good lass," says the alpha.

Something heats inside me. Who does he think he is, speaking to me like that? He is a prisoner, someone from the wolf clans no less, and I'm daughter of the king. I glare at him but he has already turned his attention to Ryan.

He turns the boy around, then pulls him backwards into the bars, hooking a large arm across his chest. He grabs his good shoulder to hold him steady. Ryan whimpers, his breathing growing rapid, as the alpha takes hold of his other forearm and runs his hand down it.

The alpha's eyes flick to mine. "Why do the guards think you're here?"

"I. . ." I force myself to meet his gaze, even though I feel suddenly warm. "I told them I was from the brothel."

He smirks and my cheeks flame. "That should work."

He makes a sudden movement.

"FUCK!" roars Ryan.

The horrible wolf in the next cell chuckles. The alpha grins, too.

"Ah, be quiet, you big wuss." He musses Ryan's hair as the boy mutters obscenities under his breath. He shoves him gently toward me. "You'll need to make a sling for—"

"I know," I snap.

I lead Ryan to the wall and sit him down, grabbing the fabric from my satchel and crouching before him. His face is bright red and his breathing is shuddery as I slide the bandage beneath his forearm, then bring the top end around the back of his neck.

"You don't like being told what to do," observes the alpha.

"No one likes to be told what to do."

"Some people like it." I can hear the smirk in his tone and I look up at him, confused. He shakes his head. "Never mind."

He watches me in silence as I tie the two ends of the bandage together above Ryan's collarbone.

I'm just finishing up when the main iron door screeches open.

I still, panic writhing inside my stomach as I imagine what Sebastian will do to me if he catches me here.

A woman's sultry laughter seeps through the darkness and I let loose a breath.

"Who's been a good boy?" she coos, as if speaking to a dog, and I tense. "Who's a good boy and deserves his treat?"

The horrible wolf who whistled at me chuckles. "I've been a good boy," he leers. "You can come in here, sweetheart."

"Oh, yes?" Her sweet rose-scented perfume permeates the dank air as her footsteps get closer. "And what about you?

They say you're an alpha. Is that true? I've always wanted to bed an alpha."

I look over my shoulder.

A pretty woman with long blonde hair leans against the bars of the alpha's cell. Her lips are painted bright red, and her cheeks are rosy. Her dark cloak hangs over one shoulder and reveals that she's not wearing anything underneath.

She flutters her eyelashes, but the alpha keeps his back to her.

"No?" she coos. "Are you sure? How about now?"

She drops her cloak, revealing her naked body. I tense, my eyes widening. I have never seen anyone unclothed before. A muscle feathers in the alpha's jaw and his gaze remains on me.

"Very well, pet." She pouts. "I suppose you'll just have to watch."

She unlocks the door to the next cell and saunters inside, hips swaying.

"That's it, sweetheart," leers the horrible wolf, looking her up and down. "Get over here. I've got something for you."

He pushes her to her knees and my heartbeat starts pounding too fast, too hard, as she smiles up at him. What is she doing? Why is she. . .?

The alpha before me shifts to the side, partially blocking them from view. "It's time to leave, Princess."

His low voice doesn't cover the wet sucking sound that comes seconds later, and the horrible things the wolf is snarling under his breath in the next cell. All the warmth drains from my body and I'm frozen.

Is she. . .? With her mouth?

"Princess." There is a command in the alpha's tone.

I'm distracted by the blur of movement in the shadows of the cell beyond as the wolf flips the woman over so she's on her hands and knees, and mounts her from behind.

If you wish to be taken like a common mutt, that can be arranged tomorrow night after the ceremony. Sebastian's threat floods my mind and my heart beats faster, a trapped bird unable to escape its cage.

The man grunts, thrusting harder, his face twisted and ugly. The woman's hair swishes in front of her face as her whole body jerks. Her hands slide through the dirt and her knees scrape against the cold hard ground. She must be in pain. And the sounds she's making. . .

Dots dance in front of my eyes.

Tomorrow night. Tomorrow night this will happen to me.

The shadows tighten around me, bind me. I can't move. I can't breathe. I am trapped. A prisoner. I'm always a prisoner. I cannot escape this.

Who knows, perhaps I will throw you into the kennels afterwards.

The woman's moans become louder, high-pitched.

"That's it," snarls the wolf. "Take it, you dirty little bitch."

"*Yes*," she cries back. "*Yes*."

Perhaps I will even let this alpha have a go with you, seeing as you have denied him his kill.

My throat tightens. I can't swallow. I can't breathe. I clutch my chest. The darkness swims around me. The air is liquid and I'm drowning in it.

"Princess," the alpha barks. "Look at me." His rough voice cuts through the swirling whirlpool that is sucking me under—strong and demanding obedience.

Slowly, I turn my head.

"That's it. Keep your eyes on me." He's crouching down so he's almost at my level, big hands curling around the bars between us. I don't know when he moved. "Deep breaths."

I do as he says, and some of the tightening of my chest loosens.

"That's it. Breathe in. Breathe out." The raging waters become lapping waves as his voice washes over me. "Breathe in. Breathe out."

Everything feels far away. Horrible sounds echo around the cells, but I keep my gaze fixed on the face in front of mine. I keep breathing. His expression is unreadable.

"That's it. Easy now." His voice is surprisingly gentle. "Good lass." I snap back into my body. "Are you okay?"

"Fine," I say, my tone clipped, my voice hoarse. Because I'm not, and he knows it, and now I am weak. I avert my gaze, but something pulls it back again. "I'm fine."

He studies my face, and I study his. He is younger than I first thought. Beyond the warrior physique, the layers of grime, and unkempt hair, there is brightness in his eyes and a youthful glow to his skin. I think he may be in his mid-twenties at most.

The noises behind him get louder and faster. "You'd best be taking your leave now, Princess. The lad's okay. You did a brave thing coming here."

I turn to Ryan, who is watching me with a strange expression.

The horrible wolf roars.

Ryan's nose wrinkles. "I wish I'd never fucking come here," he mutters again.

I take a deep breath, then stuff the spare bandages and the water flask back in my satchel. I throw on my cloak, pulling the hood over my head. It takes me two attempts to do up the fastening due to my trembling fingers.

I hurry out of the cell and lock it behind me.

The alpha stalks across his cell as I pass, his eyes dark. I'm only a few paces away when he says something.

I halt. "What?"

For a moment, all I can hear is the horrible panting sound from the next cell.

"He won't touch you," says the alpha—his voice barely audible.

"Who?"

"Sebastian. He won't touch you." His tone is so dark, so certain. I turn to face him—raising my head to meet his gaze.

"He is to be my husband," I say softly.

Again, I am reminded of the rugged mountains when I look at him. His stance is dominant, powerful, and his face could be carved from rock. His eyes, though. . . those eyes. . . something that looks like remorse, or regret, passes over them.

"No," he says, his voice equally quiet. "No, he isn't."

Does his plan for escape involve murdering Sebastian? Something inside tells me I should feel *something* about that. Sadness. Gladness. *Anything.*

I feel nothing.

I wonder if my body, this vessel that I trap my soul within, is slowly turning to stone. A statue for men like Sebastian to look at that has no purpose, no desire, no feeling.

And yet. . . as the alpha stares at me, something stirs.

I swallow hard. Then I look away—averting my eyes from the horrible wolf and the naked woman—and hurry to the main iron doors.

I feel alpha's eyes on my back as I'm let out of the kennels.

Chapter Three

I am to be wed tomorrow, and I cannot sleep.

I lie in bed, the covers pulled up to my chin, and listen to the wind howling outside of the window. Shadows dance across the ceiling, and there is a bite to the air now there are only embers in the grate.

I was trained for this.

I was trained to be beautiful and silent and obedient. I forged a prison for my wild and angry soul and I waited for the day to come when I was to be wed.

A small part of me dreamed that one day I would fall in love like the princesses in my mother's stories, that one day I would be free.

But I always knew there would be no happy ending for me.

So I waited and I dreaded.

And now it is here.

Tomorrow I will wed a man who makes Wolves fight as if they are dogs. Who threatened to take me like a mutt. Whose leery eyes make my skin crawl.

A man who I do not know, I do not love.

He won't touch you.

The alpha's promise resounds in my mind. I should tell someone what he said. I should tell someone he means to escape. I should tell someone he made a threat to the lord, to my betrothed. He is a wolf. An enemy.

Yet I lie here in the darkness, listening to the wind howling outside the castle.

And I remain as silent as I was trained.

It was an idle threat, anyway. There is no way that he can escape.

We are both prisoner to these walls.

Still, I glance at the silver letter opener on the bedside table before sleep finally takes me.

***

Sometimes I dream I am a statue in the palace gardens.

People wander around me, commenting on my shape, my form.

Her eyes look almost alive, they say, *when the light hits them.*

And all the while, I'm trapped inside myself. Screaming. But my lungs are stone and my lips are hard and my mouth tastes like old cemeteries. So no one hears me, no one cares.

Other times, I'm back in that church and I'm so scared I think I'm going to pass out.

I don't cry, though. Father doesn't like it when I cry. And the priest is in front of me with his crop.

I didn't sin, I protest.

Oh, child. All women sin. Your mother was a sinner, and you are a sinner too. Do you want the Sun Goddess to be angry? No? Good. Turn around.

Other times, I'm running. I'm running through the forest as fast as I can. The wind is in my hair, and twigs snap beneath my bare feet. I am free, but I am afraid. Because something is chasing me and I fear what will happen if it catches me.

My mother's voice ricochets off the trees as I burst into the moonlight.

Wake up, Aurora.
Wake up!

***

My eyes jolt open.

Rain hammers against the walls, and the fire in the grate is completely out. As my vision adjusts to the darkness, I realize what woke me. There is faint shouting coming from somewhere within the castle.

I frown, my breath misting in front of my face.

Outside, something howls. The wind?

The door to my chambers bursts open and I sit upright, grasping the bedsheets.

"What is the meaning–?" The words die in my throat.

The horrible dark-haired male from the kennels prowls into the room. He's still wearing the green kilt from earlier, but now he wears a linen shirt and boots as well. He smells acrid, like sweat mixed with something else unpleasant.

His gaze hones in on me and there's something predatory in it. "Hello, sweetheart."

Visions of his face, twisted and red, as he mounted the woman in the cells, flash before my eyes.

Two other men flank him, wearing the same green tartan. The bald one is tall and muscular with a dark beard and a serious expression. The other has ratlike features and mousy-brown hair that hangs to his chin.

Blood drips from their daggers onto the flagstones.

My heart stills. Time slows down.

One of them—the muscular one—closes the door behind him.

"You were right about her, Magnus," says the ratlike one. "She's quite a beauty." He sniffs the air and grins. "Mm. So sweet and innocent too."

"Aye." Magnus's thin lips curl into a twisted smile. "Not for long, though."

I scramble from the four-poster bed and almost trip over my covers. I grab the letter opener from my bedside table and brandish it before me. Even though it is made of silver, it is a pathetic means to defend myself against three bloodthirsty Wolves.

They know it too.

The ratlike one snickers as Magnus stalks closer.

"Leave now." My voice is shaking. "And Lord Sebastian will let you live."

"Your lord is a bit busy right now," says Magnus. "It's just us, and you. I thought we could take the time to get to know each other better. What do you say?"

I want to clutch my arms over my body as he looks me up, but I do not want to lower the small blade. My nightdress is too thin and the ratlike one leers at my breasts. My nipples are hard due to the cold.

"Get. Out," I hiss.

Magnus chuckles. "Come on, sweetheart. There's no need to be like—"

The door to my room swings open.

"*Out.*" A low growl comes from the doorway.

The three males stiffen.

The alpha stands there. He's wearing a crumpled white linen shirt and high boots as well as his red tartan kilt. His face looks like it is carved from thunder and stone. "*Out.*"

Magnus swallows, before a smile twists back onto his face and he turns. "It's just a bit of fun—"

"*Now,*" says the alpha.

The alpha is bigger than the other three wolves, and there's something in his eyes that promises death. Magnus seems to realize that, and shakes his head.

"Come on, lads. Time to get the fuck out of here." He grins and gives me a mock bow. "Until we meet again, Your Highness."

The alpha shuts the door behind them. My mouth is dry and my head is whirling. Is he my savior? Or does he have something even worse in mind?

"Are you hurt?" he asks.

I hold up the letter opener and curse my trembling hand.

"I'm sorry about them. Their whole clan—" His green eyes darken. "They'll pay for it later."

"You need to leave."

"Aye. I do." He swallows, and his gaze moves from the wardrobe to the crescent moon through the window. As the silence extends between us, I hear more shouting in the castle. "Do you have a warm cloak?"

"Why?"

"It's cold outside."

"I don't see why that is of any relevance to me," I say, my voice higher in pitch than I'd like it to be.

A flicker of regret crosses his face. "Aye, you do."

A humorless laugh escapes my lips and I step back. "You can't possibly think I'm going with you."

"You are, Princess."

"You. . . you won't hurt me," I say.

He sighs. "That's where you're wrong. I won't kill you. And I won't lay a finger on you in the way those bastards were threatening. But you're coming with me. And if I have to overpower you in order to make that happen, I can't promise that won't hurt."

I narrow my eyes, tilting my chin up. "I helped you, earlier."

"Aye, you did. And I appreciate that, Princess. I really do. It doesn't change the fact that I'm taking you with me."

When he steps forward, I brandish the letter opener before me. "Stay back."

The blade is laughably small in relation to his huge build, but he raises his hands placatingly. "Please calm down."

Emotions that have lain dormant inside me for years awaken.

"How dare you tell me to calm down."

Every time my father, or the priest, or my brother dismissed me for daring to show emotion, flashes before my eyes and feeds the wildness growing inside me.

"You come into my chambers in the middle of the night," I slice the blade through the air, "thinking you can steal me from my bed." I cut the space between us. "And you act as if I am overreacting?"

I jab the letter opener at his stomach and he grabs my wrist.

I still. His hand is callused and strong as it wraps around the bone.

"*Get off me*," I hiss.

He bends my wrist and the tiny blade hits the stone floor and clatters. Crouching down, he picks it up. He winces when the silver comes into contact with his skin.

"You can have this back when you behave yourself."

When he pockets it, I kick his chest. He grabs my ankle, putting a hand on my lower back to steady me. Our eyes meet, and my breath hitches at the intensity of his expression.

"What do you want with me?" I ask.

"I think you can help me end this war."

I shake my head. "Kidnapping me will only worsen it. You're going to get yourself killed, you fool."

"If that is the price I must pay to save my people, I will gladly pay it. So, what will it be, Princess? Will you grab your cloak and walk out of this room with me? Or am I going to throw you over my shoulder? You have a choice. It's not a very good one." He mimics my words from earlier, a grim smile on his face. "But it's a choice nonetheless."

"You bastard." I shake my head. "You can't possibly think you'll get all the way out of the castle."

I can hear shouting and the thunder of hooves in the grounds below.

"See? They're coming for you." I jerk my head toward the window, and a strand of red hair catches in my mouth. "If you go now, you have a chance to—"

Before I know what's happening, he's on his feet, and I'm over his shoulder. I shriek, punching his back.

"Are you insane?" I snarl. "They'll skin you alive for—"

He throws open my wardrobe and the words die in my throat at the inopportune moment for my threat.

In the current circumstance, guilt should not flood so powerfully through my chest at the sight of the wolf coat that hangs there. Nor should I want, desperately, to tell him that it was there when I arrived.

The Wolves have been attacking my people for centuries, yet I can't bring myself to agree with some of Sebastian's more barbaric practices.

He stills, the muscles in his back tightening.

Then he grabs a different fur and heads out of my chambers.

I punch him between his shoulder blades again, but I do not put my full force into it.

Perhaps it's because his mood has darkened and I'm afraid. Or perhaps it's because a small part of me is glad I'm being taken away from my fate with Sebastian, despite how frightening this wolf may be.

"You won't get away with this," I growl, regardless.

"I will. Now be quiet."

"Where are you taking me?"

"Home."

Chapter Four

Shouts fill the castle and torchlight flickers as I'm carried through a labyrinth of stone corridors.

I struggle against my captor, but his thick arm only tightens around my waist.

I do not know where I'd run to even if I did escape him. Sebastian? My father? Would that be any better? Would it be worse?

Trapped as I am, something wild seems to have knocked loose inside me. It rattles around in my chest and I do not feel the hopelessness I should be feeling. The anger I have caged since my mother died surges hot and free through my veins.

I am not stone. I am not a statue.

I am fire.

And somehow it has taken this man, this beast, to make me see it.

I pound against the alpha's back. "Get off me, you bloody horrible brute." My hair catches in my mouth. I kick my bare feet and hit nothing but air. "Get off me. You'll die for this, you horrible—" I cut myself off as we turn a corner.

There are two guards lying in a pool of blood. The alpha steps over the bodies, and I'm forced to stare down at their lifeless faces as he continues onward.

The reality of my situation slams fully into me.

These men are dangerous. They're killers. They're Wolves.

Of course being taken away from my homeland by the enemies of my people is worse than staying. Of course it is. And yet...

The alpha cuts through one of the servants' passageways, almost as if he knows where he is going, even if I am lost, and a scream from a lady-in-waiting pierces my ears. She catches my eye as we pass, then runs in the opposite direction, her dark hair falling free from her cap.

The alpha won't make it out of here.

They'll imprison him until the full moon, then skin him alive.

The thing that's knocked loose in my chest becomes frantic. My heart pounds wildly in my chest.

"She's gone to get help, you horrible brute," I hiss at him. "There are guards stationed only a couple of minutes away."

"Aye?" he says, his voice low. He quickens his pace, half running down the servants' staircase. "Thank you."

I cling onto his shoulders, my fingers digging into his muscles, my body jolting against his back. "I wasn't... I wasn't trying to help you!" I say, shrilly.

Although I wonder, as I say it, if that is entirely true.

The alpha goes left, then right, bursting into a wider corridor. I recognize the mural of warriors slaughtering Wolves on the wall. It shows our victory in the Battle of the Beasts a century ago, and it is close to the western entrance hall.

He is almost free of this place. I am almost—

"Halt." A male voice cuts through the quiet.

The alpha stills. Two guards block the corridor ahead. They have the sigil of the Southlands, a sun, painted onto their shields. My father's men.

"Is that the princess?" one says incredulously.

The other chuckles. "Oh, I don't envy you, dog. Do you know what they do to your kind up here?"

The rattle of swords signals three more guards stepping into the corridor behind us. I breathe in sharply.

"Don't kill it," says one of them—a burly looking man with the silver star of the Borderlands on his breastplate. "Lord Sebastian will want to spend some time with this one."

The alpha's body stiffens. "I'm going to need to put you down for this, Princess," he says softly.

My breath hitches as he slides me down his front, and places me on the flagstones. The guards are charging, but everything feels still. His eyes bore into mine and they are as green and alive as the forest.

Don't run, he seems to be telling me. *Don't run.*

He pushes me aside. I flatten myself against a mural as he dodges the swing of a sword. He grabs his attacker's head and twists. A sickly crack fills the hall before he hurls the body into the next soldier, who skids into the wall. He roars, and charges.

Blood and muscle and steel blur in front of me as he takes on three men at once.

He is a force of nature. He swings, and blocks, and dodges each lethal blow that comes his way. He impales one soldier on his own sword, then rams another into the far wall—

smashing his head against the stone with such force that the chandelier above trembles.

My body trembles as though the decision that's rattling inside my body is a tangible, living thing.

I should run.

But I don't want to stay in this castle.

There are two paths ahead of me and I am lost. I do not know which one to take.

The alpha picks up a sword from the floor. He thrusts it through the chin of another guard, causing blood to spill from his mouth.

The horror of it forces me to face what the alpha is. A killer.

I flee down the corridor to my right, my bare feet slapping against the cold ground. My hair flies loose behind me, and my long nightdress bunches at my ankles. I'm breathing fast, and my heart is pounding.

I run wildly, frantically. This place is new to me and, though it is supposed to be my home, it is cold and unfamiliar. I am lost in a labyrinth of stone and there is a beast in here and I do not know the way out.

"Princess, wait."

I turn.

The alpha stands in the corridor behind me. His shirt is slick with sweat, and his biceps strain against his sleeves. He walks slowly, carefully, toward me. He's like a predator, trying not to scare his prey.

"Princess, do you really—"

He tenses when he reaches me, as if he hears something I cannot, then hooks an arm around my waist. My breathing sharpens as he draws me into a shadowy alcove. He pulls my back flush against his chest.

I am aware of every ridge of his torso, and the quick pounding of his heartbeat. His breaths are hot and uneven by my ear. His scent floods my nostrils—heat and sweat and the mountains. It overwhelms me. I still, even as my blood pounds through my body and my heartbeat hammers in my ears.

A scream builds in my chest, and he clamps his hand over my mouth.

"Find her!" Lord Sebastian snaps. "Find her now! She is my betrothed and I will not have her taken from me. If they touch her, if they defile her, she is of no value to me! Do you understand?"

I feel the slight growl building in the alpha's chest.

For a moment, we are both breathing fast as Sebastian rants, just a few feet away, about the importance of my purity. Slowly, the alpha drops his hand from my mouth. It's as if he's daring me to scream.

"I need her with her virtue intact. Do you understand?" says Sebastian. "Find her. Find her!"

"Yes, my lord."

The voices fade away.

I breathe out slowly. For a moment, neither of us move.

The alpha drops his arm and I step away. His face is as dark as thunder as he stares down the corridor.

"Do you really want to stay?" he asks.

"What difference does it make? I am a prisoner either way."

"Aye." He runs a hand over the back of his neck. "And I can't promise you it won't be dangerous up in the Northlands.

My people don't much care for humans. But I promise you that I'll protect you." He swallows. "And I'll give you the choice. Run now, and I won't follow. Come with me, and no one will touch you. I swear it on the Moon Goddess."

He holds out his hand for me to take. I am trembling as the decision builds in my chest. My soul is rattling against its prison, wild and screaming.

The alpha's gaze is unwavering. It's as though there is no doubt in his mind what I will do.

"What do you want with me?" I ask.

He drags his teeth over his bottom lip, as if deciding whether to tell me. "Sebastian has something of ours. We want it back."

I let out a bitter laugh. "You want to hold me ransom. You think he will make a trade."

"Aye," he says.

And there it is. My "choice". The two paths that lie before me.

A choice between two men. Two killers. Two monsters.

Only it is not much of a choice at all, is it? Again, I am nothing more than a prize—an object—to be passed between men. A burst of hysteria builds up inside me and spills out of my mouth in a manic giggle.

"There it is," I say. "That's what this is all about! Well, you heard what the lord said. If I am defiled then I am of no value to anyone."

"That's not why I'll keep you safe."

I stare at his open palm, then I look down the corridor in the direction that Lord Sebastian went in.

"I heard what he said to you," says the alpha, his voice quiet. "At the dog fight." When I meet his eyes, there is a surprising amount of anger contained within them. "I will keep you safe. Then I will set you free. I swear it."

I do not know if it is that word—free—that makes my heart beat faster, or whether it is the look on his face. Even though I am a statue, and statues don't move, my fingers twitch at my sides.

"I swear it, Princess," he says.

And somewhere beyond the adrenaline that's pumping through me, a thought begins to form.

If I can gather intelligence on the Wolves, perhaps I can finally prove to my father that I am more than just a prize to be won.

And, if I help my father win his war, he will have no use for Sebastian.

Perhaps I can escape my fate on my own terms.

"What does Sebastian have that belongs to you?" I ask.

There's a click behind me and the alpha looks over my shoulder.

"Step back, my lady." A guard grabs my arm and pushes me behind him, his musket trained on the alpha. "They're silver bullets, so don't do anything stupid. Hands behind your head."

Slowly, the alpha raises his hands and clasps them behind his neck.

"On your knees, dog."

"Wait—" I start.

"It's okay, my lady. He'll be punished. I can take it from here—"

The decision, the choice, that has been rattling around in my chest since I laid eyes on the alpha, erupts out of me.

I grab a torch from the wall, and smack the guard in the head with it.

I expect him to fall down to the ground, unconscious, like the guards did in stories my mother would tell me as a child.

Instead he grunts, then turns to me. The mild confusion on his face quickly turns to anger.

I stagger back, dropping the torch.

"What's going on?" he says, his face reddening. "Have you. . . lain with him? She who lies with a beast—"

The alpha darts forward and breaks the man's neck, then shoves him aside.

He holds out his hand.

I suck in a deep breath.

I'm doing this to help my kingdom, I tell myself. Not because— even with blood on his shirt cuffs, and dirt on his face, and one of my guards, dead, at his feet—he is looking at me with kindness.

No one looks at me with kindness.

I place my hand in his.

His palm is warm and rough as his fingers curl around mine—sealing my fate. It is only then that a flicker of confusion crosses his face. Perhaps I imagined it, because a moment later, he gives me a small smile.

"Come," he says. "More will be on their way."

Together, we bolt down the corridor, into the western entrance hall. The door is already open, and the night spills onto the checkered floor tiles.

I smell the pine trees of the forest, and the rain-drenched grass. The cold breeze tickles my skin, so fresh I can taste it.

The wind howls, or perhaps it is the Wolves that await.

Alongside the beast, I break out of the labyrinth.

Chapter Five

Twigs and stones dig into the soles of my feet as we run into the copse of trees that lead to the Western Gate.

The wind whips my hair into my face, and rain is falling between the branches, seeping through the thin material of my nightgown. The sound of howling and the clash of steel follow us, coming from the outdoor kennels somewhere behind us. The night is thick with the woody scent of fire.

I should be alarmed. Yet all my senses are trained on the alpha's hand, clasped around mine. I feel the ungodly strength in his fingers, and the callouses that make his hand so very different to my mother's, the only hand I have ever clasped before this one.

Heat seems to spread from the place where our skin touches and it travels up my arm.

I took his hand willingly. I don't know what that means, but he will not let go. I am certain of it. He let me make my choice, but now it is made, I have a feeling there is no going back.

A sweet burst of panic surges through me. Am I really going to do this?

The alpha turns and swings me off me feet and into his arms. I yelp, and reflexively hook my arms around his neck. His eyes latch onto mine—bright even in the darkness.

"No time for second thoughts, now, Princess," he says, rain running over his full lips.

"Put me down, you brute!"

"No."

He continues onward, through the nursery of ash trees.

Over his shoulder, thick smoke curls into the moonlight from the courtyard. More howls fill the night. And it hits me. This is not an escape attempt. This is a siege.

"You planned this," I say under my breath.

"Aye."

The blood in my veins turns to ice.

I may not want to marry Sebastian, but these are *my* people being attacked by Wolves. And I am willingly leaving with one of them. And he is a killer. They all are.

"Put me down!"

"You don't want me to do that."

The small gem of truth in what he says makes my insides twist. "You have no idea what I want."

"What *do* you want?"

A strange jolt of adrenaline—of *something*—floods my system. I don't have an answer. No one has ever asked me that before. And why should they? It doesn't matter what I want. Statues do not want, or feel, or need.

The alpha's eyebrows dip in question, or confusion.

"I want. . . I want you to put me down."

His gaze moves to the Western Gate that looms ahead, and the corner of his lip tugs up. "No you don't."

"You said I had a choice." Raindrops roll into my mouth.

"Aye. And you made it. And as you can't seem to tell me truthfully what it is that you want right now, I will take that as your final decision."

The Western Gate is open—though it should not be—and a group of men in kilts wait on horses in the shadow of the dark whispering trees beyond. They glance in our direction, and the alpha's arms tighten around me as he stalks toward them.

I open my mouth.

"I'm not leaving you, Princess. And that's the end of the matter." There's a dark finality to his tone. This is a man who is used to having the last word.

"You're a monster," I mutter—though I don't quite mean it. He's a killer, maybe. But I'm not sure he's a monster.

"Aye," he says just as half-heartedly. "So you'd better do as you're told."

A hot flash of fury ignites inside me. I want to tear into this man—this wolf—who thinks he can pick me up whenever he pleases. I want to pummel my fists against his chest and shriek until my throat is raw.

The force of this feeling—so unfamiliar—scares me into keeping it at bay. I push it into the cage in my mind, and lock it away.

When we clear the gate, Magnus is waiting atop a horse and my blood cools.

"Got yourself a wee snack for the road?" he says.

"She's under my protection." The alpha stalks past him toward a grey mare near the front of the group. "Easy there, Dawn," he says when the horse whinnies.

Everyone is staring at me, and I must look bedraggled and pathetic.

"*Put me down!*" I say through gritted teeth.

The alpha slides me to the ground. My nightdress is turning translucent in the rain, and I cross my arms over my chest. His expression softens and he throws the fur cloak over my shoulders, pulling it in around my collarbone.

"Can you ride, Princess?" he asks.

I can. My mother taught me when I was a child. Being on horseback made me feel free. Perhaps that is why my father forbade me to ride after her death.

Keeping this information to myself may be helpful if I need to escape. It is best, I have found, to let people underestimate me.

So, I shake my head.

He lifts me onto the beast. A couple of the men stare at me, but when he growls, they make themselves busy by adjusting their packs, or checking their weapons.

When I'm settled, the alpha's gaze darts around the shadowy group of eight and his brow creases.

"Where's Ryan?"

I scan the shadowy male faces and see the boy with the dislocated arm isn't here.

"The wee lad?" A burly man with red hair and a thick beard shakes his head. "Not seen him."

"Fuck's sake!" the alpha curses.

For the first time tonight, he looks worried. He darts a look over his shoulder at the Western Gate, then up at me. He flexes his fingers by his sides.

"*Fuck*," he mutters.

A moment later, the boy half runs, half stumbles through the gate and some of the tension in the alpha's expression softens.

Ryan's coppery hair is plastered to his forehead and he's clasping the hand of a brunette girl around his age. She's wearing the uniform of the kitchen maids, and has an angry scar across her cheek.

My eyes narrow in distaste at the brand on her neck—one of Sebastian's ways of identifying the Wolves he has working for him in the castle.

"Ah, seeing to matters of the heart, I see," says the red-haired guy.

"Or cock," says another, with an arched eyebrow.

A few of the men chuckle.

"Shut up, dickhead," snarls Ryan, glaring up at him. It does not escape my notice that he is no longer wearing the sling. Wolves really do heal quickly, then.

"Oi!" says the alpha, slapping the back of his head. "Get on your horse, and stop pissing about." His tone is stern, but there's a glint of amusement in his eyes.

In a swift movement, he mounts the horse behind me. The heat of his body seeps through the thick furs I am wearing and makes my skin hum. He reaches for the reins, caging me within his arms.

"Ready, Princess?" His voice is a rough breath on my cheek, and I shiver.

The bare branches of the trees ahead reach for one another over the overgrown road like forlorn lovers. To my right, the mountains are jagged and wild and alive—so unlike the flat terrain of the south that submits to the feet that tread upon it.

The alpha asked me what I wanted and I couldn't answer.

Now, a word beats fast with my pulse.

Freedom.

I want to be free from my fate.

If I do this—if I can gather intelligence that will help my father win his war—I may be able to free myself from Sebastian.

"Yes," I say, and some of the tension loosens in my chest.

"Let's go," says the alpha.

The thunder of hooves competes with my heartbeat as we ride into the forest.

The man with the red hair appears beside us. His eyes glint with amusement, even in the darkness, as he raises an eyebrow at the alpha.

"Don't mean to overstep," he says. "But who's the lass?"

Chapter Six

"That's none of your concern," says the alpha over the sound of hooves.

He's leaning into me as we put space between us and the castle, and I feel his hard body against my back. Trees loom up on either side of us.

"It will be our concern if the bastards come after us," says the red-haired man. "I happen to like my balls attached to my body."

"I don't know why," replies the alpha. "You hardly ever use them."

The musky smell of horse floods my nose, mixing with the scent of damp earth. I cling on to a ridge at the front of the saddle, knuckles wet and white, my thighs gripping the beast for dear life as it jolts forward. The spindly winter-worn branches overhead provide little shelter from the wind and the rain, yet I'm not cold.

I do not know whether it is the body behind me that keeps me warm, emanating heat even though he is only wearing a sodden shirt. Or the fur he wrapped around me. Or perhaps it's the speed of my heartbeat, pumping blood laced with adrenaline through my veins.

Whatever it is, I think it is also keeping the fear I should be feeling at bay, too. Because I'm being kidnapped by the enemy, and I don't even care. In fact, with each tree we put between us and the castle, another knot in my chest seems to untangle. There will be time for fear and panic, I'm sure. Now I feel as if I'm flying through the darkness.

I'm a prisoner. But I'm free. And I wonder how both of these things can be true at the same time, yet know they are.

The red-haired man glances at me again. "She's a beauty, for sure. That doesn't mean you can just swipe the lass. What's the king going to say?"

"What makes you think I didn't take her on the king's orders?" says the alpha, and I stiffen. "Not your king," he adds in a whisper against my cheek.

I frown, confused. There is only one king—unless you count the false king my brother is fighting a war against over on the continent. And surely the Wolves are too unruly, too disorganized, to be fighting for him.

"Because I happen to know what the king ordered us to take from the castle. And I know it wasn't a bonnie lass in her nightgown." He meets my eyes. "Who are you? And don't let this big oaf frighten you."

"I'm not afraid," I say.

My voice is quiet. It is drowned by the hooves pounding the forest floor, and the wind rustling the branches, but the wolf's eyes latch onto mine curiously.

It must be true what they say about Wolves having hearing stronger than the gods intended.

I shiver.

"She's none of your concern." The alpha's tone is firm.

"She's the princess, Fergus," Magnus drawls behind us.

A smile spreads on Fergus's face, too big to be genuine. "Tell me he's joking. Tell me you didn't kidnap the daughter of the king. Because I know—I *know*—you're not that much of a hot-headed fool."

The alpha shrugs behind me. His body feels relaxed—despite the jolting of the horse and his hard muscles.

"For the love of the Goddess!" roars Fergus. "Put her down!"

"It's a bit late for that," says the alpha.

"They'll have our hides for this," says Fergus.

"They'll have your hides if they catch you anyway," I mutter under my breath.

I feel the soft laugh in the alpha's chest. Fergus looks sharply at him.

"This is madness," says Fergus, exasperated. "They'll come after us."

"Aye, probably."

"What were you thinking?"

"I was thinking that seeing as we can't find what it is we're looking for, the princess can be used as leverage to get it."

"Oh, aye? Because it seems to me it's not just young Ryan who's making reckless decisions based on his cock tonight."

My heart thumps a little faster at the impropriety of what he's suggesting. The alpha promised that no one would touch me. I assumed that meant him too.

The alpha says nothing.

"See sense!" roars Fergus. "Put her back! We'll drop her off at the nearest village if you're worried about the lass, but—"

A low growl sounds in the alpha's chest. "She's coming with us, and that's final."

Fergus gives him a long hard look, before glancing at me. An unreadable expression crosses his face. A mixture of exasperation and something else. Sorrow, perhaps?

He shakes his head. "She's a human," he says softly. "She's not—"

"I'm bringing her to the king. I won't hear any more about it."

The alpha's body jerks as he digs his heels into the horse and we speed ahead of the pack, leaving Fergus and the conversation behind.

There's a shift in his mood. His corded forearms are strained, and a dark cloud seems to hang over us. Self-preservation should persuade me to stay quiet. And yet. . .

"My father is the king," I say.

"He's *your* king. He's not ours."

We always thought the Wolves were too wild and unruly to unite behind anyone. The history books say the clans have been at war with one another, as well as us, for hundreds of years.

"I didn't know you had one," I say.

"Do you know a lot about Wolves, Princess?"

"If you are anything to go by, I know they are lacking in manners."

He chuckles darkly. "Oh, aye? Anything else?"

"I know you do as you please. Killing. Stealing. Invading the Southlands." I think about what Sebastian said, about how Wolves take their women. I remember what Magnus did to that woman in the cell. My cheeks flame. "Doing other. . . beastly things."

"It seems you have the measure of us, Princess. We're all animals up here. Running rampant around the mountains. Howling at the moon. Eating princesses for breakfast."

I tense and he laughs.

I don't know whether or not he is joking. The church says Wolves hunt our kind when the moon is full. What's more, there are many stories of Borderlands men being sent north to protect our lands, and only their bones being found, months later.

"Do you eat people?"

He laughs again. "Hush, we've got a long ride ahead of us."

That doesn't sound promising. And yet, I cannot quite stop myself from wanting to provoke him anyway.

"Did you hit your head when you were in that fighting ring?"

"Huh?"

I gesture to the right, remembering that the mountains were on that side of us before we entered the trees. "The north is *that* way, you fool."

"You know, not many people speak to me like that."

"Not many people kidnap me and hold me hostage."

"I'm not people." His lips are close to my ear, and his warm breath tickles my cheek. "I'm an animal, remember."

I shiver, something stirring deep inside me. I open my mouth to retort but he shushes me.

"We're heading west for a few miles. If we go north right away, we'll hit the Border Wall. Now shush. We've a long ride, and you're giving me a headache."

We ride throughout the night. The steady sound of the hooves and the low murmur of conversation from the Wolves behind us adds a soft lull to the crisp air.

My head keeps rolling on my neck as I fight sleep. My body was tense and alert when we started this journey. Now, I do not have the strength to keep myself upright. I sink back into the alpha's chest, as improper as that might be. He's so warm against the chill in the air.

When we clear the forest, though, my eyes jolt open and I sit upright, a wave of wakefulness surging through my body.

The sun is rising, painting the sky pink, and the rain has stopped.

We've reached the high stone wall that separates the country of the Wolves from the rest of the kingdom. And part of it has been brought down. Through it, there's an expanse of rugged terrain that stretches as far as the eye can see.

I could see the distant north from my chambers in Sebastian's castle. But up close, the scenery is even more breathtaking.

The grass is a green more vivid than I have ever seen, interspersed with fern and heather that rustles in the breeze. Small lakes, filled with dark water, reflect the sunrise. And the shape of the land. . . it looks almost unnatural for land to be shaped this way. Hills and mountains burst up from the earth as though they are alive. The ones in the distance touch the clouds. And. . . is that *snow* upon some of the sharp peaks?

The air smells like grass and rain, and it's so crisp I can taste it.

"We ride to Loch A'ghealach, then we rest the horses." The alpha's voice cuts through the silence.

He digs his heels into the mare and we're flying, leaping over the crumbling pile of rock. I gasp as we clear the border wall, and I feel the alpha smile behind me as we leave my homeland behind.

"Welcome to the Northlands, Princess," he whispers.

Chapter Seven

I was a sickly child.

The High Priest said my weak temperament came from my mother. Bad blood, he'd said. It was thought I would die of the same illness that took her.

Before that haze of death and burning herbs and the blurry insides of the room I didn't leave for months, I remember my mother taking me to the countryside in the south. It was just her, and her lady-in-waiting, and me.

I must have only been about four, but I still remember the fields of golden crops, and the rolling hills—scattered with farms and small villages—and the cabin in the woodland by a great blue lake that we stopped at.

I suppose our early memories shape us in some ways, and I wonder if that small taste of adventure stirred something inside me all those years ago. Something I buried within me. Something that set me on a path that would one day lead me here—sitting on the back of a large grey horse, caged within the arms of the enemy, surrounded by Wolves.

My captors talk among themselves as we ride for what feels like hours. The sun rises high into the sky, and we don't stop, though I am weary and the horses are slower. I wonder if the Wolves are worried they are being pursued.

They should be.

Sebastian and my father will have sent people to retrieve me by now. Not because they care that I have been kidnapped. But because both men need me to secure their future alliance. And because both need me untouched.

I don't know how I will feel if they find us. I do know my captors will meet certain death.

If the alpha is worried, he doesn't show it. He remains silent, but he feels at ease behind me, his body pressed against my back, my thighs held within his.

It is highly inappropriate for us to be this close, for him to be this familiar with me. Every time the thought occurs to me and I stiffen, trying to put some space between us, he nudges me back again. After a while, whether it's the lull of his warmth, or the ache in my bones, or the fact I am distracted by the surrounding terrain—I stop bothering.

I find myself thinking about my memory of the southern countryside once more. The scenery back then, which filled me with such awe at the time, was so. . . *soft* compared to what we pass as we ride deeper into the Northlands.

The grass I played in with my mother was trimmed, the sunlight was warm and kind, and the hills were curved and gentle. Even the lake, which seemed to me like it stretched on forever, was blue and soft and still.

Here, the landscape is *alive*.

It is rugged, and harsh, and dangerous. The mountains jut out of the earth in stiff, jagged peaks, and the grass on the sides of the rocky road is so long it tickles my feet. Above, the sky is filled with rolling grey clouds that cast shadows on the land as the wind howls. Even the air has a harsh bite to it.

There is nothing gentle here.

Before long, it seems, the sun is setting again—and I remember my mother's lady-in-waiting telling me stories about how the gods and goddesses of the night staked their claim on the Northlands before they went to rest, making the days shorter and the nights longer so the creatures that revered them had more time for worship.

A shiver ripples through me as the shadows lengthen.

The alpha's arm momentarily tightens around my waist as if he senses it.

Soon, the sky is a dusky blue, and we're stopping at the edge of a great loch surrounded by mountains. The water is so black it looks bottomless, and it churns in the wind.

"A word," calls Fergus, gesturing to a copse of evergreens by the shore as he gets off his horse.

The alpha sighs, his breath tickling my cheek. "Aye. In a minute."

He dismounts the horse, and the coldness wraps around me in his absence.

"Need a hand, Princess?"

I don't answer him as I glance down at the earth. I'm aching, and I'm not wearing shoes. I do not want to seem weak, though. I take a deep breath, then shift my leg over the beast. Before I can jump off, the alpha grabs me by the waist and lifts me down.

When my feet touch the ground, my legs crumple and the alpha hooks an arm around my front and pulls me into him.

Damn it.

"Steady, Princess," he says. "I suppose you're not used to riding. Never mind. I've got you."

He scoops me up into his arms while the other men dismount around us.

"What are you doing?" I snap.

Those nearest to us avert their eyes, some grabbing flasks from their packs to fill at the loch, others gathering branches to make a fire on the bank.

"Stop manhandling me! I'm quite capable of walking by myself."

"Aye. I'm sure you are. But as I'm already carrying you, I may as well put you down by this nice tree over here."

He gently places me by a tall evergreen away from the group, where the sweet scent of pine is thick in the air. The earth is hard and cold. When he stands and whistles at Ryan, I pull my knees to my chest beneath the fur cloak.

The alpha crouches in front of me, and a wave of his heat washes over me once more. The warmth must be a wolf thing, because he is only wearing a damp shirt over his kilt.

"Back in the castle, I told you that if you ran, I wouldn't chase you. I need you to know that is no longer the case." In the dusk, his eyes are the color of the deepest part of the forest. "If you run, I will catch you. We're not in the south any longer. Understood?"

We're in the middle of nowhere. I have no idea where I am. Where does he think I would run to?

I give him a look. "I'm not a fool."

"No. I'm sure you're not." He glances at my hair, which must look like a tangled mess right now. "You do have fire in your soul, though. So be good, okay? I'll be back in a moment."

He stands before I can retort, and whistles again. Ryan walks over, tailed by the girl he rescued from the castle.

"Get the princess some food and water. And keep an eye on her. This is important, so no pissing about."

Ryan lifts his chin, chest puffing out slightly as he solemnly nods. "Aye. I will take care of her."

The alpha glances at me, the corner of his lip slightly lifting, before he stalks across the camp to Fergus.

Ryan hurries to his horse, gathering supplies from his pack, while the girl merely stares at me warily. I avert my gaze from the brand on her neck.

"Hello," I say. "I'm Aurora."

"I know who you are."

Hostility radiates from her. I understand why. I am betrothed to the monster who must have captured her.

Even though our people are at war, I do not want her to think me a monster too.

"What is your name?" I ask.

"That's none of your concern."

Something hardens inside me. I was trying to be nice.

Before I can respond, Ryan is back, passing me a stale loaf of bread and a leather flask filled with water. All I can think about is easing the gnawing ache of hunger that's been building in my stomach all day.

"Thank you," I say, gulping down the ice-cold water.

I stare at the bread for a moment before deciding there is no ladylike way to eat it. I tear into it, washing it down with another swig from the flask.

When I'm done, the girl is still eyeing me warily. Ryan, however, seems relaxed beside her.

"How is your arm?" I ask him.

Slowly and stiffly, he stretches it out—clenching his fist a couple of times. "It'll be alright. I'll be fighting again in no time." Even in the growing darkness, I see the flush in his cheeks. "I. . . er. . . Thank you for what you did for me."

"You don't need to thank me. I'm sorry you were in that position."

When his female friend whispers something in his ear and tugs on his good arm, he nods, then glances at me. "We'll be over here if you need anything."

They go and sit a few feet away.

"She's alright, Becky," I hear him murmur to her. "She's not like the others."

The men sit around the fire, drinking an amber liquid that I think is alcohol. They're far enough away that I can't hear their conversation. Though I can see the looks they throw at me every now and again, some hostile, others curious, others predatory.

By the water, the conversation between the alpha and Fergus seems heated. Fergus gestures wildly, and the alpha's face is like stone. When the red-haired man points at me, I avert my gaze.

I am clearly unwelcome here.

I do not know how long I sit here, the conversation and laughter becoming more raucous around the fire. The alpha has stepped into the trees with Fergus, and Ryan and Becky are now deep in conversation.

Every part of me aches, yet I am alert as a rabbit surrounded by Wolves.

I feel horribly alone.

When I accidentally catch Magnus's eyes, a slow grin spreads across his face and he says something to the ratlike man who sits beside him. I quickly look away, pulling my knees closer to my chest.

They both get up and saunter over, and my pulse begins to race. I can smell the alcohol on the air and see the intent in their eyes—even in the near darkness.

Ryan jumps to his feet. "Magnus—"

"Sit down, lad," says the ratlike one with a grin, brushing him aside. "This doesn't concern you."

"Hello, sweetheart," says Magnus as he prowls forward. "It's cold out here. Perhaps you can keep us warm."

My insides twist. "You're disgusting," I say, pushing my back closer to the tree, grasping along the ground for something, anything, I can use as a weapon.

"Now, now, that's not very nice," slurs Magnus. "We're only being friendly. I can think of much better uses for that pretty little mouth than insulting us."

My fingers close around a rock as he gets closer. My pulse is racing as I stumble to my feet.

"Leave her alone," says Ryan.

The rat pushes him back.

There's a crunch as the alpha steps on a twig beside me, and his warmth wraps around me.

"If you're cold, Magnus, there's some whisky in my pack that'll warm you up," says the alpha. "I suggest you go and drink it before you and I have a problem."

His tone is easy, but the sleeves of his shirt strain against the muscles in his arms and his jaw is a hard line.

A hush falls over the camp. The air is tense as if the rest of the Wolves sense that blood might soon be spilt.

But then Magnus cracks a grin. "Hear that, lads? More drink for everyone!" He slaps the alpha's arm before sauntering off to collect his prize.

The alpha watches him go before sitting down by the tree. When my breathing has steadied, I sit down beside him, my fingers still curled around the rock.

His profile is stern as he watches the others. He doesn't speak. He doesn't reassure me. I suppose there is no point. He has probably realized the same thing I have.

I am in danger here.

I have made a terrible mistake.

Dread curls in the pit of my stomach as I stare at the group of Wolves. The night becomes darker, and the conversation becomes quieter. Gradually, snores add to the crackle of the fire and the lull of the wind.

Though my eyelids are heavy, and though the alpha sits beside me, I do not dare close them—not even for a moment.

When the last of the Wolves has fallen asleep, the alpha stands.

Up, he mouths, gesturing with his head.

He holds out his hand. I frown, but cautiously, I take it. I wince when the sharp stones dig into my already sore feet. The alpha's eyebrows dip. He puts a finger over his full lips, then scoops me up again.

This time, I do not protest for fear of waking the others.

He takes me to his horse, tied to a tree a short way from the sleeping pack, and puts me in the saddle before mounting behind me. Before I can ask him what's going on, we're riding away from the others.

I look over my shoulder. Only Ryan stirs, but when the alpha pushes his finger to his lips, he nods and settles back down beside Becky.

"Where are we going?" I ask when the camp is a small dot on the other side of the loch.

"We'll be making the rest of the journey back alone," he whispers roughly against my cheek. "I won't have them threatening you."

"You can't just tell them to leave me alone?" I say. "I thought you were supposed to be the big bad alpha."

He lets loose a quiet laugh. "Aye. I suppose I am. But what did you notice about their kilts?"

I think of the different patterns the eight men were wearing—some blue, some green, and only Ryan's red like the alpha's. "You're from different clans," I say. "You're not *their* alpha."

"No, I'm not. And while some respect my status, others. . . less so."

"Like Magnus," I say bitterly.

"Aye," he agrees darkly. "And if he were to directly challenge me, I couldn't let it stand. But when I'd killed that despicable prick, it would really damage what we're trying to do here in bringing the clans together. It's for the best that we make our own way." He pauses. "Because I really want to kill that despicable prick."

Something warms in me at that—though I realize it's not very ladylike to revel in the idea of someone being killed.

"Where are we going?" I ask, my chest feeling a little looser.

His arm tightens around my waist. "I'm taking you to the Wolf King."

A spark of panic ignites inside me. Curiosity pulses through me, too. "Who *is* the Wolf King?"

"You'll see."

"And what? You're just going to hold me for ransom for something you think Sebastian has stolen from you?"

"Aye."

"What do you think he has?" I sigh, and my breath mists in the darkness before me. "What exactly is going on?"

Chapter Eight

"Do you know the story of the Elderwolf?" the alpha asks.

Away from the camp, the night is black as pitch. I can barely see, but I can hear the wind stirring the water of the loch we ride beside, and smell the rain-drenched evergreen trees and the masculine scent of the man behind me.

"The first wolf?" I say. "Yes. Everyone knows about that." He lets the silence extend, waiting for me to fill it.

"He conspired with the Moon and betrayed the Sun and the first men," I say. "He was cursed to roam the earth on four legs, and live in a manner as beastly as his actions were."

The word "beastly" slips out. It is the word the High Priest always uses when he tells this story. With the alpha as my only audience, alone together in an unfamiliar kingdom, I wonder if I should have been more careful with my word choice.

"Aye. I suppose you would tell it that way in the Southlands." He merely sounds pensive. "It's true, we were cursed. But that's not quite the way the story goes."

He shifts behind me on the horse, and his thigh brushes against mine. I sit straighter.

Even if I bring valuable information to my father when I am free, he will disown me if he ever finds out I'm sitting with a wolf's arm resting on my lap.

The alpha gently nudges me back again.

"The Elderwolf lived here long before the first men arrived," he says, "when all kinds of ancient dangerous creatures roamed the earth. The Moon—or *Ghealach* as we call her—would watch him as he endured. Impressed by his strength and his will to survive, she fell in love with him. Now, some say the Moon herself was a wolf, while others say the Wolves were merely her favored ones, but whichever is true, she would send her creatures to protect him."

The alpha's voice is low and soothing, and I find some of the stiffness in my limbs softening as the darkness wraps around us.

"He began to leave her gifts and offerings, to thank her. And so began a secret courtship that lasted many years. They fell deeply, and irrevocably, in love."

No one has told me a story since my mother passed, and I relax against his chest.

"When the first men invaded the Northlands, the Elderwolf was gravely injured. The Moon left her post in the sky to come to him—though it was forbidden. She shared her wild and dangerous power with him, and he was able to transform—to heal, and to seek vengeance on those who had tried to kill him." I hear the smile in his voice. "It was a blessing."

"A blessing? You said you were cursed."

"Aye, we were. But the ability to transform into a wolf was not the curse."

"So what *was* the curse?"

It is fascinating to hear this story from the alpha's perspective. In the south, our religious texts tell us the power to shift was the punishment for the Elderwolf's betrayal and the story ends there.

In the north, it seems, there is a whole other chapter.

"The Elderwolf embraced his new power," he continues. "You see, it felt as if the wolf was part of him all along. And perhaps it was. Perhaps that was why he and the Moon were drawn to one another in the first place. Unfortunately, the story doesn't end there. Because the Sun is a jealous and vengeful goddess."

I flinch. If I am honest with myself, I have had blasphemous thoughts about the Goddess of the Southlands. Usually while being made to repent for my sins by the High Priest.

But to voice those thoughts aloud. . .

"When the Sun found out, she set out to punish them both. The Moon was banished. She was given to the God of Night to be locked within his prison in the sky. And the Elderwolf? Well, the wolf inside him was caged—only ever able to break free of his chains when the Moon was the closest and her power could reach him."

"On the night of a full moon." The wind rustling through the trees almost swallows my words.

"Aye."

My eyebrows knit as I piece together what he's telling me, and why he's telling me.

"You're saying the Elderwolf was once able to change whenever he wanted," I say. "That the curse wasn't that he had to transform into a wolf, but that the power was taken away from him."

"Aye." The alpha's voice comes out low and dark. "But the Sun had underestimated the power of the Moon's love. So distraught to have been parted from him, to see him suffer from her prison in the sky, she ripped out her own heart. She cast it down to the earth so he could keep it, and he could always be close to her power."

I frown. "And he found it?"

"He did. It landed in the center of Glen Ghealach, high up in the Northlands, and created the valley itself. And when he found it, he kept it close. Until one day, the Sun led the first men to him. Though he fought bravely, though he protected the heart that had been entrusted to him, there were too many of them. He was slaughtered, and the Moon's heart was stolen."

"You think it's real?"

"Aye, we do. Of course, the story is steeped in myth—but there is evidence throughout history of a relic that has passed between hands. A type of rock, we think." He swallows. "And there is evidence it holds the power for us to shift whenever we choose, to be free."

His longing for freedom stirs something inside me as I finally understand.

"You think Sebastian has it. That's why you planned the siege at his castle. That's why you took me. That's what you want to trade me for."

"Aye," he says, his voice dark as shadow and laced with intent. "We're searching for the *Cridhe na Ghealach*—the Heart of the Moon. Because with it, we'll have the power to shift when we want. With it, we'll have the power to win this war."

Chapter Nine

We'll have the power to win this war.

We ride onward.

The night is quiet except for the sound of the horse's hooves and the whisper of the wind in the trees. It emphasizes how alone we are out here. How alone I am—with a man who is plotting against my father.

His chest rises and falls steadily against my back.

"What makes you so sure Sebastian has what you're looking for?" I ask.

I sense him deciding whether or not to answer. "I have my sources."

"You have spies in Sebastian's castle, you mean." I recall his certainty that he was going to escape when I tended to Ryan's wounds. "They let you out of the kennels, I presume?"

"Aye. And they confirm what . . . what someone from the Lowfell Clan has been telling us." His tone darkens and I get the impression that whoever this someone is, the alpha doesn't care too much for them.

"But you didn't find it."

"It wasn't where we thought it would be."

I think of the carnage we left behind at Sebastian's castle; the dead guards in the entrance hall, the flames in the courtyard, the shouting and the cries of death. "Your siege was pointless, then."

His arm tightens around my waist. "I wouldn't say that."

My heart thuds faster as I realize I may be out of my depth.

I have no doubt Sebastian will wage war to get me back. I am his property, and I have been stolen from him. He will not let that go unanswered. But he does not care whether I live or die. Not really.

And the alpha is naïve if he thinks Sebastian will trade this powerful relic for me.

I am worth nothing.

I wonder what will happen to me when the Wolves finally figure that out.

***

We stop in a clearing by the bank of the loch, and the alpha dismounts.

It's so dark all I can make out is his shadowy form. The air is thick with the scent of pine and grass, and water moves and ripples somewhere behind him.

"We're resting here until morning. Come," he says.

I fold my arms. "You do realize both Sebastian and my father will send their armies north to find me? They'll ride day and night to capture my kidnapper. It won't end well for you if they do."

It won't end well for me, either.

"People really don't talk to me that way."

"Yes, you said."

"They call this place Glen Marb—the Valley of Death," says the alpha. "It was a battleground, centuries go. They say the souls of the Wolves who died here haunt the valley, seeking vengeance. If you listen carefully, you can hear them howling."

My insides tighten when I hear hollow wails in the distance. I snap my head toward him, alarmed.

He grins. "Just the wind. A silly superstition, but Sebastian believes it. He won't send his men here. We're safe until morning. Come."

This time, when he puts his hands around my waist and lowers me to the ground, I don't fight him.

I am a princess, and he stole me from my bed and brought me here. He *should* be serving me. That's what I tell myself, anyway. I am fed up of feeling weak.

If we were in the palace, and I was dressed up in one of my favorite dresses at one of the balls, things would be quite different, I'm sure.

I wince when my feet touch the sodden earth. The alpha's big hands tighten around my hips, the heat seeping through my nightdress. My cheeks flush. Men are not supposed to stand this close to me. Especially big alpha warrior men who are plotting against my father.

"*Ghealach*," he curses under his breath. "Your feet."

Above, the clouds shift, illuminating the valley and the moonlit loch. My gaze is fixed on the alpha. He's looking at my bare feet and a flicker of something. . . shame, perhaps. . . crosses his face.

"You're hurt." He swallows, shaking his head. "Forgive me, Princess. I forget sometimes, how fragile humans are."

"Fragile?" I slap his wrists and he finally releases me. "We may not all be big oafs like you, but that doesn't make us fragile."

One of my soles hurts from running barefoot out of the Borderlands castle. I must have cut it on a stone or twig when we escaped. I want to take a look, but not with the alpha looming over me.

"Let me see." He steps forward.

"I'll be fine, it's just a cut."

His nostrils flare. "You're not fine. I can smell blood."

"Firstly, that's horrifying," I tell him, folding my arms. "And secondly, if it bothers you so much, then next time you come crashing into a lady's bedchambers, let her get dressed before you kidnap her."

His face falls. "Aye. I should've done that. I'm sorry. . . I truly am." The sight of a big bloodthirsty warrior sheepishly apologizing causes a strange feeling of power to surge through me. Until he steps forward. "Now, if you'll just let me take a look—"

"No."

"Let me see!"

"If you come any closer, I will. . . I will take my leave of you!"

He stills and I think I've won, but the corner of his lip twitches. Slowly, he raises his hands.

"Okay." His tone is placating, at odds with his large physique. "Okay. At least sit down. I'll water the horse, light us a fire. Okay?"

He leads the horse down to the loch.

I shiver, and pull my furs closer. It is never this cold in the King's City.

There's a copse of fir trees nearby, so while he's fussing with the horse, I select some dry twigs and branches, and a flint rock. By the time he returns with a flask, I'm sitting and warming my hands by a small fire. The crackle of flames adds to the sound of the wind and the water.

He looks at me curiously.

"I didn't think you'd know how to do that," he says.

I tuck my knees beneath my chin, basking in the heat that washes over my face. "Do you know a lot about princesses, wolf?"

"It seems not." He sits down beside me, and nods at the flames. "Did your father teach you?"

He sounds skeptical, and he's right to be. The only thing my father taught me was how to act like a lady so that he could parade me around in front of suitors.

"My mother." I chew my bottom lip. I'm unused to people asking me questions about myself, and it feels strange. "She was from the Snowlands, originally."

"Ah, well, I hear it's pretty cold over there."

"Yes." I pull the cloak closer around me. "The clue is in the name."

The alpha laughs, a soft, surprised sound. "Aye. That it is." He hands me his flask. "If you won't let me tend to it, at least clean your cut. I don't want to have to take you to the healer when we get to the castle."

I pick up on the darkness in his tone. "You don't like healers?" I wash the blood off my sole. There's barely a scratch there and I've always healed quickly. It should be fine in a couple of days.

"This particular healer is an obnoxious prick who I'd rather we avoid."

The shadows curl around us, and my breath mists in front of my face. I nod at his pack. "Shouldn't you be putting up the tent?"

"The tent?"

"I thought we were staying until morning. Where am I going to sleep?"

A slow smile spreads across his face. "You can check for a four-poster bed in there if you like, Princess. But I'm pretty sure I forgot to pack it."

"You want me to sleep on the floor?"

"Aye."

"Where are you going to sleep?"

His eyebrows dip in confusion, before he nods at the ground.

"You're going to lie down beside me as if you were. . . as if you were my *husband*?"

"Well. . . not exactly like that, no." There's a wicked glint in his eye and I flush. "Now, behave yourself and lie down. You'll catch your death of cold if I move away." He lies on his back, clasping his hands behind his head. "I know, it's scandalous. I won't tell anyone if you don't."

When he winks, I huff and lie on my side, turning away from him.

The grass is surprisingly soft. I'm not sure if it's because the mountains block the wind, or if it's the alpha's strange body heat—but some of the stiffness in my body eases.

"What is your name?" I ask, suddenly.

"Callum." His voice is soft, and lilts slightly, as though he's surprised I asked.

"Callum?"

"Aye." He sounds amused. "Is there something wrong with my name?"

"No. . . I. . ." I glance at him over my shoulder. I take in his hard jaw covered in stubble, his wild hair, and his large biceps, bulging against his sleeves. "I expected you to have a more. . . brutish name. The name Callum makes me think of a mischievous young boy."

He chuckles. "Believe it or not, I was a mischievous wee lad once." His eyes glint playfully in the firelight and I can almost imagine it.

It warms something inside me, and I look away before he catches me smiling.

"It's nice to meet you, Callum. I'm—"

"Your name is Rory," he says, and I bristle. Nobody calls me that, and it's far too familiar for a wolf who has stolen me from my bed.

"I'm *Princess* Aurora."

He merely chuckles.

Before long, all I can hear is the crackle of the fire and Callum's breathing.

I don't know how I'm going to sleep under these conditions.

I've been taken by the Wolves. Tomorrow, I'll be presented to the mysterious Wolf King. And right now, I'm lying beside a man who is not my husband.

I gasp as the realization of where I should be right now crashes over me.

Callum stiffens. "Princess?"

I roll onto my back. "I was supposed to marry Sebastian tonight. I should. . . I should be his wife right now."

Callum turns his head to the side. "Aye."

A warmth builds inside me. I don't hide the slow smile that spreads across my face as I turn my gaze to the infinite sky.

I feel Callum's eyes on me for a moment longer, before he too looks toward the stars.

"I told you he wouldn't touch you," he says.

Chapter Ten

I'm warm. Hot, even.

My eyelids are heavy and when I open them, pink sunlight floods my vision.

Strange dreams of large Wolves and moonlit woods ebb away, leaving me confused. I'm not in my bed. Grass tickles my cheek, and the air is crisp. My nightdress is damp with dew, and a chorus of birds and wind and rippling water resounds around me.

There's another sound, too; low, steady breathing.

Something heavy presses down on my waist.

My eyes widen as it all comes back to me.

The alpha, the siege, and being taken from my homeland.

What's more, Callum has me tucked against his chest. He must have pulled me to him while he slept. I must have let him. *Goddess!*

I try to shuffle away, but a soft snarl vibrates in his throat. My pulse quickens as I push at his heavy forearm. This time, his growl is low and dangerous. His fingers are splayed across my torso, holding me to him.

My breath hitches.

I have never been this close to a man before.

I glance over my shoulder. Despite his threatening sounds, his eyes are closed and his face is soft with sleep.

I slap his arm. "Get off me, you big oaf! Get off!"

He groans, then rolls onto his back.

"Good morning to you, too, Princess." His voice is rough as he opens his eyes.

My cheeks are flaming, but he doesn't seem embarrassed. I wonder if he's used to waking up beside women he has just met. He's handsome, I suppose, in a bloodthirsty warrior kind of way.

I sit up, pulling my fur cloak closer to me to shield me from the cold.

I focus on the mountains that surround us instead of the crease on the side of Callum's face where the grass has left a mark, or the soft smile playing on his lips.

As well as illuminating the rugged scenery, the dawn exposes me.

Usually, in the morning, I would bathe, and my hair would be brushed and styled on top of my head. I'd be presented with pretty dresses, and ladies-in-waiting would fuss over me—cinching in my waist, and concealing my flaws.

I would sit in front of the mirror for hours, sometimes, tinting my lips and hiding the shadows beneath my eyes. I was supposed to be perfect before anyone saw me.

Away from all that oppressive finery, I feel naked.

My mouth tastes bad, and my eyelids are puffy, and my muscles ache. I know my skin will be unnaturally pale.

Callum is watching me.

Does he have no manners at all? Does he not know how rude it is to stare at a woman when she has just woken up?

My throat tightens. I need to get away from him.

I scramble to my feet, and wince as I march away from our little camp.

"Going somewhere, Princess?"

For all he knows, I could be running away. If he knew I could ride, perhaps he wouldn't sound so amused.

"I'm going to wash." I clamber down the rocks to the loch. "You Wolves may be content to fester in your own filth, but *I* am not."

I tiptoe to the water's edge.

The loch stretches on for miles in either direction, the rippling surface reflecting the mountains and the pink sky above. Just ahead is a small island, covered with evergreen trees. Shallow waves lap the smooth stones by my filthy feet.

The morning air fills my lungs, and, as I exhale, the anxiety leaves my body.

I'm out of my depth, and I just woke up beside an alpha in the Northlands.

But I have never seen such a beautiful landscape. It's so wild, and peaceful, and *free*.

"I wouldn't do that if I were you, Princess," says Callum. "The water's pretty—"

I shriek as I step into the shallow water. The icy temperature jolts through my body and I shudder.

"Cold," finishes Callum.

He's rolled onto his stomach to watch me. There's a wide grin on his face.

"I'd rather be. . . a little cold. . ." I begin, trying to hide the violent chatter of my teeth, "than caked in dirt. . . although you clearly don't feel. . . the same."

"I don't feel the cold, remember, Princess? Isn't that why you were snuggling up to me all night?"

"*I was not!*"

"You know, I could get completely naked right now and jump into the loch and the temperature would have no effect on me whatsoever," he continues, as though I haven't spoken. "In fact, you're right. I *am* caked in dirt. I think that's exactly what I'll do."

"Don't you dare!" I demand as he gets up and tugs his filthy shirt out of his kilt.

"My dirtiness is clearly offending you, Princess."

"The only thing that is offending me, Callum, is your complete lack of decorum." Something unreadable passes over his eyes, though he continues to smirk. "Now, why don't you make yourself useful and sort us some breakfast?"

He laughs at that—loudly and unabashedly. "Very well, Your Highness. Don't take too long. The water's cold and it'll be noon before we arrive at the castle. That's a long time to be shivering. Although, I'll happily warm you up again after."

His teasing tone provokes something that sounds almost like a growl from me. It seems to delight Callum.

"Go away," I say.

"If you're not out in five minutes, I'll be coming in after you."

Despite how much he is antagonizing me, I find the corner of my lip twitching once he has disappeared.

He is clearly in good spirits this morning, and for some reason, that fills me with warmth.

Until I realize why he is so happy.

By noon, he'll have done his job and delivered me to the castle, and I'll be at the mercy of the Wolf King.

Chapter Eleven

I take my time washing myself.

For the first time in my life, I relieve myself behind a tree.

I spend a few minutes drinking in the view, too—standing on the shore and watching my breath plume in front of my face as the sun slowly rises above the loch.

Back in the castle at the King's City, I only ever saw the sunrise through my murky bolted window. The servants would already be bustling through the courtyard below, and the ladies-in-waiting would be fussing around me.

I can't remember a time when I have been in the presence of such vast, unending silence.

I breathe in. Then out.

Small waves lap the pebbles by my feet.

By the time I make my way back up the rocks, at least fifteen minutes must have passed, and I'm shivering.

The bottom of my nightdress is sodden, and strands of my hair stick to my wet face. I feel better though. Fresher. The cold seems to have shocked some of the dread right out of me.

Callum, to my surprise, has relit the fire even though he was in a hurry for us to set off. He sits in front of it with his thick forearms resting on his raised knees. He seems totally at ease, eating a piece of bread.

He'd said he was going to come into the water after me. I'm about to ask him what kind of alpha makes false threats, when he lazily turns his head.

He looks me up and down, seemingly taking in the gooseflesh on my exposed ankles, and the chattering of my teeth. He smirks.

The point he is making couldn't be clearer.

I didn't listen to him, and now I'm suffering for it.

"Cold, Princess?"

"If you were a gentleman—"

"Not a gentleman." He grins. "Wolf."

I shiver, and I'm not sure if it's the temperature, or the look in his eyes. "You're a sadist, that's what you are."

My stomach growls, and he pats the ground beside him. I hesitate for a moment before sitting. He breaks off half of his piece of bread, and passes it to me.

It's stale and hard, but it eases the pang in my stomach.

"I thought we were in a hurry," I say when I'm finished.

He shrugs, leaning back on his hands. "The king can wait."

"You would leave your king waiting?"

I am nervous enough about this meeting without us showing up late. Does Callum not realize that his king may instantly realize I am of no value?

He shrugs, and my insides twist.

When he looks at me, his face softens. "I told you, I won't let anyone harm you."

My jaw clenches, and I stare into the flames. "If your king decides to execute me, there's not a lot you can do, Callum."

"Look at me, Princess." His tone is dark and commanding and it stirs something inside me. "I don't break my promises."

I look away, and rub my cold feet. "How does one become the Wolf King, anyway? I thought you had alphas, not kings."

He tears off a chunk of his bread and chews.

"We do. The alphas lead their clans. And the king is the alpha of the alphas, I suppose." He swallows his mouthful. "It hasn't been easy, getting the alphas to fall into line. Not all have, not yet, anyway. We're not known for submitting to others. But we were losing this war with your people. Something had to be done. We had to unite behind someone."

I clasp my hands together tightly. I got a taste of the violence of Wolves at the dog fight and the siege. Whoever has got these men—this man—to submit to him must be frightening indeed.

"What is he like?" I ask.

Callum shrugs. "He's alright, I suppose." His tone is warm, and that, more than anything, eases the panic a little.

I've always thought myself to be a good judge of people, and despite his lack of decorum, I do not think Callum is a bad man. I do not think he would support someone who was.

Although, sometimes good men can be deceived.

"I thought you didn't feel the cold," I say, noting how close his legs are to the fire.

"I don't. But the warmth still feels nice."

"Why don't you feel the cold?"

He cocks his head to the side. "Why do you ask questions as though they're accusations?" When I merely glare at him, he shrugs. "It's my wolf blood."

He pops the last chunk of bread into his mouth, and I watch as he chews then swallows. I can't help but remember what he said earlier.

"Do you. . . do you really eat people?"

His eyes widen. He looks me up and down, and I feel naked under his scrutiny.

"As much as I'd enjoy feasting on you, Princess, I will refrain," he says.

I get the impression he's telling a joke. "Okay. Well. . . good."

He grins as he gets up. "We should go."

He holds out one of his big hands. I take it and let him pull me to my feet. He pours the remaining water in the flask over the fire, dowsing the flames, before stamping on it a few times. We walk to the horse, which is tethered by a fir tree.

"Wait there a moment," he says, before heading down to the loch to refill the flask.

The sun has risen now, and the sky is a bright morning shade of blue. The mountains around us are unspoiled and there are different shades of green everywhere. To our left, the sun glints off the surface of the loch. The air smells like pine and woodsmoke; it's so different to the dirty smells of the city. I breathe it in deeply.

"You're allowed to be impressed, Princess," says Callum gently as he comes up behind me.

"It's. . . beautiful," I admit.

"Aye," he says softly. "It is."

When I turn to face him, he's looking at me.

He averts his gaze. "Come on," he says, his voice a little rough.

He hoists me up on the horse, then mounts behind me.

Soon, we're back on the road, and on our way to the castle.

Chapter Twelve

The wind picks up around us as we ride out of the valley. It is as wild and untamed as the feelings that whirl around in my stomach. Even the mountains seem to move as the gust blows through the grass and the trees.

But the mountains remain whole. And so must I.

I can't let anyone see I am afraid of the fate that awaits me when we reach the Wolf King.

After a few hours of riding, due to my insistence, we take a break to eat some more bread and hard cheese. Much to Callum's exasperation.

If I'm honest, I'm not hungry. Every hour we ride brings us closer to the Wolves and a part of me wants to delay what is coming, to prepare myself.

We're just about to set off again, and Callum is packing up the horse, when the sky opens.

I gasp. I have never seen rain like this—so wild and loud and wet. It even makes the rain I've experienced over the past couple of days seem tame. It runs down my face, my lips—

making my hair stick to my cheeks and seeping through my furs.

It rains in the King's City, too, of course. But there, it's nothing more than moisture in the air and patters on the cobblestones; a moment's reprieve from the heat from the Sun Goddess. And even then, if I am ever caught out in it, one of the King's Guard will put a parasol over my head and usher me indoors as if I will break if the water touches me.

Dolls are not supposed to get wet, after all.

It frustrated me at the time, but I wonder now if they were right. I think I am breaking. The stone statue I dream about is cracking beneath the raindrops.

Before I realize what I'm doing, I'm turning my face toward the sky and stretching out my arms—welcoming the feeling of cold water on my skin.

I laugh.

I am here, and I am human, and I am *alive*.

A footstep causes the laughter to die in my throat as the realization of where I am and who I'm with crashes through me.

Slowly, I turn to face him.

I have always thought of rain as an equalizer of men. It doesn't matter if you're dressed in rags or finery, the rain will soak you and make you look smaller all the same.

It is different with Callum. It is like the rain strengthens him.

Water rolls off his kilt, and his tree-trunk calves are muddy. His shirt sticks to his muscles and emphasizes how big they are.

I look up at his face—fearing the disgust I'm sure I'll see in his eyes, and wondering if he'll scold me, or backhand me, like my father would if he'd witnessed such a scene.

He is looking at me as though I am the strangest, most wonderful thing he has ever seen. There's a broad smile on his face, and it's that, more than anything, that makes me realize how dangerous this man—this wolf—is.

This is someone who has no need to conceal his emotions, because who would dare judge him or take advantage of him because of them? He looks like if he decided to punch the ground, he would cause an earthquake.

Heart thumping, I drag my gaze away.

"I'm glad the rain pleases you, Princess," he says. "There's plenty more of that where we're heading. Now come, we'd better be on our way."

***

An hour later, I am no longer laughing, nor pleased.

The rain has stopped, and I am bedraggled and miserable.

"You need to find me some suitable clothes to change into when we arrive," I say. "You can't present me to your king like this."

"You can change into one of my shirts and—"

"Something *suitable*, Callum."

He sighs. He sounds resigned. "Aye."

"Well. . . good." Some of the nerves in my stomach steady.

If I was back home, I'd spend the entire day preparing for something like this—bathing, braiding my hair, selecting the perfect dress; one that would convey whatever message my father was trying to send.

I'd be demure and sweet, or fun and flirty, or a tempting prize to be won.

I would be more confident about meeting the Wolf King if I had access to my finery and my costumes. But at least if I can change out of my nightdress, I can make myself somewhat presentable.

We fall silent for a while, and the wind beings to calm as we take an overgrown road through the grass and fern.

The sounds of bird calls that I've not heard before and running water surround us.

The sun is higher now. It does little to warm the Northlands air, but I close my eyes for a moment and bask in the light regardless. When I open them, I notice how it turns the vein-like streams coming down the mountains silver.

A strange sense of peace settles over me. I find myself sinking back into the man behind me.

Even if I bring my father valuable information about the Wolves and their king, he'll still find something to punish me for when I get home. What does it matter if I relax for a while? Even if I am sitting inappropriately close to a man who is not my betrothed.

I glance down. Callum's thighs are huge, and they rub against mine through his red tartan.

A rumor I heard the ladies-in-waiting whispering back at the palace comes back to me, about how Wolves wear no undergarments beneath their kilts.

I stiffen. If that is true, he is sitting *way* too close to me.

"It's going to be alright, you know?" Callum says, misreading my tension.

I can't exactly ask him about his undergarments, so I decide to follow his track of conversation. "You don't know that."

"I told you, I'll protect you. I take care of my own."

I'm about to tell him I'm not his, and as such, that means very little to me. But an image of muscle and blood, and the sickening sound of cracking bone, flashes behind my eyelids.

"You didn't take care of Ryan," I say quietly.

His knuckles whiten as he clenches the reins on my lap.

I tense. It was the wrong thing to say.

Although it is a valid fear of mine. Because how can he tell me he will take care of me—the daughter of his enemy—when he was going to kill a young man from his own pack?

I don't think he's going to respond. I hear him swallow.

"No." His voice is rough. "No. I didn't. I should've dislocated his arm back at the castle, when I saw him loading up his horse."

"Your regret is you should have hurt him *earlier*?"

"Aye. I let him disobey me because I knew about the lass he wanted to save. I was too soft on the lad."

"Dislocating someone's arm is hardly taking care of them, nor being soft!"

"It's better than killing them for *your* betrothed's amusement!" His tone is harsher than I've ever heard it, and cool shame floods my system.

"It's not as if I have a say in who I marry!"

"No? I thought you said there was always a choice, Princess."

I grit my teeth. "Yes. And the choice was to marry Sebastian and survive, or refuse him—rendering myself

96

useless to my father. I made my choice to survive, and I would make it again."

"Aye. And I made my choice, too," says Callum, his tone a little softer. "I chose to rough up the lad in the ring so you'd take pity on him and spare him."

My breath mists in front of my face as I breathe out slowly. "You couldn't possibly know I would do that."

"I didn't," he says. "Not for certain. But I could smell your fear, and hear your heartbeat. I could sense your repulsion of the men sitting beside you, and I could feel you didn't want to be there in that hall. And yet, you didn't show it. And when your eyes met mine, I could see the steel in them. I could see the determination, and the strength, and the fire in your soul. Most people would've looked away from me if I'd looked at them the way I looked at you, but you didn't. And I felt the hatred in that gaze. You hated everyone in that room, and you hated me. Goddess, you hated me. You hated me for what I was about to do to the lad." He lets loose a half-laugh that sounds almost like a growl. "No. I didn't know for certain. But I was pretty sure."

Something tightens, then loosens, inside me.

I'm not sure why his words are having such an effect on me. Perhaps because he is right. Perhaps because, in a room crowded with people, he was the only one who noticed me. I cannot remember a time when anyone else has ever really looked.

"I noticed something else about the way you were looking at me, Princess." His voice is lighter, almost teasing.

My eyebrows knit together. "What?"

"You thought I was handsome." His voice is alight with amusement now. I can hear the stupid grin on his face.

"I did not!" My face flushes as I elbow him in the side.

He roars with laughter. I'm surprised he doesn't upset the horse. She's probably used to carrying around big brutes like him, poor thing. I'm about to ask if that's true, when we reach the crest of a hill, revealing the valley below.

A rugged castle made of stone stands in the distance. It's beside a loch with water so black it looks bottomless. Beyond, there is a backdrop of mountains, and a forest that stretches into the distance.

My stomach clenches.

"There she is," says Callum. "Castle Madadh-allaidh. No doubt the rest of our party will have alerted the king that we're on our way. Are you ready, Princess?"

I swallow, steadying my writhing nerves.

I will myself to be stone. No, steel.

I nod. "Yes."

Callum tightens his arm around my waist in what I think is supposed to be a reassuring gesture.

He takes the reins with both hands, digs his heels into the horse, and we gallop down the hill toward the castle.

Chapter Thirteen

The castle courtyard is full of Wolves.

They look like men and women, but I know what lurks beneath their skin. It's obvious in the way they dress and wear their hair wild and loose, shouting at one another across the stone yard in accents as thick as the grime that coats them.

The air is loud and smelly and wild as the wind whips my hair into my face.

Ahead, the castle waits for me, like a dangerous beast, with walls made of crumbling grey stone. It's tall and angular in appearance, with a turret that casts a long shadow over the courtyard.

As we ride to the heavy wooden doors ahead, a couple of men who are noisily sparring drop their swords to stare at me. It's as if they can sense what lurks beneath my skin as well. I am the daughter of their enemy king. What would they do to me if they knew?

My heart beats faster.

Callum hooks his arm around my waist and pulls me closer to him. His body is warm, and I can feel his heart beating steadily against my back. It is a stark contrast to the chaos around us.

"I was a wee lad the first time I came here." His voice is a rough whisper that tickles my ear—and I wonder why he is telling me this now when there are clearly more important things to be concerned about. "It was the first time I'd ever been to the south."

I swallow, focusing on Callum rather than the couple of women carrying dead rabbits, who have stopped their conversation to turn their attention toward me.

"This isn't the south," I say quietly.

"It is when you're from Highfell."

His tone is light and conversational, and I wonder if he is trying to distract me from the other Wolves that are now casting their gazes in our direction. He pulls gently on the reins of the horse and we come to a stop not far from the castle doors.

"It's the real north up there. Harsh and wild, with nights so dark you can barely see in front of your face. When my father brought me down here, he told me all southerners were soft. But our clans were at war with one another. And that first time I came here, I was afraid."

He shifts behind me, then dismounts the horse. I stiffen, gripping the ridge on the saddle as the cold air seeps through my furs to my nightdress.

Even though most of the Wolves are openly staring at us, his gaze doesn't move from mine. There's something so still in it that it eases the panic rising in my chest.

"But no harm came to me." He smiles softly. "And no harm will come to you. Not while I'm at your side. Okay?"

He holds out a big hand. I swallow and raise my chin—pushing the fear deep down. I can't let these people think I am weak.

I swing my leg over the horse, then, tentatively, I take his hand.

His fingers are rough and callused and they close around mine.

He helps me slide down the horse, one of his hands clasping my waist. I wince when my feet touch the stone, and his jaw tightens as that hint of shame crosses his expression once more. I expect him to scoop me off my feet again. He seems to be in the habit of doing so and a pathetic part of me wants him to. I ache and my soles hurt and I'm tired and dirty. I want to bury my face in his chest so I cannot see everyone looking at me. I want to pretend I'm not here.

He squeezes my hand before looking over my shoulder at the twenty or so Wolves who are clearly watching us.

"Don't you have work to be doing?" His voice is light, but there's no mistaking the authority in his tone. "If you have enough time for idle gossip in the middle of the day, I'm sure Mrs. McDonald would welcome your help peeling potatoes in the kitchens."

The smaller man who was sparring gives an exaggerated shudder. His accent is so thick I can only pick up the words "kill" and "dragon", but there are a few titters in the crowd and Callum grins. I get the impression that whoever Mrs. McDonald is, she's not very popular.

Whether that's the case or not, the tension seems to break and the people in the courtyard go back to their business—though a few eye Callum and me curiously. Some of the unfriendly looks seem to be directed at Callum as well as me, though he either doesn't notice, or doesn't care.

"Peeling taties?" A female voice comes from somewhere behind Callum's large physique. "You could've told them I had some horse shite for them to sweep up. I wouldn't mind the afternoon off."

Callum's grin widens. "Aye? Got plans, have you?"

"Oh, a nice dram of whiskey. Soak in the bath. I've not had chance for one in a week."

"I can tell."

Callum turns, revealing the girl standing behind him. She looks around my age, slightly taller than me, with long brown hair that's tied in a loose ponytail with a red tartan ribbon. She's pretty—even with dirt smearing her cheek, and the fact that she's dressed like a man in breeches and a linen shirt slick with sweat.

Callum may be teasing her, but I can tell she hasn't bathed in a while as well. She's giving off a strong smell of horses.

She narrows her eyes at Callum, though the corner of her lip twitches. "Cheeky bastard. You survived?"

"Sorry to disappoint."

They embrace. He pulls her close, and her arm grips the back of his neck as she burrows her head into his shoulder.

"I was worried about you, Callum," she mumbles. "So worried."

And I feel like someone has just punched me in the gut. My blood pumps cold and it is stupid for my body to be reacting this way. Because he is a wolf and an enemy.

And of course he has a woman back home. Because despite all his faults, he is strong and brave and kind.

I swallow and try to calm my racing pulse.

Callum stiffens, then turns to look at me as they release one another—his expression confused—as though he senses the raw emotion surging through me. The girl's eyebrows knit together as well. Her eyes narrow on my bare feet, on the damp fur cloak, and the dirty nightdress beneath.

She gives Callum a hard look, and his jaw tightens almost imperceptibly.

"Who's this, then?" she asks, putting her hands on her hips.

"This is Rory," says Callum—and there's a shift in his tone. It's almost as if he's daring her to challenge him. "She was one of Sebastian's prisoners."

I frown, wondering why he isn't being truthful to his wife, or lover, or whoever she is to him. Even though I suppose it is not quite a lie.

"She's not one of us," says the girl.

Callum's eyebrows raise. "Does that matter?"

"I suppose it depends on *who* exactly she is. And what you hope to achieve by bringing her here." She gives him another appraising look, then brushes him aside. "Are you okay, lass?"

Surprise blooms in my chest at the question. "I. . . yes. Yes. I'm fine."

She arches an eyebrow as if she doesn't believe me. "Aye? Well, if any of these louts give you any trouble, you come find me. I work in the stables." She gestures to an archway leading out from the courtyard.

"I'm sure I'll be fine." I stand straighter.

I don't want to come across as weak and powerless. I chose to come here—however ill-advised that may be. I don't want to be a victim. I am a princess.

"Hm," she says, taking the reins of Callum's horse. "For the love of *Ghealach*, get her something decent to wear."

"You realize I'm your alpha, right?" he says, eyes glinting playfully.

"Aye." She sighs dramatically. "And that's why I spend my days sweeping up after you." She pats the horse's neck, gives Callum a fond look, then leads the horse away. "Come on, Dawn."

"Fi," he calls after her.

"Aye?"

"Are the others back yet?"

Her brow furrows. "No. I thought they'd be arriving with you."

He frowns as she leaves, clearly troubled. He offers me a half-smile. "Probably hungover."

He puts his hand on my lower back to nudge me toward the castle. I stiffen at the inappropriateness of it. His woman friend is still in sight. His eyebrows knit together, but he drops his hand.

"Come on," he says. "Let's get you into some fresh clothes before we meet with the king."

I straighten my back, hold my head high, and walk toward the castle—trying my hardest not to limp when my muscles are screaming and stones dig into my feet. Callum doesn't say anything. And thank the Goddess he doesn't pick me up either.

He leans over me to push open the heavy oak doors, and we step into an echoey entrance hall.

I catch a glimpse of a dark mezzanine, draped with green tartan, and a large oil painting of a great black wolf, before Callum nudges me through a door into a long corridor.

Out of sight of the other Wolves, my body sags.

"Why did you tell your wife I was a prisoner?" I ask.

Callum's brow furrows.

"My wife? What are you—?" Suddenly, he throws his head back and roars with laughter. It makes me jump as the sound echoes around the cold space.

"Fiona? She's not my wife! *Ghealach*! Don't let her hear you saying that. She'd not be best pleased with you!"

Something that feels traitorously like relief blooms in my chest. I swallow, pushing it down. "Oh. You're inappropriate with *all* women then?"

He laughs. "I gave her a *hug*, Princess. She's my oldest friend. But wife? No. Whatever gave you—"

He halts and looks at me searchingly, his head tilting to the side. His smile broadens.

"What?" I fold my arms across my chest.

"So *that's* what that was all about."

"What are you talking about?"

"You know, Princess, that as a wolf, I have exceptionally good senses." His eyes glint in the torchlight. Then he starts moving again. "You were jealous," he says.

Chapter Fourteen

"I was not jealous!"

I march ahead of Callum. My bare feet slap painfully against the flagstones. I have no idea where I'm going, but I need to get away from the aura of amusement he is emitting, and the wide grin on his face.

I was. . . caught by surprise when he hugged that woman. That's all. He's a wolf! An enemy! I was *not. . . jealous* he might have someone back home.

I'm so flustered that as I turn a corner, I barge into a servant. She yelps, and her basket of potatoes spills onto the floor.

"Oh, Goddess!" I say.

"Watch where you're going—" She sniffs the air, and her lips curl into a snarl. "*Human.*"

I take a small step back.

"What are you doing here?" she growls, advancing. "Your kind isn't welcome—"

Suddenly she stiffens. The girl's eyes widen at something over my shoulder, and she bows her head in deference. Her cheeks flame.

Callum stands in the doorway behind me. He picks up a potato that has rolled into his boot, then walks over and places it in her basket.

"Everything okay, Kayleigh?" he asks.

"Aye," she mumbles. "Thank you."

She rushes off, presumably toward the kitchens, leaving me feeling rattled.

"She *hated* me," I say. I'm used to indifference within the walls of the palace, but not hatred.

"Can you blame her?"

I swivel round to face him. "I have done nothing to her. And she looked like she wanted to kill me."

He sighs. "You're a human, Princ—" He stops himself from saying my title. "Rory."

He walks past, and I fall into step beside him.

"Kayleigh's father was killed by Sebastian's army in an attack on their village, just north of the Borderlands," he tells me as we navigate the gloomy corridors. "Her mother was taken—she's presumed dead too. The humans burned the whole village. That girl, she barely escaped with her life. So, aye, she doesn't like humans very much."

"That. . . That's awful." I say. "I wish we weren't at war. I wish so many people did not have to die. But if the Wolves stopped invading our lands, then perhaps we could find peace. Three villages just south of the Borderlands were raided in the last month alone. Many of my people have been killed, too."

He looks like he's going to reply, but he runs his hand over his mouth instead. His callused palms make a scraping noise as they brush over his stubble.

There's a weary look in his eye—as if the facts I stated are tiring to him.

"Anyway, that's why I didn't tell Fiona who you really were. As Wolves, our hearing is a lot stronger than yours. If I'd have told her, the whole courtyard would have known you were the daughter of our enemy king, and betrothed to a man who has single-handedly tortured and killed many of our people."

"Oh," I say, softly. "They would have turned on me instantly."

"Aye," says Callum, darkly. "When the others are back, they'll find out who you are soon enough. I'd prefer to present you to the king first. It'll be easier to protect you if he makes it clear you're not to be touched."

A feeling, darker than the surrounding shadows, fills my chest. "What makes you so sure he won't execute me to send a message to Sebastian and my father?"

"Because he wants the Heart of the Moon as much as I do," says Callum. "And because I know him. And because. . . well. . ." He lowers his voice. "He owes me."

My gaze darts to his face, curious, but he's looking ahead.

When we reach the foot of a stairway, my shoulders droop again. Exhaustion is taking its toll on me, and the thought of mustering up the strength to climb who knows how many stairs is not a pleasant one.

But there will be some fresh clothes waiting for me at the top, at least.

Before I can step forward, Callum has scooped me up into his arms and is walking up the stairs.

"Put me down!" I protest, but my heart isn't in it, and my hands automatically clasp around his thick neck.

His warmth seeps through the fur cloak I'm wearing and my body seems to soften into his. One of his hands is curled around the bottom of my thigh, and I can feel his rough palms through my thin nightdress. A burst of heat surges through me.

Callum's jaw tightens, and he clears his throat.

"You're tired," he says. "And I gave you the dignity of walking past the others into the castle, but there's no one around now."

I'm surprised he considered how I would have felt to be picked up in front of all those Wolves.

Then I remember what Sebastian said at the dog fight—about Wolves preying on the weak. He must have known I needed to seem strong.

"I'm fine," I say.

"You're not fine. There's no need to put airs on around me. We know each other too well now." He carries me to a first-floor landing, leading me past a number of closed doors. His green eyes glint. "I mean, we've already slept together."

Heat floods my cheeks. "Don't you dare go around saying things like that!"

"But it's true!"

I punch his chest. It's like hitting a rock and he doesn't even flinch. He merely chuckles as he carries me to a door near the end of the corridor. A narrow window lets in a slit of cold sunlight, and offers a glimpse of the mountains and the dark waters of the loch outside.

He puts me down and his nose twitches.

"Isla?" he says, looking over his shoulder.

Seconds later, a pretty girl around my age with long mousy-brown hair rushes out of one of the nearby doors. She's wearing a dress made of the same red tartan that Callum's kilt is made of. She squeals when she sees him.

"Callum!" She throws her hair over her shoulder, then flutters her eyelashes. "I've run you a bath—just how you like it—and there's some fresh clothes laid out on your bed."

She doesn't seem to notice the weary look on his face as she loops a strand of hair around her finger and continues to chatter.

"I was hoping you'd be back in time for the full moon. And the equinox feast, I'm glad you didn't miss it. How was the siege? Some of the others were worried you'd not be returning, but I knew. Don't you worry about Callum, I told them, he's—"

She cuts off.

She straightens, her eyes darkening. "Who's this?"

"This is Rory," says Callum with a tired smile. "I need you to grab her some fresh clothes. A dress and some shoes." He pauses, thoughtful for a moment. "Put her in the clan colors."

Her smile disappears. "*She* can't wear the clan colors."

"I wasn't asking for your opinion on the matter, Isla," says Callum.

Her cheeks turn red and she lowers her head.

"Of course." She stomps over to the door she just emerged from. "Come on then." She shoots me a cold look over her shoulder.

Callum gives me a reassuring nod. "I'll be right out here."

Taking a deep breath, I head after Isla. She leads me into a room, and shuts the door before hurrying to a wardrobe at the far wall.

I linger awkwardly by the single bed against one wall.

"These are your chambers?" I ask.

She huffs as she sifts through the fabric. "Aye."

The room is small but comfortable. As well as the bed, there's an armoire and a dressing table with a mirror on it. A narrow window looks out onto the mountain. The scent of rose petals permeates the air.

A moment later, she thrusts a red tartan dress into my hands and some leather boots.

"Thank you," I say.

"I want them back, later." She scowls, flicks her hair over her shoulder, then exits the room.

I breathe out slowly. Even though we're indoors, my breath mists in front of me.

I suppose I'll need to get used to people hating me. It will only get worse when they find out who I really am.

I inspect the dress. It's simple—much less complicated than some of the dresses I wear at home. As I have no servants to help dress me, that is a good thing.

The fabric is thick red tartan, the same as Callum's kilt. I hope that this is a good choice. Callum said he looks after his own, and it makes it seem like I am part of his clan. I only worry about what his actual clan will think of me wearing their colors. If Isla is anything to go by, they won't be happy.

I take a couple of deep breaths to steady my nerves, then I peel off the fur cloak and wet nightdress, and change.

The boots are worn and a little too big for my feet, but I welcome the warmth.

111

I asses myself in the mirror.

I wince at the face starting back at me. My skin is pale and my eyelids are puffy. There are errant twigs caught in my tangled hair and I wish I had a brush and a hair tie. I don't look like a Southlands princess at all.

I look wild.

How can I possibly face a king looking like this? How can I possibly face *Callum* looking like this?

Panic rises, and my eyes burn as I frantically run my hands through my hair.

If I'm not perfect, how can I get through this?

"Everything alright in there?" Callum's steady voice permeates the door.

I close my eyes, then take a deep breath.

I am strong. I am stone. I am a statue.

"Yes," I say.

"Good. Let's get this over with, shall we?"

I pinch my cheeks, bringing a little color into them, raise my chin, then nod to myself.

I will survive this.

I head out into the corridor. "Okay. I'm ready to meet your king."

Chapter Fifteen

Callum falls into step beside me.

I should be taking note of the way through this labyrinth. I should be mapping out the exits, and memorizing the rooms in this castle where the Wolves await.

Instead, my attention is ensnared by the man beside me. His eyes travel over my messy hair, then linger on tartan dress.

He swallows before focusing on the corridor ahead.

My throat tightens. "Is there a problem?" I ask, pulling my fingers through the tangled knots of my hair.

I do not want to be nervous about meeting with Callum's king. But my stomach is turning over and over. If I'd just had a little more time to get ready—to compose myself and present myself in a way that is more fitting for the occasion—then perhaps this strange ball of energy inside me would have subsided.

"No." He shrugs. "You look—"

"Don't say I look nice. I don't. I have not slept properly, I've been on a horse for two days, and I haven't even had time to bathe!"

"I was going to say you look like a wolf."

"That's not a compliment!"

He grins. "But you do look nice."

"So you're a liar as well as a killer?"

"I'm only one of those things, Princess." We head down a stairway. "And I seem to remember *you* hitting a solider on the head when we were at Sebastian's castle, so perhaps I'm not the only violent one here."

"I didn't kill him," I protest.

"No, you didn't. It was a pretty weak hit." He raises his eyebrows. "We'll have to do something about that if you're to stay here with us for much longer."

"I saved you!"

The corner of his mouth tilts. "You caused a minor distraction, I suppose."

I cannot believe he is referring to the single most outlandish thing I have ever done in my life as a *minor distraction.*

I have only known Callum for a couple of days, yet he is already the most irritating male I have ever encountered.

We head down another flight of steps, then through a narrow corridor. The different stages of the lunar cycle are carved along the stone walls. There's a set of double doors at the end of the corridor with a colorful coat of arms hanging over it, depicting a wolf and a moon.

That must be where we are heading. I wonder if the man behind those doors will be cruel like the king I know.

"It's going to be okay, you know," says Callum softly. "The king is—"

He halts. All the muscles along his jaw tighten. For a moment, he is not the teasing Callum with mischief in his eyes.

He's the Callum who was in that dog-fighting ring—still and solid. A warrior. His biceps bulge against his sleeves.

He pushes me against the wall, and presses his palm over my mouth.

I inhale sharply. He doesn't move for a moment and his heat burns me. He puts a finger to his lips, and I nod.

He steps back, takes my hand, and pulls me back the way that we came.

Whatever he has heard, or smelt, has obviously rattled him. Danger lies ahead.

We're almost at the end of the corridor when the doors open behind us.

"Callum!" says a man behind us. "Where are you going?"

"*Shit*," Callum curses under his breath. He takes a breath, composing himself, then turns around. "Duncan, I need to speak with James."

The man in the doorway is shorter than Callum, and has blond hair scraped into a bun. He's wearing a blue tartan kilt— so he's not one of Callum's clan. He grins, then gestures behind him.

"Come inside," he says.

Callum pauses for a beat before he sighs. He heads back toward the door, his hand still clasped around mine.

I push down my panic.

When I first met Callum, I told him I had faced worse monsters than him.

I survived my father, who treats me like cattle to be traded to the highest bidder. My brother, who gained pleasure from demeaning me and humiliating me. Even the High Priest, who would beat me for my alleged sins.

I can face the Wolf King. Even if he is so fearsome that males like Callum have submitted to him.

Callum and I walk into a room that reminds me of a darker version of the council chambers back at the palace. There are fiery sconces on the stone walls, interspersed with carvings of lovers and Wolves and wars and moons. They might depict the story Callum told me about the Elderwolf and the Moon Goddess. A large green patterned rug is lying across the flagstones, faded where feet have walked across it. The air smells like woodsmoke, even though there is no fire lit in the grate. A thread of cold daylight comes in through the narrow window.

My attention is taken by the long table at the back of the room. And the four men sitting behind it.

The man—the wolf—in the center is obviously the king.

He is huge, with a shaved head, broad shoulders, and a thick neck.

On one side of him, there's a male with an unruly beard, and on the other sits a short male with long brown hair.

My gaze snags on another male sitting further away from them at the end of the table—the only one who is not looking at me. He's sitting with one arm over the back of his chair as he peels an apple with a small knife. He is strikingly handsome, with a sharp jawline and dark hair. Unlike the others, he is wearing breeches, not a kilt.

A strange feeling jolts through me. Recognition, perhaps, though I am sure we've never met.

Callum stiffens.

Duncan sits down at the empty seat at the left hand side of the table, and my attention flicks back to where it should be right now.

The Wolf King.

There's something predatory in his gaze as he looks me up and down. His kilt is the same color green as Magnus's. Callum implied that Magnus's whole clan was horrible. Yet when Callum spoke of the king, his voice softened.

It doesn't make sense.

I want to run away from this man, but I must play along.

I bow my head and curtsey. "Your Majesty."

There's a beat of silence, then all the men behind the table roar with laughter. All except the male with the apple who sits at the end.

"He's not the king," says Callum darkly. "Where's James?"

"He had business to attend to," says the male I mistook for the Wolf King. "Did he not tell you? He left me in charge in his stead."

Callum's eyes narrow. "Aye. Course he did."

"You're welcome to challenge me for the title, if you wish." The big man leans forward, resting his sizeable arms upon the table. "As it's my castle you're in, I don't imagine it'll go well for you. Nor do I imagine James will be happy if I throw the whole lot of you out."

A muscle twitches in Callum's jaw. "When will James be back?"

The man shrugs. "How should I know? A couple of weeks, maybe." His attention moves back to me. "I'm Robert. You can call me Your Majesty, if you like." His grin twists into a leer, and a couple of the others snicker. "The real question is, who are you? And what are we going to do with you?"

Chapter Sixteen

There is a ball of nervous energy inside me.

I walked into a den of Wolves, and they're looking at me like they're going to devour me. And this is before they've even discovered my true identity; the daughter of their enemy king.

It is only the dark-haired man draped over the chair at the end who seems disinterested in my fate.

"You're not going to do anything with her," says Callum. There's a deathly calm to his tone. "She was Sebastian's prisoner, and now she's with me. I wanted to speak with James, but as he's not here, we'll be taking our leave."

He grabs my hand.

"No," says Robert, softly.

Callum stills, and a thick tension spreads across the room, mingling with the heady scent of woodsmoke. He releases me.

"No?" he says, his voice equally quiet.

Robert nods at me. "Who is she?"

I raise my chin. My eyes flit momentarily to the narrow window and the mountains beyond—the freedom that I desire. "I'm—"

"Her name is Rory," says Callum. "A kitchen maid. Not that it's any of your concern."

A flicker of irritation cuts through the fear. Must it always be this way for me? Men discussing my future as though I have no say in it myself.

A crunch momentarily distracts me as the man at the end of the table bites into his apple. His eyes are on me, now. Glinting.

Callum shifts so that his body shields me from him—even though the man posing as the king is clearly the bigger threat.

"Why did you bring her here?" asks Robert.

"That's none of your concern," replies Callum.

Robert laughs darkly. "I won't have a human walking freely in my castle. Though perhaps she can stay with me and keep my bed warm."

A low growl vibrates in Callum's chest and the humor disappears from Robert's face. Beside him, Duncan rises and his hand moves to a sword in his belt.

It was foolish to come here, to think it would end differently than this.

These men will fight for me. And if Callum loses, will I be killed? Or will my fate be even worse?

I let a childish dream of freedom, and a wolf with kind eyes, ensnare me. Now I am in more danger than ever before.

Callum's hand curls into a fist at his side.

"Oh, let him keep his pet." The man at the end of the table finally speaks. His voice is as smooth as silk, and, to my surprise, he speaks with a Southlands accent. "Did I ever tell you about the time my mother let me keep a rabbit?" He looks at Robert, before going back to his apple. "When she took it from me, I cried."

No one speaks for a moment. Silence hangs over us like a shroud. Robert sinks back into his seat and scrapes his hand over his stubble.

He chuckles. "Very well. Keep your pet, Callum. But she earns her keep."

"I can find a use for her," says the man with the Southlands accent.

"No," says Callum.

The dark-haired male leans forward, resting his chin on his hand. "You know, little rabbit, I was in your king's army, once. Perhaps we've already met."

There's something pointed in his words and my whole body stills. Does he know who I am?

Callum clasps my hand, but his heat is not enough to thaw the ice that spreads through my veins.

"She's under my protection," he says roughly.

Tension radiates from him as he pulls me out of the room and into the corridor. I almost stumble. He is silent as he leads me back through the labyrinth.

I shouldn't have come here. I should have stayed with my people, and done my duty. I was foolish to think I was clever enough to survive this.

Callum squeezes my hand, as if he senses the direction of my thoughts, and my pulse steadies a little.

Then I pull out of his grasp.

He gives me a puzzled look.

"It's inappropriate," I say, quietly, as we climb the stairway.

He laughs, surprised. "That's what you're concerned about right now?"

"Well. . . no, Callum. I'm more concerned that I'm in a castle full of Wolves, my life is in danger, and your plan has failed."

Callum stops outside a room. "I'll keep you safe, Princess. You have my word."

"And what? You're just going to fight every single wolf in this castle, are you?"

"If I have to."

He leans over my shoulder to push the door open, revealing bedchambers. His, presumably. A large four-poster bed dominates the space and my blood heats.

I have never been in a man's bedchambers before.

"Go on," he says. He walks forward, nudging me through, then closes the door behind us.

He drops into a leather armchair by a window that looks out onto the loch.

There is a large armoire on one wall, and a chest at the foot of the bed. The dark wooden floor is covered with a tartan rug, the same color as his kilt. Above his headboard hangs an oil painting of a rugged landscape. There's a copper bathtub, filled with steaming water, in front of the fire in the hearth. I look at it longingly.

"I'm sorry I put you in that situation, Princess," says Callum.

I shift on my feet. "What do we do now?"

He blows out air. "Honestly, I'm not sure. I don't think anyone would be foolish enough to try anything with you under my protection. But I don't like it. And if they find out who you are. . ." He shakes his head. "Either way, it looks like you'll be staying with us for a while longer yet."

"That man. . . The one with dark hair who was sitting at the end of the table. He knows who I am."

Callum runs a hand over his full lips, then leans back in his chair. "Aye. I think so too."

"Who is he?"

His expression darkens. "His name is Blake. He's the most dangerous male in the Kingdom of Wolves, and he has the power to either help us, or destroy us. There's a feast tonight. I'll speak with him then. And I need you to come with me."

Chapter Seventeen

It takes everything in me not to crumple into a pile on Callum's floor.

"A feast?"

Back home, I'd relish the idea of going to a feast.

The balls, the gatherings, the summer festivals—I lived for those events. As stifling as they could be, they were the only times when my father saw me as useful—even if I was just a prop to him, or a trophy to dangle in front of visiting kingdoms.

But I have been riding for two days, and I haven't bathed properly, and I don't have my clothes or my servants or my make-up.

I shake my head. "No. I'm not in the mood for a feast. I will retire early tonight, and you can speak to Blake alone."

Callum sighs. "Why don't you sit down?"

He nods at the big four-poster bed to my side and my cheeks heat. I'm an unmarried woman. He can't possibly expect me to sit on his bed.

"I would rather stand."

"I'm not leaving you alone. You're coming with me."

"No."

He arches an eyebrow. "No?"

This man is a mountain, and he's used to getting his own way. There is only one card I can play to get the upper hand here.

"If you drag me into your Great Hall, I will tell everyone who I am!" I fold my arms. "It will cause carnage. And what will you do then?"

"That would end worse for you than it would for me, Princess," says Callum. "Believe me."

"So you're not going to protect me?"

"Oh, I would protect you from the Wolves outside these doors. But if you're going to do something reckless, it's me you'll have to contend with."

I feel as if he's just doused me with cold water. "You're threatening me?"

"Aye," he says. Though I've seen him threaten people before—with his muscles hard, and his posture dominant—and he doesn't look like that now. He looks relaxed, his expression soft, a playful glint in his green eyes.

"Is that how you became the big, strong alpha?" I demand. "Threatening women you kidnapped?"

"Not quite."

I fight the urge to ask him how he became an alpha, pushing down the intrigue that blooms inside my chest at how this infernal Kingdom of Wolves actually works. Now is not the time.

"Well, what are you going to do to me?" I ask.

The armchair creaks as he leans forward, and his heat and scent wash over me. "I'd start by telling everybody about our secret."

"What secret?"

"About our. . . sleeping arrangement last night." He clucks his tongue. "What will people think? A princess and a wolf. The scandal!"

My cheeks heat, and a feral sound escapes my lips.

A slow smile spreads across his face.

"What kind of gentleman are you?" I demand.

"I'm not a gentleman, remember? I'm a wolf." The amusement doesn't leave his expression as he nods at the bed. "Sit down."

"No."

He rises from his seat, and his body swamps mine. I have to tilt my head back to meet his gaze. "You must be tired," he says.

He steps forward and his chest bumps into mine. I stumble onto the bed, quickly pushing myself upright. My hands sink into the soft downy quilt.

His chest is right in front of my face. One of his buttons must have torn off in the siege, and I catch a glimpse of the skin and toned muscle beneath his shirt.

I swallow.

"Is this how you get your way? By pushing people around?" I ask.

"It's one of my methods of persuasion, aye." He crouches in front of me, placing one of his knees on the tartan rug. "I don't usually have to work so hard to get someone to do something. You're very stubborn, aren't you?"

He puts a hand on my thigh, and all the muscles in my body clench.

He quickly removes it.

"Come with me." He sighs. "Please. This is my fault. I put you into this situation. Let me fix this."

There is something so earnest in his eyes, so. . . lonely. . . that I fight the urge to touch his cheek.

Despite his infuriating arrogance, I can tell this is a man who feels the weight of his responsibilities and decisions. This is a man who bears that weight so others don't have to.

Something softens inside me, and vulnerability flickers in his eyes as if he senses it.

I sigh.

I'd rather speak with Blake in different circumstances. If I was feeling rested and sharp, I'd be more confident I could gain the upper hand. But I cannot deny that I am curious about the dark-haired wolf with the Southlands accent.

I'm sure my father would be interested to know about a wolf who claims to have served in his guard, too.

"Fine." I roll my eyes. "I'll come to your feast. But I need to wash first."

Callum smiles. When he steps away, the air feels lighter and I can breathe again.

He nods at the copper bathtub behind him. "Take it. It'll make you feel better."

"Where are you going?"

"I'll be outside." He leans against the doorframe. "Unless you'd like me to help you with your bath?"

I make a strangled sound at the thought of being naked in front of Callum with his hands on me. "How can you say such things?"

"What? It was a genuine offer!"

"No it wasn't! You're trying to annoy me."

He grins. "Maybe a wee bit. You're cute when you blush."

My cheeks flame and I hate myself for it. "Brute!"

He chuckles as he steps into the corridor.

"We have a few hours until we'll need to head to the Great Hall," he says over his shoulder. "Wash and get some rest. You'll need your strength. Feasts here. . ." He drags his teeth over his bottom lip, his eyes glinting. "Well, let's just say they can get lively."

And with those ominous words, he shuts the door behind him.

Chapter Eighteen

A floorboard creaks, and my eyes jolt open.

It takes me a moment to realize I'm lying on Callum's bed.

My body heats. Before today, I'd never even been in a man's bedchambers before—let alone fallen asleep on their soft quilt with my hair soaking their pillows. At least I had the grace to clothe myself in the tartan dress after my bath. Even if my feet are bare, and my skirts have risen to my thighs.

I can smell him on the sheets, soft and masculine, and my cheeks flush.

The room is dark, though a fire is crackling in the hearth, emitting a soft glow. When I glance at the narrow window, I notice the crescent moon outside. It is nighttime already.

Beside the window, Callum sifts through his wardrobe. He's wearing his kilt, but his shirt now hangs over the arm of his chair.

I bite my bottom lip.

I saw him topless when he was in the fighting ring, and his hard muscle had seemed fearsome. Now, I find myself admiring his broad shoulders and the way that the muscles in his back shift as he pulls out a shirt.

His skin glistens, and his hair is darker, as if wet. He must have washed, too.

"Good sleep?" he asks without turning.

I shut my eyes, my breath hitching.

"I know you're awake, Princess. Your heart is hammering." The floorboards creak as he turns. "You're not afraid of me, are you?" He sounds concerned—ashamed, even.

The air shifts as he approaches. My pulse quickens and I'm not sure why. I do not fear him, even though I probably should. He breathes in sharply, then places something on the bedside table beside me.

"If it makes you feel safer," he says.

I open my eyes. The letter opener he took from me during the siege now sits beside a half-burned candle.

I push myself up onto the pillows and take it, turning it in my hand. The silver gleams in the dim light.

I frown. "You would give me this?"

"I don't want you to fear me."

I stare at the tiny knife, then at the size of Callum, and fight the urge to roll my eyes. "I don't think I could do much damage with this."

An answering grin spreads across his face, and he shrugs. "Small things can be deadly, too."

He places his shirt onto the bed, and crouches in front of me. His face is close to mine, and I fight the urge to drop my gaze and look at his bare chest. He closes his fingers around my hand, and brings it close to his neck so that the blade is almost touching his skin.

My breathing quickens. "What are you doing?"

"Go for the throat." His voice is rougher than usual.

I swallow, then nod. The air heats, becomes unbreathable.

He pulls away and I exhale. He releases a long breath too, and I wonder if I wasn't the only one affected.

Turning around, he shrugs on his shirt, and buttons it up.

"I don't fear you," I say, quietly.

His shoulders soften.

"Good. You have no reason to." He nods at the blade, clutched in my hand. "The other Wolves here. . . and the particular wolf we'll be meeting with tonight. . ." His expression darkens. "Be on your guard, Princess. And stay close to me."

I place the blade in the pocket of my dress.

Callum holds out his hand. "Ready?"

My stomach is roiling, but I allow him to pull me to my feet.

He offers me a half-smile. "You know, these feasts can actually be quite fun."

"Apart from all the Wolves who want to kill me."

"Aye. Apart from that."

He leads me out of his room.

Callum said Blake was the most dangerous man here.

I suppose I'll soon find out whether or not that is true.

As we head down the stairwell, Callum reels off a list of all the foods we can expect to eat this evening.

I'm barely listening. I keep having to disentangle my hand from his, only for him to reach for me and enclose my fingers within his once more. I'm not even sure he realizes he's doing it.

This kind of overfamiliar behavior would not be tolerated in the Southlands, and I wonder whether all Wolves are this physical, or whether it's just Callum.

I don't hate it, though, and that in itself is rather disconcerting.

I'm a betrothed woman—even if I'm supposed to marry a cruel and horrible man. My father would kill me if he saw me holding hands with the alpha of Highfell. I don't even want to think about what he would do to Callum.

Callum's familiarity, however, is not enough to distract me from the high-pitched screeching that hits my ears when we walk into the next corridor.

Callum must notice my wince, because he chuckles. "You don't have bagpipes in the south?"

He points ahead. There's a young boy—around ten years old—standing at the entrance of the Great Hall. He has a blue tartan bag nestled beneath his arm, and his cheeks are as red as his hair as he blows into a pipe.

He looks like he's about to pass out.

"Just be thankful you don't have wolf hearing," he whispers darkly. "I had to listen to the wee lad practicing." He gives the boy a thumbs-up as we pass by. "Great job, Brodie!"

An extra shrill note rings my ears as Brodie puffs out his chest with pride.

A soft laugh escapes my lips.

Callum's gaze snaps toward me as we enter the Great Hall, a warm smile spreading across his face.

"What?" I ask.

He shrugs. "You have a nice laugh."

When we walk into the entrance hall, my smile fades.

In the Southlands, we thought the Wolves were too unruly to unite against us. For the centuries that we have been at war, they have fought among themselves, as well as with us. It has been our greatest advantage.

Yet here, within the walls of this castle, there must be over one hundred Wolves. They shout and laugh and insult one another as they sit along four long tables that are laden with food.

The air smells like ale and woodsmoke and roast venison.

At the end of the hall, beneath a coat of arms that depicts a wolf and a moon, there's a raised dais. At the table atop it sits Robert, the acting Wolf King.

Callum takes my hand and leads me toward him and the four equally menacing men that sit with him. There's a lull in the crowd as we pass by.

I'm not sure why he's taking me toward Robert's table. The Wolves sitting there look like the scariest in the hall—each donning a different tartan. Callum drops into one of the vacant seats at the end of the table, and gestures that I do the same.

Trying not to show my fear, I sit down beside him, the small letter opener pressing into my thigh. Not that it will do me much good if everyone turns on me. It seems like that may be a possibility. Everyone is looking in my direction.

Can they smell that I'm a human? Or are they wondering why I'm wearing Callum's clan colors?

Callum, however, seems perfectly at ease. His legs are spread, and his elbow rests casually on the table. When Robert looks at him, Callum meets his eye.

There's a moment of tension. Then Robert leans back in his seat and forks up a piece of meat before going back to his conversation.

The raucous laughter and merriness resumes—even if some of the Wolves look at me with a mixture of curiosity and hostility.

I spot Fiona, the girl I thought was Callum's wife, at one of the tables. She's wearing a dress like mine, made of red tartan, and her brown hair hangs in waves down her shoulders—though there are a couple of strands of hay in it.

She grins and turns back to the person next to her. Isla is sitting at the same table, and she scowls when I catch her eye.

Beside me, Callum grabs a plate and starts piling it with food—potatoes, roasted turnips, venison, thick meat gravy, and blackberry sauce. He places it before me, then helps himself to a plate.

I ignore my grumbling stomach.

"Weren't we supposed to be keeping my presence discreet?" I whisper.

"The alphas sit at this table." His voice is the same volume as mine as he scans the Great Hall. "And I'm an alpha. It would have looked stranger if I'd not sat here."

He stabs a chunk of meat with his fork and puts it into his mouth.

"Where's Blake?" I ask.

"No idea. Whenever he crawls out from wherever he's lurking right now, he'll come sit at this table too."

My eyebrows raise. "He's an alpha?"

Blake looks strong, but he isn't big and muscular like Callum or the other males sitting at this table. His accent also indicates he doesn't originate from the Northlands.

"There's been some debate over the matter," says Callum, his voice low. "The last person who questioned it hasn't been seen for a while." He nods at the entrance to the hall. "Ah. There he is."

Blake stands in the doorway.

Like earlier, he's dressed in dark breeches rather than a kilt, and wears a black shirt that is perfectly fitted to his hard chest and torso. His hair is dark, and a couple of errant strands curl against his forehead.

He scans the Great Hall, a bored look on his face.

When his eyes lock onto mine, a wicked smile spreads across his face.

He heads toward us.

Chapter Nineteen

Many of the men in this Great Hall remind me of beasts. But there's something different about the dark-haired male who prowls toward us.

It's not just that he wears breeches instead of a kilt. It's the calculated disinterest on his face, and the fluid way he moves.

He reminds me more of a cat than a wolf.

People much bigger than him watch him warily as he passes by.

When he stops in front of our table, Callum leans back in his seat, a look of dislike etched onto his face.

"Brought your pet to the feast, I see?" says Blake.

He's almost as tall as Callum, though not as muscular. He looks like he's in his early twenties like Callum, too. I catch his scent of shadows and pine—like a forest at night.

"We need to talk," says Callum.

A slow smile spreads across Blake's face, and dimples puncture his cheeks. "So we do." While Callum's voice is low and rough, Blake's is smooth like silk. "After we eat."

He looks at the door on the left-hand side of the hall and Callum inclines his head.

Blake drops into a seat by Robert and starts a conversation.

"I'm not a pet," I say quietly.

Blake meets my eyes and smirks.

Again, I feel that small tug of recognition. I wonder if I saw him at my father's palace. If I did, what on earth is he doing here?

"No. Course not," Callum says absently, stabbing a potato.

"What if he says something about me to Robert?"

"He won't. He's a self-interested prick. He'll want to find out what you're doing here in case there's a way for him to exploit it," continues Callum, lowering his voice. "There are too many ears in this hall. We'll speak with him later." He nods at my plate. "Enjoy your food. It's good, I promise."

***

The Great Hall gets louder with bagpipes, shouting, and slurred song as the night progresses. I'm starting to enjoy the music, although that could be because a small troop of musicians have taken over from ten-year-old Brodie.

While it's difficult to imagine anyone could turn into a wolf, the people at the feast move, and shout, and dance, as though no sense of propriety binds them. A fight has broken out by the entrance, and a man and a woman are kissing against the far wall.

I watch, fascinated, as I eat.

I count six different clan colors running through the hall— two different blues, a yellow, two greens, and the red that Callum wears. That means the Wolf King, whoever he is, must have united six clans. Perhaps seven. Blake, dressed all in black, is certainly set apart from the rest, and I wonder if his people are elsewhere.

People approach Callum throughout the evening—speaking to him deferentially and dipping their heads when addressing him. Some ask about the siege and the whereabouts of the other Wolves who still haven't returned. Callum tells them he's sent someone out to look for them, his jaw tensing as he relays this information.

He must be worried about Ryan. I am, too. I've no doubt Sebastian will have sent men after me. What if they caught up with the group Callum and I left behind?

A couple of hours into the feast, Blake finally gets up. He weaves through the crowd and exits the Great Hall through the door he nodded at earlier.

Callum waits a couple of minutes before rising. "Ready?"

My limbs are stiff, either from the horse-riding or from sitting down for so long, but I let Callum steer me through the boisterous crowd. His huge body creates a protective bubble around me.

When we reach the door Blake went through, Callum puts a hand flat on my stomach and I still. His warm breath tickles my ear.

"Just to warn you, Wolves tend to use this room on nights such as this when they want a bit of. . . privacy."

"That's good, isn't it? That's what we want."

"Aye," he says carefully. "But others may want privacy for a different reason. If you catch my drift?"

I don't, but I nod anyway.

"When we get in there, I'll need to tell Blake I've taken you prisoner," he says. "That's not the way that I see you, okay?"

He opens the door and hustles me inside.

The room is warm and dark, full of nooks and alcoves and small round tables where candles flicker. It smells like woodsmoke and spice, and it takes my eyes a moment to adjust.

There's a woman straddling a man on the leather armchair to our right. The top of her dress is pulled down, exposing her breasts, and the male has his mouth around one of her nipples. She rocks against him, moaning softly.

I gasp, jerking my head in the opposite direction.

Callum nudges me forward. "It's okay. Keep walking."

We head toward the hearth at the end of the room. There are two armchairs facing it, and Blake sits back in one of them, his long legs stretched out in front of him toward the crackling flames.

When we reach him, I look for a third space to sit down, but Callum hooks his arm around my waist and drops down into the vacant armchair—pulling me down onto his lap. When I try to get back up, his arm tightens around me.

Blake watches our almost imperceptible struggle, his dark eyes glinting.

He leans forward.

"Caught yourself a little rabbit, have you, Callum?" he says.

Chapter Twenty

My mouth dries.

Blake's gaze pins me to the spot, while Callum's thick arm holds me against his chest.

I'm not used to being so close to a male. Back at the palace, I had to dance, and smile, and sweet-talk nobles at social gatherings. If any of them had held me like this, they would have been executed. This is not appropriate. And it's certainly not the way I wanted to meet the male that Callum said is the most dangerous wolf in the Northlands.

But it is the strange heat pulsing beneath my skin that finally makes me try to shuffle out of Callum's grasp.

"Behave," growls Callum, and I stiffen.

He has not used this tone on me before, and panic surges through me. Have I misjudged this male?

But then I remember he was going to tell Blake I was his prisoner. I do not see how that can work to our advantage, though. If Blake knows who I am, then it only makes me look weak.

Before I can decide how to react, Blake takes my hand in his and presses his lips to my knuckles. I freeze.

"It's a pleasure to meet you, little rabbit," he says.

A low growl rumbles in Callum's chest and the corner of Blake's lip quirks before he releases me.

"You remind me of someone I saw back at the Southlands palace," says Blake. "Did you know that the daughter of the king has red hair, just like yours?"

"Give it a rest, Blake," growls Callum. "I know you know who she is."

Blake sighs, before leaning back in his chair and reaching for a glass of wine on the round table beside him. "Very well. Let's be direct with one another, if you don't want to play."

"Where's James?" asks Callum.

"There was a disturbance near the border. He went to sort it." Blake sips his wine. "You intend to trade her for the Heart of the Moon, I suppose?"

"Aye."

"If the Wolves find out who she really is, they'll tear her apart."

I frown. Must they speak about me as if I'm not even here?

But then Blake's eyes move to mine. Curiosity ripples off him. "Why did you choose to come here, little rabbit?"

"She didn't choose. I took her," says Callum. "And I've just told you why."

"Very well. I'm interested in how this is all going to play out. I'll keep your secret."

"If Magnus gets back before James, he could cause some trouble," says Callum.

"Are you asking for my help, Callum?"

"Aye," Callum grits out.

"Say please."

Callum's thighs tense beneath me, and I can feel the restraint in his chest. If he launches himself at Blake like I sense he wants to, we're going to be in trouble.

"Please," I say, giving him a hard look.

Blake's grin widens, and again I notice the dimples in his cheeks. "Looks like your pet has better manners than you, Callum. Very well. I'll deal with Magnus." He turns his attention back to Callum. "And you can put your rabbit in a hutch for safekeeping. The chambers in the western tower are empty—"

"She stays with me," says Callum.

Blake puts his glass down on the table. In a sudden movement, he reaches for me.

Callum grabs his wrist, stopping him.

I'm jolted forward.

"Look at you," says Blake. "You're like a dog guarding his favorite chew toy. What happens when you decide you want to play with it?"

"She's my prisoner," says Callum.

Blake chuckles. "Please. You're not a kidnapper, Callum. You're a savior. Perhaps you told yourself that you brought her here for the Heart of the Moon, but we both know the truth. You saw a woman who needed saving, and you wanted to be the one to do so. She'll stay in the room in the tower where we can both keep an eye on her."

"No," says Callum.

"You truly wish for me to believe you're holding her captive?" Blake arches an eyebrow. "Fine. Prove it. Make her do something." His lips curve into a smile. "Tell her to come and sit with me."

"That is not—" I splutter.

"The day I feel the need to prove myself to you is the day I relinquish my title as alpha of Highfell," says Callum.

Blake somehow manages to look bored even with Callum tightly gripping his wrist. "If you want my help, you'll put her in the tower."

"No."

"Fine. Keep her in your room. Have her sleep in your bed."

Panic, mingled with something else, surges through my body.

"Out of interest, have you had many dealings with noblemen in the south?" Blake continues, conversationally. "I have. They're a primitive lot. Did you know they require their brides to be untouched? Did you know, on occasion, they check?"

The blood drains from my face and Callum's biceps clench. "What's that got to do with anything?"

"Well, I'm curious, Callum. How do you expect to get her betrothed to agree to a trade when it's only a matter of time before you have your cock buried inside her?"

My cheeks flame. "That's not—"

"That's enough, Blake," growls Callum. "She'll be staying where I can keep an eye on her."

"The room in the tower is close to my chambers, and to yours. Do you think anyone would be foolish enough to try anything with either of us so close? She'll be perfectly safe."

"She's too valuable to risk."

"And what of the Heart of the Moon?" asks Blake. "How valuable is that? How will you trade her—"

I jerk forward, freeing myself from both of them and stumbling across the flagstones. Both turn their heads toward me.

Callum's body is hard with tension, whereas Blake seems merely intrigued.

I've had enough of this charade. Blake knows who I am, and he seems to have the measure of Callum, as well.

"Does my opinion factor into the equation?" I ask. "Or are you going to keep on speaking about me as if I'm not here?"

Blake's eyes gleam, while Callum looks a little sheepish. He releases Blake, and the dark-haired wolf leans back, resting his elbow casually on the arm of his chair.

"What is it that you want, Princess?" Callum asks, seemingly realizing the pretense is over.

Freedom. That is what I want. I want to be free from Sebastian, and to not have my fate determined by powerful men.

For that to happen, I need to be alone so I can figure out my next move.

I can't plot against the Wolves, and find out more information about the Heart of the Moon and the Wolf King, if I am kept in Callum's room, in his bed.

"I'll need my own chambers," I say. "If Sebastian found out that I'd shared a room with another man, I'd lose my value. You heard what he said back at the castle."

The muscles along Callum's jaw tighten. He sighs and inclines his head.

"Very well," he says. "But I have a condition. And I don't think you're going to like it."

Chapter Twenty-One

It could be my imagination, but Callum looks a little uncomfortable.

Blake, however, is grinning. He has one ankle on his knee. Again, he reminds me of a cat. This time, a cat who has found a couple of mice to play with.

Whatever this condition is, it cannot be good for me.

"You know, I didn't take you for someone who would engage in such an archaic tradition, Callum," says Blake.

"Aye, well, it'll keep her safe until we can get the Heart of the Moon."

"The Heart of the Moon. Yes. That's the reason." Blake's eyes glint in the firelight.

"What condition?" I ask.

"I'll tell you when we get upstairs." Callum gets up. "Come on, it's been a long night. You must be tired."

"You really should challenge him for the title, you know," says Blake.

Callum turns back around. "Who?" His tone is weighted.

"Rob, of course." Blake picks up his wine glass. "Who else?"

"That would cause trouble, and you know it."

"You're the rightful second in command. They're going to think you're weak."

"Only weak men feel the need to assert their dominance."

"For once, you and I agree on something," says Blake. "Others do not. You need to play the game sometimes, Callum."

"And you should take a break from the game every once in a while, Blake. There are more important things than power."

Blake's gaze falls onto me for a moment, before a slow smile spreads across his face.

"Not for me," he says.

***

My eyelids are heavy when Callum and I stop on a small, torchlit landing in the castle's turret.

My breath mists in front of my face, but the labored climb has me hot and bothered. I'm not used to so much exercise. Callum hasn't even broken a sweat.

"You said there was a condition," I say, suppressing a yawn.

"Aye." Callum pushes open a small wooden door. "It can wait until morning."

He nudges me inside.

The room is small and filled with books. There are piles of them on a writing desk and they fill the rickety shelf beside it.

There are even some stacked on the floorboards in one corner.

Against the wall, there's a single bed.

There's a scent in the air that seems familiar, but I can't place it.

"Can Blake truly deal with Magnus?" I ask.

My insides twist with hate when I think of the wolf who burst into my bedchambers back in the Borderlands. He threatened me. Twice.

I'd have thought Callum would be better equipped to deal with a male like that. While Callum has been gentle with me, I saw him in the fighting ring. I know he would be a terrifying opponent.

Blake emitted a dark undercurrent of violence too, but it seemed more calculated and sharp—like a blade rather than a hammer.

"Blake has leverage on a lot of the Wolves here." Callum's eyes harden on the candle that flickers on the bedside table, as though it displeases him, before he continues. "He's got something on Magnus. I don't know what, but if anyone can keep him in check without me murdering him and losing his clan's support, it's Blake."

When Callum opens the wardrobe, a low growl rumbles in his chest. It's full of clothes.

"The prick knew I'd agree to you staying here," he says. "He's had someone prepare the room."

He pulls out a white nightdress and hands it to me. It looks like it's exactly my size.

"It's clean," he says.

"Oh. Thank you."

I shift from one foot to another and Callum chews the inside of his cheek. For the first time since I met him, he seems at a loss for what to do next.

There's a strange energy in the air.

"Um. . . You can go now," I say.

His eyes widen. A slow grin spreads across his face, lightening his features.

"What?" I ask, folding my arms.

"I've not been dismissed since I was a wee lad pestering my parents," he says. He inclines his head.

He walks to the door, but lingers in the doorway.

"I'll come for you in the morning. And we'll talk about my condition for having your own room. If you agree, I'll show you around the grounds."

"And if I don't?"

He raises an eyebrow. "You'll be sharing a room with me for the rest of your time here."

Something in his expression changes, and I wonder if he can hear the quickening of my pulse.

"Good night, Princess," he says, his voice a little rough.

He walks out of the room and closes the door behind him.

The thought of being pulled onto his lap, his hard thighs beneath mine, flashes through my mind. I push it away.

"Good night," I reply quietly.

Though he doesn't respond, I am sure that with his wolf hearing, he heard me.

Chapter Twenty-Two

I have been alone since my mother died.

The loneliness has always spread through my body like rot. Even though I am continuously surrounded by people, it has lurked beneath my skin and threatened to consume me.

This morning, when I wake up alone, it feels different.

It's an alone where I can hear my own thoughts; they mingle with the gentle patter of rain against the thin window.

For once, I don't have to perform to anyone, because there are no ladies-in-waiting ushering me out of bed. Instead, I can lie bundled up in the soft quilt in a room filled with intriguing piles of books and sweet-scented herbs.

This morning, I'm not the king's daughter, or Sebastian's wife, or a princess with duties.

I am just. . . me.

A thrill surges through my body.

There are so many things I should be worrying about—the Wolves, the inevitability of Sebastian's army finding me, Blake telling the acting Wolf King who I am.

And Callum.

Callum, and whatever condition he wants me to agree to in order for me to keep my own room.

Callum is so unlike anyone I have met before. He is lacking in decorum, and he continually behaves in a manner I am not used to. He teases me, and asks me questions, and *touches* me.

And the worst thing is, I'm not sure I dislike it.

Right now, I feel at peace. Content.

Free.

I lie here for around twenty minutes, savoring the feeling.

My eyes catch on the wardrobe. I was too tired to investigate last night, but I'm curious about what clothes are in there.

Today, I intend to learn as much about the Wolves as I can, and I'm hoping I'll have a little more control over how I present myself than I did yesterday.

I stretch, my limbs aching from being on horseback for two days. I limp across the room and throw open the wardrobe.

I'm pleasantly surprised by what I see.

There is an array of dresses waiting for me. They're all made from dark materials—black, greys, and navy blues. I skim my fingers along them, noting most are simple enough for me to put on without assistance, and all are well made.

There's an elegant black dress in particular that catches my eye—made with silk and intricate lace. It emits power. I run my fingers over it.

It is not appropriate for today, though. I want to fit in, not draw attention.

I notice a couple of pairs of breeches in here, too.

In the Southlands, women do not dress in such garments. My father would probably disown me if he saw me wearing clothes like these.

Perhaps I'll try them another day.

Instead, I select a simple brown dress that should make me look non-threatening, and put it on.

I'm pulling my fingers through my hair when someone taps against the door.

My breath hitches because I know who it will be.

"Can I come in, Princess?" asks Callum.

When I open the door, he's wearing the same clothes as last night. A couple of the top buttons of his cream linen shirt are undone, and the sleeves are rolled up to his elbows. His jaw is shadowed with stubble, and I wonder if he slept.

His eyes are still bright, though.

"You look nice," he says.

Compliments seem to come so easily to him, and they seem sincere. It is unnerving.

I walk toward the window so that he can't see my smile. "Thank you."

The sky is full of grey clouds, and rain ricochets off the loch. The scenery, and the weather, is so different to the sun-drenched city beyond the Southlands palace walls.

Callum comes to stand behind me and his scorching body heat burns into my back.

"Miserable day, isn't it?" he says. "It rains a lot up here. I don't suppose you're used to such weather down in the south?"

"Have you ever been? To the south? Beyond the Boderlands, I mean."

"Everything's south when you're from Highfell." I hear the smile in his voice. "Aye, I visited King's City once. About. . . hm. . . must have been five years ago."

"To cause trouble, I presume?"

He laughs. "No. I was looking for someone. I thought she might be there."

A strange feeling surges through my body. "You were looking for a lover?"

"A lover? No." He sighs. "I was looking for my mother."

I glance up at him. He's staring out of the window, a pensive look on his face. Something softens inside me.

"Why would she be in the Southlands?"

He chews his bottom lip. "She went missing one night. My father thought she was taken by humans. She was presumed dead. But. . ." He shakes his head. "I never bought it. I think she ran away."

My eyebrows knit together. "Why would she do that?"

Callum swallows. "My father was. . . he was a difficult man."

"Oh," I say, softly. "Did you find her?"

He offers me a sad smile. "No."

A long silence stretches between us as we both stare out of the window. The trees beyond the loch whisper in the breeze, and there are no people in sight.

Again, peace washes over me.

Until Callum sighs.

"So, about this condition I have for you staying in here. . ." he says.

I turn to face him, and I have to tilt my head back to meet his gaze. "What is it?"

He pulls a small black box from the pocket of his kilt. He stares at it for a moment. Then he exhales, before passing it to me.

I frown as I open it.

Inside, there's a red tartan ribbon with a crimson jewel attached to the front.

"What is this?" I ask.

"It's. . . erm . . . a necklace." Callum rubs the back of his neck.

I take it out of the box. The length is short.

This is not a necklace. It's a collar.

He has the good grace to look a little sheepish.

"It's an old tradition." Callum clears his throat "When an alpha is in an. . . intimate relationship. . . they can ask their partner to wear one of these. It signals to the rest of the pack that they're spoken for."

He swallows, and his jawline hardens. His eyes smolder with intensity.

"If you wear this, it signals that you're mine."

Chapter Twenty-Three

The red strip of material hangs from my fingertips, and my jaw sets. Indignation rises within me. He cannot possibly expect me to put this on. It is degrading.

"It's a collar," I say.

"Don't think of it that way."

I drop it back into the box and thrust it back at Callum. "I won't wear it."

"It's not much different than a wedding band—"

"And you'll see I am not wearing one of those, either."

"You would have worn one, if I'd left you at the Borderlands."

"So that is my choice? To belong to Sebastian, or to belong to you?"

Callum's jaw tightens. "Surely I'm the better choice. Aye?"

My gaze dips down to his crumpled shirt, straining over tensed muscles, then back up to his eyes. They burn into mine and my heart beats a little faster.

The first time I saw Callum, I thought him a monster. He looked like one in that fighting ring, his broad chest bare, his torso as hard as rock.

Yet the true monster that night was sitting beside me. He threatened to take me like a common mutt on our wedding night. He said he'd throw me into the kennels after for Callum to use in the same way.

The thought filled me with fear. But I know now Callum would never have hurt me in that way.

Even though he is a powerful enemy of my people, I cannot deny the truth.

He is the better choice.

I swallow. "That is not the point."

"No," says Callum, raising his eyebrows. "The point is, it'll keep you safe. No one will touch you if they know that you're mine."

"People will already know you brought me here. Wearing this is needless."

"No, Princess, it's not." He shakes his head. "Telling people. . . It's not the same. We may not have noblemen and ladies like you have in the south. But we have rules, and laws, and traditions. Like, if I were to challenge Rob and win, I would take his clan and title." He nods at the item in my hand. "Wear this, and you won't be harmed. It's wolf law. Unbreakable. Inevitable. Just as we are bound to the Moon and must shift when she touches us."

I note how the red jewel refracts the morning light.

"Would you wear one of these?" I ask.

"Course I wouldn't. It's different."

"Why?"

"Because. . . Because I'm an alpha!"

"And I'm a princess!"

He groans and rubs his face. "You're impossible. That's what you are."

"And you aren't?"

He folds his big arms across his chest, and I fold mine, taking a step toward him.

"I agreed to come here in exchange for my freedom," I say. "Belonging to you while I'm here, then being shipped off back to Sebastian when you're done with me, is hardly freedom, is it? That was our deal. That was *my* condition."

A strangled noise escapes his lips. "Don't you see? This gives you your freedom! You can stay in this room, you can wander around the castle by yourself if you wish." He points at the window. "You can even go for walks outside. No one will touch you. You'll *be* free."

He steps forward, so that we're only inches apart, and his scent envelopes me.

"The full moon is getting closer, Princess. We've got a wolf inside of us. All of us." He puts a hand on his chest. "It affects us as it gets closer. It brings out certain. . . instincts. You're not safe. Not unless you wear this. Not unless people think you're mine."

I shake my head. "No. It's demeaning. I'm not doing it."

Callum closes his eyes. "*Ghealach*, give my strength."

He walks past me, drops the small box on the bed, then walks to the door.

"Where are we going?" I ask.

"*I'm* going to get some breakfast. *You* can stay here and think about your choices. Wear that, or have me at your side twenty-four seven." He leans in the doorway, and the corner of his lip quirks. "Unless that's what you want, Princess?"

"No!" I march toward him. "I'm hungry. I'm coming too."

He laughs, darkly. "Oh, I don't think so."

I put my hand on his stomach in an attempt to push him away, then I still.

His torso is solid, and I can feel the ridges of his muscles through his linen shirt. His body heat sears my fingertips.

I have never touched a man like this before.

My gaze flits up to his. The humor has gone from his eyes—and just for a second, before he blinks a couple of times—I think I see his irises change shape.

I pull away as if I have been burned, and take a big step back.

"I'm sorry," I mumble—then hate myself for apologizing. Hasn't he manhandled me enough times since we met?

He looks at me curiously, his expression softening.

"You don't have to apologize for touching me, Princess." He raises an eyebrow. "Now, if you want to apologize for being as stubborn as an ox. . . well, that's a different matter." He looks at the small box on the bed. "Think about it. I'll be back shortly when you've considered your options."

And with that, he turns and leaves me alone.

I sigh and go and sit on the bed.

I pick up the small box, and look at the offending item inside once more.

In my lifetime, I have done many things I have not wanted to do to ensure my survival. I didn't want to marry Sebastian to help my father secure the north, but I was planning to do it regardless. Because I feared what would happen to me if I didn't.

Putting this on would be the wise thing to do. If Callum is telling the truth, it would allow me to freely walk around the castle and learn about the Wolves. Who else in the Southlands would ever have such an opportunity?

On the other hand, it is degrading. Even if I cast aside what my father would think, I have to consider my future. My people would never respect me if I put this on.

What's more, Callum got frustrated with me when I refused. I don't know why, but that satisfied me. He is so big and strong and in control—it makes me wonder what will happen if he loses it. What will happen if I provoke the wolf behind the man?

I drop the box back down onto the mattress beside me. If anything, I'd like to see what Callum does if I offer a little resistance. He deserves it for not bringing me any breakfast.

My stomach grumbles as I continue my exploration of my new chambers.

There are books everywhere. I pick out *A Healer's Encyclopedia*, *A Collection of Diseases and Ailments*, and *A Compendium of Poisons* from among the titles. One dusty tome in particular catches my eye. *Experiments: Book One* is handwritten in an almost illegible scrawl across the thick spine.

I open it on a random page.

Wolves Healing Times is written in blotchy letters across the top of the parchment.

Tool: Iron knife. Insertion made along Subject Thirteen's lower torso, one inch deep. Healing time approximately three minutes, significantly faster than when cut with silver. If the blade was poisoned, would the substance linger beneath the skin? Test theory tomorrow.

Goddess! Did the former resident of these chambers write this book? I shudder, yet cannot help but flick to another page.

If I remove a wolf's organs, will they grow back? is written along the top of the parchment.

Someone knocks on the door, and I look up, startled, dropping the macabre book on my mattress. It lands with a thud, and releases a cloud of dust.

Has Callum realized he was harsh to leave me alone without breakfast? Or is it someone else?

I tiptoe to the door. "Who is it?"

"Can I come in?" The voice is female, and familiar.

Before I respond, Fiona walks into the room, bringing the earthy scent of horses with her. She's carrying a tray that has a teapot and chipped cup, a bowl of steaming porridge, and a small pot of honey atop it.

"On Callum's orders." She brushes aside a stack of papers and sets the tray down on the writing desk. "I'm also under strict orders that I'm not—under any circumstances—to tell you Callum was the one who told me to bring it up to you."

She grins over her shoulder, her brown eyes glinting.

"So why did you tell me?" I ask.

"Because he's a good man. And I don't see the point in hiding that."

She turns and leans back against the desk, her gaze narrowing on the small box on my bed. From her expression, I wonder if she disapproves of it as much as I do.

"He told me who you are, and why he brought you here," she says. "He also said you were being difficult."

I fold my arms. "Well, what does he expect?"

"He expects you to treat him as your alpha, and to do everything he says. And he doesn't know what to do with you, now he's found out you won't."

"He doesn't like people saying no to him, does he?"

"Oh, I think he does, actually. He's not used to it." She nods at the collar. "You don't want to wear it? Why?"

I assess her, wondering whether to tell her the truth. Back home, the ladies who would keep me company at balls, or on walks in the grounds, would go along with anything I said— wanting desperately to gain my favor and the favor of the king.

I get the impression that, for once, I can have a candid conversation. Perhaps she'll even understand.

"My whole life, I have been treated like a prize or a possession. I thought. . ." I sigh. "I don't know. I thought it might be different here. Like, maybe I could be something, or someone, else. If I wear that thing, I just belong to another man. It's the same as back home."

She nods. "Aye. I get that. You know, it's freer up here for females than it is in the Southlands. We can fight, and work in the stables, and we have a say in the clan politics. But you'll have noticed that there were no females sitting at that alpha table in the Great Hall last night. And there are certain old wolf traditions that, in my opinion, should be wiped out." She nods at the small box. "If it makes you feel any better, Callum doesn't like it as a tradition, either. And wearing it *will* give you the freedom to go about the castle without fear." She bites her bottom lip and looks like she's deciding whether or not to tell me something. "Honestly, I'm surprised he decided to give it to you. The cost is as high for him as it is for you."

My eyebrows knit together. "What do you mean?"

"Perhaps he'll explain it to you sometime." She pushes off from the desk and walks back to the door. "You should wear it though. The full moon is coming and you're a human." Her eyes darken in the morning light. "You'll need all the protection you can get when she rises."

Perhaps she is right, but I cannot bring myself to put on the collar.

***

The next few days pass by in a similar manner.

I wake up aching and sore—my muscles stiff from the journey here. Callum visits in the morning. Fiona brings me porridge and berries and fresh tea at breakfast time. And a lady-in-waiting visits in the evening to bring me potted pies, and cuts of meat and bread.

When I am alone, I explore my small bedchambers while the rain patters against the window.

I read more of that horrible book of experiments, flicking through pages titled *The effects of wolfsbane on a wolf's ability to heal*, *The order in which a wolf's bones break when they shift*, and *Provoking the inner wolf: A half-wolf's response to emotional trauma*.

I am certain I do not want to meet the person who stayed in this room before me.

I find myself looking forward to Callum's visits—where he inappropriately sits on my bed, or stands by the window, and shares snippets of his life with me.

He tells me about his clan's castle, which is so far north that it barely sees sunlight, about hunting in the forests as he was growing up, and about breaking his leg when he was a boy—climbing down into Glen Ghealach to find an old temple dedicated to the Elderwolf.

Despite his frustration with me that first morning, he doesn't push too hard about the collar.

"You know, some would think it an honor to wear," he tells me one morning.

"Like who? Isla?" I cross my arms. She practically swooned over him when we first arrived at the castle. I bet she would love to "belong" to him.

A slow grin spreads across Callum's face at that. "Aye. Like Isla."

I scowl and tell him to leave.

"But I'd prefer it if you wore it, Princess."

A traitorous smile crosses my lips that I quickly hide from him.

I know I should just end this stupid morning ritual—yet I cannot quite bring myself to do it. The days are peaceful, and a part of my soul I didn't even know was broken feels as if it is slowly starting to heal.

Strangely, Callum seems to be enjoying our newfound routine as much as I am. Though he appears increasingly disheveled each morning.

A small seed of guilt begins to sprout in my chest.

Is he not sleeping because of me? Has he been standing guard at night?

It is a conversation with Fiona, on the third night when she brings up my dinner, that finally seals my fate.

"Have you had word of the others?" I ask her, cutting into a piece of venison pie as I sit at the desk. "The ones who escaped Sebastian's castle with us?"

She's lying on my bed, her hands clasped behind her head, her dirty boots on my bedspread.

I have never had a friend before. My days were full of false smile and fake laughs. Everyone was too afraid of my father to say anything that wasn't superficial. A small part of me wonders if it could be different with Fiona, but I push the thought away. Why would she want to be friends with the daughter of an enemy king?

"No," she says. "We think something's happened to them. Callum's sent a party out to find them. He wants to go too, he's worried about the lad—"

"Ryan?"

"Aye. But. . . well. . ."

I put down my fork, frowning. "Why won't he go?"

She turns her head and arches her eyebrow pointedly.

"Oh," I say quietly, my appetite waning. "Because of me."

***

The next morning, I wake up early and watch the sun rise over the loch.

When I'm finally traded back to my people, I'm determined to be of more value to my father than a prize to be given to Sebastian. If I can prove that, I will be free on my own terms. And if wearing the collar will allow me to do that, I should do so.

It will allow me to explore this castle, and find out its secrets. I'm doing this for *me*, not for Callum.

Before I can think too much about it, I open the box, pick up the collar, and fasten it around my neck.

It's restrictive—a reminder that I am allowing myself to belong to yet another man. Or at least for it to look that way. The jewel is cool against my skin, and I feel its weight—heavy and prominent—just as I'm sure I will feel the weight of this choice in the days to come.

Feeling a little light-headed, I sit down on the edge of the mattress, and clasp my hands together.

It's not long before there's a heavy knock at the door. My heart jumps into my throat as I stand up.

"Come in," I say.

When Callum enters, his gaze instantly dips to my neck. His jaw tightens.

"If I wear this, I can keep my own room and wander, unsupervised, through the castle," I say.

He runs a hand over his mouth. "Aye." His voice is a little rough.

"Okay," I say.

He sucks in a deep breath. "Okay. But if you wear that in public, there are things that will be expected of you. Things that will reflect badly on me, if you take no heed of them." His eyes are serious—verging on stern—as they bore into mine. "So, we need to go over some ground rules."

Chapter Twenty-Four

"Ground rules?" I narrow my eyes.

Callum sighs, then nods at the bed. "Why don't you take a seat?"

"I'd prefer to stand."

He huffs out a laugh. "This is the first rule—if I ask you to do something, I need you to do it."

"Why?"

"Because I'm an alpha. And it's expected."

"So alphas are so fragile they cannot bear to be challenged on anything?" I cock my head to the side. "I think you are a lot more similar to Southlands lords than you realize."

A soft grunt of displeasure scrapes against his throat as he folds his big arms. I have to stop myself from staring at the way his biceps strain against his sleeves. I have to suppress my smile, too. Why is it so satisfying to get a rise out of him?

"No," he mumbles. "It's not like that."

The corner of my lip twitches. "What is it like?"

He sighs. "Okay, I suppose it is a wee bit like that. I'll look weak if you challenge me. And if I look weak, that puts you in danger. Aye?"

I roll my eyes. "Fine. But if you ask me to do anything degrading, I swear on the Sun Goddess, I will make you look so weak—"

"I won't, Rory. I promise I will not ask you to do anything that will cause you harm, nor compromise your morals or integrity. And in return, while you will be mine, I will be yours, too. I will be your alpha. And I promise to take care of you. For as long as you're here, with me."

I am held captive by his gaze. Something stirs inside me, warm, and it spreads through my body and seems to thaw my soul. "Oh," I say, softly.

I should find everything he is saying abhorrent.

But for the first time since my mother died, someone is offering to take care of me. I've been alone for so long that a part of me has forgotten how that feels.

I turn away from him and go and sit on the bed so he can't see the effect he's having on me.

"There's another thing," he says.

He follows me, then crouches down. The floorboards creak beneath his weight. He runs his thumb along the ribbon around my neck, and I forget how to breathe.

"People know I do not like this as a tradition," he says. "When they see you wearing it, they're going to think one of two things. One is the truth. They're going to think I'm hiding something from them and protecting you because you're important. We cannot let them think that."

"Because someone might challenge you?" I ask.

"Aye. And I'd win, make no mistake about that."

I fight my smile. It would seem like arrogance if anyone else said it, but with him, I actually believe it.

"But it would cause a messy political situation, and James, the king, wouldn't be too pleased with me."

"What is the other option?"

"If you're wearing that, people are going to think we have been. . . intimate. . . with one another. Do you understand what I'm saying?"

The memory of what Magnus did to that woman in the kennels floods my mind. He had her on her knees, moaning, as he thrust into her from behind. Sebastian said that that is how all Wolves take their women.

People will think I have done that with Callum.

My gaze drops to his broad chest, and his shirt collar, unbuttoned to expose his thick neck. His hands are on the bed by my thighs, and I think of them grabbing my hips. I Imagine him flipping me over and taking his pleasure from me.

A spark of heat flickers inside me.

"If you wear that, people are going to think you're my mate," he says. "It is the only other explanation for why I would have given you this. And we must encourage this explanation."

"Your mate?"

"It's a wolf thing. Rare, but powerful. Stronger, even, than love. Two souls chosen by the Moon Goddess to be together, their fates entwined. So. . ." He gives me a sheepish grin. "I may have to touch you from time to time—"

"You do that anyway."

"And you may have to act as if you actually like me, Princess."

"I do like you."

His smile widens. "Well, that's good then, isn't it? Because I like you too. Now, can you agree to all this?"

I must act as if he is my. . . lover? The thought makes my heart race a little faster.

Slowly, I nod. "I suppose. If I must."

"Good. Now, come. There's something I want to show you."

***

The dark waters of the loch ripple. On the far side, there's nothing but green craggy mountains. To our left, there's a large forest.

The wind is gentle today. It whispers through my hair and carries the scent of peat and heather. Swords clang in the castle courtyard behind us, but we're beyond the outer walls, and our spot is deserted. A few people looked in our direction when we passed by, but the dark cloak I found in the wardrobe hides the collar well enough.

I said that I'd wear it, I didn't say I'd display it.

Callum and I sit on the damp grass. He pulls out a hunk of bread he stole from the kitchens and breaks it in two, passing me half.

I take a bite, then stretch out my legs, wincing at the ache that pervades.

"You're still in pain from riding?" he asks, arching an eyebrow. "*Ghealach*, it's been. . . what. . . four days?"

"We can't all be big muscly Wolves like you."

He laughs. "Aye. That may be true. Four days. . . Do all humans take this long to heal? Because if so. . . perhaps we won't need the Heart of the Moon to beat you after all. . ."

There's a teasing glint in his eye and I raise my chin. "You know, I may not be a big bloodthirsty warrior, but I'm sure there are things I can do better than you."

"Oh aye? Like what?"

I shrug. "I have some skills in healing and apothecary." I'd had to. I tended to my mother a lot as a child then developed an interest in it after she died. I always wondered if I could have saved her, if I'd just known the right combination of herbs. "And I do a lot of needlework, too, back home."

He tears off a chunk of bread with his teeth and chews. "You like to sew?"

"I wasn't allowed to do much else. I was ill for a lot of my childhood. And my father would never let me go out and do the fun things the other children were allowed to do." I shrug. "It wasn't appropriate for my station. So I found my own ways to pass the time."

"What kinds of things do you like to sew?"

"Dresses, mostly. I love fashion." I swallow. "And my mother taught me how to embroider. I liked to create the scenes she would tell me in her stories as a child. I would pretend I was living in them." I shake my head. "It's silly, really."

"No," he says. "It doesn't sound silly at all. What else do you like to do?"

"Well. . . I like to read, I suppose."

"Another thing you're probably better at than me." Callum rests his arms on his raised knees as he looks out onto the water.

"You can't read?"

"I can. Not well. My mother taught me when I was a wee lad, but my father never thought it was important. He—"

Callum stiffens, and the hairs on the back of my neck prickle. We both look over our shoulders.

Blake leans against the outer wall of the castle around three hundred feet behind us. He's speaking to a girl who is carrying a dead pheasant, but his eyes are on me. His gaze drops to my neck, and the corner of his lip quirks.

"Blake," growls Callum. "What does he want?"

When the girl leaves, Blake walks toward us with his hands in the pockets of his breeches.

Halfway across the grassy expanse, he halts.

Callum sniffs the air, then jumps to his feet.

The two of them turn their heads toward the hill on the other side of the castle.

"What is it?" I ask, alarmed, as I get up.

"Horses. Fergus. Magnus. And. . . and Ryan." Callum's body is rigid, his breathing hard. "They're coming. I can smell them. And blood. I smell blood. Lots of blood." He swallows, and his face whitens. "Ryan's blood."

Chapter Twenty-Five

Something seems to pass between the two males.

Blake inclines his head. He walks back toward the castle, the breeze ruffling his dark hair.

In the distance, I hear shouting and the thunder of hooves.

"If Magnus tells anyone who she is, I'll kill you." Callum is breathing hard, his teeth gritted and his jawline tense.

Even a hundred feet away, Blake hears him, looks over his shoulder, and arches an eyebrow. He says something I can't hear, and a low growl vibrates in Callum's chest.

"Don't you think I know that?" he says. "Just get on with it and be quick."

Blake's lips curve, but he walks a little faster and disappears around the castle walls.

Callum is breathing fast. "Stay close to me."

We hurry across the grass, Callum taking care to keep stride with me. When a cry of pain rattles through the air, he breaks into a run. I chase after him.

I stumble into chaos when I reach the courtyard, and I lose sight of him.

The air is loud with raised voices, and Wolves are gathering. It feels like the hours before a storm—when the air is thick and static—and something is about to break.

A voice to my left shouts something derogatory about my father, another promises to take something from Sebastian and kill it slowly. Another yells that all Southerners will die.

The skin on my arms turns to gooseflesh. The crowd has swallowed me, my shoulders are knocked by big muscular arms, and I catch flashes of weapons and clan colors and eyes filled with hate. I need to find Callum. If these Wolves realize I'm the king's daughter, I'll be torn apart.

I don't think a collar will save me now.

I'm not sure even Callum can. A part of me wonders if he will even notice if they descend upon me. Someone from his clan has been injured. He is distracted. He has more important things to be worrying about than me.

I push toward the center of the crowd and the metallic scent of blood hits me in a wave. My stomach turns. Crimson paints the cobbled stones ahead.

Callum stands deathly still in the eye of the storm.

He says something to Fergus and Becky, the young kitchen maid rescued from Sebastian's castle. He grabs the pale body slung over one of one of two horses, and holds it over his shoulder. Becky lets out a cry that's audible, even over all the noise. Her face is streaked with tears and blood.

My heart stills. Ryan.

He is barely breathing. His eyes are closed, and there's a purple mark across his cheek where he's been struck. His shirt is drenched with blood and his copper hair is slick with sweat.

I hurry closer, causing a male in a blue kilt closest to the horses to curse at me.

"Watch where you're going, lass. You—" His nostrils flare, then his features harden. "*Human*. Hey!" He looks around him. "There's a southern bitch –"

Callum turns around, and time seems to stop.

A low growl reverberates from his chest, vibrating at such a frequency it rumbles around the courtyard. He has growled a few times in my presence, but this time, it is pure animal.

It reminds me of what he is. A wolf. A killer.

An alpha.

A hush falls over the courtyard.

Eyes flick toward the source of Callum's displeasure, and the wolf in the blue kilt steps back. The mob looks at me.

The hairs on the back of my neck raise as a whisper passes from mouth to mouth. *Human.*

I want to run, to hide, but I can't. I'm surrounded.

A gust of wind sweeps my hair out of my face, exposing my neck.

And the collar.

Another current of emotion passes through the crowd. Someone growls. A female spits on the floor.

"She's mine," says Callum.

My mouth dries at the power he commands.

His gaze seeks mine, and I raise my chin. He nods, and I nod in return.

Then time speeds up again. With Ryan over his shoulder, Callum strides toward the castle doors.

"Fergus, go get the healer." Callum says the word *healer* as though it tastes bad. "Isla, look after the lass—"

"I'm going with you," growls Becky.

Isla darts forward, but Callum meets Becky's determined gaze, sighs, then inclines his head.

"Rory," says Callum. "This way."

Isla's eyes turn to ice when they drop to the collar around my neck. Her lips pinch together.

Callum doesn't need to tell me twice. Even if I wasn't surrounded by Wolves who wanted to kill me, I would follow.

Not because of Callum's stupid collar. Because of the body in his arms—dripping with blood.

I am connected to that boy.

I spared his life, in the dog-fighting ring. I tended to his wounded arm in the kennels. He put me on this path that led to the Kingdom of Wolves. And it was surely my people, looking for me, that did this to him.

He cannot meet his end this way.

"Slut," Isla mutters as I pass.

I bite back a retort, not wanting to add fuel to an already inflammatory situation.

I feel the eyes of the surrounding Wolves burning into my back as I hurry through the castle entrance. The big oak doors swing shut behind me.

***

I follow the group through the castle.

We pass the kitchens, then head down a stairway to a dark room beneath the castle. We must be in the infirmary. There are shelves filled with small jars and pots along the walls, and a workstation littered with books and herbs and glinting metal tools against one wall.

There are a couple of cots, and Callum gently places Ryan onto one of them. He kneels down beside him and presses against the wound in his side. Blood spills between his fingers.

Ryan's breathing is raspy, each shuddering breath sounding like it could be his last. Callum looks like he's in pain.

There's a strange scent in the air, and the walls close in on me as I recognize it. It smells like death. The pain and the grief and the inevitability of what will come hangs like a shroud over us, and reminds me too much of those hours I spent with my mother before the end.

My heart pounds against my ribs. I don't know what to do.

Becky, grasping onto Ryan's hand on the other side of the bed, starts to cry. It's as if she has realized what is going to happen too.

"*Ghealach!*" curses Callum. "Why isn't he healing? He shouldn't be bleeding this much. Where the fuck is—?"

The door opens, and Blake enters. Despite the obvious animosity Callum holds for the male, some of the tension seems to leave his shoulders.

It's strange—the power seems to shift in the room, too. Even though Callum is the more muscular of the two males, he seems smaller, somehow, as Blake stalks forward.

"What took you so long?" says Callum.

"Magnus took a little persuading." Blake kneels beside Callum, and Becky growls as he lifts up one of Ryan's closed eyelids. "Make that noise at me again and I'll rip out your tongue."

Becky looks as if she's about to launch herself over the cot at him, but Callum raises a blood-slicked hand.

"It's alright, Becky," he says. "Blake's our healer here at Castle Madadh-allaidh."

I distinctly recall Callum referring to the castle's healer in a derogatory manner on the way here. Now I know why.

Blake is not what I expected of a healer. He is nothing like the fusty old men who worked for the High Priest and did little to ease my mother's suffering.

I watch as he unbuttons the cuffs of his sleeves, then rolls them up—revealing corded forearms, and a nasty scar just beneath his elbow.

"What's wrong with him?" I ask, thinking back to that horrible book of experiments I found in my chambers. "I thought Wolves healed quickly."

Candles flicker in the infirmary, and the light dances across Blake's chiseled features. "Come on, you know the answer to that, little rabbit."

"Why should I?"

Blake clucks his tongue. "So, you've wandered into a den of Wolves with no idea what weakens us? That's not very smart, is it?"

"Now's not the time, Blake," growls Callum.

"I expect stupidity from him," Blake continues. "You. . . no. Small and fragile things cannot afford to be stupid. They're too easy to break."

If Callum didn't have both his hands pressing into Ryan's side, I think he would have broken Blake. He certainly looks like he wants to—his jawline is hard.

Yet, oddly, beneath the thinly veiled threat, it feels almost as if Blake is trying to give me a piece of advice.

His eyes are glinting as if he's challenging me to find the answer.

I think back to that book again. There was an experiment that declared a substance that affected a wolf's ability to heal, and, in large doses, was deadly.

Dread fills me.

"Wolfsbane," I say.

"Good girl," says Blake.

Chapter Twenty-Six

Wolfsbane.

The air is sucked out of the infirmary. Callum tenses, and a cry tears from Becky's lips.

In the book I read, it didn't seem like there was a cure.

"Can you fix him?" The plea in Callum's voice breaks something inside me.

"Perhaps." Blake walks over to his workstation, and selects a pipette.

He takes a sample of Ryan's blood and holds it up to the torch flickering on the wall.

"What are you doing?" I ask.

"Identifying the strain."

Callum's gaze seeks mine. I can see he is lost, floating away, and looking for something to hold onto. Even though we barely know each other, he wants it to be me.

I know that feeling. I felt like I was drowning when my mother was dying. I wanted to grab onto someone, anyone— my father, my brother, the ladies-in-waiting—so that my head would remain above the water. Only, they always remained out of reach.

I will not remain out of Callum's reach.

My gaze flits back to Blake. "Can he be cured?"

"There's only one person in the Northlands who knows the antidote," says Blake.

"You?"

His lips curve into a smile. He goes back to the workstation and starts mixing something in a beaker.

"Keep pressure on the wound," he tells Callum.

When Blake returns, he tips back Ryan's head and pours the liquid into his mouth. Ryan chokes.

I step closer, peering over Becky's head. "That's the antidote?"

"Yes."

"What is it made of?"

"If I told you, I'd have to kill you." His tone is light, but I have the distinct feeling that this is not an empty threat. "Keep hold of him."

"I am holding him," growls Callum. "Fix him."

"How does it work?" I ask.

Ryan's eyes jolt open. His back arches off the cot, and his shoulders bend in an unnatural way. He screams.

Blake clamps his hand over Ryan's mouth, forcing him to swallow the liquid that he's trying to spit out.

"Is that necessary?" snaps Callum.

"Get off him!" shrieks Becky. "You're hurting him. Stop it!"

I watch the gash in Ryan's side, fascinated. The blood loss is slowing. Blake is hurting him, yes. But he's *fixing* him, too.

Becky doesn't see it, though. She throws herself at Blake. With his free hand, he grabs her arm.

"Take her outside," he says.

Callum looks at me, and I see the question in him, the plea.

"Come on, Becky." I gently touch her shoulder. "Let's—"

"No. The rabbit stays." Blake glances at Callum. "*You* take her."

Callum's posture straightens. "If you think for a moment that I'm leaving her alone with you—"

"Do you want me to fix him?"

Callum swallows. "Aye, but—"

He winces when Ryan lets out a bloodcurdling scream.

"Then take the girl outside, and leave your pet," says Blake. "She is of more use to me than you."

I bristle at being called a pet, but he's right. I can help.

Callum is too emotional. Whatever fight Ryan has ahead of him, it is clearly going to be painful—and Callum looks as if he wants to take the pain away.

The easiest way for him to do that would be to get rid of Blake. Yet Blake seems to actually know what he is doing. He is fixing him, in a way that no one was ever able to do for my mother.

"It's okay, Callum," I say, gently. "You should take Becky outside."

I know Callum will not be happy to leave me, or Ryan, so I search for a way to make him feel like he is in control of the situation.

"Someone needs to find out what happened," I say. "Others could be in danger. You should go with Becky and speak to Fergus."

Callum takes a deep, shuddering breath. "You're sure?"

"Yes."

Blake puts his hand on Ryan's wound when Callum gets up.

Callum's eyes narrow on him. "If you touch her—"

"Yes, yes, you'll kill me in an undoubtedly unimaginative way. Don't worry. I don't harm things that are useful to me."

Callum's warmth floods me as he touches my shoulder and squeezes lightly.

"I'll be fine," I say.

He takes Becky's arm and leads her, sobbing, away. "If you need me, I'll hear you."

"I know."

They head out of the room, and he closes the door behind them.

"Others could be in danger?" Blake rolls his eyes. "You're a manipulative little thing, aren't you?"

I glare at Blake. I do not like being called that. I wasn't being manipulative. I was trying to help. "I got him to leave, didn't I?"

Blake smirks. "Get a needle and thread from my case on the workstation. And the pot of white ointment."

I hurry over. The pot sits amid an array of glass jars, pestles, and dried herbs. I grab it, then flip open his case. There's are cold metal scalpels in there, alongside the items he's asking for.

When I have them, I kneel by his side.

"Put the ointment on the wound."

"What is it?" I twist off the lid. It smells sharp, like alcohol.

When I smear it onto the gash in Ryan's side, he shrieks. Blake grabs his shoulders and pins him down.

"It's to kill the bacteria. Wolves heal fast, but wounds can still get infected. Now, sew it up."

"Sew it up?"

"Yes. Imagine you're sewing a dress."

I look at him. Was he listening in on mine and Callum's conversation?

He nods at the wound. "Go on."

I grab the needle and thread. Hand shaking slightly, I hover above the wound. I am by no means queasy when it comes to blood and wounds, but this is something I haven't done before.

Blake leans over me, and I catch the scent of dark forests as he pinches the flesh on both sides of the wound together. He takes the needle from me.

"Like this." He punctures the skin with the needle, and Ryan shrieks again as he pulls the thread through. "Then, create a knot. Like this."

He hands the needle back to me.

I mimic Blake's movements as I pull the needle through his flesh.

"Wolfsbane is an intriguing poison," says Blake. "It attacks the wolf inside us. Stops us from healing, lowers our temperature, drains our strength."

With each pull of the needle, the wound gets smaller, and I feel more satisfied. My hand is no longer shaking by the time that I'm done.

"How does the antidote work?"

"It forces the wolf to fight back." He points at the thread. "Now pull here, tighten it. . . There. Good. Now, cut the thread."

He passes me some scissors, and I do so.

"How did you discover the antidote?" I ask.

He walks over to his workstation, and wipes his hand on a rag. "You don't want to know."

I focus on Ryan. He's already less pale, and his breathing is steadier. "Will he be okay?"

"That depends."

"On?"

"The strength of the wolf."

When Ryan faced Callum in the fighting ring, he was courageous. He faced his fate with strength and dignity. "He's strong."

"Not particularly." Blake drops the now bloody rag, and smirks when I glare at him. "It was a weak strain of wolfsbane. He'll recover."

I breathe out slowly. It's like a weight is lifted from my chest.

I don't fight the smile that spreads across my face.

Blake looks at me curiously. Then his gaze flits lazily to the door.

"You seem to be in some pain yourself, little rabbit," he says. "Muscular pain, from your journey here, I presume. If you come to my chambers tonight, I have just the thing to help."

Callum strides back into the room.

"He's in recovery," says Blake, before Callum can speak. "You can take him to his chambers, if you—"

Blake's gaze narrows on Ryan, and he snatches something from the boy's pocket.

"What's that?" Callum holds out his hand.

Blake turns over a bloody envelope. Instead of giving it to Callum, he passes it to me.

I frown.

Aurora is written in elegant calligraphy across the front.

Heart beating fast, I turn it over. The wax seal has a star in its center; the sigil of the Borderlands.

My skin turns cold as I rip it open and read.

A present for you, my love.

Think of the boy as a betrothal gift. I know you were fond of him from our time at the dog fight.

I'll be seeing you soon.

Yours,

Sebastian

Chapter Twenty-Seven

Ryan's chambers are warm and quiet.

A fire crackles in the hearth, casting light onto Callum's face as he sits in the wooden chair beside it. He's changed out of his blood-soaked clothes—as have I—and he's bathed. His hair is damp and brushed back from his face. He looks younger and more boyish when he's clean.

Becky snoozes in a chair next to the bed, and Ryan breathes softly as he sleeps. Alongside my relief at his recovery, a swell of satisfaction blooms in my chest. He is going to be okay. And I helped.

Still, a dark shadow hangs over me.

"What are we going to do about Sebastian?" I ask.

"Don't worry about that."

"Not all of your people have returned. He hurt Ryan because of me. And if he has more of your men. . ."

Callum runs a hand over his mouth. "It's not your fault. We'll get him back for this, I promise you."

Something twists in my gut. Now, more than ever, I do not want to go back to Sebastian. And, after spending time with

Callum, my initial plan of giving my father information about the Wolf King is getting less appealing.

Yet, if I stay, people will be tortured and die because of me.

I'm not sure if I can stomach it.

"I should go back," I say.

"No." Callum's eyes blaze into mine.

"You're going to trade me for the Heart of the Moon, anyway. Why not do it now?"

"No." This time his tone is final. "We'll find another way."

***

I'm not sure how much longer we sit there, but it feels late by the time that Callum walks me back to my chambers.

"Thank you for earlier," he says. "What you did for Ryan. . . I appreciate it."

"It was nothing," I say, embarrassed by the emotion blazing in his eyes.

"No. It wasn't."

Callum follows me into my room. Someone has been here in my absence, and lit the candles on the desk and the bedside table. They emit a soft glow, and flick shadows over the books and the small bed. They do nothing to fight the cold, though. My breath plumes in front of my face.

It has been a long day, and the adrenaline that was pumping through my body earlier has desisted—leaving me with aching limbs and heavy eyelids.

"Let me help," says Callum.

"What?"

He stands awkwardly beside the bookshelf. His height and broad shoulders seem too big for the small room. His head almost touches the ceiling.

When he drags his teeth over his bottom lip, an uncharacteristic vulnerability flashes behind his eyes.

"Blake said you were still aching. And the way you were walking up the stairs. . ."

"It's unsettling that you know these things, you know?"

He offers me a lopsided grin. "Aye. Not much is private around here. Imagine being a young pup, up to no good, and your mother being able to hear your racing pulse as you lie to her about your whereabouts."

"Were you often up to no good?"

"Oh, always."

I let loose a soft laugh, and his eyes brighten.

I shift from one foot to the other, suddenly very aware that we are alone in my chambers after nightfall. I swallow.

"It's not bad, the aching. Blake said if I went to his chambers, he would give me something for the pain."

Callum's expression darkens. "Blake was trying to provoke me. I doubt he has anything that could help. The wolf inside us fights off most pain relief. And if he did have something, it'd be in the infirmary, not his bedchambers." A sheepish look crosses his face. "But I can help you, if you'd like?"

"How?"

He nods at the bed. "Lie down. On your front."

"I will do no such thing!"

He laughs, softly. "I mean no harm, Princess. Nothing improper, I swear it. I promised you no one would touch you, and that extends to me."

I eye him suspiciously. "Well, what are you going to do?"

"Just massage some of the tension out of your muscles."

"That seems like you'd be touching me."

"Aye, I know. . . but it's not. . . I mean. . . it's not like I'd be. . ." He shakes his head. "*Ghealach*! You've got me tongue-tied."

He looks down at his feet. When he runs his hand over the back of his neck, there's a ghost of a smile on his lips.

"What I mean to say, Princess, is that I'm offering a massage purely for its medicinal properties. Just as a healer might offer a soldier treatment after battle. If you want it, that is?"

He shifts his weight from one foot to another. If I didn't know better, I'd think this arrogant, powerful alpha was nervous.

I suppress my smile. Why does that give me so much satisfaction?

I glance at his hands, by his sides, and my amusement disappears as I imagine them on me. They're so big and strong, I can't help but wonder what they would feel like. It would be wrong for me to let him touch me like that. I'm not supposed to let anyone touch me.

But it's not as if anyone would ever know. And if it's for medicinal purposes. . .

Heart racing, I lie down on my front on the bed. "Okay," I whisper.

He sucks in a deep breath before approaching. The mattress dips as he sits down beside me, and a wave of his heat washes over me. He smells like the outdoors and the mountains.

Tentatively, he brushes my hair off my neck and I tense.

He unfastens the collar, and places it on the bedside table.

"You don't need to wear that when it's just us," he says.

"Fiona said you don't like it. As a tradition."

"No. I don't."

He puts his hands on my shoulders and all my nerves come alive. His skin is hot, and his fingers are strong as he kneads my muscles. I breathe out slowly, my body softening under his touch.

"Why?" I whisper.

His hands move down, and his palms stretch across my back and make me feel tiny in comparison to him.

"My father was a. . . difficult male." His fingers are on either side of my waist as he runs his thumbs in gentle circles down my spine. I have to suppress a moan. "He was the alpha of Highfell before me, and he believed that leadership was all about dominance and bending others to your will. If you're not a wolf, you're a sheep, he would say. He did not treat his people well. Nor did he treat my mother well."

His hands move back up to my shoulders.

"He was possessive. Jealous. Angry. When he'd lose his temper, he'd say it was the wolf that made him do it. It wasn't. It was him."

He swallows.

"I don't want to be like him. I wanted to be alpha to look after my people, to protect them. Not to dominate them. But I feel it sometimes—that flicker of anger, or that twinge of jealousy. I wanted to hurt Blake earlier, when he invited you to his chambers." He laughs darkly. "When does protectiveness become possessiveness? Can you even be an alpha if a part of you doesn't like to be in charge?"

He runs his thumb over the back of my neck, leaving a trail of heat in his wake. I fight back a whimper.

"The collar, it's a symbol of dominance. And I don't like it. When I am with a female, I want it to be because we are equal. I do not want to become my father. I do not want my people to think that is who I am. And I don't want *you* to think that's who I am, Princess." He trails his hands over my upper arms, and sighs. "So no, I do not like you wearing that thing. It is a reminder of everything I do not want to be."

"What do you want to be?"

He pauses, and for a moment, all I can hear is his breathing and the soft flicker of the candle by the bed. "A good man."

I swallow. "I think you're a good man."

I probably shouldn't think that about a wolf who stole me from my bed, but I do. I have met monsters, and Callum is not one of them.

"That means a lot, Princess." Callum's voice is rough, and I know he's being sincere. "It really does."

Candlelight casts shadows across the wall beside me, and despite the heaviness of the conversation, my body is weightless beneath Callum's hands. He moves them over my shoulders, kneading and pressing his fingers into my aching muscles.

"Is this okay?" he asks.

"*Yes.*"

My blood is heating in my veins. Even though the chambers are cold, I'm hot.

He may be relieving tension from my muscles, but it seems to be building up in a different way. I want more. I want him harder, firmer, lower.

My breathing quickens. There's another ache building between my legs. As his fingers lightly brush my waist, all the heat in my body seems to pool at my core.

Callum stills.

Cold disappointment floods me.

"What's the matter?" I glance over my shoulder.

Panic surges through my body when my gaze lands on Callum's face.

I scramble forward, reaching for the silver letter opener on my bedside table, as I push my back against the headboard.

Every muscle in Callum's body is tense. He shuts his eyes. But not before I see what is behind his eyelids.

His pupils are dilated. His irises are a different shape, and brighter, somehow.

They are not Callum's eyes. They are not the eyes of a man. They have changed.

They're the eyes of a wolf.

Chapter Twenty-Eight

My grip on the silver letter opener is so tight that my knuckles are white.

The door is maybe a ten-foot dash from where I am, but I don't think I can make it.

Every story I've ever heard about Wolves crashes through my mind; stories about torn flesh, massacred villages, blood and gore and murder.

At some point since I was taken, I let myself forget the cold, hard truth.

This male can turn into a wolf.

Callum is breathing heavily, and his hands grip the bedsheets on either side of him.

"It's okay." His voice is as rough as gravel. "You're safe."

"Your eyes. . ."

"I know."

My breathing is fast, and my hand trembles as I brandish the ridiculously small weapon in front of me. "Are you going to turn into a wolf?"

His jaw clenches. "No. I can't. Only on a full moon."

I glance at the window. The candlelight is reflected in the glass. Beyond it, the mountains hide the shape of the moon.

"It's not a full moon," he says, a hint of amusement in his tone, as if he knows I'm checking.

"But I saw. . . your eyes."

"Aye." He lets out a shaky breath. "That happens sometimes. When I get a bit. . . emotional. I'm sorry. I didn't mean to frighten you."

I exhale. "You're not going to change?"

"No. You're perfectly safe."

I frown. "Are you sure?"

He laughs, though it sounds a little forced. "Aye. I'm sure."

My toes uncurl from the bedsheets. I move a little closer to him, and he tenses.

The floorboards creak as I slip off the bed. Warily, I approach.

He shifts his body in tandem with my movements, so that he's facing me—his thighs slightly parting as I step between them. My legs brush against his kilt. His broad chest moves up and down deeply.

He smells like the outdoors, like the Northlands winds have clung to his skin and his clothing—but there's heat beneath it. Like spice and woodsmoke. And he's warm. So warm. How can a male radiate such heat?

His face tilts up, and candlelight flickers across his closed eyelids. The movement exposes his throat to me, and I hold the silver blade between us.

I take a shaky breath. "I want to see."

Slowly, he opens his eyes.

My breath catches in my throat. His irises have expanded and changed shape. They're still green, but brighter, and within them there are flecks of yellow and gold. His pupils are dilated and they're as black as the depths of the forest at night.

They're wolf's eyes.

They are fascinating.

I have heard many stories about Wolves, but they all depict their brutality and lack of mercy when they raid our villages. I didn't know their eyes could change when they looked like men, nor look so beautiful.

I touch his cheek. The muscles in his forearms flex as his grip on the mattress tightens.

"It happens when you're emotional?" I ask. "What emotion are you feeling?"

"The same emotion as you, Princess."

"I'm not feeling anything."

He smiles, softly. "You might be able to hide your emotions from Southerners, Princess. You forget that I'm a wolf. I can sense things. Your heartbeat. . . your scent. . ." He swallows, hard. "It changes."

My fingers inch down the side of his face, touching his rough stubble. "Don't smell me."

He laughs and it sounds like a growl. "I can't help it."

"I'm not feeling anything."

"Okay."

His eyes don't move from mine. They are wary and alert, but there's something almost vulnerable dancing around those flecks of gold.

The air feels thick and heady and strange. Static, almost. And tension coils in my lower stomach.

Despite the chill in the room, I am hot.

I have a male in my chambers after nightfall, even though I am betrothed to another. He's an alpha of an enemy kingdom. He's plotting against my father.

I know everything about this is wrong, but when his hands shift on the bedsheets, I want him to place them on my hips.

His gaze dips to my mouth, and I forget how to breathe.

I want to brush my lips against his.

I want to know what it's like to kiss a man. Would Callum be soft and gentle, or hard and claiming? The latter would have scared me a week ago. Now, it heats my blood.

He closes his eyes and takes a deep breath.

When he opens them again, he averts his gaze to the floorboards between our feet. My hand drops to my side.

"It's getting late." Callum clears his throat. He stands, and I have to step back. "I should go."

Disappointment carves a hole in my chest. "I thought you were going to stop my arms and legs from aching."

He gives me a soft smile. "I think you want me to ease a different ache, Princess. And while, under different circumstances, I'd be happy to oblige, under these circumstances, it wouldn't be right."

My cheeks flame. "That's not. . . how dare you suggest. . . I'm the Princess of the Southlands!"

It is strange that even though his eyes look like wolf eyes, I can see the glimmer of amusement in them.

"Nonetheless, I don't trust myself right now." He bows his head. "Good night, Princess."

"Yes, good, you should go," I say, raising my chin, pretending it was *I* who dismissed him. "It is late. Good night, Callum."

He releases a shuddery breath as he exits my chambers.

Part of me wants to chase after Callum, and another wants to keep the door closed and never let him back inside again.

After dropping the letter opener on my bedside table, I sit on my bed and put my head in my hands.

I don't know what is wrong with me.

I feel like I am playing with fire—and there's a small dark part of me that *wants* to get burned.

Later, when I'm in my nightgown and settling down to sleep, I tell myself it was all just a lapse in judgement. I've had a long day, and the adrenaline made me want things I have never wanted before. That's all.

I didn't really want to kiss him. I didn't really want him to touch me. That would be wrong. I am an unmarried woman, and that would go against everything I have been taught to believe. It would take me even further away from my duty to my kingdom.

But it occurs to me, in the dark of night, that if Callum *did* touch me, Sebastian would not want me anymore.

I close my eyes, pushing down the dark thoughts this revelation has created.

When I finally fall asleep, I dream of Callum's mouth on my skin, his rough hands on my body, his strong arms holding me close to him.

And then I dream of unfamiliar wolf eyes, watching me, from deep within the forest.

Chapter Twenty-Nine

"You look frustrated this morning, Callum," says Blake at breakfast the next day.

He saunters over to the alpha table and seats himself beside the acting Wolf King.

"Aye, that he does," says Robert, not bothering to lower his voice. "Something to do with the Southern lass, do you reckon? I wouldn't be going around looking like I had a stick up my arse if she was wearing *my* collar."

He goes on to describe the horrible things he would do to me to relieve his frustration, much to my disgust, while two other Wolves roar with laughter.

Beside me, Callum's jaw sets.

"What do you reckon, Blake?" asks Robert, realizing that Blake doesn't seem to be listening.

The dark-haired wolf is sitting with one arm slung over his chair, seemingly staring at the tapestries that depict different stages of the moon hanging from the walls.

Lazily, he turns his head. "About what?"

"The lass!"

I feel Blake's eyes on me, just for a moment, even though I'm staring down at my porridge. My fist tightens around my spoon.

"She's adequate, I suppose," he replies.

I look up just as he grabs an apple and saunters out of the Great Hall.

Robert laughs as he continues his disgusting monologue about me. Rage builds inside my chest.

I wonder if he'd be so amused if I slipped some wolfsbane in his tea.

Callum puts a hand on my leg, and I start.

"I'll kill him for you, if you like," he says.

His voice is quiet, but the air feels charged for a moment. A furrow appears in Robert's brow, so I know he heard him, and Callum smiles at him. Threateningly.

Robert turns away and re-joins the conversation the other men are now having about Blake.

"Does Blake even like the lasses?"

"I think so. I've heard some screams coming from his room late at night."

"Aye, but they're not the good kind."

"I've heard he has some dark tastes. . . Never wanted to ask."

I turn back to Callum. "Would you really kill him for me?" I ask.

"Aye. I hope you don't ask. Because it could cause me some serious problems when the king returns."

I smile as I go back to my porridge.

I'm less amused when Robert looms over our table twenty minutes later.

"I said you could keep her if she earned her keep," he says. He walks off before Callum can respond.

"I could get a job in the infirmary," I say. I don't want to do anything to appease that horrible wolf, but I must admit, I'm curious. I wonder what I could learn about healing and Wolves if I had the opportunity to do so. "I don't mind. I have nothing else to do while we wait for your king to return, so I may as well make myself useful."

Callum's eyebrows raise, then he shakes his head. "No. I appreciate what you did for Ryan, but I don't want you alone with Blake." He gives me an assessing look. "If you truly want a way to pass the time, I may have an idea."

"What is it?"

"Our cook, Mrs. McDonald, is always complaining that she needs help peeling potatoes in the kitchens."

***

The past week, a restless energy has been growing within the castle. The Wolves are angry about the attack against Ryan, but there's more to it than that. It feels like the days before a big storm where the air is close and humid.

It feels like something big is about to happen.

I see less of Callum during the week than I did in my first few days here. It is partially because I'm spending my time in the kitchens.

When I first arrived here, someone made a comment about the cook, Mrs. McDonald, being like a dragon, and they were not wrong. She is truly a formidable woman—with greying hair and a sharp tongue. She is constantly shouting at me.

LAUREN PALPHREYMAN

Her hatred doesn't come from the fact that I am human; rather that I am incompetent in the kitchen. I have no idea how to make a stew, I burn the bread, and I'm constantly knocking things over.

I have never had to do these things before. People always served me my meals, so it's no wonder I'm useless. I have a feeling that even if Mrs. McDonald knew I was a princess, she would not sympathize.

I don't like being constantly scolded—for the first few days it was difficult to bite my tongue. But there's actually something refreshing about someone being unguarded around me—not fearing that I'll have them executed if they speak to me in a way I do not like.

It makes me feel. . . normal.

The other plus side of being so useless is that after a few days the kitchen maid Kayleigh, who snarled at me for making her drop her potatoes on that first day here, starts to take pity on me—even if she is still cold. She begrudgingly shows me how to dice an onion, and grumpily walks me around the kitchen gardens one day to show me the different herbs.

On the fifth day, when she cuts herself, I offer to take her to the infirmary and she blanches—clearly terrified of the dark-haired wolf who occupies it. I help her clean it so it doesn't become infected.

After that, she is a lot more pleasant, and even starts to gossip with me.

"What's Callum like in the sack, then?" she asks one day.

"In the sack?"

"You know, in bed."

I flush, remembering people are supposed to think I have been intimate with him. "Kayleigh! Can we change the subject, please?"

She giggles. "You Southerners are so shy. I bet he's good. I'd be shouting about it from the rooftops if I had a male like that in my bed."

Callum hasn't been anywhere near my bed again since he massaged me, though.

He tells me he is busy. He's trying to stop the Wolves from attacking Sebastian in retaliation for what he did to Ryan. Their best move, he says, is to wait until the return of the Wolf King—when he can put his plan into play and get hold of the Heart of the Moon.

But there is more to it than that.

Even though he has spent time with me every day—eating dinner with me in the Great Hall, and teasing me about Mrs. McDonald—he is more guarded around me. He's certainly been less physical and seems to avoid touching me.

I should be glad about that. Yet I'm worried I have offended him in some way. Or perhaps he has just lost interest in me.

I ask Fiona about him one day, when she shows me the stables on my lunch break.

"Don't take it personally," she says. "As the full moon gets closer, the wolf gets stronger. It brings certain. . . animalistic traits to the surface."

"Like what?"

"Like the need to hunt, to kill. . . to fuck."

My eyes widen and I splutter, "Goodness!"

She laughs and gives me a half-shrug. "All I'm saying is, he's trying to suppress the wolf around you, that's all."

There is an irony, I suppose, that for so many years, I tried to suppress my emotions and now Callum is doing the same. I think of that recurring dream I had, where I was a statue in the palace grounds. I haven't had that dream since I came here.

In fact, I no longer feel like stone at all.

I feel as if I'm finally waking up.

As the days pass, a restlessness grows inside me. It's wild and dark and aching. It is as if my soul is responding to the crackle of energy that pulses through the castle as the full moon approaches.

And I feel *alive*.

The day of the full moon, I'm dismissed from the kitchens early. Apparently, the Wolves fast during the day, and hunt during the night, so there is no work to be done.

It is raining, so I spend my day reading.

I find myself thinking about my mother's symptoms and searching for answers within the countless medical tomes within these chambers. I wasn't allowed access to such books at the palace—they were reserved only for the healers and the educated men—and I wonder if I may finally find my answers here.

I'm distracted, though. My skin itches, and every time I see the word "wolf" on the page, I think of Callum's eyes. Every time I shift position on the bed, I think about how he massaged me. Every time I catch the smell of woodsmoke drifting from one of the rooms below, I'm reminded of his scent.

Twilight arrives, and my room is painted in grey shadow. I'm reading about how a wolf bite can activate the wolf gene in a half-wolf, when someone knocks on the door. I drop the book.

I expect Callum to walk into my room, but instead, Fiona enters balancing a tray laden with bread and cheese, and a fresh jug of water.

Disappointment swells within me.

Is Callum not going to visit me tonight? I thought he would.

Fiona arches an eyebrow as she sets down the tray, as if she knows what I'm thinking.

"He sent me to tell you to stay in your room," she says. "He says you're not to come out for any reason."

She's even scruffier than usual. Her shirt is untucked and her dark hair is loose down her shoulders. I catch the scent of alcohol on her breath, and her cheeks are rosy.

"Where is he?"

"There's a ritual on the night of a full moon, out in the forest. We're all expected to be there to welcome the Moon Goddess. The alphas especially." She leans back against the writing desk. "Callum's there already."

I try not to feel hurt. I try not to feel anything. It shouldn't bother me that he is having a good time without me. Why should he give me a second thought? I'm just the bargaining chip that he will use to get his Heart of the Moon.

It's just, I'd started to think. . . I'm not sure what I thought. It was a silly fantasy, I suppose, that the powerful alpha of the Highfell Clan could fall for the spoiled Southlands princess.

I'm betrothed to another, anyway. Callum has always intended to give me back to him. And I have always intended to give my father information about the Wolves, so I might escape my fate with Sebastian.

How could anything ever happen between us?

I try not to think about the crude things Fiona said, about what the full moon makes Wolves want to do. If Callum wants to enjoy himself, then that is his right, and there are certainly plenty of females who would happily enjoy him.

Something dark and ugly twists in my chest. "What do you do at the ritual?"

"We drink, and dance, and cut loose." Her eyes are bright. "Then the moon rises, and we shift."

She pushes off from the desk, and heads to the door.

"No one will bother you tonight. We'll all be hunting in the forest. Stay in the castle." She nods at the letter opener on my bedside table. "Keep that close, too."

She leaves me to join Callum and the others.

As the room darkens, so do my thoughts.

The old me—the one who existed before I was taken— would have accepted that someone as important as Callum would not visit me before an important event. When I was left at home while my brother went hunting, or when I was sent to bed by my father at feasts so the men could talk, I accepted this without question.

But something is changing within me—shifting and transforming.

I deserved a visit from him. Didn't I?

The shadows grow, and in the distance, I can hear men shouting. I wonder if Callum's is among them. I try not to think about what he might be doing, and who he might be doing it with.

I'm sure Isla will be all over him tonight.

Before long, a ghostly glow fills my chambers, and curiosity pulls me to the window.

The full moon is high in the sky. I have never seen it so bright before. It paints the evergreens an ashy silver.

As I'm staring, time seems to stand still. Silence sweeps over the land. The wind drops, and the loch is deathly quiet. A howl breaks the night, followed by hundreds more. My arms turn into gooseflesh and the hairs on the back of my neck stand on end.

The Wolves have shifted.

I'm peering through the glass, wondering if I'll see any of them, when I hear a roar of pain. It's distinctly human, and sounds like it's coming from within the castle.

I breathe in sharply.

Has Ryan woken up?

Wolfsbane attacks the wolf. I've been reading about it all week. I wonder if he is unable to shift.

I move my weight from one foot to the other. I want to go to him, but I was told to stay in my room.

He screams again, and I cannot bear it. He is hurt because of me, because Sebastian wants me back and sent him with a message. My mother's voice comes to me, just as it did on the night when I went to the kennels to tend to his injuries.

Have courage, little one.

I have to do something.

I pull on my cloak and boots, pocket the silver letter opener, and hurry out of the door.

The castle is eerily quiet, and I can barely see where I'm going as I feel my way down the spiral staircase.

I reach one of the landings. The male cries out again, and I follow the sound down a sconce-lined corridor. There's a loud clatter ahead, followed by a low grunt. It's coming from one of the rooms.

Heart in my throat, I push open the door.

The room is dark, but I can see I'm in someone's bedchambers.

A regal four-poster bed with black silk bedding dominates the space. An oil lamp has shattered on the floor and shards of glass glint on the sheepskin rug.

"Ry—"

The young wolf's name dies in my mouth.

There's a male in the room, but it isn't Ryan.

He's facing away from me, so all I can see is a muscular back—a silver web of angry scars crisscrossing his skin. He's leaning against a desk and he's breathing hard.

He's wearing nothing but a pair of breeches.

"Blake?" I whisper.

I don't understand. He should be a wolf.

"What are you doing here, little rabbit?" His voice sounds strange—as dark and smooth as the night sky outside the window.

Slowly, he turns around.

He's covered in a thin sheen of sweat, and a couple of dark strands of hair stick to his forehead. There are scars on his torso, too, but my gaze is held by the strange look on his face.

I step back, my hand reaching for the knife in my pocket. "Blake... I... I thought you were... Why aren't you...? What are you doing?"

His nostrils flare.

He breathes in then sighs, his head tilting back. The tension in his muscles dissipates. "Fuck it."

When he meets my gaze again, the wolf is in his eyes.

A cold smile spreads across his face.

"Run," he says.

Chapter Thirty

Run.

Although my heartbeat skitters in my chest, I turn to stone. My feet grow roots and I cannot move. I can only stare in horror, unblinking, at Blake.

The ghostly glow from the full moon reflects off his damp skin. He stalks toward me.

"Run." His voice is different—low, and raspy.

The air is charged. It feels like lightning is about to strike.

And then he *changes.*

It only takes a few seconds, but every bone in his body breaks and shifts.

And what is left in his place. . .

Time stops.

He is as large as a wild bear. His fur is black, making him at one with the shadows. His eyes, amber, glow in the darkness. He bares his teeth and growls. Adrenaline surges through my body, cracking the stone and uprooting my feet.

Run, my brain screams.

Just as the beast leaps, I turn.

I bolt out of the room.

I knock my shoulder against the door frame as I escape, veering into the opposite stone wall, then stumbling into the center of the corridor.

There's a crash behind me. A gnashing of teeth.

My feet pound against the stone floor, propelling me forward. I do not know where I'm going. The night is dark. The corridors and stairways unfamiliar. Again, I am alone in a labyrinth of stone and shadow, and the beast is getting closer.

One word repeats in my mind, over and over again, as the sound of my heartbeat rages in my ears.

Run. Run. Run.

His claws scrape and clack against the flagstones. There's a smash as he barges into a wall, knocking an unlit sconce from its holder. His growl vibrates through my chest.

Faster. Faster. Faster.

I reach a stairway.

The wolf crashes in front of me, skidding over the stone. I change course, and he blocks me again with his teeth bared. His heat swamps me as I veer in the opposite direction.

He is leading me further into the maze, herding me like the dogs on the farms do with the sheep before they are slaughtered.

Goddess, help me.

The walls close in as I sprint past them. My hair sticks to my face, and my body is drenched in sweat. My cloak constricts me. The air is hot. Claustrophobic.

I need to get out of here. I need to feel the wind, and taste the mountains. I need the freshness of the rain to touch my face, and I need to see the infinite sky—even if it is not my goddess that lights it tonight.

I don't want to be herded into my own tomb.

I will not die tonight.

Something inside me screams.

Fight. Fight. Fight.

I hurl the silver letter opener over my shoulder. I don't wait to see if I hit my target, though he is so big, surely I cannot miss. A crash, then an aggressive growl, fills my ears. I don't pause. I wrench a large oil painting off the wall as I pass, partially blocking the path.

Ahead, there is the stairway that Callum carried me up when I arrived at the castle.

I almost fall in my haste to get down it, regaining my balance only when I reach the bottom. Then I'm in the entrance hall, and the wolf is behind me—but the doors are open and the night is ahead.

The wind rattles the walls, and it speaks to me.

Come. Come. Come.

My muscles screaming, I hurtle out into the deserted courtyard, then beyond the castle walls into the open wilderness.

The air has never tasted so fresh, and yet I am not safe. Not yet.

Heavy paws stir the wet earth behind me, and a growl is carried on the wind.

On one side of me is the loch, silver in the light of the moon. On the other, there is nothing but open space and the steep incline of the hill that Callum and I rode down when we arrived here.

I run in the other direction, past the castle and toward the thousands of evergreen trees whispering to me.

Hide. Hide. Hide.

The wind blows my hair from my face.

The air shifts as I enter the forest. It gets damper and darker. The smell of bark and heather floods my senses. Pine needles and twigs crunch beneath my boots.

A crash resounds behind me as the wolf—as *Blake*—leaps into one of the trees, using it to propel him into my path.

I change course, weaving through the tall trunks, barely feeling the branches that scratch my face.

And I'm aware he is herding me again. He keeps jumping in front of me, teeth gnashing, as he dismembers trees and scatters the undergrowth. I keep having to change course, desperate to escape his fierce jaws.

He knows this forest. He knows something I do not.

I find out what it is when I burst into a clearing.

A fast-moving river cuts the path ahead, crashing against the rocks and weaving to the right. I veer left but there is a thicket of thorns so thick there is no way through.

"*No!*"

A low, threatening sound fills the clearing.

I turn.

Neon amber eyes flash in the gloom between the trees.

The wolf stalks forward.

"Blake. . ." I say, breathless, edging back even as the river crashes behind me. "You don't want to do this."

I do not want to beg.

I do not want to die.

"Blake. Please."

He pauses, tilting his head to the side.

"You know. . . who I am." I gulp down the thick air. "This. . . is a mistake."

His eyes glint. Intelligence radiates from him, even in his wolf form.

I don't know if he understands me. I don't know if I could persuade him even if he did.

"What about the Heart of the Moon?" I try to reason with him. "If you kill me, you won't get it."

He looks up at the sky between the branches and howls. It is long and mournful, and it raises the hairs on the back of my neck.

"If you hurt me, Callum will kill you."

The way his mouth moves. . . it almost looks like he is grinning. Dread fills me. Perhaps provoking Callum is the whole point.

He snarls, and the noise is primal. There is no way to reason with him.

I veer to the side, but it is too late.

He crashes into my chest, and my back hits the undergrowth. The air is knocked from my lungs.

I push and struggle against him, my hands sinking into fur, my head tilting away from gnashing teeth. He is crushing me, immeasurably heavy and strong. I kick one of his legs and he growls.

"Get off me!" I screech.

My fingers fumble in the dirt, my heart leaping when they close around a rock. I smack him in the head with it, turning and crawling from beneath him.

He bites the collar of my cloak and drags me back, turning me over with his paws so I'm forced to look up at him.

His eyes glint, a predator pleased he has caught his prey. He licks my face, as if taunting me, his tongue hot and rough and disgusting.

My skin crawls, but I do not have enough air in my lungs to scream.

When he bares his teeth, I know I'm dead.

The river crashes behind me. The wind stirs the branches above.

Fight, it seems to say.

Fight. Fight. Fight.

I bare my teeth back, feeling something feral and wild knock loose inside me.

His lip curls above his teeth. And then a lower, more threatening growl rumbles through the forest. It stirs the trees and shakes the earth. Blake's ears prick up.

I cannot see beyond him, but something is approaching. From Blake's reaction, it must be something even worse than he is.

Blake turns. I gulp in the sweet taste of the night as I scramble from beneath him, dragging myself closer to the river.

Another wolf prowls into the clearing.

He is huge, with tawny fur and bared teeth. The ground seems to shudder as he approaches. Fear grips my heart and squeezes. Fiona's warning to stay inside the castle tonight resounds in my mind.

The wolf's gaze locks onto mine.

His eyes are green, with flecks of gold and yellow.

"*Callum?*" I breathe.

He growls, his gaze moving back to Blake.

Chapter Thirty-One

The two Wolves stare at one another across the clearing.

The air is charged. It's as if the forest itself is holding its breath. Watching. Waiting.

All I can hear is my pounding heart, and the whispering leaves as they rustle in the breeze.

Fight, they seem to be saying. *Fight. Fight. Fight.*

A growl builds behind the bared teeth of the bigger wolf— Callum. It is so low that I feel it vibrating thought my bones. The shadows seem to cower from him.

Callum would be a terrifying opponent as a man. Tall and broad with muscles that look like they're carved from rock. Now, he looks as feral as he is strong. His teeth are sharp enough to tear through flesh and his paws send shivers through the ground.

His eyes—they glow with the soul of the forest and they are *enraged*.

Blake answers with a snarl of his own. The dark wolf is standing close enough to me that I can feel his body heat. He's guarding me, I realize. Keeping his prey close. If he moved suddenly, he could rip through my flesh.

I attempt to edge backward, sharp stones digging into my palms.

A twig snaps beneath my boot.

Blake's head turns.

I recognize the intent too late to do anything about it.

Blake leaps on top of me as Callum races across the clearing. The wind is knocked out of my lungs. My pulse thunders as I push Blake's head back, my fingers sinking into black fur. His teeth catch on my cloak, narrowly missing my shoulder, but then the force of the larger wolf knocks him flying. There's a ripping sound as Blake takes part of my cloak with him.

I roll onto my front as Blake rolls back onto his feet.

Callum is close enough that I could touch him, and every muscle in his body is taut. He snarls. I eye him warily, as he glares at Blake with glowing eyes.

Blake takes off, part of my cloak between his teeth as he crashes through narrow tree trunks. Callum tears after him, stirring the carpet of wet leaves and skidding through the mud, slowing to a halt as he reaches the edge of the clearing.

He growls once more into the darkness, daring Blake to answer back.

Then he turns.

My heart stills.

Get up. My pulse screams. *Get up.*

I force my nerves to calm in the way I would when facing my father or the High Priest back at the palace.

Whatever hunting instinct Callum has within him, I do not want to provoke it.

"Callum," I say softly, warily. "It's okay. It's me."

I don't know whether the male I have come to know is in there.

All I know are the stories I have been told of Wolves. Stories of monsters who hunt and kill without reason or mercy. They destroy villages, and feast on flesh. There are even ghost towns in the Northlands, discovered by our armies, filled with nothing but bones.

The wolf standing before me is capable of all of those things, I'm sure.

The murals on the walls of the Palace show the Wolves as scrawny, and ghoul like—with dull fur, and frothing mouths, and unintelligent feral black eyes.

Callum looks nothing like that. He is majestic. The way he carries himself is tall and proud. And his eyes shine with intelligence.

He prowls toward me. The moonlight sifts through the branches overhead, and reflects off his glossy coat. I edge back, though the river crashes against the rocks close behind.

"Callum," I whisper. "You won't hurt me."

And then he is standing over me, close enough that I can feel waves of his body heat.

He stares at me—perfectly still. It's like he's trying to tell me something. He lowers his head, sinking into a bow. And I realize what he is telling me. I am safe. He won't hurt me.

Relief crashes over me and mingles with a strange, burning curiosity.

Tentatively, I raise a hand. When he doesn't move, I touch the side of his face, my trembling fingers sinking into thick fur.

He tenses and I stiffen.

The forest seems to hold its breath again. The leaves whisper.

Fool. Fool. Fool.

He nudges my hand with his head and I exhale—my breath pluming in front of my face.

I'm not sure what happens next. Will he let me go back to the castle? I try to push myself to my feet.

He nudges me back down. Before I can protest, he lies across my lap. His weight is even greater than Blake's and his heat sears me through my dress.

"Goddess," I gasp. "Callum. . . get off me, you big oaf. . ."

When I push him, he snaps at the air close to my hand.

"Callum!"

He rests his chin on the carpet of leaves.

"What are you doing? You'd better not be—" He closes his eyes. "Don't you dare go to sleep!"

He opens one lazy eye. And—even in his wolf form—I catch the glint of amusement.

And the stupid bloody brute closes his eyes again.

I try to wriggle out from beneath him, but I cannot move. It's as if there's a boulder trapping me. A big, warm, breathing, snoring, stupid wolf-shaped boulder.

I push him a couple more times, but he doesn't even stir.

I cry out, exasperated, as I realize it's no use.

"You are just as infuriating as a wolf as you are as a man!"

I lie back, and stare up at the slithers of moonlight through the branches of the trees. A breathy sound comes out of him that sounds almost like a laugh.

Around us, the leaves whisper and thick hedges rustle and the darkness creeps. Somewhere in the distance, a wolf howls.

And yet, somehow, despite everything that has just happened, I know I am safe.

***

I open my eyes to grey sunlight seeping through the branches overhead.

I groan. My back aches, and my eyelids are heavy. There's a dull throb in my temple and one of my arms is ice-cold. My mouth is bone-dry. The sound of water is tantalizingly close behind me, and small droplets of it splash my forehead as it rushes over the rocks.

I try to move to it, but I can't. I'm trapped. I cannot move my legs.

I glance down, and breathe in sharply.

Callum is curled over my lap, and he is no longer in wolf form.

His head is resting on my stomach, one big arm slung protectively over my body. He's facing away from me, his muscular shoulders rising and falling in time with his steady breathing.

And he's completely naked.

Goddess!

I stare up at the branches and steady my breathing—fighting the flush in my cheeks. Quietly, I push myself onto my elbows and look again.

My eyes trace the bulge of his biceps, then the broadness of his shoulders. An urge to touch him flares inside me.

Tentatively, I raise one hand, and hover it above his back. His body heat sears my fingertips as I move closer.

He stirs, making a soft, gruff sound at the back of his throat. Hurriedly, I lie back down again, pinning my hands to my sides.

He pushes himself up onto his forearms.

"Morning, Princess," he says.

He shifts so that his face hovers above mine. He keeps one arm over my body, cocooning me within his large frame. I keep my gaze on his, aware that if I look down, I will see a lot more than his back and shoulders.

"Had yourself a wee adventure last night, did you?"

Tension I didn't even realize was building loosens. I thought he might be angry with me for not staying in my chambers. Especially as he's been so stand-offish with me over the past week. Yet he seems relaxed. Amused, even.

"Why aren't you annoyed?" I narrow my eyes.

He looks at me curiously. "Why would I be?"

"I didn't do what you told me to do."

"If you always did as you were told, we would never have met. Plus, I'm presuming you had your reasons for leaving your room, and you weren't just out for a nighttime stroll?"

"Someone sounded like they were in pain. I thought it was Ryan."

He smiles, brimming with warmth. "There you go, then. I would have done the same."

"It was Blake."

He exhales. "Aye. I thought as much."

He sits up. The muscles in his back ripple as he stretches. He cracks his neck, then stands and rolls his shoulders. I'm not sure he even notices he's not wearing anything.

When he turns back around, my gaze drops. I cannot help it.

My eyes widen and I jerk my head back again to stare at the trees.

The only naked men I have ever seen are the statues in the palace gardens.

Callum chuckles. "What are you doing? Come on, we need to get back."

Face flaming, I roll onto my side so I'm not looking at him, and push myself to my feet. I wince. Every muscle in my body is stiff and aching.

When I turn to face Callum, my gaze accidentally drops once more before I resolutely look away.

"Come on," he says, amused.

His warmth washes over me as he steps closer and scoops me into his arms. I hook my wrists around his neck as if it's a reflex, but irritation sparks inside me. It's annoying enough that he thinks he can manhandle me whenever he pleases. It's even worse he thinks it's appropriate even when he's completely naked. "I'm perfectly capable of walking by myself!"

"Aye, I know." The corner of his lip twitches as he heads back through the trees. "I reckoned if I carried you, you'd have to stop staring at my cock."

I make a strangled sound, then punch him in the arm. I may as well be hitting a rock. "You're horrible!"

He laughs. "You're the one who can't stop looking."

I glare at him, and his expression softens.

"You've had a rough night, Princess. Are you okay?"

"Yes." I swallow. "Can you remember what happens when you're in wolf form?"

"Aye. I remember."

"Blake tried to kill me."

All the humor drains from Callum's eyes. "No. No, he didn't."

Fire blazes in my chest. I thought Callum might be different from the Southlands lords who never listened to, nor believed, the ladies in the palace. I was clearly wrong about him. I grit my teeth. "Yes, he did. You obviously *don't* remember if you think that, but the least you could do is believe me when I tell you."

Callum sighs heavily. "No, Princess. You've got me wrong. I'm not trying to dispute that he came after you. What I'm saying is he didn't try to kill you."

He chews his cheek, his expression troubled.

"He chased you to that clearing, far away from the other Wolves that were out last night. He got his scent on you so they wouldn't smell you. He took part of your cloak with him, so if they caught your scent, they'd chase after him instead."

He stares at the forest ahead, his jaw tightening.

"He wasn't trying to kill you. He was protecting you." He swallows, hard. "And Blake doesn't do anything unless it's within his own interests. So I want to know why."

Chapter Thirty-Two

Callum is quiet as he carries me through the forest.

While he was relaxed and easygoing when he awoke, his expression becomes increasingly strained as we get closer to the castle.

With every step, his jaw tightens, and his arms harden around me. His hold on my thighs gets firmer, his fingers digging into my skin through the material of my dress. A couple of times, I catch his nose wrinkling as if he smells something bad.

I sniff the air and all I can smell is the wet leaves from the forest.

I flush, wondering if the problem is me. I got hot last night as I ran from Blake, and I can't imagine I smell particularly pleasant.

"What's the matter?" I ask.

His eyebrows raise and I wonder if he's surprised I noticed. "I. . . it's just. . ." He shakes his head and gives me a small smile. "It's just a wolf thing. Don't worry about it."

When we reach the grassy expanse that leads back to the castle gate, the morning is quiet. A thin layer of mist coats the loch, and the heather and fern are dull in the grey light.

Ahead, there are a few Wolves making their way back through the castle walls, laughing and joking with one another.

They're all as naked as Callum.

"Goddess!" I turn my head, only to be confronted with Callum's hard chest. My pulse beats a little faster, warmth blooming in my lower stomach. His grip on me almost imperceptibly tightens. "You Wolves really have no modesty, do you?"

Callum chuckles. "It's only natural."

"Natural, perhaps. But it's far more *acceptable* to wear clothes when in other people's company."

"Only because that's what your society has taught you."

"So if I started prancing around without my clothes on, you'd be perfectly okay with that?"

A slow grin spreads across his face. "If *you* started prancing around with no clothes on, I think I'd like that very much, Princess."

"*Brute*," I mutter.

I expect Callum to take me back to my room, but instead, he carries me into his chambers.

There's a fire crackling in the hearth, and in front of it stands the copper tub, filled with steaming water. I glance at it longingly as Callum places me down on his bed, then turns and walks over to his wardrobe. I stare at the ceiling, determined not to look at him.

Then I glance at Callum, even though I know I shouldn't.

I'm not sure if I'm relieved or disappointed that he's pulled on a pair of loose-fitting cotton breeches. He's still topless though, his muscular back on display as he closes the wardrobe doors.

"I didn't know you wore breeches," I say.

"The way you were looking at me earlier. . ." He leans against the wall by the window, his eyes glinting playfully as he shakes his head. "I thought I'd better cover myself up as much as possible. I was feeling very vulnerable."

I sit up, pulling my knees to my chest as I lean against the headboard. "And yet, you seem to be absent a shirt."

He laughs, then shrugs. "I left my kilt in the forest. Don't tell anyone, but these breeches are actually rather comfortable. Do I look like a gentleman?"

I laugh, too, and shake my head. "No."

"No?"

"You look like a rake."

He puts a hand on his chest, his eyes widening in mock indignation. "A rake? Me? Why?"

"Firstly, there is the case of the missing shirt." My gaze drops to his chest and the ridges of his abdomen. I look at the hard V of his hips, and the line of hair trailing downward, and swallow. "Also. . . a gentlemen wouldn't wear those breeches."

"Why not?"

"Look how loose-fitting they are! And the material. . ." My gaze drops even further, before I hurriedly meet his eyes again, heat creeping into my cheeks. "I don't think you're as covered up as you think you are. Wherever did you get them from?"

"I got these from the King's City when I was looking for my mother. A market by the docks, if I recall correctly."

"That explains a lot."

"Why's that?"

"The docks are an incredibly disreputable place to go." I raise an eyebrow. "I should have known you would find yourself there."

A half-smile plays on his lips. "It was easier to blend in there as a wolf, that's for sure."

Something in the air seems to shift.

"Why did you bring me to your chambers?" I ask.

He opens his mouth as if to speak. The humor disappears from his expression and he sighs.

"I. . . the wolf hasn't quite settled down yet," he says. "I suppose I'm feeling a wee bit. . . protective of you, right now. I would rather that you were here."

"Oh," I say. "Okay."

Some of the tension leaves his upper body, and he raises his eyebrows. "Really? That was easier than I expected."

"I can be agreeable when I want to be." I shrug off my torn cloak, then I take off my boots, and shuffle back on the bed. "Plus, your bed is more comfortable than mine."

His gaze moves to my bare feet as they sink into the downy quilt, then back to my face. His jaw tightens.

"What's wrong?" I ask.

"Nothing."

He takes a step toward the bed. Then he halts, his hand curling into a fist.

Gritting his teeth, he swivels on his heel and starts pacing up and down the room. The floorboards creak beneath his weight.

My brow furrows. "Whatever is the matter with you?"

"I. . . nothing. . . It's a—"

"Do *not* say it's a wolf thing. You've barely spoken to me all week, I was chased through the forest last night, and now you're acting strange. Tell me what's going on."

He stands still and blows out hot air. "I don't want to make you uncomfortable."

Irritation prickles beneath my skin. "You don't make me uncomfortable. Goddess knows that you should. You're inappropriate, and you're the enemy of my kingdom, and last night you turned into a wolf and slept on top of me! But you don't. So stop acting as if I'm made of glass and you're afraid I might shatter, and tell me what's wrong."

He runs a hand over the back of his neck, then he sighs.

"Look, Princess, like I said, the wolf hasn't quite settled down," he says. "And you're in my bed, with the scent of another male all over you. And I don't like that. I don't like that one bit. I want you to smell like me. When another wolf is close, I want it to be my scent they smell on your skin. I want to mark you as mine. And I can think of countless ways I would do it. Countless ill-advised, highly pleasurable ways I would do it. It's all I can think about. And I know I should leave and calm myself down. But I don't want to leave. I want to stay here, with you." He shakes his head. "You smell so much like *him*... like Blake... It's driving me out of my mind."

I should leave before things get out of control. I shouldn't allow a male so say things like that to me. I definitely shouldn't *like* it.

I am held captive by his helpless gaze. Something hot is pooling inside me, heating my blood and making my skin hum.

I swallow. "Oh."

He rubs his face with both hands. "Fuck. I've frightened you."

The heat turns into angry flames. "Stop doing that."

"I know. I'm sorry." He stares up at the ceiling. "It was inappropriate—"

"No. Not that. *This.* Stop treating me like I'm some precious doll that needs shielding from the world. Stop treating me as if I can't handle things. As if I can't handle you. You *are* inappropriate. You shouldn't say half of the things you say to me. But has it occurred to you that perhaps I like it that you do? That perhaps I like it that you talk to me as if I'm an actual human being? That, perhaps, my entire life, no one else ever really has?"

My skin is burning now, and I'm breathless. It feels good to say it, to unleash it, to let something out that I think has been building up inside me for quite some time.

Callum's eyes widen. It's as if he's not quite sure what to do.

He releases a half-laugh. "No, I suppose it hadn't occurred to me."

"So, what do you want me to do?"

"About what?"

"You said I smelt like Blake. I don't want to smell like him either. Do you want me to wash?"

He exhales, then goes back to his pacing. "No. I want to wash you."

He sounds so sullen that it almost makes me laugh. "Callum!"

"What?" His lips are twitching, even though his body is tense. "I thought you liked how inappropriate I am."

I roll my eyes.

Then I glance at the copper bathtub.

Something has been knocked loose inside me. Telling him off has made me feel daring. I want to feel that way again. I'm fed up of locking up my emotions. I'm fed up of making myself smaller than I am so that others can feel bigger, stronger. I'm fed up of being shielded from the world and all it has to offer.

Curiosity flares inside me.

He protects me because he thinks he holds all the power. But the way he is acting. . . I wonder if *I* am powerful, too.

"Okay," I say. "Wash me."

Chapter Thirty-Three

Callum stills.

He's facing away from me, and the muscles in his back harden. I don't think he's breathing. I don't think I am, either.

We are both frozen in time.

Only, my heartbeat is wild in my ears. *Did I really just say that?*

He turns around.

He opens his mouth, then shuts it again.

"What?" His voice is low and gruff as gravel.

I raise my chin. "I thought Wolves had superhuman hearing?"

He lets loose a half-laugh. "Aye. But you can't possibly have said what I think you just said."

"Why not?"

The rise and fall of his chest is deeper than usual, as though he's making a strained effort to control his breathing. His fingers twitch at his side. "You want. . . You want me to wash you?"

"That's what I said."

"You realize you'd have to take off your clothes for me to do that?"

"I am well aware of how a bath works, Callum. I have bathed many times before. More so, I'd imagine, than you."

He laughs, shaking his head. There's an exasperated look on his face. "I'd imagine you've not been bathed by a male before? No?"

"When I was at the palace, people would always fuss around me while I was bathing. I do not see why this is any different."

His jaw tightens. "It's different."

"You Wolves all seem perfectly fine to wander around without wearing anything. I don't see why I should be held to a higher set of rules."

I slide off the bed and Callum tenses as I walk to the bathtub.

I'm hyperaware of him tracking my every movement, and it feels *good* to have so completely captured his attention. It feels *powerful*.

I run my hand through the water. It's warm and soothing, and the steam carries the scent of lavender as it mingles with the woodsmoke. I wonder if Isla ran this bath for him. The thought of ruining her obvious plans to seduce him provokes a burst of satisfaction that startles me.

I glance over my shoulder at Callum. He looks wary.

"What's the matter?" I ask.

"You're going to get me into trouble."

I am enjoying this far too much. "I thought you wanted to wash me."

"Aye." His eyes darken to the color of the forest at night. "I do."

I stare at the steaming water.

As much as I'm enjoying feeling in control of this situation, if I do this, it will be the boldest thing I've ever done.

I said this was no different than being bathed back at the palace, but it is and we both know it. No man has ever seen me without my clothes on before. That is something that is supposed to be reserved only for my husband.

For Sebastian.

For a man who makes males from the Northlands fight for sport. Who threatened me. Who skins Wolves alive and hurt Ryan and said he'd throw me into the kennels for Callum after he was done with me.

Sebastian sees me as nothing more than a prize, a trophy for him to keep on show, an item for him to do with as he wishes.

But what about what *I* want?

The bedchambers are silent, except for the gentle crackling coming from the hearth. I can feel Callum watching me, waiting to see what I'll do. The tension in the room is like a tangible thing, the air unbreathable.

"Princess. . ." His voice is strained. Almost pleading. Though I'm not sure what he's pleading for. I don't think he knows, either.

My fingers tremble as I undo the fastenings on the back of my dress. I pull the sleeves down, and let it fall and pool at my feet, leaving me in nothing but a black shift.

Callum's eyes are wide, and his hand is curled into a fist at his side. The distance between us feels palpable.

He doesn't move. He is that alpha from the fighting ring again; tense and ready for battle.

I don't want him to see the faint scars on my back—the ones that the High Priest gave me. So I face him when I take hold of the hem of my shift. His jaw tightens.

"Princess. . ." he says again, and I'm not sure if it's a warning or a plea.

I imagine I am back at the palace, and merely undressing for any other bath, and lift it over my head, revealing myself fully to him.

Callum inhales, his mouth slightly parting. He lets loose a shuddery breath.

He keeps his eyes on mine, his jawline hard with determination. There's defiance in his expression, too. It's as if he's fighting something.

But then his gaze drops.

And, Goddess, I feel the weight of it on my body. Though I'm standing close to the fire, my nipples harden. My breasts feel heavier, swollen. And there's an ache between my legs.

I cannot believe I am doing this. I should grab my shift and cover myself up. Yet I allow his gaze to brand my skin, and I feel *powerful*. I like the way his expression changes, his biceps tensing.

The wolf flashes behind Callum's eyes. He squeezes them shut and curses under his breath.

I step into the copper bathtub. The water is warm and fragrant as I sink down into it, letting it soothe my muscles and wrap around my body until only my head and shoulders are exposed.

Callum looks like he's in pain. I've never seen someone look so tense.

"Well?" I say.

The ghost of a smile plays on his lips. He blinks a few times, and he arches an eyebrow. "Have I told you that people don't speak to me that way?"

"Several times."

He huffs a laugh. Shaking his head, he crosses the room. With each step he takes toward me, my heart beats a little faster.

When he reaches the tub, he sinks to his knees, bringing his face close to mine. His warmth and heady scent mingle with the steam.

"You're sure about this?" he asks.

"It's not a big deal," I say, though I feel more daring than I have ever felt in my life. "People bathe me all the time. It's just a bath."

His eyes glint as though he can see through my lie.

He drags his teeth over his bottom lip, and for a horrible moment, I think he is going to walk away.

He laughs again, and shakes his head.

He reaches for the bar of soap and the cloth that sit on the tray on the floor, then trails his hand in the water. He doesn't touch me, but I feel his heat on my torso as though he is. He lathers the soap between his big hands—releasing the scent of soap suds into his bedchambers.

The humor disappears from his eyes. "I can smell him on your face."

I remember how Blake licked me last night.

I sink beneath the water, and rub my cheeks. When I emerge, Callum's muscles seem a little less tense.

"Better?" I ask.

"Aye." He gives me a soft smile. "Much."

He runs the soapy cloth over my shoulder, then down my arm. I can feel the heat of his palm, even though his skin is not touching mine.

I revel in the strangeness of this new feeling. No one has touched me this way before. I should feel vulnerable and exposed. Goddess knows, I am those things. But my body is soft beneath his touch, and it feels as if his hands were made for me.

He moves the cloth over my collarbone, causing my pulse to spike, and watches the trail of soapy suds he leaves in his wake. His hand seems so big when it's on my body.

My gaze moves back to his face.

Despite the heat that's pooling between my legs that has nothing to do with the warm water, his expression almost makes me laugh.

His jaw is set with determination, and I don't think I've ever seen someone look so focused.

His hand dips beneath the waterline, slowly moving down my chest. I feel his thumb brush against the swell of my breast and I know he must be able to feel how hard my heart is beating.

Why do I, so badly, want to tease him?

"I thought you said you weren't ever going to touch me," I say.

"I'm not touching you." His serious eyes follow his hand as it trails back between my breasts. "I'm touching the cloth. And the cloth is touching you."

A laugh I didn't know was building erupts from my lips.

"What?"

"Nothing. . . just. . . you." I look pointedly at his hand, splayed across my chest. The cloth is barely visible beneath it. "I would definitely consider this as you touching me."

He grins. "You'd know if I was really touching you, Princess."

I do know, I want to tell him. I know he is touching me because my whole body is on fire and there's something inside me that aches to be released and no one's hands have ever brought me to life like that before.

His expression darkens as if he's sensed the direction of my thoughts.

He shuts his eyes abruptly, hiding the wolf.

"Why do you do that?" I ask.

"Do what?"

I touch his cheek, dampening his skin with my wet hand. "You shut your eyes every time it happens. Are you embarrassed by the wolf?"

"Embarrassed? No. Never." He opens his eyes, revealing those strange yet beautiful irises. "I'm proud to be a wolf. But I don't want to scare you."

"I've already told you that you don't."

"You're very strange."

"So are you."

I trace his jaw with my thumb. Slowly, he moves his hand up to the back of my neck. His grip is firm, yet my body softens at his touch. His face is inches from mine, and his warm breath tickles my skin.

My pulse thunders in my ears.

"Rory." His voice is strained, barely louder than a whisper. He presses his forehead against mine, bringing his lips closer.

"You need to tell me to leave. I want to be a better man, but I don't think I can be."

"Callum—"

The door opens behind us and adrenaline and shame surge through me.

"What on earth have I walked in on here?" Blake's amused drawl comes from the doorway and a look of fury crosses Callum's face as he jerks back, his shoulders stiffening.

I sink further beneath the water, cheeks flaming as I glare over my shoulder at the male leaning against the doorframe.

"I had fun last night, little rabbit." Blake's lips curve into a smile. "We should do it again sometime."

Callum gets up, water running down his arms, and crosses the room in a couple of strides. He grabs Blake by the collar of his shirt, and slams him into the wall.

"Before you do something you regret, Callum," says Blake, his voice choked. "I have a message from the king."

Chapter Thirty-Four

I am exposed.

Even though my cheeks flame, the bathwater seems suddenly cold. The grey light coming through the window is revealing.

I'm not supposed to let any male see me undressed, and there are now two of them in the room.

What's more, Blake is clearly amused by the situation.

For a dark moment, I hope Callum chokes him.

After a couple of seconds, he steps back.

Blake doesn't quite manage to conceal the large gulp of air he takes before brushing down his now-crumpled shirt, the collar askew. His hair is ruffled, and his cheeks are slightly pink. He still manages to look smug, though.

"Which king?" growls Callum.

Blake leans against the doorframe and lets his expression settle into one of boredom. "Ours." There's something almost sarcastic in his tone.

"What message?"

"You know, you really ought to watch that temper of yours, Callum."

"And you ought to watch your back."

"Oh, you're far too honorable a wolf for me to worry about that."

"Goddess, Blake! Are you going to tell me the message?" growls Callum. "Or am I going to beat it out of you?"

Blake's eyes glint. He clearly enjoys provoking Callum. "He's in trouble. He needs your help."

"What trouble?" Despite the anger rippling out of Callum, I catch a hint of concern in his voice.

"Perhaps we should go somewhere private to speak. When you've finished washing your pet, of course."

My blood heats, and I straighten as I try to compose myself.

I catch the flash of interest in Blake's eyes when he catches sight of my upper back. He might have seen the scars that brand my skin. I sink down quickly, and the water sloshes over the side.

"You don't look at her. You look at me." Callum moves sideways so his body blocks me from view. "Get the fuck out of my chambers. I'll meet you downstairs."

Blake pushes off from the wall. "Look at you, dressing like a Southerner to impress the Princess. Breeches? Whatever would your father say? Goddess rest his soul."

Callum's entire body tenses. I remember what he said about his father. Whatever their relationship was, it obviously wasn't an easy one. Blake has crossed a line.

Something hardens inside me. I forget I'm naked and vulnerable.

I want to get under Blake's skin.

"Do the other Wolves know?" I ask him.

"Know what?"

"That you're ashamed of being a wolf."

"What makes you say that?"

"You weren't at the ritual last night." I recall the groans of pain that drew me out of my chambers, and the struggle on Blake's face when I walked in on him. "You were trying not to shift."

His head tilts, reminding me of a cat deciding whether it wants to play with a mouse. "Do *you* know?"

"Know what?"

"Why your mother died?"

All the blood drains from my body. Time slows. I am no longer a living, breathing, thing.

I am rage.

"That's enough." Callum's voice pulls me back into my body.

"She died of a disease," I snarl.

"Did she?" says Blake.

"*Out.*" Callum growls. "*Now.*"

Blake steps back into the corridor.

"Wait." I cringe at the desperation in my voice.

Both males turn to me, but only Callum seems surprised at my outburst.

"Do you know what she died of?" I ask Blake.

"No," he says. "But I'd like to. Wouldn't you?"

He turns on his heel, and disappears from sight.

Callum shuts the door. The wolf is in his eyes, provoked by anger this time. His expression softens as he looks at me. "Are you okay, Princess?"

My heart is beating too fast.

"Yes," I say quietly, though I'm not sure if I am.

I feel exposed again. Small. Silly. What was I thinking? I should not have been this bold. Nothing good could come of it.

Callum grabs a shirt from his wardrobe and pulls it on. "I'm sorry, Princess, but I have to go. I need to find out what's going on. If James is in trouble. . ."

"Blake could be lying."

He runs a hand over the back of his neck. "He wasn't. His heartbeat was steady. I believe him. Finish your bath. I'll come for you later."

He heads across the room, fastening his buttons. When he's opened the door, he looks over his shoulder. His eyes darken, and he blinks a couple of times before blowing out hot air.

"It's probably for the best," he mutters.

I'm not sure whether he's talking to me or himself as he heads into the corridor and closes the door behind him.

***

I finish my bath quickly.

I'm not sure how to feel about what just happened. It's the boldest thing I've ever done, and if my father ever found out, I'd be severely punished.

Still, Callum's touch lingers on my skin. I think he was going to kiss me, and what's more, I wanted him to. He has provoked a restlessness inside me that I have never felt before.

I almost miss the days when I felt nothing at all.

I dry off, and when he hasn't returned, I dress and head back to my chambers.

I hurry past Isla on my way, trying not to react as she mutters something derogatory about me to her friend.

Mrs. McDonald told me I didn't have to help in the kitchens today, so I spend my time poring over the medical books in my chambers.

Blake's words about my mother have taken root in my mind. I cannot get rid of them.

I read until darkness creeps through my window, and I have to strain to read the blurred ink on parchment.

When Callum still hasn't come, I wonder whether he's ridden out to some Northlands village to find the king. It angers me that he would go without telling me.

Yet after the events of last night, I am finding it hard to keep my eyes open.

I shut them.

I'm in the forest, lying on my back.

The moonlight seeps through the branches overhead.

Callum's face hovers above mine. His body pins me to the fresh earth and his body heat sears into me. He is naked, and I feel the hardness of him against my hip.

A growl reverberates through my chest, though I am not sure if it is coming from him or me as his lips move to my jaw, my neck, my collarbone. My legs wrap around his waist.

And I am on fire.

Flames rage inside me, longing for release.

It is suffocating. The heat. The furnace. The weight of him. The pressure building at my core.

I sink my fingernails into his back and he groans as his mouth moves lower, and one of his hands moves higher.

There is an ache between my legs where heat pools. An unbearable ache.

"Callum," I gasp. "Callum."

The air is still, crushing, unrelenting.

The leaves rustle.

We are not alone in the forest.

He nips my ear with his teeth and a spark of heat rushes through me. I moan as my back arches.

My gaze locks onto the wolf, standing in the shadows.

It crashes through the undergrowth toward me.

My eyes jolt open.

My pulse is racing and my body is on fire. The ache from my dream is still there. I'm breathing fast and the covers stick to my skin. Liquid heat pools between my legs.

It takes me a moment to get my bearings—the single bed, the books and pots on the shelves, and the night casting my chambers in shadow.

There's a crash outside my door.

I bolt out of bed.

"Stay away from her." Callum's rough voice reverberates through the door. I fling it open.

Callum has shoved Blake into the wall, like he did this morning. Yet there is something more threatening about the position in the darkness. Callum seems bigger and more unruly. Blake is tense, his eyes narrowed. He is fighting back this time, with his hand curled around Callum's neck.

Both males look as if they are struggling for breath.

They turn to look at me, and I inhale sharply.

Callum looks feral. There is no other word to describe him. His eyes are as bright, and as wolf-like, as they were when he was in wolf form. His breathing is ragged and hard.

"Go back inside," says Blake. *"Now."*

"Callum?" I say softly.

He releases Blake and turns to face me. He looks different. Wild. The wolf-like desire to hunt gleams in his eyes.

He stands there, perfectly still.

It should scare me. *He* should scare me. Yet my pulse is quickening for a different reason entirely.

"Callum? What's wrong?"

He stalks toward me.

Chapter Thirty-Five

Callum is no longer the male I have come to know. He is no longer gentle and protective and kind. He is the wolf that chased Blake in the forest—wild and feral and hungry.

His muscles are tensed, and his biceps look like they're about to rip free from his rolled-up sleeves. His forearms are corded and they're like steel.

And the scent of him—Goddess, the scent of him—is somehow dark and primal and powerful.

His eyes glow in the darkness, and they are locked on mine.

My whole body is hot. Aching. Restless.

What is wrong with him? What is wrong with *me*?

I cannot decide whether to run away from him, or run toward him.

I am ensnared. I can't move, even though the Northlands winds seem to rage inside me.

The air pulses as he gets closer and heat radiates from him.

"Callum!" A sharp female voice slices through the darkness.

He spins around and growls. His power rumbles across the small landing as Fiona comes into view, panting. She halts at the top of the winding staircase and her stance widens—as if she's getting ready to fight. Even if she's only wearing a thin nightgown, and her brown hair is loose.

"Callum!" Command laces her tone, despite the wariness on her face. "Go cool down."

He snarls and the sound is deep with menace. He prowls toward her.

She tilts her head back and grits her teeth. The wolf flashes behind her eyes. Callum's hands are in fists at his sides.

"*Cool. The fuck. Down.*" Fiona prods him in the chest with each word. "*Now.*"

He growls, and I cannot help but marvel at Fiona's courage. She doesn't even flinch.

I fear for her, though. Callum is not himself.

I try to reach out to him with my thoughts, as if my will alone could stop him from harming her.

Calm down. Calm down!

Callum's broad shoulders soften. Something in the air shifts.

He pushes past her and stalks down the stairs.

Fiona's body deflates, and the wolf disappears from her eyes. I exhale and crumple against the doorframe, even though tension coils within me.

"Well, that was. . . interesting," says Blake.

I'd almost forgotten he was there.

He leans against the stone wall, the torchlight flickering across his face. The top few buttons of his shirt are undone where Callum grabbed him. He cocks an eyebrow at Fiona.

"Breathe a word of this to anyone, and I'll end you." She points her finger at him. "Now, piss off."

He dips his head deferentially. He almost looks like he's bowing. Fiona flinches, and I'm not sure why.

He pushes off from the wall and saunters past her down the stairs.

"I mean it, Blake," she hisses. "Not a word."

The darkness does not reply.

She looks troubled. When she notices me looking, she composes herself and offers me a smile.

"Are you okay?" I ask.

She laughs, and whatever darkness that was plaguing her lifts. "You're asking about me? Aye. I'm fine. Are you alright?"

"Yes." I bite my bottom lip. "What. . . what was wrong with him? Is he okay?"

"Callum? Oh, aye. That big oaf is just fine. He'll be mortified, later, though. It's. . . it's a wolf thing."

When I fold my arms, she grins.

"We might want to have this conversation somewhere private." She gestures over my shoulder.

I step aside, and she enters my room.

She settles on my bed, leaning against the wall and stretching her bare feet over the side of the mattress as I shut the door.

"Why was he acting like that?" I ask.

I sit down beside her, though keep a little distance between us. I'm not used to anyone being this comfortable around me.

"He's become. . . a wee bit attached to you since he brought you here. And it's the night after the full moon. The wolf hasn't quite settled yet." She chews her bottom lip. "This is potentially a bit. . . awkward. . . but were you, perhaps, relieving some tension earlier?"

There's an aura of wicked amusement rippling off her.

I frown. "What do you mean?"

"You know, scratching an itch? Easing some frustrations?" When I just look at her blankly, she whispers, "You know. . . *touching yourself*?"

My cheeks flame. "What? No!"

Her eyebrows raise. "No? Hm. You were feeling a wee bit. . . restless?"

My face is on fire. I stare at the bookshelf across the room, the dream I had about Callum flashing through my mind. "No!"

Fiona chuckles softly. "It's nothing to be embarrassed about. Your scent. . . it changes depending on your emotions. Fear. Anger. *Arousal*. As Wolves, we can often pick up on these shifts. Particularly when we're attuned to a certain person."

My heartbeat thumps against my chest, mortification wrapping its cold fingers around my heart.

"He could smell my dream?"

"Ah, so you had a dream?" She grins. "I'm not sure exactly what happened. My guess is he sensed the shift in you and came to stand guard, in case any other Wolves sensed it too. Like Blake."

"Blake?" My blood turns cold, and dislike pulses through my body.

"I'd wager that's what set Callum off. Once he let the wolf take over. . . well. . . his attention will have been consumed by you." She shakes her head. "I've never seen him get that worked up before."

She swallows, and all the color drains from her face.

"And then. . . Callum and I. . ." She pinches the bridge of her nose. "In front of Blake. . . shit."

"What?"

She wrings her hands together. "I challenged Callum, my alpha. And he backed down."

"And that's bad?"

"Aye. That's bad. It's—"

"A wolf thing?" I arch my eyebrow.

"Aye." She sighs and her breath plumes in front of her face. "It gives me the right to openly challenge him for alpha of Highfell."

I'm slightly concerned for Callum, but my curiosity is spiked. "A female can be alpha?"

"Aye. Though it's rare. Archaic traditions make it hard for us to gain the status."

"Will you challenge him?"

She lets out a dark laugh. "No. Course not. I have no designs on the role."

"So why are you worried?"

"Because if Blake tells anyone and it becomes open knowledge, Callum and I will have to fight it out. Physically. Publicly." Her stare is dark and blank. "Wolf law."

She tries to look like she's unaffected, but she fiddles with her fingers.

"Blake won't tell anyone," I say.

"He'd better not."

"He hasn't told anyone about me yet."

She gives me an almost pitying look, as if I'm being naïve. "He's not doing that out of the goodness of his heart, Rory. He's playing some sort of game."

246

I stop myself from rolling my eyes. I'm not a fool. "I know. He has us all where he wants us. You challenging Callum for alpha would disrupt that. He won't tell."

Fiona's stare is puzzled. Appraising.

"You seem to understand that snake better than any of us," she says.

"I grew up in the palace, in a den of vipers. I would be a fool not to learn their language."

"I hope you're right." She shuffles off the bed, and heads to the door. "Can I ask you something, Rory?"

Her gaze is so penetrating I have to force myself to meet it. I don't want her to look too deeply inside me. I'm afraid she'll see that I'm a viper too. Didn't I allow myself to be taken here, to gain intelligence on the Wolves that I could use to barter for my freedom?

"Do you want to go back home?" she asks. "To the Southlands? Your father? Sebastian?"

Every muscle in my body hardens, and every bone stiffens.

No, my soul is screaming, but I'm that statue in my dreams again and I can't get the words out. *No. No. No.*

I am not ready for that question. I am not ready to admit I want to neglect my duty, my kingdom, my role as the princess.

I am not ready to give voice to the truth.

I am a traitor to the Southlands.

"Why do you ask me that?" I have to fight to keep my voice even.

"Because you're right. You *do* speak their language." She shrugs. "I think you could be more useful to us than a hostage to be traded for the Heart of the Moon. Don't you?"

I don't respond. I may not want to go home, not truly. That doesn't mean I want to commit treason.

She closes the door behind her—leaving me alone with my thoughts and the darkness.

I am restless as I get back into bed.

My mind whirls over everything Fiona said. My thoughts are like daggers. I am destined to either betray my kingdom, or betray Callum by telling my father all I've learned about the Wolves since I got here.

Through my guilt, I keep thinking about Callum prowling toward me with his eyes dark with intent.

What would have happened if Fiona hadn't arrived?

Would he have thrown Blake aside and kissed me? Would he have carried me to the bed? Would he have eased this ache that consumes me?

Heat surges through my body and throbs between my legs.

I'm on fire as I imagine his mouth on mine, his hands gripping my hips. I slide my hand up my thigh, and imagine it's his. I'm aching. I need it to stop, I need—

Someone knocks on the door and I breathe in sharply. I know, without opening it, that it's Callum.

Cheeks flaming, I slip out of bed, and prowl across the room. I open the door a crack, my heart hammering.

Callum's eyes are human once more. His expression is soft, remorseful, even. He's soaking wet, and his shirt and breeches cling to his body. As usual, he's emitting heat.

"May I come in?" he asks.

Chapter Thirty-Six

I step back, giving Callum access to my chambers.

He closes the door softly behind him, and turns to face me.

The scent of the outdoors clings to him and his hair is ruffled and damp. I wonder if he's been in the loch, even though the night is pitch black outside my window.

His face is serious, and something in his eyes seems lost. Nervous, even.

He runs a hand over the back of his neck, and releases a long breath.

"I'm so sorry." His voice is rough. "The way I behaved earlier... I... I want you to know I'd never hurt you. Ever."

His eyes bore into mine, and in them there is a silent plea that I believe him.

He's standing so close that I could touch him. Goddess, I want to. Yet neither of us move. His hands remain firmly at his sides, his forearms corded, as though he's making a concerted effort to show me he can behave like a gentleman.

A shameful part of me doesn't want him to.

"I know that," I whisper.

The air feels warm and tight. Stifling. I need to break this tension, somehow, before it breaks me.

"Did you get the message from your king?"

"Aye. He needs my help. I'll have to ride out in the next couple of days to meet him."

The tension thickens. I swallow.

I note how the moonlight reflects off his skin. "It's a little late for a swim, isn't it?"

He huffs a laugh. "Aye. A wee bit. I had some extra energy I needed to get out of my system."

I think of the feeling that's been crackling beneath my skin all evening. I think about what I was about to do before he knocked on the door.

"Did it work?"

His jaw tenses. "Not really."

"And now you've come back."

"I can't keep away."

There's something so raw in his voice that my stomach jolts.

"I wanted to show you. . ." Tentatively, he puts his hand on my cheek. "I wanted to show you I can be gentle."

I feel, again, as if I have swallowed the Northlands winds. That they're billowing inside me, raging inside my chest, demanding I release them.

I force myself to remain steady, to not reveal the wildness that's building inside me.

Even though I want that release.

Even though I want to scream and bite and tear into something. Into him. I want the storm that has been building for days—or perhaps since Callum first set foot into my bedchambers during the siege and threw me over his shoulder—to finally break.

From the way he is breathing, I wonder if Callum is containing something too. I've seen what he cages inside him—so different to the storm building in my chest, yet just as wild. I touch his chest, so I can feel his heart pounding. I wonder whether the beast within will stir.

"Show me, then," I say.

His eyebrows raise. He smiles.

He cups my cheek. He brushes his lips against mine. True to his word, he is gentle, restrained.

Yet his kiss unleashes something violent within me.

"I've wanted to do that for a long time, Princess—"

My fists curl into his shirt, and I pull him back.

I catch the flicker of surprise in his eyes before his mouth clashes against mine.

One of his hands slides into my hair and he tilts my head back. He parts my lips with his tongue, and a low sound scrapes against his throat and vibrates through my core as he tastes me. His scent of woodsmoke and the mountains floods my nose, and I am burning and drowning in him at the same time.

A soft whimper escapes me.

"Fuck." His voice is rough and raw against my lips.

He grabs my hips and pulls me closer, and I press myself into him—desperate to ease the ache that's building.

His kiss deepens as he backs me into the wall and slides his thigh between my legs. I breathe in sharply at the spark of pleasure that ripples through me.

I grab him tighter, my knuckles pushing against the hard muscle beneath his shirt. His tongue moves in hot, deep strokes against mine and he tastes like pure heat. All I can think of is more.

My senses are heightened to everything—the grip of his fingers around my hips, the scrape of his stubble against my jaw, and the hardness of him. Wet heat pools at my core.

Is this what it is like to be a wolf? So attuned to every sensation.

It is overwhelming. Yet it is not enough.

I shift against his thigh and moan at the friction it causes. A low growl vibrates in his chest, and his grip tightens around my hips.

I still. I've gone too far. I'm out of control. I need to calm down. I need—

His kiss becomes more gentle. Urging. As if he's coaxing me.

"Don't stop."

He presses a trail of kisses against my neck, leaving a line of fire that makes me whimper, then nips my earlobe with his teeth.

"I can handle it. Don't stop."

I see the wolf in his eyes.

His mouth is on mine again—his kiss deep and claiming. The ache between my legs builds and I cannot stop myself. I roll my hips, pressing against him, harder, faster. My breathing is shallow. I feel desperate. Wild. Feral.

I hook a hand around his neck, pulling his mouth even further into mine, meeting each deep stroke of his tongue with a thrust of my own. His fingers tighten and he growls.

The hard length of him is pressing against my hip.

I want to touch him, to coax more low, rough sounds from his lips. When I shift, and run my fingers down his chest, he presses himself closer to me—stopping me from slipping my hand between us.

"I can't handle that," he says, with a dark, breathy laugh.

He moves his hands down my back, pulling me to him. My nipples are sensitive against the thin material of my nightgown as they rub against his chest with each ragged breath. And I want more.

I rock against his thigh, the heat building, a flush spreading over my body.

Whatever was knocked loose in my chest when Callum hurled me over his shoulder back at the castle has escaped again. It rages inside me, primal and wild and free. I am no longer a princess, or a prisoner, or a statue. I am no longer trapped in a cage, or a castle. There are no chains nor wedding rings to bind me.

Callum groans against my lips as if he can sense the change in me.

There is something tightening inside me, burning, building.

And then it crashes over me. Callum thrusts his tongue roughly against mine, claiming my release as it surges through me. My knees buckle and he holds me, stopping me from falling, as my breath comes out hard and fast against his lips.

He growls, the sound as low and animal as I have ever heard it.

He curses under his breath.

And before I'm aware of what's happening, he scoops me into his arms. My legs wrap around his waist, my core pressing against his hard torso. And then we're on my single bed—the frame creaking with the weight of him—and he's on top of me, his forearms on either side of my head as he hovers over my face.

His wolf eyes hold mine, as wild and feral as they were when we were in the forest. His jawline is hard, his biceps big and tensed—as though he is still holding back.

I touch his cheek, running my thumb over his swollen lips.

He rolls his hips once against me, those wild eyes never leaving my face, and I moan as his hard length presses against my core.

He growls again as he shifts down, peppering kisses down my jawline, my neck, my collarbone. His eyes glow in the darkness as he puts his mouth around my nipple and sucks hard through the fabric.

I cry out, my back arching off the bed.

His mouth is on mine again, hot and deep and claiming.

I sink my teeth into his bottom lip.

He growls, and grabs my wrist, pinning it roughly against the mattress. And the strength in him—Goddess, the strength in him! Exhilaration and raw heat surge through my body.

Then he stills.

Every muscle in his body tenses.

"Callum?" I whisper, my voice breathy and strange.

He sucks in a shaky breath. Then he lets out a half-laugh. "Perhaps I can't control myself."

He staggers back off the bed.

His breathing sounds pained. I'm not sure if it's water from the loch or sweat that shines on his skin.

"Fuck."

"What's wrong?"

I sit up and he jerks back, his muscles twitching. His gaze snaps to the narrow window and the weak moonlight, then back to me.

"Callum?"

"I feel. . . I feel. . . strange."

I slide off the bed and step toward him. "Callum, tell me what's going on."

"I feel. . . I feel like. . ." His hands clench in fists at his sides.

When he meets my gaze, he looks. . . wary.

"Callum. . . it's okay," I say softly, as though coaxing a wild animal.

I'm not sure what is wrong with him. Every muscle in his body is taut and strained. His biceps bulge against his shirt and his jaw is set. Perhaps that feeling of need that pulses through my body pulses through his too.

He told me before he wouldn't let anyone touch me, himself included. Is that what he is worrying about? Touching me?

Or is he trying to hide the wolf inside him?

"I'm not afraid," I tell him.

A vein pulses in his neck.

"I don't feel. . ." he starts, shaking his head. "It's not. . ."

"It's okay," I soothe.

I pad across the cold floorboards toward him, but when he growls, I still.

"Don't," he says, and there is power in his command. I freeze, my expression hardening.

"Tell me what's wrong."

He takes a deep breath. Then he turns to the door.

"What are you doing?" My voice is sharp as it cuts through the shadows.

"I must go."

I feel like I'm being doused with ice-cold water. I have just shared something with him that I have shared with no man before. Something that is forbidden to me. And now he is just going to leave?

Something inside my chest shatters like glass, sharp and painful.

I swallow, then raise my chin—trying to look like a noble lady even though I'm wearing a nightgown and have just experienced something I shouldn't have.

"Yes. You must," I say. "It was inappropriate for you to come here at this hour. I am the princess of the Southlands, and I am betrothed to another man. You have taken too many liberties with me."

His shoulders tense, and his face falls. "You're right. I'm sorry, Princess."

My heart breaks. I want him to fight for me, to tell me that he's never giving me back to Sebastian.

But I put on my mask, and do not let him see.

His footsteps are hurried as he leaves, as though he cannot get away from me fast enough.

I stare at the closed door, my breathing ragged.

I want to scream. I want to tear through the forest and howl into the wind. Instead, I do what I always do, and swallow it. I swallow the feelings and the hurt and the rage. I let the darkness wrap around me, the shadows dousing the flames in my soul, until I am cold and empty.

Later, as I lie down on my pillows, and recall what happened, something occurs to me.

Callum was scared.

Tomorrow, I will find out why.

Chapter Thirty-Seven

There's a knock at door, waking me.

How can I face Callum this morning?

I lock away the shame that creeps through my body when I remember how bold I was, when I remember how angry I was when he left. I lock away other feelings too—feelings I do not want to acknowledge. Feelings that heat my blood, and rattle my soul. I push away the strange dreams of Wolves and mountains and monsters in the dark, too.

I take a deep breath. "Come in."

"Hello, little rabbit."

My stomach drops and I jolt upright, the sheets dropping to my midriff.

Blake leans in the doorway. He's wearing dark breeches and a well-fitting black shirt. He looks like a villainous prince from the kinds of stories my mother would tell me. His dark hair, slightly messy like he's been running his fingers through it, only adds to the effect.

I am *not* in the mood for him this morning. "What are *you* doing here?"

I glance at my bedside table, looking for the silver letter opener I brought here. There is only a pile of medical books, an almost burnt-out candle, and Callum's red tartan collar on its surface.

"Looking for something?" he asks.

He pulls a small cloth package out of his pocket, and unwraps it to reveal my silver blade within. I'd forgotten that I'd thrown it at him during the full moon.

He holds it out to me and it gleams in the cold sunlight.

Warily, I slide out of bed, and pad across the floor toward him. He tracks my movements. When I reach for it, his lips part slightly.

I drop my arm to my side. "Why do you want me to take it so much? What have you done to it?"

"Nothing."

He seems to study me. He's tall, and I have to look up. I feel like he's challenging me, and I don't want to back down. I cannot help the small burst of interest that sparks inside me, too.

Like Callum, Blake is an alpha. He must be around the same age, too. He has the Southlands accent, and says he worked in the King's Guard. How did he rise to such a high position among the Wolves?

"Why did you choose to come here, little rabbit?" asks Blake.

"I didn't. I was kidnapped."

"Hm." His eyes gleam, as if he knows I am lying.

He removes the letter opener from the cloth and his skin hisses as the silver touches his skin.

He flips it over so he's holding the blade, and offers me the hilt.

"I've done nothing to it," he says. "Take it."

I let him hold it for a moment longer, knowing it is burning his skin. Then I take it. His gaze flits to my hand, my face. Curiosity blazes in his eyes.

His expression settles back to boredom as he walks over to my bookshelf.

"Get out of my chambers," I say.

He runs his index finger along the dusty spines. "Are you sure they're your chambers?"

A horrible feeling washes over me. I glance at the piles of medical tomes, the strange pots of herbs, and that dark book of handwritten experiments that I've been reading.

I told myself I never wanted to meet the previous inhabitant of this room.

I stare at Blake's back as he thumbs through the books.

"This was your room, wasn't it?" I say flatly.

"This *is* my room. I no longer reside here, but I use it for some of my most interesting possessions."

I don't like the way he says that—as if he's storing me in here, too. "Get out, Blake. Callum won't be pleased when I tell him about this."

Blake turns and props an elbow on the bookshelf. "Did he not tell you?"

"Tell me what?"

"Callum's not here."

I frown. "You're lying."

A dimple punctures his cheek. "He rode out this morning. He's gone to find the Wolf King."

My insides turn to ice.

Chapter Thirty-Eight

Callum has left? After everything that happened between us?

Last night, I betrayed my kingdom when I kissed him.

Despite that, he has ridden out to find the Wolf King—someone who will undoubtedly either execute me or send me straight back to Sebastian. And he didn't even say goodbye?

Shame spreads through my body. Shame that something that was so monumental to me obviously meant nothing to him. I wonder how many women he must have kissed for that to be the case.

I force my expression to settle into one of indifference.

I will not let this serpent know that his news has rattled me.

"I knew he would be riding out to find his king soon. I just hadn't realized he had gone yet. If you're trying to create trouble, you will find none here."

The corner of Blake's lip quirks. "Pity, I do enjoy trouble."

"Why are you here?"

"I'm looking for something." He slides a blue leather-bound book from the shelf. "Ah, here it is."

I don't catch the full title, but I see the word *lore* in elegant calligraphy across the front, and a dusting of golden stars on the spine.

He tucks it beneath his arm and walks to the door.

"What book is that?" I ask.

He pauses and his shoulders stiffen. He clearly doesn't want me to know what he's reading. When he turns around, though, his expression is unrattled.

He nods at the pile of medical books by my bed. "Are you trying to find out if you could have saved her?"

My fist tightens around the silver blade. His voice is casual, as though the death of my mother was meaningless. "That's none of your concern."

"What were her symptoms?" When I merely glare at him, he shrugs. "Don't you want to know whether *I* could have saved her?"

My breathing is fast. "You couldn't have. You would have been a child when she died."

"As would you."

He waits. I hate that he knows how desperate I am for answers.

"She had cold sweats, fevers, shaking, and pain," I blurt before I can change my mind about confiding in him. "She would hallucinate sometimes, and heal slowly. She was. . . weak. She got weaker every day."

"Was she worse in the morning or the evening?"

I remember her frail form in the four-poster bed as sunlight seeped through the palace shutters. "Morning."

"Was she treated for her illness?"

"Yes."

"A potion or brew, I presume?"

I nod, remembering that foul-smelling herbal liquid that was forced down her throat. Remembering the taste of it from when they fed it to me when I got sick, too.

"And did your father love your mother?"

"What's that got to do with anything?"

"Answer the question."

I grit my teeth. "My father doesn't love anyone."

Blake shrugs. "That sounds like no disease I know of." He moves out into the landing and pauses. "Be careful, little rabbit. Fiona has gone too. Isla has been left in charge of your welfare. You're alone among the Wolves."

When he's gone, I walk over to the window with my fist clenched. I'm not sure whether Blake was trying to scare me or provoke me, or both. How dare he try to bait me with questions about my mother? Regardless, I cannot believe Callum has left me alone.

Mist hangs over the loch and twists around the peaks of the mountains. The vastness of the landscape makes me feel small.

I wonder how long Callum will be gone for. I want to give him a piece of my mind.

But I dread his return, too.

Because when he comes back, the Wolf King will be with him.

***

For the next couple of days, I'm glad to have my job in the kitchens. It distracts me, and stops my thoughts from becoming too dark.

Callum thinks wearing his collar will keep me safe, but it seems that without him here in the castle, the hostility aimed at me is palpable.

When I head to the kitchens in the mornings, Magnus and his rat-faced friend shout lewd comments as they pass on their way to training. While picking herbs in the kitchen gardens one afternoon, Isla whispers something behind her hand to her friend and snickers as she swans by. And only Mrs. McDonald and Kayleigh speak to me—everyone else merely eyes me with contempt. They do not want a human in their midst.

The strip of red tartan around my neck prevents any further trouble, at least.

I eat as much as I can during lunch so I do not have to stray downstairs after dark when the alcohol comes out and the bagpipe music starts playing. I ignore Isla's comments, and Magnus's leers. And I spend the rest of my days reading, while the anger inside me grows thorns and shoots.

Why has Callum left me?

Is he okay?

On the third morning, I wake at dawn. The sun has not yet risen, and the air smells strangely like perfume and roses. I slept restlessly, and dreamt of Wolves and wilderness and darkness.

I turn to my bedside table to reach for Callum's collar.

My heart stills.

No.

I jump out of bed and frantically shift books aside, sending parchment fluttering onto the floorboards.

My blood turns to ice, then to fire.

The collar is not there.

Someone has been in my chambers.

A hurricane rages in my chest, much wilder than the winds currently ratting the window of my bedchambers.

Isla.

It has to be her.

I stomp across the room, wrench open the wardrobe door, and change into the first dress I can find. *How dare she.* I storm down the spiral staircase into a corridor. I'm going to the Great Hall, and I will show Isla that it was a mistake to provoke me. I will show her what happens when she steals from the princess of the—

I make impact with a mass of dark hair and stringy muscle and stagger back along the torchlit corridor. My stomach drops and my feet grow roots that bind me to the stone floor.

"Hello, sweetheart." Magnus leers. A slow grin spreads across his face, revealing a missing tooth.

His two friends, the male with ratlike features, and the muscular male with a dark beard, stand on either side of him—both in their green kilts, blocking my path.

For a moment, I cannot move. Then my instincts kick in.

I turn and try to run back down the corridor, but the bigger male grabs my arm.

"Get off me!"

I try to wrench away, but his grip is like steel.

"Where are you going, sweetheart?" drawls Magnus.

The air is sour with sweat. Magnus's gaze travels up and down my body, and my skin turns cold wherever it lands.

I grit my teeth and glare up at him. "When Callum finds out—"

"Callum isn't here. And you're not wearing his collar." He steps closer to me, and his acrid scent floods my nostrils. I almost gag. "That makes you free game."

"You will pay for this." I try to pull away but the bigger man's hand tightens around my arm. "Callum will kill you, you fools."

The three of them laugh and the wild and thorny thing that has been growing inside me for days sets alight.

"I will make you pay for this."

"There's no need to be like that," says Magnus. "We can all be friends here. Now, the way I see it, we know something about you that you don't want our acting Wolf King to know about, *Princess*. What will you do for us to stop us from—"

The warmth from another person washes over my back and a slender hand clasps my neck. Time slows down as I feel the whisper of silk against my throat. My heart is racing so fast I think it will burst from my chest. The gloomy corridor sways around me.

I force myself to calm down, and everything comes back into focus. Curling my fist, I get ready to fight.

Only Magnus and the other two men have already staggered back with fear in their eyes.

"We're sorry. We didn't know." Magnus's expression is wary. "We thought she was Callum's. We never would have. . . if we'd known she was she was yours. . ."

When they get no response, they back away, then scurry toward the Great Hall.

Heart in my throat, I spin around.

And I find myself face to face with Blake.

I'm breathing fast as my mind races to process what just happened, what is still happening. "I. . . what are you. . .?"

His gaze drops to the collar that now sits around my neck. *His* collar.

Chapter Thirty-Nine

I reach for the collar. Blake's fingers curl around my wrist before I can rip it off.

"I wouldn't do that if I were you," he says.

He's standing too close. His body heat bores into me, despite the cool expression on his face. The shadows wrap around him, and his dark shirt and breeches make him look at one with the darkness.

My breathing is fast, and I'm not sure if it's because of the danger I just escaped, or the danger I'm now in. I try to calm my nerves.

I lift my chin. "Why not?"

"Because I will not offer it to you again."

I choke out a laugh. "Why would I want this?"

The firelight from a nearby torch dances across his eyes. "You have no friends here, little rabbit. Callum is gone. Fiona is gone. Ryan is weak. And Callum is not as well liked as he may think. There are many more animals like Magnus who will take advantage of the situation you find yourself in."

"What makes you any better than Magnus?"

His expression is devoid of any emotion. There's a chill in the gloomy corridor, and my breath plumes in front of my face and mingles with his.

"Did you ever wonder why I have a Southlands accent?" he asks. "My mother was a human. She lived just south of the Borderlands. One night, a pack of Wolves raided her village. One of them forced themselves on her, and the consequence was me." His tone is smooth, like dark silk.

"I tracked him down, of course, many years later. He cried when I showed him exactly what he had created." His eyes bore into mine, and inside them there is nothing but darkness. Yet I relax my arm in his grip. "There is nothing more deplorable than rape."

While his expression is unreadable, his gaze is intense. It is as if I am one of the strange books in his chambers that he is trying to read. Understanding seems to pass between us.

When he releases my wrist, I drop my arm to my side.

The air is thick with silence. I feel as if I should say something, but words evade me.

I open my mouth.

He turns and walks away, torchlight and shadows flickering across his profile as he passes the sconces on the stone walls.

"Come to my chambers at nightfall," he says.

My eyebrows lift but before I can say anything, he disappears around the corner.

I'm rooted to the flagstones. I'd planned to confront Isla, but after the experience I've just had, I'm shaken. Not only by what Magnus planned to do, but by Blake as well.

I decide to head back to my bedchambers.

On the way to the stairwell, Isla and a pack of her friends round a corner.

"Lose something?" she asks sweetly as I pass.

I spin around. All the rage that has been building in my chest longs for release.

"Where is it?" I snarl.

"I don't know what you're talking about." Her voice is falsely sweet, and she smirks to indicate that she knows exactly what I'm talking about. She smells like rose perfume, the scent that lingered in my chambers this morning. The three girls standing around her snicker.

"Do you think he will want you if you steal from him?" I ask.

She swishes her dirty blonde hair over her shoulder and steps closer to me.

"Do you really think he wants a Southern, human whore?" She makes each word sound more poisonous than the last. "Once he's tired of you, he'll find a wolf. He'll find his mate. And when he's ready—"

Her gaze snaps to Blake's collar. Her eyes widen in surprise, before a look of wariness crosses her face.

Then she releases a harsh laugh.

"You've moved on fast, haven't you?" She steps back into her group of friends. "Come on, let's go to breakfast. I'm starving, and this Southern slut is ruining my appetite."

They walk away, whispering and giggling.

"Don't steal from me again," I say.

Isla doesn't respond, but her shoulders stiffen.

***

There is a storm coming.

I feel it as nightfall approaches.

The air is static and close and the Wolves seem more excitable than usual. I can hear them outside, shouting and laughing and brawling within the castle grounds. I wonder if that's a wolf thing. Perhaps they can sense the storm and it agitates them in some way.

It makes me glad I have protection while Callum is away, even if it is Blake I must turn to.

I sit cross-legged on my bed and examine the collar he put around my neck.

It is black and featherlight, with a faint pattern on it made up of crisscrossing blacks and greys and other shades of night. It's made of silk, and I run it through my fingers. At its center, there's a black obsidian stone that absorbs the light from my candle.

I cannot decide whether to go to Blake's chambers or not.

There are many reasons not to. For one thing, it would be completely inappropriate for me to visit a man's bedchambers. Especially alone, after dark.

For another, Callum told me Blake was the most dangerous wolf in this entire kingdom.

And yet, the story Blake told me about his mother haunts me. A moment of understanding passed between us in that corridor. I wonder if we both have broken souls.

Maybe he's not as bad as Callum thinks.

Curiosity flares within me, too. If his mother was human, does that make him a half-wolf? Why are the Wolves here so afraid of him? And why did he protect me?

As the candle burns low, flicking shadows over the shelves that creak beneath Blake's books, my intrigue finally outweighs my trepidation.

I want to know why he has invited me to his chambers, and I'm certain he won't harm me. Whatever his game is, I think he needs me in one piece in order to win.

Thunder rumbles through the castle walls as I slide off my bed, signaling the arrival of the storm.

I pull on my boots, and creep down the spiral staircase.

The torches in the corridors flicker violently, as if the flames are as excited by the storm as the Wolves that shout and roar in the Great Hall. I stick to the shadows, flattening myself against the wall as a couple of drunken Wolves pass by on their way to the festivities.

When I reach Blake's door, I take a deep breath.

The last time I was here, he shifted and chased me through the forest. I'm not sure what I'll be faced with this time.

I gather my nerves, and I knock.

I wait a few seconds. The rain hammers against the castle, and there's a flash of light through the narrow window at the end of the corridor as lightning strikes.

There's a thud within Blake's chambers, followed by the sound of someone stumbling.

The door opens a crack.

Blake's dark hair is messy, as if he's been running his hands through it, and his skin is clammy. The top few buttons of his white shirt are undone and his sleeves are rolled up to his elbows to reveal corded forearms.

His eyes are bloodshot.

"What are you doing here?" he asks.

Behind him, his room is a mess. The black sheets of his four-poster bed are crumpled, there are books all over the floor, and his desk is littered with small glass jars.

My brow furrows. "You told me to come at nightfall. . ."

"Oh. Right." His words are a little slurred. He tilts his head to the side. "Why would a rabbit seek out a wolf?"

His usual scent of dark forests is mixed with a faint aroma of alcohol. There's another scent in the air too—herbal and familiar. It puts me on edge.

"Are you drunk?" I ask.

"No." He starts to close the door. "Now's not a good time."

Thunder rumbles down the corridor, and Blake flinches.

I put my hand on the door, keeping it open, as a flash of lightning reveals the handwritten label on one of the jars.

"Is that wolfsbane?" I push past him into the room.

He sighs, then closes the door.

I pick up the jar. The lid is off, and it's releasing the dangerous scent I recognized. I turn to him. "What is this? Are you trying to poison yourself?"

"Course not." He slumps onto the end of his four-poster bed, and threads his fingers through his dark hair. "Go away."

As well as wolfsbane, I note lavender, dried chamomile, and some valerian root on his desk. I pick up a pot reading *milk of the poppy*. There's a decanter full of clear liquid beside them, and when I sniff it, I wince at the pungent alcoholic odor.

Thunder rattles the jars, and Blake's knuckles whiten as he grips his hair.

"Are you trying to make a sleep aid?" I ask. "Why the wolfsbane? Unless. . ."

Callum told me they didn't have painkillers up here because the wolf inside them would fight it off.

"You're using wolfsbane to weaken the wolf and give the other ingredients time to work, aren't you? Why do you need a sleep aid?"

The room lights up, and the force of the thunder makes the mountains tremble. Blake's whole body hardens and a rough sound scrapes the back of his throat. "*Fuck's sake.*"

"Goddess! You're afraid of the storm!"

He removes his hands from his hair, and slowly looks up at me. "If you tell anyone, I will kill you."

I know the dark image he cultivates is important to him. I believe he will do what it takes to prevent that from being shattered.

"I know," I say.

When the thunder sounds again, he shuts his eyes, his chest inflating as he takes a deep breath. He groans and lies back on the bed, his feet planted on the floorboards.

"It's only a storm," I say, placing my hands on my hips.

"Thanks for that. Very helpful."

"Why are you afraid?"

"None of your business."

I hover by his desk, unsure of what to do.

As I'm debating, he half crawls up the bed and slumps on his pillows, groaning again. I sigh. Tentatively, I approach.

"I think you've taken too much," I say.

"Oh, do you? Well, thank goodness that Callum's little pet, who only learned of wolfsbane a couple of weeks ago, is here to offer me her sage advice." He turns away from me. "Go away."

He smells of sweat and soap and the forest. His shirt clings to his muscular back.

"Seriously, Blake, you don't look good."

"Maybe it's because you're irritating me."

"Or maybe it's because you've just taken poison, you fool. Where's the antidote?"

"I'm the healer. Not you."

"You're a mess. And your potion hasn't worked. You're not asleep, are you?"

Lightning floods the room and he curls in on himself as he braces for the thunder that cracks through the sky moments later.

I sigh, and perch on the edge of the bed.

"You know, I used to be afraid of storms. When I was a child."

"Piss off."

I smirk, then something softens in me. Though part of me is glad to have seen him in this way—sure I will be able to use it to my advantage at some point—he's in a such a pitiful state, I cannot help but feel a bit of sympathy for him.

When I was afraid as a child, my mother would sing to me. I try to recall her melody.

Softly, I start to hum.

The tune always brought me comfort, and I hope that it will do the same for him.

When she sang it, I would imagine myself running through the wild grass, the moon shining, the stars clear and bright. And I would know that I was not alone. I was safe.

Blake's shoulders soften, and he releases a gentle sigh. "I'm serious. If you speak of this, you're dead."

I shush him and continue with the soft melody.

I have not thought of this song for a while, and I find myself getting lost in it as the thunder rattles the castle, and lightning illuminates the loch through the window.

It is not until I hear a gentle snore that I stop, startled.

Despite the storm outside, Blake is asleep.

He's rolled onto his back, and one of his arms is flung above his head. I take the opportunity to openly look at the angry white scar that marks his forearm near his elbow. It looks like a bite from a very large beast. A wolf, perhaps.

His expression is peaceful, and it's a stark contrast to the dark violence he usually emanates. He looks almost pleasant, handsome, even, without the smirk on his lips or the cunning ambition glinting in his eyes.

His chest rises and falls softly.

I blink, suddenly aware that I've been staring too long.

I stand abruptly and cross the room.

"I prefer you when you're sleeping," I mutter as I close the door and head back to my chambers.

***

I will have my revenge on Isla.

I'd like to have my revenge on Magnus, too, but that awful wolf seems to be giving me a wide berth. He's not been in the Great Hall or running drills in the yard for the past couple of days.

In fact, most Wolves seem to be avoiding me. It seems Blake's collar acts as a larger deterrent than Callum's—even though I've not seen the dark-haired wolf since the storm.

The negative side of this is that Kayleigh will no longer speak to me in the kitchens. Her face turned white when she first saw the black strip around my neck, and since then she's wanted nothing to do with me.

Isla, however, has taken every opportunity to call me a slut, and to giggle with her friends about me every time I see her.

She knew how much danger I'd be in without Callum's collar. She *wanted* someone to hurt me. And what's more, she hasn't given it back.

I cannot let it stand.

I get the idea from the potion Blake made on the night of the storm.

I take some wolfsbane and some buckthorn from his stores in the infirmary, and crush them into a powder. I'm not trying to kill her. I just need to neutralize the wolf so the laxative properties of buckthorn can kick in. I want to humiliate her a little.

When I'm left alone in the kitchens, I pull out the small vial with the powder in. I pop out the cork, and hover over the bowl of mashed potato I'm intending to set down in front of Isla and her friends.

Someone grabs my wrist, and I turn.

"Is that why you chose to come here, little rabbit?" Blake's eyes gleam with curiosity. "To poison us all?"

If he's embarrassed about the other night, he doesn't show it. He's as well put together as usual, with his black shirt emphasizing his toned chest, and an unreadable expression on his face.

My heart pounds. If he tells anyone what he just caught me doing, I'll surely be killed before Callum can return.

"Only Isla. For stealing from me."

He brings the vial to his nose, and inhales deeply. "Wolfsbane. Death is a harsh punishment for theft. I didn't think you had it in you. Though, if you're going to kill her, perhaps you could use a different method? Poison is my trademark. They'll think it was me."

"It's not. . . I'm not going to kill her!" My cheeks flame. "The wolfsbane is just there to neutralize the wolf!"

He smells the vial again, then he grins and dimples puncture his cheeks. "Buckthorn." He shakes his head, plucking the vial from my fingers. "You've put too much wolfsbane in. This *will* kill her." He nods at the mashed potato. "Isla is lactose-intolerant. A nob of butter should have the desired effect."

He pushes the cork into the vial, then pockets it. "Mind if I keep this? I have a better use for it."

He walks across the kitchen and pauses in the doorway. His gaze is appraising as he looks me up and down. "You're a devious little thing, aren't you?"

Strangely, it doesn't sound like an insult.

My breathing doesn't return to normal until I can no longer hear his retreating footsteps.

Later, after Kayleigh and I have finished serving the food, I sit alone at the end of one of the tables in the Great Hall with my bowl of stew and mashed potato. As usual, everyone is giving me a wide berth.

About halfway through the meal, Isla stands up with a panicked expression.

Her stomach growls so loudly that the chatter in the hall desists.

She releases gas, and her cheeks turn bright red.

A number of the surrounding Wolves, including her friends, roar with laughter. I suppress my smile as I look resolutely in the other direction.

Blake catches my eye from the alpha table and winks before going back to his conversation with Robert.

Isla flees the Great Hall.

***

Later, I sleep better than I have in the days since Callum left. Until a loud sound wakes me. I sit upright in bed.

Outside, men are shouting.

I hurtle to the window.

The sun is rising and the sky is painted crimson. People on horseback thunder down the hill toward the castle. The male at the front wears red tartan.

My heart jumps into my throat.

Callum.

He's home.

I pull on a dress, then run out of my chambers.

Chapter Forty

I sit on the edge of Callum's four-poster bed and wait.

All my life, it seems, I have been waiting for something. Waiting to be dismissed by my father, waiting to be wed to the highest bidder, waiting to be seen. To be heard.

To be used.

To be *free*.

I have been waiting for Callum, now, for days.

I am tired of waiting.

Since he's been gone, something wild and ugly has sprouted in my chest and grown thorns.

I knew he would need to leave at some point, but he left without saying goodbye. He kissed me then abandoned me. He left me to the Wolves.

What's more, he left to retrieve the Wolf King, who will either trade me for the Heart of the Moon in the coming days or realize I'm of no value to him, and execute me. What is to be my fate, now he is here?

It's always been part of my plan to be sent back to my people. I wanted to make a trade of my own with my father;

information on the Wolves, and the Wolf King himself, in exchange for my freedom. I have plenty of that now.

The more time I've spent with Callum the harder I've realized that will be. I do not want to betray him. In fact, I'd started to wonder whether I wanted to leave him at all.

I wonder now if I have been foolish, and misinterpreted his affections like a naïve princess with a silly crush.

I am envious of the Northlands winds that rattle the window and howl against the stone walls. How good it would feel to unleash that rage with no thought to the consequences.

My muscles tighten when footsteps approach the door. It bursts open, and my breath catches in my throat.

Callum stands in the doorway, and he looks every bit the fierce warrior I feared he was when I first met him.

He is covered in dirt and blood and gore. His shirt is drenched in it and sticks to his muscular torso and chest. There's mud smeared across his face, and it has dried in his hair, slicking it back from his forehead.

His breathing is fast and agitated, but when he sees me, a broad grin spreads across his face. It is infectious. I have to fight the twitch at the corner of my lip.

"There you are!" he says. "I was worried when you weren't in your chambers and I found this."

He lifts up his collar, and the red stone glints in the firelight.

"I . . . where did you find that?"

His forehead furrows. "It was beside your bed."

I grit my teeth as he shuts the door and places it on the small table by his armchair. Isla must have slipped into my chambers when I came down here.

He turns and looks at me, his brow creasing. "Is something the matter?"

I let out a laugh—sharp like splintered glass—and his frown deepens.

"You've been gone for days, Callum, and you're truly going to ask me that? Have you forgotten I am the princess of your enemy kingdom? That our people are at war? That your people despise me?"

That you left me alone after the moment we shared.

His eyes sharpen. "Did something happen while I was away?"

"Does it matter? You still left!"

His expression softens beneath the grime. He steps toward me and when I tense, he halts. He sighs, rocking back on his heels and leaning back against the table.

"I'm sorry, Princess. I didn't want to go. We got word that the situation had worsened not long after. . . after I left your chambers. The king could have died. I had to leave straightaway. I had no choice."

I swallow. "There's always a choice."

"Not always. Not in this."

"You *chose* not to say goodbye."

He runs a hand over the back of his neck and winces. I note how his shoulders are slumped and he's using the table to support himself.

Is he hurt? Has he slept? Is that blood his? Worry threads through my anger. I can't back down, though. Not until I've had my say.

He meets my eyes, and there's a plea within them.

"I'm sorry. If there was another choice, I would have taken it." He shakes his head. "Did you at least get my note?"

"Your note?"

"Aye. I left it with—" His gaze drops to the black collar around my neck and his eyes narrow. "What's that?" His voice is dangerously low.

I have never seen him stand so still. Irritation flares inside me. How can he be jealous when he left me to fend for myself?

"You know what it is," I say.

He swallows. "Why are you wearing it?"

"Because you left me alone, and Isla—"

"Did he hurt you?" His voice is rough.

"No. He protected me."

Callum's eyes flash with emotion. I cannot tell whether it's anger or hurt. "Blake doesn't protect anyone. Not without a price."

"Has it ever occurred to you that he's not as bad as you make him out to be?"

"He is every bit as bad as I make him out to be! And I leave for a few days, and I come back, and you're wearing his collar?"

"I had no choice."

"I thought you said there was always a choice. And what? You chose *him*?" His voice is dark, and his breathing shallow. "Did he touch you?"

Rage jolts through my body, and I straighten. "How dare you ask me that."

"Did he?"

I jump to my feet. "You left me, Callum!"

"Take it off." The command in his tone makes my muscles tighten.

I step toward him. The scent of the outdoors and battle clings to him; wet earth and steel and mountains. "I am not one of your pack, and you have no right to order me around."

He closes the space between us. I'm not sure if the heat that stokes me is coming from him, or whether it's burning inside me, but my breathing is fast and my cheeks flame.

I'm angry. So angry. There is a wilder emotion inside me too. And it wants release.

His eyes narrow. "Take. It. Off."

He has a wolf inside him.

And it want to provoke it.

"No," I say.

He crashes to his knees and cries out. The unlit candle sitting on his small table falls onto its side, and the floorboards splinter beneath the strain of catching him.

"Callum!"

He grabs his shoulder. "Fuck."

All the heat drains out of me, and I drop to floor in front of him. "You're hurt."

"I got shot. Silver. Thought I'd got all the bullet out." He releases a soft, pained laugh. "Obviously not."

I lift his chin. "Let me see."

"It's nothing." He shrugs me away. "Don't worry yourself, Princess. I'll be fine."

"I'll be the judge of that."

He lets me undo the buttons of his damp shirt, and I push it off his shoulders to reveal his strong, muscular chest.

My breath hitches at the sight of him.

He's dripping with sweat, and it highlights the ridges of his torso, and his large biceps.

He was shirtless the first time we met, but then, the sheer size of him was threatening. Now, a completely different feeling stirs inside me.

Until my gaze moves to his shoulder.

The veins spreading from his bullet wound are black. It's not healing, and I catch the scent of something herbal among the blood. Something that makes my stomach turn.

"It'll be fine." Callum's eyelids are drooping. "I've been shot with silver before. My body will push it out, eventually. It's just. . ." He takes a deep, wheezing breath. "Just a wee bit painful in the meantime."

"Callum." I try to sound gentle, but my heart is pounding. "The bullet had wolfsbane on it. You're not going to heal on your own. I need to go and get—"

"No," he growls.

"He has the antidote."

Callum's eyes blaze. "I'd rather die than have *him* in here."

"No you wouldn't, you stubborn wolf!"

I stand up, and he grabs my ankle.

"No."

He's so weak that when I jerk away, he has to slam his hand against the ground to stop himself from toppling over.

His chambers spin around me, and fear tightens around my heart.

I shake my head. "I won't let you die."

He looks up at me, pale and drenched in blood and sweat. There's a plea in his eyes. *Don't do this.*

"You're going to be okay," I tell him. "I need to get him."

"Rory!" he roars after me.

I bolt out of his room, and run as fast as I can toward Blake's chambers.

Chapter Forty-One

I burst into Blake's room.

He's draped in an armchair by the window, and doesn't look up from the book he's reading—the blue tome with stars on the spine that he took from my chambers.

"Please, do come in, little rabbit." He flicks to the next page. "No need to knock."

"He's hurt. You need to come. *Now*."

"What's wrong with him?"

"Wolfsbane."

His expression is unreadable, but he gets up.

He places the book on his writing desk, which has been tidied after the other night. In fact, the space is now immaculate; the bed is made, books are neatly tucked into the shelves along the wall, and the sheepskin rug by the hearth no longer glints with shards of broken glass.

He pulls a black leather case out of a drawer in his armoire, then heads to the door. I fall into step beside him.

When we enter Callum's chambers, my stomach drops.

He's pulled himself up onto the bed and his downy quilt is red with his blood. His breathing is raspy, and he's barely moving.

"Callum?" I bolt across the room and grab his hand.

His fingers don't curl around mine like they usually do. His skin is cold.

Dots dance in front of my eyes as Blake kneels by my side.

He grabs Callum's shoulder and inspects the wound. "Why didn't you ride back earlier, you stubborn fool?"

Callum's eyes are glazed. I'm not sure he can hear what Blake is saying.

The chambers swim around me.

I recognize the look on his face. My mother had that expression not long before she died.

"Hold his shoulders." Blake's command jolts me back into my body.

I lean over the bed as Blake produces a small vial of translucent liquid from his case.

"Brace yourself," says Blake. "He's not going to like this."

I force myself to breathe, even though the air is thick with the scent of blood and poison. It mingles with the heavy woodsmoke coming from the fireplace.

I nod, remembering how hard Ryan fought against the antidote when it was given to him. Callum must be double his size and strength.

Blake uncorks the vial and tips about half of it on the wound. It hisses, and my muscles tense, readying for a fight.

Callum doesn't react.

A wave of nausea rolls over me. "Come on, Callum. *Please.*"

Blake brushes me aside and grabs Callum's hair in his fist. He tips the rest of the liquid into his mouth, clamping his hand over his lips. When he pulls away, the translucent liquid dribbles down Callum's chin.

Blake sighs, and panic fizzes in my chest.

"Why isn't it working?" I ask.

Blake stares at Callum and his expression is unreadable.

"If this is how you wish to go, then don't let me stop you." He rests his forearms on the mattress and leans closer. "Don't worry, I'll look after your pet when you're gone."

"Blake," I warn.

Callum's eyes flicker open for a moment.

"You know, I haven't decided how I'll fuck her first." Blake's voice is low and seductive. "With my fingers, or my tongue."

Callum's head rolls to the side and he grunts.

The corner of Blake's lip lifts. "What do you think I should do? There are so many possibilities. Perhaps I'll have her ride my face."

Callum growls, but the noise dies in his throat as his back arches up from the mattress.

"Stop it!" I snarl.

Blake leans closer, his voice dropping to a whisper. "Or perhaps I'll have her on her knees before me while I sit on James's throne, my fist in her hair, her lips moving up and down my cock as I fuck her mouth."

Callum's eyes jolt open. They are enraged, and they don't move from Blake's. He grips the bedsheets.

"I wonder—" continues Blake.

"That's enough!" I lurch at Blake.

He hooks his arm around my waist, pulls me onto his lap, and slams his lips against mine.

I stiffen. Every muscle hardens as my blood turns to ice. For a moment, time is moving too quickly and too slowly at the same time.

It all floods back—Blake's mouth crushed against mine, his strong arm holding me to him, the feeling of his thighs tensed beneath me. He's barely breathing. I don't think I am either. I jolt away and raise my hand to slap him.

Only, before I make impact with his face, the air is knocked from my lungs.

There's heat and muscle against my back and my chest as the three of us crash to the ground. The floorboards groan, or perhaps it's Blake as his head hits the floor. Callum's growl vibrates against my ear. The scent of male sweat floods my nostrils.

I scramble from between them, my hair in my face, my breathing fast.

Blake gets the upper hand for a moment, and I almost stagger into the copper bathtub as they roll over on the ground. I dart aside, grabbing onto the mahogany bed post, as Callum pins him down and wraps his hands around Blake's neck.

"There he is," says Blake, on a choked breath.

Callum's eyes are feral. All the muscles in his arms are pronounced. Fury ripples from him in waves. It is almost inconceivable that he was lying on the bed, close to death, just a moment ago.

Blake tilts his head to catch my eye. There's blood dribbling from his nose.

"A little help," he says through wheezing breaths.

My heartbeat slams against my ribs. My mind isn't processing what is happening. I feel as if I've floated out of my body and I'm watching from far away. Callum was dying and Blake kissed me and now they are fighting. "Why on earth would I help—?"

My gaze snaps back to Callum's face, and the wolf that is now glaring behind his eyes. The wolf that is fighting both Blake *and* the wolfsbane.

"*Aurora*," Blake chokes.

I crash back into my body.

"Callum," I say.

Despite the fury etched into every muscle of his body, his gaze snaps to mine. The distraction is enough for Blake to slam him onto his back. Callum groans, resting his head on the floorboards, the fight draining from his body.

"Fuck," he moans.

"I know, I know," Blake soothes. Blood is dripping from his nose, and it glints in the morning light.

"One of these days, Blake," Callum murmurs.

"Yes. Yes. I'm sure you'll try to kill me."

Blake pushes himself to his knees. Callum grabs his wrist before he can get up fully. "Why?"

A sly smile spreads across Blake's face. "Because I need you alive."

He lightly slaps him on the cheek a couple of times. Then he gets up and walks to the door.

"Don't ever touch her again," says Callum.

Blake glances over his shoulder at me. His expression is cold. A mirror of my own expression, I'm sure. He turns swiftly away and disappears into the corridor.

"Princess? Are you alright?"

My gaze snaps to Callum and my eyebrows raise with a thousand questions. "*You're* asking me that?"

He offers me a soft smile as I crash to my knees beside him.

Chapter Forty-Two

I press my forehead against Callum's, and let his heat envelope me.

My eyes burn. I cannot bear the thought of him being taken from me.

"I thought I was going to lose you," I whisper, my throat thick.

He puts his hand on my cheek, his palm rough and firm. "I'm okay."

"You weren't waking up. I thought. . . I thought. . ."

"I'm right here." His tone is gentle; there's a hint of amusement there too.

"What's so funny?" My breath mingles with his.

"If I'd known getting injured would cause you to be so nice to me, I'd have done it sooner."

I pull back slightly, and frown. "Don't say that."

His skin is pale and he's coated in a layer of sweat and grime. I can smell the battle on him—blood and earth and steel. But his scent of the mountains seeps through and warms me with its familiarity. Black veins spread from the wound in his shoulder. They are fainter than before, but he must be in pain.

The wolf has gone from his eyes, and it is the man who now watches me.

"I thought of you every hour I was away," he says. "All I could think of was getting back to you. I shouldn't have left you. I won't do it again."

My throat thickens. I try to harden my heart. I try to freeze the warmth that spreads through my veins. Because it's not true.

He will trade me for the Heart of the Moon to save his people, and soon this will be over.

"You will," I whisper.

His jaw hardens. "No." His voice is rough and raw. "No. I won't."

I touch his face, my fingertips brushing over his stubble. "Callum, you brought me here for a reason. And now the Wolf King has returned—"

"I will find another way."

"Callum—"

He slides his hand to the back of my neck and pulls my forehead to his. "I will find another way."

His breath is hot on my skin, and my blood heats up. Our lips are almost touching. I long to sink further into his warmth, to take comfort in it. Even though it would be foolish. Even though it would destroy this wavering barrier between us and leave me open to all the pain that is yet to come.

He gently strokes the back of my neck, and my eyelids close.

It makes me feel safe, and warm, and cared for.

I wonder, when I am sent back home, whether I will ever feel this way again—whether I will ever feel *anything* again.

Without thinking, I kiss him.

He groans softly as he parts his lips. It makes me want to climb on top of him. I want to be closer to him in any way that I can.

But he is injured, and I know how much it will hurt if I succumb to these feelings completely.

I pull away.

"You're not going back to him." His tone is so steady and strong that I almost believe him.

He tugs me back down, and I nestle my head against his good shoulder. He sighs, and his breathing and heartbeat become steadier as the minutes pass by.

"Princess, will you do me a favor?"

"Yes," I say—surprising myself with how quickly I agree.

"Will you take Blake's collar off now?"

I jolt upright and he watches me with sleepy eyes.

"Goddess! I forgot I was wearing it." I pull it off, and toss it to the other side of his chambers. It hits the foot of his armchair by the window.

Shame surges through me as I recall the argument I had with Callum before I knew he was injured. I *wanted* to provoke him. I feel worse when I think of the things Blake said about me, what he *did* to me. He *kissed* me.

"I didn't choose him over you, Callum. I would never do that. Isla—"

I turn back to him, but his eyes are closed. There's a soft, satisfied smile on his face and his bare chest moves up and down steadily. "Mm?"

"I'll tell you later." I put his arm around my neck. "Come on, let's get you into bed."

I try to nudge him to his feet, but I think I'd have more luck trying to pick up one of the mountains outside. So I nestle beside him on the floorboards, and let his warmth cocoon me.

His arm tightens around my shoulder, pulling me close, and he sighs again.

Soon his gentle snores fill his chambers.

***

It is late at night when Callum and I sit on his bed, leaning against the headboard, eating bread and cheese that one of the servants brought us. They helped me change the bedding while he slept, too, so his quilt is no longer stained with blood.

The change in him is evident, even in the flickering candlelight. He slept all day. Color has come back to his cheeks and his eyes are bright. He no longer smells like a battlefield after I helped him wash the grime from his skin, and his wound is almost completely healed.

He's changed from his battle-worn kilt into his loose-fitting cotton breeches, and rests his forearms against his knees. He gave me a shirt to wear too, because my dress was covered in his blood and I didn't want to leave him to change in my chambers.

I sit with my knees close to my chest, the material pulled down to my calves. It is revealing and feels intimate to be wearing his clothes. It smells like him too, and I can barely concentrate as I tell him what happened while he was away.

He is listening attentively, though, and his gaze darkens when I tell him I suspect Isla stole his collar from me.

"Are you sure it was her?" he asks.

I snap my head toward him. "Yes."

"I'm not saying I don't believe you, Princess. I'm just surprised, I suppose. I knew the lass had a wee crush on me, but to defy her alpha like that. . ." His eyebrows knit together. "She gave you the note, though?"

"What note?"

"The note I—" Understanding dawns on his face. He drops his chunk of bread onto the plate, and rubs his face with both hands. "Fuck. No wonder you were so angry with me."

"You wrote me a note? Before you left."

"I'd never have left without saying anything at all." His jawline hardens. "I'll be speaking with Isla about this. I promise you, Princess. She won't bother you again."

I roll my eyes. "I can handle Isla."

He grins. "You can?"

"Yes. And you're missing the point. Why didn't you just come and tell me you were leaving?" When he opens his mouth to respond, I give him a sharp look. "And don't say you didn't have time."

He runs a hand over the back of his neck and stares at the foot of the bed.

"I should have gone back to your chambers to say goodbye, I know that. But before, when I was kissing you, tasting you, when I had you beneath me on that bed. . ." My cheeks flush, but he doesn't seem remotely embarrassed. "I lost control of myself. I felt the wolf—"

"I'm not afraid of you. I've told you. The wolf doesn't scare me."

"But *I* was scared. The only time I feel out of control like that is when the moon is full. No one has made me feel that way before. And *I* was afraid."

"You're afraid of losing control with me?"

"Of course I am."

Something sad blooms inside my chest and my throat thickens. I look away, my jaw tightening. "Oh. Right."

"That upsets you?" I hear the confusion in his voice.

I shrug and force myself to bite into my bread. "No. I understand." The bread is dry as it makes its way down my throat. "You need to trade me for the Heart of the Moon. You said you wouldn't touch me. I'd be worthless to Sebastian if you. . . lost control around me."

Callum doesn't respond. All I can hear are the flames crackling in the hearth, the wind outside, and my own angry heartbeat. Carefully, he stacks my plate on top of his and places them both on the bedside table.

He puts his hand gently on my jaw, and turns my head so I'm looking at him.

He looks more serious than I've ever seen him. Perhaps even a little. . . sad.

"Do you truly think that?" His brow furrows. "Do you truly think I give a shit about Sebastian? That I would give him the slightest bit of consideration when it comes to you and me? Princess, I made a promise not to touch you because it's the right thing to do. And it's a promise that gets harder to keep every day, every hour, every second I'm around you. But I must. Because I took you."

He shakes his head, and his voice thickens. "I took you from your home, and your bed, and your people. I made you my prisoner, Aurora." His eyes are shining, and he turns his attention to the posts at the end of the bed. "You think there's always a choice, but there's not. Not without freedom. You can't choose me when you're not really free."

I'm blindsided. Emotions hurtle around my chest like the winds rattling the windows.

"Callum, you didn't take me prisoner."

I'm not sure if I'm relieved, or confused, or amused, or heartbroken. It is overwhelming. And yet, for once, I don't want to push the emotions away. I want to embrace them. I want to *feel*.

I shift on the bed, and turn his face toward mine. "I chose to come. And I'm glad that I did. I have never felt more free than when I am with you. And. . . well. . ." I take a deep breath. "There's another thing."

His eyebrows knit together. "What is it?"

I chew my bottom lip. "I was planning on giving my father information about the Wolves once you had sent me back. I was going to use it to get out of my marriage with Sebastian."

Callum stills. At some point during our time together, I let myself forget he is a fierce warrior, though it is obvious now from the tightening of his jaw, and the tension he emits. Was I foolish to admit this to him?

He told me before that he would die to save his people.

"Are you still planning to do that?" he asks.

"I don't want to marry him, Callum."

"Aye. I know that. But. . ." He puts his hand on my cheek. "What you've just told me. You cannot tell anyone else. If the king finds out. . . Please tell me you understand that?"

"I'm not a fool."

Something like relief blooms in his eyes. "No. You're not." A soft smile plays on his lips, and he shakes his head. "My wee spy."

The word *my* stokes something inside me.

"You're not concerned?" I ask.

"It makes no difference to me." He shrugs. "You're not going back to him."

"And, so you see, I was never really a prisoner to begin with."

He drops his hand, and sighs. "You might think that, Princess, but I disagree."

"Oh, for the love of the Goddess, Callum! Will you stop being such a big bloody. . . gentleman!"

He raises his eyebrows, and stills.

His gaze drops down to my body, and the shirt I'm wearing, and something unreadable flickers over his expression. "A spy, not a prisoner, huh?"

When he meets my eyes again, mischief dances amid the darkness.

"I never thought you'd ask me not to be a gentleman, Princess."

He drags his teeth over his bottom lip, as if considering something. Then he grins. In a sudden movement, he flips me onto my back and climbs on top of me—caging me between his arms. He brings his mouth to my ear, and I shiver as his warm breath touches my skin.

"But I'll be happy to oblige," he whispers.

Chapter Forty-Three

My insides tighten.

Callum's warm breath heats my skin, his lips almost touching my neck.

His shirt has ridden up to my hips, and I can feel the cotton of his breeches against the bare skin of my thighs.

My legs are parted to accommodate him, my core pressed against his hard stomach. When he shifts, my breath catches in my throat as a jolt of need courses through my body.

And the scent of him—Goddess, the scent of him—he smells like heat and male and the mountains.

He groans into my ear, and the sound vibrates through me.

"You don't know how many ungentlemanly things I've thought about doing to you." His voice is low, and his accent is even thicker than usual.

He brushes his lips against my neck, then shifts so his face hovers above mine. His solid weight presses down on me. His forearms are flat on the pillow on either side of my head.

I should feel trapped, held prisoner by his body. The strength of him, the sheer size of him, should make me feel weak. He is alpha of Highfell, a warrior and a wolf. I should be afraid.

Yet I feel something else entirely.

It is stirred by the quickening of his breathing, and the look in his eyes—there is dark intent there, but a hint of something else too. Awe, perhaps.

That first moment I saw him, standing stern and warrior-like in Sebastian's fighting ring, I would never in a million years have imagined that one day, we would be in this position. I thought him a monster. A brute. Someone to be feared. Hated, even.

I wonder if that is what is going through his mind too, as he brushes a strand of hair from my face.

"What ungentlemanly things?" I ask.

A slow grin spreads across his face. "Kissing you."

"Gentlemen kiss their ladies."

He raises an eyebrow. "Is that so?"

"Yes. There is a moment in the wedding ceremony where the groom kisses the bride."

His eyes glint with mischief. "Hm. It seems I'm not quite as well versed in the ways of gentlemen as you, Princess. You'll have to teach me. Do gentlemen kiss their ladies like this?"

He brushes his lips against mine. The kiss is gentle. Chaste. *Frustrating.* I want to buck against him—grab his hair, pull him closer to me. But my arms are pinned by my sides by his body, which holds me in place.

"Yes! And I told you to stop being a gentlemen, damn it!"

His grin widens, becomes wolfish.

"How will I know how *not* to act like a gentlemen, if I don't know how they behave in the first place?" His tone is teasing, his demeanor calm. It frustrates me even further. He knows he has total control here. And what's more, he is enjoying it.

"Do they kiss like *this*?" he asks.

He lowers his mouth to mine. This time, his kiss is deep. Rough. Claiming. I can't breathe, I can't think. There is only him, his mouth, his tongue moving in deep dominant strokes against mine, his groan that rumbles through my body and makes me quiver.

My hips move of their own accord, pushing my center against his bare torso, desperate for the friction.

I whimper when he pulls away, his breath still mingling with mine.

"Well?" he asks, his voice low and rough. The wolf flickers behind his eyes, fighting with the mischief that glimmers there.

"No." The word escapes on a breath. "They don't kiss like that."

"Hm. Interesting. How about this?"

He shifts, moving down my body so he hovers over my chest. Eyes on mine, he lowers his mouth to where my nipple is peaked, visible through the thin material of his shirt. He clamps his lips around it and he sucks hard.

I cry out as my back arches from the mattress.

It should hurt, yet I thread my fingers into his hair and pull him closer as he gives my other nipple the same rough treatment. He chuckles, then moves his hand to my breast, squeezing and rubbing as he sucks—causing raw liquid heat to pool at my core.

I moan as the ache builds. My hips buck, and I cry out in frustration. His eyes are still on mine, even as he brushes his teeth against my breast and gently bites.

I gasp. "*Callum!*"

He lifts an eyebrow, then carefully, lazily, detaches himself. He doesn't stop palming my breast. I arch into his hand, wanting to curse the material between us. His breathing is heavy and his cheeks are flushed. He is not as in control as he is implying.

"I asked you a question, Princess," he says. "And until we get to the bottom of it, I'm not going to be able to move on to my next lesson."

He pinches my nipple between his finger and thumb and an almost feral sound escapes my lips. The wolf becomes dominant in his eyes in answer to my call, before he pushes it back.

"No. That's not very gentlemanly at all!" I gasp.

His grin widens. "No? Good. Because, there's another place I've imagined kissing you for weeks now. You'll have to let me know whether it's gentlemanly or not."

There's a question in his eyes. My breathing is fast as I nod, my head brushing against the pillow.

I watch, entranced, as he lowers himself further down the bed. He pushes himself up, and kneels between my legs. His gaze sweeps up and down my body and his face darkens.

He is a vision of power and dominance. For a moment, he reminds me of a statue of a warrior—impenetrable, his expression serious. Only his chest moves up and down, deeply.

There is the same intent on his face as there was when I first saw him in that fighting ring.

Slowly, he slides his hands up my hips, hitching up the shirt and exposing my midriff and my underwear. I feel all of his attention hone in on the place between my legs that throbs with need. A low, almost inaudible growl builds in his chest, before his gaze moves back to mine.

My breathing is fast. I am completely at his mercy, and I do not know what he is going to do next. I am captivated. I cannot move. Cannot think. Not beyond the restlessness that builds like a storm in my chest, and the fire in my veins, and the ache that consumes me.

He shifts, and plants a soft kiss on my torso. The feel of his mouth and his stubble against my bare skin is almost too much to bear, and I whimper.

Then he lowers himself even further and my breathing becomes frantic.

He plants a kiss on my most intimate place, and I cry out as a jolt of pleasure surges through my body. He glances up at me, his mouth inches away from my core. His breath is warm through my underwear.

I should be pushing him away. I should not be so exposed, so brazen, so wanton with a man. Is this the kind of thing that happens in a brothel? I do not know. This is certainly not the way that a lady is supposed to behave. Least of all a princess.

Yet I lie there, my legs parted.

He cocks an eyebrow—and I know the question he is asking is not just part of his game. He is asking permission. If I play along, he will take this even further. How far, I do not know.

All I can think of is *more*.

"No," I whimper. "Gentleman do not do that."

He smiles, but his eyes darken. He slides down my underwear and tosses it aside, and my heartbeat hammers in my chest as he exposes me fully to him. His breathing becomes ragged, his shoulders hardening.

"Fuck. You're beautiful," he mutters, as he looks at me where no man has ever looked at me before. His eyes lift to mine once more. "Do they do this?"

He lowers his head and lightly kisses the sensitive bundle of nerves. I cry out as heat and surprise surge through my veins. Before I can process what he has just done, his mouth is on me, fully, completely. Hot and wet and hungry. He devours me. My back arches. My hips buck, and he grabs them, growling like a wild animal being disturbed from his prey, as he plants them firmly against the mattress.

He slides his tongue along my center, and I moan. I have never felt anything like it. He flicks, and licks, and sucks as though he cannot get enough of me, and the storm inside me becomes frantic. I want to lose myself to it. To this feeling. To him.

I reach for him, threading my fingers into his hair, pulling his mouth closer to me. I rock, shamelessly, against his face. He growls, sliding his hand up the shirt to roughly palm my breast.

"Fuck," he groans against me, and I shiver.

I do not feel like a human or a princess. I feel primal. That wildness builds with each lap of his tongue, each squeeze of my breast, each time he rubs my nipple with his thumb. I am writhing beneath him, my legs spread fully for him, my fingers clenched in his hair.

He moves his hand away, and I'm about to protest when he slides a finger inside me.

I cry out at the pressure of it, at the friction. He moves his hand at the same pace as his tongue—deep and fast and rough. It builds, and I rock harder, needing more. Needing him.

He groans, the noise vibrating through me, then he slides in another finger, spreading me wider, opening me up even more to him. It is too much to bear.

"Callum. . . I'm going to. . . It feels. . . I. . ."

I cry out, my breathing fast, as release crashes over me, through me. The world blurs. There is only this feeling, wild and raw, pumping through my veins. I feel like the wind that tears through the Northlands, and the animals that rage through the forests. He growls, his mouth clamping over the bundle of nerves, tasting me as I come undone beneath him.

When I finally settle back into my body, I'm panting, splayed out on the bed.

Callum kisses me gently between my legs, his eyes on mine—the wolf is prominent behind them. When he pulls away, his lips are moist. He drags his teeth over them, a low growl scraping against his throat. He climbs back over me, and gently kisses my mouth.

I moan against his lips, brushing my fingertips down the side of his face.

I am aware of his hard length, pressing against my bare thigh.

I should feel embarrassed, yet I do not think I have ever felt so relaxed in all of my life.

He looks down at me, and smiles softly.

"Well?" he asks, mischief in his expression. "Does a gentleman do that?"

Chapter Forty-Four

"I do not believe that gentlemen do that," I whisper.

Callum grins.

The wolf is still in his eyes. His irises are forest-green and glint in the flickering light coming from the hearth. I feel warm and soft and weightless. It makes me even more aware of the solidity of his body, which hovers over mine, and the hard length that presses against my bare thigh.

Another lick of heat pulses through me.

What would it be like to make him lose control in the way that he just did to me?

I do not know much about men, but I know if I touched him. . .

His eyes darken as if he knows the direction of my thoughts.

I try to slip my hand between us, but his body is flush with mine. So, I nudge his big shoulder. Conflict mingled with something else crosses his features before, warily, he lets me push him onto his back.

I prop myself up on my elbow. I am transfixed by his body. I take in his large biceps and the dusting of hair on his chest. I cannot help but recall the first moment I laid eyes on him, when I found the size and strength of him threatening.

Now it stirs something very different to fear inside me. How can a male be built this way? His sculpted frame rivals that of the marble statues of the gods that line the King's Approach to the palace. Hard and powerful and commanding attention.

Only, his cheeks are flushed, and his lips are swollen, and his chest moves up and down quickly. I have done that to him. Despite coming undone beneath him just moments ago, letting him have total control of my body, I feel powerful. What else can I do to him?

I touch his chest. He watches my hand as I run my fingertips down the ridges of his torso. I reach the hard V of his hips, and cast my gaze downward.

His arousal is obvious, visible through the thin material of his breeches. I hover my hand above it, my heart hammering in my chest. Callum seems to stop breathing. I think I have as well.

I have never done this before. Never touched a man. I have never wanted to until now. Will he finally lose control around me? Will he bend me over and take me in the way Wolves take their women?

Before, that frightened me. Now, heat pools between my legs in the place that is already slick and wet.

Tentatively, I move my hand down.

Callum lets out a low growl of frustration and grabs my wrist before I can touch him. In a sudden movement, he pulls me back to the pillow, turns me onto my side, and pulls me against his chest. His whole body is tense, flush against mine. His heart hammers against my back.

"What are you doing?" I growl.

"We have a big day tomorrow." His voice is strained. "You'll meet with the king. You should get some rest."

A swell of disappointment grows in my chest. "You don't want me to touch you?"

"More than anything, I want you to touch me." He swallows. "But it wouldn't be right. I'll give to you, but I won't take from you. That's where I draw the line."

I huff. "You are a gentleman, after all, then?"

"I'm a wolf and an alpha. I must have my honor."

His hard length presses against my behind.

I shift slightly. He hisses through his teeth and puts his hand flat on my stomach, fingers splayed. He holds me still against him. "Princess, that's not a good idea."

"If you don't like it, do something about it."

"Speak to me like that again, and I shall bend you over my knee," he growls in my ear.

Indignation spreads through my body, heating and pooling between my legs. He chuckles and kisses the back of my neck, causing another thrill to surge through me.

"And I do like it," he says. "I like it very much."

"Then, why?"

"One day," he promises darkly. "One day, I will show you what happens when you touch a wolf."

He strokes my bare stomach, his hand beneath my shirt.

"Now, go to sleep," he says.

The movement of his hand is gentle and soothing, and—weightless as I am—I soon find my eyelids drooping and my body relaxing into his.

"The Wolf King is truly back?" I ask.

"Aye. He'll address everyone tomorrow morning. We'll speak with him then."

"Are you worried?"

"No," he says, but I catch a hint of hesitation.

"What happened? Why did he need your aid?"

"He was visiting one of the outlying clans, trying to drum up support for the war. He ran into Sebastian's soldiers not far from here. The force of the army was much larger than it usually would be to siege a fairly insignificant castle, and they had better weapons than I've ever seen them fight with before. They took the whole castle and fort, and we barely escaped with our lives. Some didn't."

"He's coming for me," I say, horror replacing the warmth in my body. I knew this was coming, and for a while, I'd let myself forget. I was a fool.

"Aye." His chest hardens against my back, and he pulls me a little closer, his hand firm on my torso. "They're getting close."

"Does the Wolf King know they were there because of me?"

He hesitates again. "No. I think James presumed they'd got wind he'd be visiting and the attack was in his honor. I haven't told him about you yet."

Silence falls over us, thick and heavy. All I can hear are the dwindling flames in the hearth, and the wind blowing against the castle walls. Words don't need to be said.

When the Wolf King finds out I am the princess of his enemy, things could go badly.

"He won't hurt you," Callum says, finally.

He sounds so certain that I want to believe him.

Yet it is a while before I fall asleep.

I dream of wolf eyes, watching me through the trees.

***

The weak morning sun shines on the two dresses laid out on Callum's bed. Callum retrieved them for me, not wanting me to encounter any Wolves while wearing only his shirt. Now he sits his armchair, looking out of the window, with a pensive look on his face. He's fiddling with the button of his cuff.

If today wasn't such a big day, I might be worrying that he regrets what happened last night.

But today, I meet with the Wolf King. I have no time to be dwelling on stubborn alphas, or the things that he did to me with his tongue.

I look between the two costumes I instructed Callum to bring me.

The first impression I make with his king is important and I have a difficult choice to make.

One garment is white and simple. It would make me look innocent and demure, like a perfect princess, a perfect doll.

The other is the black dress that caught my eye when I first arrived here. It's striking, with intricate lace sleeves and a high collar. It is something someone important would wear, someone powerful. I run my fingers down the dark material, tempted by the power it seems to hold.

The two are polar opposites.

"Which one would your king like best?" I ask.

Callum slides his gaze from the mountains, to me. "Hm?"

I place my hands on my hips. "Which dress?"

"They're both bonnie. You'll look beautiful whatever you wear."

I exhale. "That's not the point."

He raises his eyebrows and looks confused.

I shake my head. "Never mind. You are truly useless."

He grins, then shrugs, moving his gaze back to the window. I cannot tell whether it is what we did last night that troubles him, or the upcoming meeting with the king.

Either way, I have more important things to be worrying about right now.

I eventually settle on the white dress, deeming the black too threatening. I was dressed in white the first time I was paraded in front of Sebastian, and though the outcome wasn't favorable to me, it gained the best outcome for my kingdom.

I comb my fingers through my hair, then pull on my boots.

"I'm ready," I say, finally.

He turns his head, and offers me a genuine smile, his eyes bright in the morning light. "You look perfect."

"Are you sure?"

"Aye." He opens his mouth as if to say something, then seems to think better of it. He runs a hand over his mouth, then turns his gaze back to the grey sky. "We'll head down in half an hour."

I don't think I can wait that long. Not with Callum in such an odd mood, my thoughts consumed with what I let him do to me last night, and my doomed future creeping ever closer.

Something black catches my eye on the stone floor by the armchair—giving the whirlwind inside my chest a focal point. I pick up Blake's collar.

He said he needed Callum alive. For what purpose?

He said some other horrible things about me, too. And he kissed me.

"I'm going to return this," I say, holding up the collar.

Callum turns his head to look at me, his eyes momentarily hardening on the obsidian stone at the collar's center.

His nostrils flare, then he smiles.

"Okay. But if you're not back in ten minutes, I'm going to murder him."

I nod.

Glad to have something to do, I head to Blake's chambers.

Chapter Forty-Five

I enter Blake's chambers without knocking.

He's in his armchair again, reading that book he took from my room.

He turns the page, then reaches for a teacup on the table beside him. From the fresh herbal scent in the room, I'd wager it is full of peppermint tea.

He takes a sip, then goes back to his book. "Have you met the last person, other than you, who burst into my chambers unannounced?" he asks.

"No?"

"That's because they're dead."

"Am I supposed to be scared?"

"Yes." He flicks the page. "You smell like wet dog, by the way. I knew Callum wouldn't be able to resist playing with his new toy."

I hold up his black collar to show I won't be wearing it anymore. "I've come to return this."

He shrugs, not lifting his gaze from his book. "You can put it on the desk."

Irritation flares inside me. Is he not even going to look at me?

Deep down, I know it's not just annoyance at Blake that flickers beneath my skin and makes my chest feel tight. It's fear too; I'm afraid of this unchartered territory I find myself in.

I'm playing a game and I don't know the rules any longer.

I'm lost among Wolves, and I think I am falling for one of them. I shared something with him last night that is forbidden to me. And he has been distant with me all morning. And soon, I must meet with his king—a male so fearsome that the other Wolves fall behind him.

I thought if I came to the Northlands, I could win the right to choose my own fate.

But the Wolf King is the one who holds all the cards here, and I do not know what moves I need to play in order to win.

I take a deep breath, forcing my emotions down and hardening my soul. I focus my attention on the wolf before me instead.

He looks as disheveled as he did on the night of the storm. Perhaps even more so.

He's wearing the same clothes as last night. His white shirt is untucked and there are a few spots of blood on his unbuttoned collar. His dark hair is messy, and his feet are bare as he rests them on a footstool.

The candle beside him flickers, and is almost burnt out, even though the morning light permeates the narrow window behind him.

I wonder if he's slept at all.

"Are you going to apologize?" I ask.

His gaze slides to mine as if I've finally caught his attention. "I saved his life. You should be thanking me."

"You said. . ." My cheeks flame. "You said some very inappropriate things about me."

A stupid dimple creases one of his cheeks. The smile doesn't meet his eyes. "Come now, you can't be acting shy any longer. Not after whatever you and that big oaf got up to last night."

"You. . . you kissed me!"

"It was hardly a kiss."

A tornado rages inside my chest, rattling my bones, and I need to release it. I toss his collar onto the floor between us. "Here."

As soon as I've done it, I regret it.

I don't know much about Wolves, but these collars are important to the alphas. Blake may be different than the others, but he is an alpha nonetheless.

For a moment, we're paused in time. Neither of us moves, and the air is heavy and silent.

He slides his feet off the footstool, and rises.

A part of me wants to step back, but I make myself hold my ground. I won't cower. Not before him.

He surprises me by crouching onto one knee before me. He picks up the collar, then looks up.

His body heat envelopes me, and I catch the scent of dark forests and peppermint tea.

He moistens his lips, and for some reason, what Callum did to me last night crashes into my mind. Followed by one of the horrible things that Blake said. About having me ride his face.

When Blake smirks, I realize that was exactly his intention.

I have had many things to be angry about. My father, selling me off to the highest bidder. My mother dying. My brother's cold indifference. The High Priest's cruelty. It is now that wild fire spreads through my veins. And when Blake slowly rises to his full height, I slap him across the face with all the strength I have.

The crack echoes around his chambers as his head jerks to one side.

I pull back, stunned, my heartbeat the only thing I can hear, my palm stinging. I cannot believe I just did that. I have never hit anyone in all my twenty years of life. Princesses don't hit people.

They especially don't hit Wolves. Or alphas. Or alpha Wolves that other alphas seem to fear.

Callum described Blake as the most dangerous male in the Kingdom of Wolves, and I just slapped him. Goddess!

As the mists of rage and confusion ebb away, I notice Blake is smiling. His cheek is bright red and his eyes dance.

"The rabbit has grown some claws," he says.

"Don't touch me again."

"Likewise." He walks back across the room, tossing the collar on the table, before dropping into his armchair. "Out of interest, what will you do if I touch you again?" He arches an eyebrow. "Put buckthorn in my tea?"

I narrow my eyes. "Wolfsbane."

He smiles, then leans back in his seat and rests his ankle on his knee. He grabs his book and starts reading, as if he's finished with me, as if I'm no threat.

I decide he is not worth any more of my time. I have more important things to worry about. I turn on my heel and stride back to the door.

"Aurora," says Blake.

"What?"

"You're not planning on meeting the Wolf King dressed like that, are you?"

Don't bite. Don't bite. Don't—

"What's wrong with this dress?" I ask, turning back around.

"You look like a pretty little doll." The way he says it doesn't sound like a compliment.

"Perhaps that's the point."

"This is not the kingdom of men."

"Meaning?"

"Do you want to face the Wolf King as a queen or a doll?"

"I'm not a queen."

He quirks an eyebrow. "Are you a doll?"

"I'll be either if it gets me out of this alive."

He smirks. "James likes his women bold."

"I don't trust you."

"Probably wise. But I'm not lying."

I scowl as I head out his chambers.

As much as I hate to admit it, I'd gone to Blake's chambers to release some of this pent-up fury. If anything, I now feel even more unsettled. My mind is reeling as I navigate the stone corridors, and make my way back to Callum's room.

Is Blake lying to make a fool out of me? Or was his advice supposed to help me? I cannot figure it out. What should I do? How should I navigate this dark and treacherous forest when it is the big bad wolf that gives me directions?

Callum is still staring out of the window when I arrive. He looks up as I enter, and concern flashes in his eyes.

"Are you okay, Princess?" His expression darkens. "Did Blake upset you?"

"I. . . no. . ." I shake my head. "I'm fine."

He swallows, then nods—exhaling before turning back to the mountains. "Good."

"You regret it, don't you?" I try to sound confident, as if it doesn't bother me that he's acting distant after what happened last night, but my voice wavers slightly.

He turns back to me, his eyebrows lifting. His expression softens. He walks toward me, swamping me with his huge frame. I step back, and he steers me to the bed. When the backs of my legs hit the mattress, I sit down.

He crouches down between my legs and places his hands on my hips. His face is more serious than I've ever seen it.

"No," he says. "Never. In another life, in another situation, we'd have spent this morning in bed with me between your thighs." The corner of his lip lifts as my cheeks flame. "But due to the current situation we're in, I admit, I'm a wee bit. . . troubled this morning."

Some of the anxiety building in my chest diminishes, only to be replaced by a greater worry. "So you *are* worried about the king."

He sighs. "There is a chance he may not be best pleased about. . . how protective I have become of you."

Something warms inside my chest at the sincerity in his expression. "You don't need to tell him."

"He'll know."

"How?"

"My scent is all over you."

Heat floods my face, and the reason Blake knew something had happened between us becomes evident. A part of me wonders if that is the reason Callum was happy for me to visit Blake in the first place.

"Oh. I should wash, then."

"Ah, you see, that's what's troubling me. I want you to smell like me. I like it. I want every wolf to know, James included."

I fold my arms. "That doesn't sound sensible."

He grins. "Aye, well I never said I was sensible. Besides, there's no time now for a bath. Not unless you want to go for a swim in the loch."

He raises his eyebrows, and I smile—remembering how cold the water was when I washed at Glen Marb. From the grin on his face, I think he is remembering it too.

He sighs, his breath misting in front of his face.

"We should go."

He brushes his lips against my forehead, and my hands reflexively move to chest, my fingers gripping his shirt. He's so firm and solid beneath it and I want to take comfort in that strength—to take comfort in him. His hands momentarily tighten around my hips.

Heat flares inside me, despite the words he mumbles against my skin. "It's time to meet the Wolf King."

Chapter Forty-Six

The castle corridors outside Callum's chambers seem colder, the shadows longer. The torches on the wall flicker as we pass, as if possessed by the same nervous energy that builds in my stomach.

When I descended the kennel steps that night in Sebastian's castle, I felt as if I was walking into the jaws of a great beast.

Now, it has swallowed me.

When I meet with the Wolf King, I will find out whether it is to chew me up and spit me back out again.

Or worse.

Callum walks by my side, his hand pressed against the small of my back. The warmth he radiates is of little comfort. Not when he is uncharacteristically quiet. His heavy footsteps echo off the stone walls, steady and slow, as though he is delaying the inevitable.

As we reach the stairwell, loud voices pierce the gloom from the lower floors of the castle. Some agitated, some excitable, some tainted with anger. It reminds me of the noise one hears on the day of an execution in the King's City.

Perhaps there will be an execution today.

And yet, all I can think about is the dress I am wearing. It's white and long-sleeved.

The perfect doll—that is what Blake said I looked like.

I've had little choice over so many things in my life—who I'd marry, where I'd live, what my purpose should be. But my clothing—the way I present myself—that was a choice I always had.

And I was good at it. My dresses were disguises, my make-up a mask. I could choose to blend into the background of a meal in the Great Hall, or be the focal point in a grand ball.

I had that choice this morning. I thought I had made the correct one, and yet Blake has gotten under my skin.

Should I have chosen differently?

"Does the Wolf King have a wife?" I ask as we make our way down the stairwell.

"Hm? No."

"What kind of women does he like?"

Callum's eyebrow cocks up, as if he's surprised by the question. "I don't know. Bonny lasses, I suppose."

I sigh. "His last lover, who was she?"

"That'd be Claire." He lets out a half-laugh. "She was a fiery one. Kept him on his toes, that's for sure."

Blake's words come back to me.

James likes his women bold.

He was telling the truth.

I halt on the bottom step. "Goddess, Callum!"

Callum's eyebrows knit together. "What's the matter?"

My heart pounds against my ribcage as my mind reels with choices. I glance at the door ahead, knowing the corridor behind it leads to the Great Hall where I will meet my fate. I look over my shoulder at the stairway.

I take a deep breath. "I need to change my dress."

"Rory—" Callum's tone is a warning, but I've already turned around. I run back up the stairs, almost tripping over my skirts. Callum is close behind me. "We don't have time for this!"

I run into his chambers and close the door in his face. "Send someone in to help me."

I hear him slam his hand against the wall outside, then curse under his breath. "It's just a dress." His tone is pointedly even—as though he's trying to reason with a petulant child. "It doesn't matter—"

"Send someone to help me!"

"Goddess, give me strength," he growls. "Fine. But if you're not out in five minutes, I'll throw you over my shoulder and take you down to the Great Hall regardless of what you are, or are not, wearing!"

***

Ten minutes later, I step back into the corridor donning the black dress. It is strange, but after a couple of weeks of wearing clothes that make me fit in, I feel more myself, wearing it.

It is a beautiful piece of clothing, and I wonder where it came from.

The sleeves are made of intricate lace that is shaped into leaves and thorns and branches. One of the servants helped me cinch in the corset at the waist, and the collar is high. I pinned back my hair to accentuate it, and pinched my cheeks to bring some color to them, though my face must still be pale. My long skirts rustle as they trail across the floor.

Callum is pacing up and down and his hands are in fists at his sides.

"Finally!" He spins around, eyes blazing. "You—"

He swallows, then blinks a couple of times. His lips part and his eyebrows raise. Taking a deep breath, he dips his head deferentially—his eyes never leaving mine.

"Your Highness," he says.

I grab my black skirts, and walk past him. "It's just a dress." I flash him a smile as I repeat his words to him.

He huffs out a laugh as he falls into step beside me. He keeps looking at me, then averting his gaze when I catch his eye.

"You know, I forget sometimes. Who you are. I mean. . . I don't forget. I know you're the princess. Well . . I. . ." He exhales. "Goddess, you've got me tongue-tied. What I mean to say is that you look nice."

I hide my smile, though I'm sure it's evident in my tone. "Thank you, Callum."

"It makes me think—"

"What?"

He sighs. "Nothing. A silly fantasy."

I throw him a curious look, but he merely smiles sheepishly and gestures ahead.

The Great Hall is full of noise when we reach it, though it barely competes with the beating of my heart. Brodie, the small freckled boy, is playing bagpipes again by the open double doors. In another situation, I might tell him that he has improved. The screeching has started to actually sound like music.

Instead, I let loose a shaky breath. I need to reserve all of my energy to keep my head held high, and to stop myself from running.

"Is he in there? Your king?"

"Not yet, thank the Goddess. He likes to make an entrance."

I take a deep breath. The air tastes like woodsmoke and whisky.

"He won't harm you," says Callum, touching the small of my back.

There's a mass of Wolves in the Great Hall already, shouting and laughing as they wait.

"Even if he doesn't, the others might," I say. "My people have just attacked your people once more. Who is to say that the whole room won't turn on me?"

He cups my face in his big hand, and bends to rest his forehead against mine. "I won't let that happen. I swear it."

I run a hand over his chest, feeling the strength in him, before resting my palm against his heart.

It beats steadily. Calm. Unafraid.

I'm not sure I believe this will work out in my favor. But Callum seems confident, at least.

He brushes his lips against my forehead, running his hand over the back of my neck.

"Come," he says.

He takes my hand, then leads me through the doors.

The tables have been pushed to the sides of the hall, where the tapestries that depict the story of the Elderwolf hang.

Callum pushes through the tangle of limbs. Those nearest to us move aside to let us pass. Some look at me strangely, confusion and curiosity dancing in their eyes. I wonder if my dress lends a clue as to who I really am.

I suppose I no longer look like a kitchen maid.

I look like the daughter of their enemy king.

I keep my head high, though my grip on Callum's hand tightens. He squeezes back as he leads me up the steps onto the wooden platform where the alpha's table usually stands.

In its place, there is now a large wooden throne. It is simple, but the back has been carved into an image of trees twisting up to a full moon.

The alphas of the clans stand on either side of it—six in total including Robert the acting Wolf King.

Callum leads me to one side of the platform.

From the far end of the line-up, Blake catches my eye.

He looks very different from the disheveled male I encountered earlier. He's changed out of his scruffy clothes, and is wearing an elegant black coat with silver buttons, over a dark shirt and breeches.

"How did it go with Blake, anyway?" asks Callum under his breath.

"I. . . kind of. . .well. . ." I fight the flush of embarrassment. "I hit him."

Callum's eyebrows lift. "He let you hit him?"

"No, Callum. He didn't *let* me hit him. Why would you say that?"

"You're very small." He grins as I glare at him. "You're not going to hit *me*, are you?"

"Oh, be quiet."

He looks at Blake, who is straightening his cuffs, and his expression darkens. "He may look like a wee weasel, but he's more capable than he seems. He was in the King's Guard for a time, if you believe his stories. He's a deadly warrior when he chooses to fight rather than stab people in the back, or poison them. It's hard to believe you could just walk into his chambers and hit him."

"Perhaps that's how I did it. Because you males have such difficulty in believing women could do such things."

"Hm, perhaps," says Callum.

Across the room, Blake smirks, and I'm sure he's listening.

I'm trying to think of something I can say to annoy Blake, when the bagpipe music stops.

I breathe in sharply. Callum tenses, his hard bicep brushing my arm. A hush descends over the Great Hall. For a moment, the air is thick with silence.

The pipes start playing again, but it's a more regal piece with a slower rhythm.

"It'll be okay," mutters Callum, and I'm not sure if he's speaking to me or himself as the crowd parts to create a walkway in the center of the room.

My heart beats fast. I think of the little that I know of the Wolf King. He united seven warring Northlands clans and big brutish alphas follow his command.

He likes bold women.

I need him to like me if I am to escape execution, and to avoid going back to Sebastian.

Be bold, I tell myself, though my insides are twisting and a storm is billowing in my chest. *Be bold*.

I raise my chin as all gazes turn to the back of the Great Hall.

The Wolf King steps through the wooden doors.

He looks like no king I have encountered before. Tall and muscular, he wears no crown or fancy jewels, and dresses simply in a cream shirt and kilt. His sleeves are rolled to his elbows, revealing tattoos inked on his corded forearms. His tangled hair is brown, and it brushes his powerful shoulders. I cannot quite tell his age, but I'd wager he is around thirty.

He commands all the attention in the room, and as he strides toward us, the Wolves drop to one knee.

As he gets closer, and my pulse races faster, I notice that his kilt is predominantly red, like Callum's, but it's a different pattern. It seems to contain the colors of all the clans.

He walks up the steps of the platform, his boots thudding and shaking the wood. The alphas all dip their heads deferentially, Callum included.

I, however, cannot stop staring.

The Wolf King's eyes land on mine, and he frowns. Slowly, he walks toward me. Callum tenses, and my insides clench.

Be bold.

He seems to appraise me for a moment.

"It's customary to kneel in the presence of a king," he says. His voice is low and powerful, thick with the accent of the Northlands.

I always thought my wedding day was the moment my whole life was building toward, but now, I think perhaps it was this one.

I have one moment to make an impression. One moment to show I am not a useless doll. Nor a pawn to be played in a game between men. Nor a statue, made of stone, with nothing inside.

I spared Ryan in that fighting ring. I chose to come with Callum to this Kingdom of Wolves. I bartered with him for my freedom.

Be bold, my pounding heartbeat demands. *Be bold.*

I swallow and raise my chin.

"A real princess does not kneel to a false king," I say.

There's a collective intake of breath within the Great Hall. A few of the alphas step forward. Shouts ring through the room. Robert's hand curls around his sword.

I can barely focus on the disruption I have created. The hall is blurring around me. The adrenaline that pumps through my veins makes everything seem faraway.

I brace myself. I wait for the Wolf King to strike me down, to push me to my knees, or throw me into the dungeons.

As my pulse calms, I notice his displeasure is focused on Callum—who has stepped forward, his arm in front of mine. His head is no longer dipped, and his hard gaze is locked on the Wolf King in direct challenge.

My insides twist. *Goddess, what have I done?*

Across the platform, Blake's lips curve into a wicked smile.

I try to think of something, anything, I can do to make this right, to make it look like Callum is not challenging his king.

Then the Wolf King's jaw tightens as he stares at Callum.

"A word, please, Brother," he says.

My eyebrows lift as James walks past us both, heads down the steps leading down from the platform, and through a door behind the throne.

Callum scans the Great Hall as a mixture of hostile and intrigued faces stare up at us. When he doesn't find what, or who, he is looking for, he turns to Blake.

He gives me a hard look before turning on his heel and following the Wolf King through the door—leaving me alone with the Wolves.

Blake saunters over with his hands in his pockets. He stares out at the room.

"Well, it was bold, I'll give you that," he says.

Chapter Forty-Seven

"You said be bold," I hiss.

"Yes, look him in the eye, answer his questions, don't cower before him. I didn't expect you to challenge his claim to the throne!" Blake laughs, and it's a real laugh, too. Not contrived, like usual. "That was excellent. Not for you, obviously. But for me, that was truly entertaining."

"Shut up, Blake."

The Great Hall is filled with agitated voices. Someone shouts, "Death to the Southlands king!"

I chew my bottom lip. "Callum is the Wolf King's brother?"

I am standing on the precipice of a storm that could break at any moment. All it will take is one wolf to charge onto this platform, one alpha to draw his sword. Robert certainly looks like he wants to as he mutters darkly to the large red-haired male beside him.

I glance at the door behind the throne. If the worst happens, that is where I will run. I would rather take my chances against the Wolf King with Callum at my side, than this unruly mob with only Blake for company.

Blake is completely at ease beside me, his hands in the pockets of his breeches. It is as if he is looking out onto one of the Northlands lochs on a peaceful morning.

His eyebrow cocks up. "He didn't tell you?"

There's an irritating smugness to his tone. He knows damn well that Callum didn't tell me, and he is clearly trying to get a rise out of me.

An ugly feeling of betrayal twists with the anxiety building in my stomach. Why would Callum have kept something so important from me?

I want to voice my concern, but I do not want Blake to see my weakness. I swallow. I focus on one of the tapestries that shows the Elderwolf howling at the moon so I don't have to look at the sea of hostile faces.

"They have a. . . complicated relationship." Blake's voice drops to a whisper—answering my unasked question anyway.

I try not to take the bait, yet I cannot fight the curiosity that flares within. "How so?"

Blake's lips curve into a smile as if he's pleased I'm willing to play his game with him.

"Their father started all this." He inclines his head at the crowd of Wolves in the hall. "Bringing all the clans together. He was the first Wolf King. When he. . . died—"

Blake puts a strange weight on the word, and his eyes glint in the morning light that seeps through the narrow windows.

"—it left the position open. It was assumed one of his sons would take the title, though things do not work the same way here as they do in the Southlands. No one is entitled to the position based on the blood that runs in their veins. Rather, it is based on the blood that they spill. Any wolf can win the throne."

"By challenging the current king?"

Blake inclines his head. "The appointment is more political than they will admit, though. Without the backing of at least half of the clans, the title means nothing."

"There would be continuous civil war, I suppose."

A half-smile plays on Blake's lips. "Indeed."

"What has that got to do with Callum and James?"

"James had more backing with the clans here. He is. . . more similar to his father. But Callum had support from some of the outlying clans." He drops his voice lower, and I have to strain to hear him over the rabble. "It tipped the scale in his favor."

"So he should have won?"

Blake shrugs a shoulder. "If he'd beaten James."

"He lost the challenge?"

"He forfeited."

My brow furrows. "Why?"

"That's the question, isn't it?" says Blake, his eyes glinting with intrigue. "A question many Wolves are still asking. And by asking the question—"

"It weakens James's claim to the throne." I lower my voice because I do not want anyone to hear me. Surely this is a treasonous thing to say. "You don't know who would have won if they'd actually fought. By walking away, Callum made his brother look weak."

"Which James is not particularly thankful for."

My insides clench at the knowledge. Callum's strange sense of calm as we walked into this den of Wolves, and his assurance that he'd be able to talk his king into letting me stay, clearly relied on their familial bond. Yet it seems their relationship is complicated—maybe more so than Callum realizes.

That same kindness and sense of loyalty that drew me to him could wind up being my downfall. Has he been too generous in trusting his brother?

I try to settle my violent pulse, wondering what they are speaking about behind the closed door.

"You look exquisite, by the way," says Blake, his voice smooth like honey. My head snaps toward him, but he is staring at a spot of wall above the oak doors at the opposite side of the hall. "You should never pretend to be less than what you are."

My jaw tightens. That is rich, coming from him. Blake is a male whose entire persona seems contrived. He continually wears a mask of disinterest to hide his true intentions, whatever they may be. "And you don't pretend?"

Dimples puncture his cheeks. "I'm always pretending."

The door behind the throne opens and both of us look over our shoulders.

Callum stands in the doorway, looking tense. He gestures me over with a strained smile. His glaze slides to Blake and hardens. He says something I cannot hear and Blake inclines his head.

"As the king commands," he replies.

My heart is in my throat as I walk past the throne and down the steps toward Callum. This is it. This is the moment when my fate will be sealed.

Blake looks bored as he follows closely behind.

"Calm yourself," he whispers, his tone dark. "Wolves like to hunt little rabbits. Your pulse is pounding so hard that even I could be tempted to give chase."

"Be quiet," I snap. "How is saying something repugnant like that supposed to help?"

"Who says I'm trying to help?"

When we reach the doorway, Callum steers me into the room. His hand is strong and comforting on my lower back.

"It'll be alright," he says under his breath. "He just wants to meet you."

Blake follows and shuts the door behind us, sealing out the noise from the Great Hall.

It is as if I have left the hurricane and now stand in the very eye of the storm.

The room we are in is small and windowless. Claustrophobic. There is no escape.

A fire crackles in the hearth and fills the air with the thick scent of woodsmoke. Above the mantel, a large rectangle of the stone wall is lighter than the rest—as though a painting or tapestry once hung there but has since been removed.

There is no furniture except for a couple of high-backed leather armchairs. The Wolf King sits in one, and his fingers drum against the arm of the chair.

Now I know they are brothers, I can see some of the similarities between them despite their different hair colors, and the ink that covers James's arms.

Tall, broad-shouldered, and well built, I can imagine both are a fearsome sight on a battlefield. They also have a similar stubbornness in the line of their jaw, and almond-shaped eyes—though James's are hazel.

We assess one another, and an uncomfortable silence spreads across the room. I will my pulse to calm and my posture to remain straight as I push down my emotions.

Be bold.

Finally, James leans forward. "So, this is the princess of the Southlands."

"She—" Callum starts to speak, but James's gaze snaps toward him.

"You've had your chance to speak, Brother." His tone is harsh and gruff.

I catch a huff of laughter from Blake, where he leans by the door with his arms folded across his chest.

I meet James's glare. "Yes."

"A lot of my men died because of you," he says. "Good men."

Callum grits his teeth and a flash of pain passes over his features. It is as though he bears the weight of those lives lost.

"A lot of my men have died because of you, too," I say, softly.

The king's jaw tightens in the same way Callum's does when he is displeased. He runs a hand over his stubble. "Our sources tell us your betrothed has the Heart of the Moon. Is that true?"

"I would not know. I only met him twice."

His gaze moves to Blake. "Are we certain he has it?"

Blake shrugs. "As certain as we can be."

James rises and I tense at the power that radiates from him. Callum shifts slightly so that his arm is in front of mine.

I fight the urge to step back.

"Has my brother dishonored you?" James's voice is dangerously quiet.

Indignation rises in me, my cheeks flaming.

"I would never—" Callum growls.

"I can smell you all over her, Brother!" James's eyes blaze as he glares at Callum. "What were you thinking? You kidnap the princess of our enemy without running it by me first, provoking the wrath of both their king's army and Sebastian's army! A plan that would have pleased me, had my men been prepared for it, and had you not gone all sappy-eyed for the lass! He has Wolves working for him, you know? Prisoners he's turned. If I can smell you all over her, they will too. How the fuck are we to trade her when Sebastian will know that you've had her first?"

My breathing sharpens, my stomach hardening. I feel as if my insides are turning to steel.

"We're not trading her." Callum's body is unsettlingly still.

"You forget your place, Brother. Don't make me put you in the dungeons."

Callum laughs, but it is not his usual easy laugh; it is dark and unfamiliar. "I'd like to see you try."

The air thickens in the room and the tension is like a palpable thing. It is like elastic pulled too tight. Callum is breathing fast and James's biceps strain against his shirt.

I need to do something, anything, to stop this from happening. If they fight and James wins, I am doomed. Callum will be locked away, leaving my fate in the hands of the Wolf King, who clearly does not want me here. If Callum wins, surely civil war will break out among the Wolves and the mob will turn on me anyway.

"I can be of more use to you here," I say, my voice quiet yet clear.

Both of them snap their heads toward me.

"You do not even know for certain Sebastian has the relic you seek." I make my voice sound stronger, more commanding. "I was raised in the Southlands palace. I know the King's City. I know its defenses. And, what's more, I know how my father's mind works. My father and Sebastian do not care for my safety—I am nothing but a pawn to them—but they care that you've taken me. It makes them look weak. They will stop at nothing to get me back, and that will make them careless."

I force myself to look the Wolf King in the eye. "If you want to win this war, you do not need some old rock that may or may not have magical powers. You need a strategy. You need me."

The first hint of a smile ghosts James's lips as he looks at me. "And why should we trust you, daughter of my enemy?"

"She chose to come here, you know?" says Blake as he studies his fingernails. "So strange for a rabbit to walk willingly into a den of Wolves."

"Is that so?" asks James.

"Aye." Callum sounds almost proud. "It's true."

James blows out hot air, then he laughs. "Fuck it. Let's keep her. Piss off some Southern cunts. No offence, Blake."

He slaps Callum's arm, then walks past us to the door.

When he glances over his shoulder at me, something unreadable passes over his face. I tense, even as Callum relaxes beside me. There's something hard in his eyes. Something calculating.

This doesn't feel right. He was too easily persuaded. Too many of his people have died because of me.

Blake watches him warily, too.

James smiles and I could almost believe I imagined it. "Come. Let us put this behind us. Tonight we feast. Make no mistake, the Southlands armies are on their way. Tomorrow, we'll further discuss how the princess can be of use to us."

Chapter Forty-Eight

The Great Hall is transformed for James's feast.

There is drinking and laughter and shouting. We eat roast venison and potatoes and vegetables smothered with butter. Fires roar in the two hearths, fighting the cold night that seeps through the narrow windows. The air is thick with the scent of woodsmoke.

As the night gets darker, the food gets cleared away and people dance raucously to the upbeat music coming from the band in the corner. The sound of bagpipes and fiddles and drums accompanies stomping feet that shake the hall.

To an outsider, it would seem like a joyous occasion. Yet the emotions inside my chest are as turbulent as the couples spinning on the dancefloor and the wind that rattles the windows.

Something is wrong.

Despite James telling the Wolves I am not to be harmed, hostile eyes have fallen on me all evening. The thought that Magnus and his friends must be here somewhere puts me further on edge. I do not want those disgusting men so much as looking at me.

And, what's more, I do not trust the Wolf King.

There was something about the way he looked at me that worries me. Whatever his plans are, I do not think they will work in my favor.

I have had no time to voice my concerns to Callum. He has been in meetings with the other alphas all day—leaving me in my chambers with Ryan at my door.

Now, we are seated at the alpha table—with Callum in deep conversation with his brother about battle tactics. As he has been for most of the evening.

I'm fiddling with my wooden beaker of water, when Blake drops into the empty chair beside me. He's taken off his black coat, and his dark shirt is unbuttoned at the collar. There's a slight flush to his cheeks.

"Hello, little rabbit." I catch a hint of whisky on his breath. "Enjoying the festivities?"

"Are you drunk?"

"Exceedingly." He leans over me to reach for a decanter full of amber-colored liquid. I have to lean back to prevent getting his armpit in my face. "Yet you are not drunk in the slightest. Something we simply must rectify."

He tops up his glass, then fills my beaker and pushes it toward me. His eyes glint in the torchlight—curious and watchful. And certainly more intelligent than his current demeanor suggests. I wonder if he is even drunk, or whether this is just a game.

"Oh, you'd like that, wouldn't you? For me to drink all this and start behaving like that."

I gesture at one of the men stumbling around on the dancefloor, who—as if knowing the point I'm trying to prove—trips over his boots and crashes into one of the tables, knocking over a chair and spilling a jug of ale.

A dimple creases one of Blake's cheeks. "Not at all. I'm merely trying to help. You seem on edge, little rabbit. Whisky helps."

"I'd prefer to keep my wits about me."

I scan the Great Hall—filled with Wolves who gave me grief before they knew I was the Southlands princess. I catch sight of Isla, dancing and giggling with a group of women. I think of what Magnus tried to do to me. I cannot suppress the cold shiver that crawls up my spine despite the blazing heat in here.

"It's a shame Magnus couldn't make it tonight," says Blake, as though he read my mind. "He got a nasty bout of food poisoning. As did his friends. They're in my infirmary. Don't worry, though. I'm taking care of them."

His voice is as dark as the night outside the castle.

The Great Hall seems to still. The music fades. All I can hear is my heartbeat, pounding in my ears.

My gaze snaps up to Blake's, and something in his eyes makes me shiver.

I recall the vial of poison he took from me in the kitchens; the one I was going to use on Isla. He said he had a use for it.

Did he use it on them?

The corner of his lip quirks in answer to my unasked question.

"Will they. . . will they survive?" I ask.

"Perhaps. Perhaps not." He shrugs. "What do you think?"

A shadow stirs inside me—provoked by the darkness in Blake's gaze. Everything else seems distant.

He is offering to kill them for me. I do not know how to feel about that. They deserve death, for what they were intending to do. But could my conscience bear it?

I swallow. "I. . . I don't know."

"Pity."

"Are they in pain?"

"Very much so."

I grab my beaker with shaking hands, clutching at the wood until my knuckles whiten.

I smile. "Good."

Blake raises his glass. And, Goddess help me, I clink my beaker against it and drain it. I wince as the hot smoky liquid burns my throat. Coughing, I place it back down upon the table.

Blake nudges the bottle toward me before getting up and walking back into the crowd.

I pour myself another whisky.

He's right. It does take the edge off.

***

"You're drunk!" Callum roars.

Hundreds of candles flicker on the tabletops, and the light dances over his handsome face.

James has gone to mingle with his people, so Callum and I are alone at the alpha table. The Great Hall is a blur of dancing and brawling and music.

I poke him in the chest, feeling the hard muscle beneath his shirt. I giggle. "*You're* drunk."

He laughs, as if he cannot believe what he's seeing.

"Aye, I am a bit. Not as much as you." He shakes his head. "You're going to be a bloody nightmare tomorrow when the hangover kicks in! Goddess! I'm a wee bit scared!"

"You're scared of me?"

"Oh aye. Very."

"You said I was small!"

"You are small. You're a small and fearsome creature."

His face swims in and out of focus. I grab both sides of his head, and push my forehead into his. "That's not a very nice thing to say."

He laughs again, and his big hands curl around my waist. "You see? Terrifying."

I dip my mouth to his ear. "That thing you did last night. I want you to do it again."

He stills, his fingers tightening, and a soft groan scrapes his throat. His expression is pained. "Let's see how you feel in the morning, shall we?"

"No. Now."

He twists me around and pulls me onto his lap. "You see? You're a small, fearsome, and demanding creature." His warm breath tickles my ear. "And, believe me when I say, if you torture me tonight, I shall repay the debt tomorrow."

"I'm not torturing you!"

I try to face him, but he pulls me back again, his thick arm hooked around my waist. His chest rises and falls deeply against my back.

"Oh, but you are. I'm hard just thinking about what we did last night, and about how much I want to do it again right now." His words turn my insides to molten gold. He nips my ear with his teeth and I gasp. "I'd slide my hand between your legs right now if I could. I'd make you come while they all danced—oblivious to what I was doing to you."

My pulse hammers in my ears, heat pooling at my core. "Why don't you do it then?"

The wolf is in his eyes, and he does not try to hide it. "Because you're drunk. And I'm drunk. And I fear you'd regret it in the morning."

I stroke the side of his face, my fingers tracing his lips. "I wouldn't."

His eyes return to their usual forest-green. "Be that as it may, I won't take that risk while you're drunk. I will dance with you, though."

"I'm not drunk!"

I push my fingers into his mouth. He nips them playfully with his teeth. I giggle.

"You are *very* drunk, Princess." He glances at the writhing mass of people on the dancefloor. "Let's dance."

"I don't know the moves."

Callum nods at a couples of Wolves, spinning around and causing mayhem as others dodge out of their path. "I don't think many of them do, either."

A grin spreads across my face, and I jump up. "Okay. Come on then."

He takes a deep breath, giving me a sheepish smile. "Aye. Just. . . just give me a moment."

He looks away from me, exhaling. I'm about to ask him what the problem is, but he adjusts his kilt, and gets up.

He puts an arm around my waist, smiles, and leads me to the dancefloor.

***

I'm happy.

The thought jolts through me like a silver bullet—unfamiliar and strange and certain.

My feet ache from dancing. Strands of my hair escape their pins and stick to my face. My chest hurts because I'm constricted by my corset, and I'm far too hot beneath my long lacy sleeves.

Yet I am happy.

I do not hide the smile on my face, or my squeal of glee as Callum spins me around—his eyes filled with wonder and delight. His hands are warm and firm around mine.

The joy that has washed over me seems to have flooded the entire Great Hall. The dancefloor has cleared a little since earlier, with some of the Wolves heading into the alcoves, but the nearby Wolves dance alongside us. They're too caught up in the music and the alcohol and their own laughter to throw any ill-feeling my way.

I have attended many dances in my twenty years, but I've never cut loose and felt so free.

Callum laughs as I spread my arms and spin around. He pulls me close. "I've just seen Fi. I need to speak with her about something." His warm breath tickles my ear and I giggle. "Come on, sit down for a moment. Let's get you a glass of water. I fear the havoc you will cause if I leave you unattended."

He grins as he leads me to one of the tables and sits me down on the bench.

"I'll be back in a moment." He kisses my forehead. "Be good, okay?"

He strides over to Fiona, who is standing by the oak doors dressed in her stable gear. It could be my imagination, but she looks a little tense.

I follow her gaze to the seat at the middle of the alpha table where James now sits. He is speaking with Robert, one hand on a tankard of ale.

As they're speaking, Blake walks past them to the band. Nearby, Brodie is watching them play. The young male's expression is a mixture of resentment and awe, and the corner of my lip twitches.

Blake whispers something to one of the band members. They change the tune they're playing to something a little slower.

I sway on the bench. The melody is familiar to me, though I cannot place it. I reach for a beaker and pour myself a glass of water.

When I turn back to the dancefloor, Blake stands in front of me.

He holds out a slender hand.

"Would you care to dance?" he asks.

Chapter Forty-Nine

For a moment I am speechless.

My gaze travels up his black shirt, now buttoned up to the collar, and lands on his face. I cannot read his expression. He seems serious, yet his eyes glint in the torchlight as though they hold a thousand secrets.

The dancefloor blurs behind him as people slow their steps to the new melody that's playing. Where have I heard this song before?

"You want to dance with me?" I ask.

"Yes."

A giggle escapes my lips, and Blake tilts his head to the side—the movement almost catlike. "Does that amuse you, little rabbit?"

I lean back against the table and take a sip from my beaker—welcoming the coldness of the water as it travels down my throat. I am hot. Too hot. And my mind feels fuzzy from all the whisky.

Blake tracks my every movement as I brush a strand of hair out of my face.

"Do you think me a fool, Blake?"

"On the contrary. Dance with me."

"If you mean to provoke Callum, he's otherwise engaged." I put down my beaker and raise an eyebrow. "You're wasting your time."

He smiles, dimples puncturing his cheeks. I could almost forget that he is a manipulative snake when he looks at me like that.

"I am not trying to provoke your master, little rabbit. *That* would be a waste of my time."

"What *are* you trying to do, then?"

"Wouldn't you like to know?"

I frown. "Callum is not my master."

"Prove it." He glances at his hand, still outstretched. "Dance with me."

The shadows in the Great Hall seem to gravitate toward him as the candles flicker, as though attracted to whatever darkness resides in his soul.

I laugh and shake my head. "Do you truly think me so easily manipulated?"

He smirks. "Oh, darling, I know exactly how to manipulate you."

"I'm not dancing with you, am I?"

"No. But you will."

"What makes you so sure?"

He steps forward, and places both hands on the table on either side of me. I breathe in sharply, inhaling his scent of the forest at night, as he dips his mouth to my ear.

"Because I'm playing a game, little rabbit." His warm breath tickles my cheek. "And a part of you wants to play too—just to see if you can beat me."

He turns his face toward mine, a challenge glinting in his eyes.

Then he steps back and I can breathe again.

"Why would I play a game with you when I am at a disadvantage?" I say. "I do not know the rules, nor the prize."

"No. But don't you want to find out?"

He holds out his hand.

My mother used to tell me stories about Night—the deity who holds the keys to the Moon Goddess's prison. He tempts mortals into making deals with him, offering them what they desire in exchange for their souls.

Blake reminds me of him right now. Dangerous and strange with eyes gleaming with dark promises.

And I hate that I am tempted. Because he is right; I *do* want to find out what he is scheming.

Yet if I dance with him, what part of my soul will he claim?

He raises an eyebrow.

I raise my chin.

Perhaps the warm, smoky alcohol I have consumed is giving me false confidence, but I do not think that Blake is as smart as he thinks he is.

I place my hand in his.

A slow smile spreads across his face as his fingers curl around mine. He leads me to the dancefloor.

He raises our joined hands, and places his other on my waist.

"Do you know the Dance of the Dawn?" he asks.

"Of course."

"This music follows the same rhythm."

He pulls me closer, and I place a hand on his shoulder. "You wish to perform a Southlands dance in a hall full of northerners?"

"We are both Southlanders, are we not?"

"Is that the game? You wish to antagonize everyone here?"

"Let's play and find out, shall we?"

I incline my head. "Very well."

I step back and he releases me.

I curtsy and he bows, as is tradition, and then we dance.

We step forward, raising our hands, palms almost touching, as we circle one another. We change direction—our gazes locked, our steps careful. Graceful. Wary. Blake's eyes track my every movement as though he is a predator, hunting his prey.

I think that people are watching us, but it would be unwise to look away from the wolf before me.

As the dance progresses, it requires closer contact. Blake's hand curls around mine once more, his other flattening on the small of my back as he spins us around. My hand rests gently on his shoulder, and I fight the urge to sink my fingers into the hard muscle as he moves us faster and faster.

His steps are graceful, his poise strong and confident. He is a good dancer. Too good.

"You said you were part of the King's Guard," I say.

"I did."

"I did not know that members of the King's Guard had cause to learn to dance." I lift an eyebrow. "Certainly not this well."

He smirks as we continue our dance around the edge of the dancefloor. "You think I dance well? I should be flattered by such a compliment coming from the princess herself."

"I *think* you're a liar. You were not part of the King's Guard, were you? You're a man of noble birth. There is no other explanation for why you can dance."

He spins me under his arm, and I inhale sharply as he pulls me back again. "Interesting theory, little rabbit. I assure you, I *was* in the King's Guard, I am *not* a man of noble birth, and there *is* another explanation."

"I do not trust you."

"Nor should you."

"Tell me the explanation."

"I already have. In a way."

"Stop speaking in riddles. Tell me what I want to know." I raise my chin. "Or I will tell everyone your secret." I smile sweetly. "I think there may be a storm coming."

I expect him to blanch, for his shoulder to tense beneath my fingers. Instead he smiles, pulling me closer.

"Go ahead," he whispers. "My account of what you were doing in my chambers late at night will be quite different to yours, I assure you." His tone is as dark and seductive as the night sky.

The heat drains from my body as we continue to circle the dancefloor. My pulse pounds so hard in my ears that it almost drowns out the sound that has chilled me to my core. I'm still dancing, but my movements no longer feel like my own. Everything blurs. It is Blake who is leading me, like a puppet master, commanding his toy.

The music has reached its crescendo, and the reason why it seemed familiar to me is now clear. I recognize this part of the song.

It is the same melody my mother used to sing to me at night.

The same melody I hummed to Blake when he was afraid.

Why would a band of Wolves in the Northlands know the tune my mother loved so dearly?

Blake is watching me curiously, his head tilted slightly to one side.

I narrow my eyes. "What is this?"

"What is what?" His expression of faux innocence is betrayed by the hungry gleam in his eyes.

"Why did you ask them to play this music?"

"It is a well-known wolf melody," he says, feigning confusion. "About the Elderwolf and his love for the Moon. I thought you might like it. Do you not?"

I try to pull away, but his hand tightens around mine. His slender fingers are like a cold vice. He spins me around. "Do you recognize it?" he asks.

"You know I do. Let me go."

"That wouldn't be wise, little rabbit. Everyone is watching us. Including James."

I look around. People are staring at us curiously from the benches, the alcoves, the sides of the hall. The dancefloor has cleared, leaving us at its center. I do not know when that happened.

The Wolf King is leaning forward in his chair, an unreadable expression on his face.

I search for Callum, seeking a lifeline out of this situation, but he must have left the hall to speak with Fiona.

I am truly alone.

My eyes meet Blake's. "I don't care. I'm leaving."

"You should care."

"Why?"

He moves forward so his cheek almost touches mine, and lowers his voice. "Because you are in danger. Do you truly believe James will let you stay?"

"No. But how does dancing with you help my situation?"

"That is the game, little rabbit. Play with me, and find out."

I'm about to tell him that I'll take my chances, when his gaze flits over my shoulder. "Too late."

He drops my hand just as a wave of warmth washes over me. Before I can turn, I'm scooped up into big strong arms. I breathe in sharply, hooking my hands around Callum's neck, my eyes widening in surprise as he claims my mouth with his.

It is not a gentle kiss. It is hard and deep and claiming. His tongue moves in strong, dominant strokes against mine. Heat floods through my body, melting the ice, as my grip tightens around his neck. I have to fight the moan that threatens to escape me. Too many people are watching.

The wolf is in his eyes when he pulls back and glares at Blake.

Blake steps back, his eyes dancing with amusement.

I feel both him and the Wolf King watching us as Callum carries me out of the Great Hall.

Callum snaps his fingers at Ryan as we pass. "Ryan, I'm putting the princess to bed. You'll guard her door while I attend to some business."

Ryan disentangles himself from his girlfriend, Becky, and grumbles as he follows us through the castle to my bedchambers.

"Put me down," I hiss as soon as we're out of earshot of the hall.

"No."

"I don't want to go to bed."

A muscle feathers in his jaw. "You're going to bed. And you'll stay there until I return."

"You're angry with me," I say as he carries me up the winding staircase to my chambers.

"No." He doesn't look at me.

He pushes the door open, then drops me ungracefully on my bed.

"Callum!"

The wolf is in his eyes. He looks like a bloodthirsty warrior. Then he blinks and releases a long breath.

"No." He shakes his head, suddenly looking weary. "No. I'm not angry with you, Princess."

I do not believe him. I wonder if it's because I danced with Blake, or whether something worse is going on. I push myself upright. "What did Fiona want?"

"I'll tell you shortly." He runs a hand over his mouth. "I need to go check on something. Stay here."

Before I can respond, he walks out of the room, closing the door behind him. I hear Ryan grumbling on the other side.

"Oi. That woman in there saved your life. Twice," Callum growls. "You can go back to smooching with your girlfriend later. But now, you'll stop being an insolent pup and you'll do as I say."

"Sorry," mutters Ryan.

"Aye. I know. Now, no one goes in, and the princess doesn't come out. Understood?"

"I can hardly stop her if—"

"You'll find a way." Callum sounds uncharacteristically brittle. "I trust you, okay? Don't let me down."

"No." I hear the sudden pride in Ryan's voice. "I won't."

***

I wake with a start.

There's a hand over my mouth. I struggle with my covers, my legs tangled in my skirts. A face comes into focus in the darkness, and my pulse steadies.

Callum crouches on the floorboards beside my bed.

He puts a finger on his lips, before pulling his palm away.

"Get dressed," he whispers, nodding at a pile of clothes he's placed by my feet. "And put on your boots."

My breathing quickens at the note of urgency in his voice. I cannot help but think of the first time he took me from my chambers. He told me to get dressed, then. I refused to do anything he said.

This time, I comply.

I hurry out of bed, my mind fuzzy from the whisky. My pulse kicks up when I see it is brown breeches and a white shirt that he has selected for me.

I have never worn breeches before. It would be improper. I have always worn pretty dresses.

I swallow. Then I turn, allowing Callum to untie the fastenings of my dress and undo my corset. His gaze burns into my back and he tenses. I suppose with his wolf sight, he can see my scars in the darkness.

I hurriedly pull on my new clothes and boots. When I turn, his jawline is hard. He fastens my cloak around my neck.

"What's going on?" I whisper.

"James," he says darkly. "I'll explain when we're safe. Come." He holds out his hand. "We're leaving."

I save my questions. The worry in his brow, and the shallowness of his breathing, are the only answers I need right now. Whatever Fiona told him, whatever he was checking up on earlier, must be bad.

I take his hand, feeling his comforting warmth as his fingers close around mine.

He leads me out of my chambers. We hurry through the dark labyrinth of the castle. We take the servants' corridors, avoiding the Great Hall, where the Wolves are still drinking and dancing despite the late hour.

We reach the entrance hall and my heart leaps.

The doors at the other end are already open, the night spilling onto the flagstones. I can taste heather and the mountains on the back of my tongue.

I can taste freedom.

Until Blake saunters across the room, his footsteps echoing around the space. He stops in front of the doorway, blocking our escape.

Callum stills, pushing me behind him.

"Going somewhere?" asks Blake.

His dark hair ripples in the breeze that comes from outside.

"Don't make me hurt you," warns Callum, his voice low, almost a growl.

"You won't hurt me," says Blake. "Because if we fight, we'll make noise. And if we make noise, your brother will come looking. I don't think he'll be very happy that you're stealing his bargaining chip for the Heart of the Moon, do you?"

Callum swallows. I've never seen him so tense. He looks as if he's weighing his options, wondering whether he can fight his way out before his brother arrives with backup.

I don't like our chances. I can hear the music and dancing from here.

I step out from behind him.

"Please, Blake," I say softly.

Blake's body is perfectly still for a moment. I cannot read him. I cannot understand what is going on in his mind right now.

Then he inclines his head and steps aside.

Callum releases a breath, then grabs my hand again.

"Run fast, little rabbit," says Blake as we pass. "The Wolves are coming for you now."

"Thank you," I whisper as we step into the courtyard.

"Don't thank me yet." He smiles. "The game is far from over."

A chill ripples through me, but Callum is pulling me across the cobbled stones. We rush to the stables, where Fiona is waiting beside the grey horse we rode here on. There are two bulky bags packed and strapped to the saddle.

"You took your sweet time," she says, hands on her hips.

She hugs Callum and he pulls her close. "Thank you," he whispers.

"Aye, well, no need to get all emotional about it." She turns to me. "Good luck, Rory. I'll see you again soon, I hope."

I return her smile, despite the worry clenching in my stomach. "I hope so, too."

Callum helps me onto the horse before mounting behind me.

And then we're riding out of the castle gates, and across the wild terrain.

"Where are you taking me?" I ask. My voice is almost drowned out by the sound of the hooves thudding against the mud, and the pounding of my heartbeat.

"James sent a messenger to Sebastian. Everything my brother said. . . it was a lie. He means to send you back in exchange for the Heart of the Moon. Sebastian is on his way."

My stomach drops, and Callum's arm tightens around my waist.

"He can't have you." His voice is hard. Angrier than I've ever heard it. "I'm taking you away from all this. I'm taking you to Highfell." He pulls me closer to him, and his body heat washes over me. "I'm taking you home."

Chapter Fifty

We ride for hours.

The night is pitch-black and I cannot see beyond a few inches in front of my face.

At one point, I hear water lapping the pebbled shore of a loch. At another, wind stirs the branches of the trees and I can smell fern and damp earth. Dark shapes loom around us.

All the while, Callum is silent behind me.

His chest is hard against my back, and his thighs are tense as they brush against mine.

I wonder if he feels betrayed by his brother, or whether he feels as if he is betraying his people by taking me away.

Or perhaps it is neither. Perhaps he is angry I danced with Blake.

When Callum took me from the dancefloor, his kiss was hard and dominant. It was as if he was staking his claim. Heat stirs inside me at the memory of his mouth against mine, despite how unnecessary and inappropriate it was to do such a thing in front of so many people.

He must realize he has nothing to worry about as far as Blake is concerned. I do not trust that male in the slightest.

"Are you okay?" I ask. The wind is violent, and my voice is barely audible over the sound of the rustling trees.

"Those scars on your back," he says softly, surprising me, "how did you get them?"

Memories flood my mind—the stained-glass windows of the Church of Light and Sun, months of sickness and grief, the High Priest and his crop.

I swallow. "It was a long time ago."

A rough sound vibrates in Callum's chest. "Was it your father?"

I turn myself to stone. A statue. Something that cannot feel pain.

"If you must know, I was sick, like my mother. The potions they gave me didn't help. The High Priest said if he. . . cleansed me of my sin, the Goddess would spare me," I say hurriedly. "And she did."

His body stills behind me. I'm not sure he's breathing. "The High Priest beat you?"

"It. . . it was only a few times—"

"Only?!" I flinch at the loudness of Callum's voice.

"Yes. Only," I snap. I don't want his anger. It stirs something ugly inside me that I cannot face. "Now drop it."

My breathing is fast, and so is his.

Until, finally, I exhale—letting the anger plume in front of my face with my breath. I touch his wrist where it rests in my lap.

"I do not wish to speak of it. Okay?"

A sound rumbles through his chest—a low growl he is clearly trying to suppress. "No one will ever touch you again."

With the heat and strength of his body cocooning me, I almost believe him.

But Sebastian is riding North to get me, the Wolves are surely on our tail, and Blake's warning rings in my ears: the game is far from over.

***

We ride throughout the night.

As the sun rises, the valley around us is bathed in orange light. With it, the whisky-induced fuzziness in my head is replaced by monotonous thumping. Every jolt of the horse rattles my brain. The sound of the birds chirping is shrill and irritating. And my mouth tastes horrible.

"How much further is it?" I say. "We've been riding for hours."

He chuckles. "Sore head, Princess?"

"That is neither here nor there."

"Highfell is a week's ride away. We're—"

"A week!"

"Aye." Amusement laces Callum's tone. "A week. The Northern Pass is the quickest route to my castle, but also the most well known. That's the route James'll use to send his Wolves after us—so we're taking a slight detour. When they don't find us in a few days, he'll call them off, and they'll go back to fighting the Southlands armies."

I frown. "That doesn't sound sensible."

My mouth is dry and I swallow.

"No?" As if sensing my thirst, Callum reaches down into one of the saddlebags and passes me a flask. I snatch it from him, and greedily gulp it down. "And why is that?"

"James's men will get to Highfell before us." I take another sip of water, savoring the freshness that travels down my throat. "They'll be waiting for us when we arrive and we'll be captured."

"If James truly wanted to capture us, then aye, that would be a good plan," says Callum. "But he doesn't care about the Heart of the Moon. Not enough. Getting hold of that thing was always a long shot. He won't want to make an enemy out of me."

He shifts behind me, running his thumb absently over my thigh.

"No. He won't bother. He'll pretend to have you, lure Sebastian out, and put his efforts into killing him. And good riddance to him, too. I only wish I could have been the one to do it."

Doubt seeps through me as I pass the flask back. "Are you sure? You seem to be putting a lot of trust in a male who just betrayed you."

Callum takes a sip, then puts the water back in the pack.

"Aye. I know my brother. If we can stay out of his reach for the next couple of days, we can put all of this behind us. I'm certain of it." He squeezes my leg. "That means we don't stop to rest until nightfall."

He chuckles as I groan.

***

It is dark when we finally stop on the shore of a great dark loch.

I sit in front of the fire Callum lit before he led the horse to a copse of trees.

My headache has eased, and though my muscles ache and I'm weary from travelling, my soul feels lighter than it has in days.

It's peaceful here. It seems as though we are the only souls around.

Perhaps I have finally escaped my fate.

When Callum doesn't return for twenty minutes or so, though, fear starts to gnaw at me. What is he doing? Has someone found him? Has he grown tired of my foul mood and abandoned me?

I'm about to go look for him when he emerges from the trees carrying some hunks of bread and cheese. The pebbles crunch beneath his boots.

Relief floods me, but is quickly replaced by a strange tension as he passes me the food, then sits on a rock on the other side of the flames. Something shifts in the air.

We eat in silence.

It is as if we both realize we are completely alone for the first time since he took me from Sebastian's castle.

Something has been growing between us since then. Strong, and pervasive, and passionate. Something we both thought was wrong.

Yet the main reason we have not been fully. . . intimate. . . with one another, is not because I wanted to maintain my honor.

It is because Callum believed I was his prisoner.

Surely, he does not feel that way any longer.

He gives me a soft smile. The firelight dances over his strong features. He takes a deep breath, and I think he's going to say something, but he sighs and takes another bite of bread.

I offer a small smile back, then go back to my food, even though my insides are clenching.

I wish I was not nervous. I wish I could walk over to him and give him what he wants—like those ladies Sebastian would send to the Wolves. Yet I am lost. Overwhelmed. I do not know what to do, nor what he expects from me.

I swallow the last piece of bread, then brush the crumbs off my breeches. I chew my bottom lip, searching for something—anything—to say to break this never-ending silence.

"This is. . . this is a nice. . . loch," I say, looking at the black water.

"Aye. That it is."

Silence falls once more, punctuated only by the crackling flames. I take a deep breath, smelling woodsmoke and damp earth.

"Can I ask you something?"

"Aye."

"Last night, when you. . . when you kissed me. . . were you angry with me?"

"No." He smiles sheepishly. "I was jealous."

I fail to suppress the twitch of my lip.

He leans forward, resting his forearms on his thighs. "I'm pleased to see my inner turmoil amuses you, Princess."

"You don't need to be jealous because I danced with Blake."

"Aye, I know. It's just. . . seeing you both. . ." He sighs and shakes his head, running his hand over his mouth.

"What?"

"I don't know. He looked like a Southlands lord, and you his lady. I didn't like that. Not one little bit. In the real world. . . you and I. . . I'd never stand a chance with you, would I? But him—"

"This is the real world."

"You know what I mean." He shakes his head. "And there you go, smiling again."

"Sorry." I bite my lip. "It's just. . . You're so strong and confident all the time. I suppose it's reassuring to know you have irrational thoughts like the rest of us."

A wide grin spreads across his face. "You think that's irrational?"

"I suppose we would never have been matched by my father. You *are* from the Northlands. Although if you had worn those awful breeches of yours, and put on a Southlands accent, I'm sure you could have infiltrated the palace. Once we'd met, I would have liked you, I'm certain of it."

"Oh aye?"

"Yes."

"Perhaps. Though you thought I was a monster when we first met."

Cold shame spreads through my body. It is hard to believe I could have thought this male, this wolf, was a monster. Perhaps I was a monster, to automatically assume such a thing.

"I know. I'm sorry for that," I say. "I've learned a lot about Wolves since then."

"Like what?"

"Well. . . I know they like to wander around naked a lot." Callum laughs. "They're horribly inappropriate. And they like to sniff people all the time." He laughs louder. "They're always fighting and brawling, and they listen to incredibly screechy music despite their very good sense of hearing. And some of them, like humans, are not very pleasant. But some. . . Some are gentle and kind and funny and caring. Some are good men."

The smile dies from his lips, an intensity crossing his features. The tangle of nerves in my stomach starts to tighten once more.

"And some of them do not know how to behave like gentlemen," I add, raising my chin.

He laughs, breaking the tense moment. "Aye, that might be true. You know, I've learned a lot about princesses these past few weeks, too."

I give him a hard look. "Like what?"

"They're very stubborn." His eyes twinkle as I fold my arms across my chest. "And very fearsome. And very small." I glare at him and he grins. "They're a wee bit spoiled."

"They are not!"

"And intelligent. They can't handle their whisky. And they pretend to be very chaste and shy, but. . ." He drops his voice to a whisper, as though telling me a secret. "They're actually very, very demanding."

My cheeks flame and he laughs, loudly.

"They blush when you say rude things to them. And they're good, and interesting, and honest, and kind. They hide their emotions, but they feel deeply. Passionately." His expression becomes serious and my blood heats up. "They care about people more than they will admit. And they're brave. Braver than any wolf I've ever known."

There's a tightness in my throat, and I swallow, trying to push it back. I do not know what is wrong with me, it's just—

"I've upset you?" asks Callum, frowning.

The backs of my eyes burn. I sniffle, trying to suppress the feelings that threaten to come. "Some of the things you said were bad."

"Goddess, I'm sorry, Princess, I—"

"Usually, people say I'm pretty." My voice is thick.

Callum's eyebrows raise. "Oh. . . you are. I didn't mean to offend you by not mentioning—"

"No." I blink a couple of times. "You don't understand. That's usually all they say. And it's not even me they're complimenting. It's a version of me. It's not real. It's make-up and dresses and them wanting to get into my father's good graces."

I take a deep breath, wiping my eyes on the back of my hand. I feel Callum watching me.

"No one. . . no one has ever tried to know me before." I take a shuddery breath, tasting the woodsmoke that twists in the darkness. His gaze is so fierce that it is hard to hold it. "Not until you."

His jaw is hard, his posture still. He says nothing for a moment, then removes his arms from his thighs, and sits back.

"Come here," he says.

My pulse is fast as I get up and walk toward him. His body heat and scent wash over me as he parts his thighs for me to stand between them.

He takes my hand in both of his. "I do want to know you. I want to know everything about you."

"I want that, too."

He runs his thumb over my skin and his touch is gentle. He swallows, hard. "You're not my prisoner anymore."

"No." I do not bother to add that I don't believe I ever really was. I am ensnared, unable to think properly, unable to speak.

There is need in his eyes. Hunger. His chest moves up and down deeply, his breathing as ragged as mine. I feel as if we are on the edge of a storm that is about to break.

He drags his teeth over his bottom lip.

He stands up, his large frame looming over me.

"Come," he says, his voice gruff. "I want to show you something."

Chapter Fifty-One

My heart is in my throat as Callum leads me across the shore. Pebbles crunch underfoot.

His hand is firm and warm around mine. I am reminded of the first time I took his hand, back in Sebastian's castle. Like now, I was nervous. Uncertain of what was to come. I took his hand anyway.

I think I will always take his hand, if he offers it to me.

My mother once told me that we always have a choice.

I chose Callum that day—when I turned my back on my people and travelled with him to the kingdom of my enemies.

Sometimes it does not feel like a choice at all. It feels inevitable. Like the setting of the sun, and the rising of the moon.

What other choice could there be? It feels as if it has always been him. This. Everything has led to this moment.

Nerves tangle in my stomach, because I think I know what is going to happen next—what Callum might expect from me. I want to give him it, yet I cannot deny that I fear it a little too.

When Callum gently squeezes my hand, he must be able to hear the pounding of my pulse.

He leads me through the copse of trees he disappeared into earlier, nudging aside an overhanging branch with his free arm. The scent of wet pine is released into the cool night air, and a few raindrops—collected among the needles—fall on me as I follow him.

I stop, my eyes widening with surprise.

I nudge past him.

"What's this?" I ask.

We're on the shore of the loch, but we're partially sheltered from the Northlands winds by the trees on one side, and steep rocky land on the other. In the center of the intimate clearing, there's a tent.

"I remembered the last time I tried to get you to sleep on the ground." Every sense in my body is attuned to him as he steps closer. "Do you. . . do you like it?"

Warmth spreads through me at the slight note of uncertainty in his tone. He seems almost nervous.

The tent is triangular in shape and it's small. It is high enough to sit or kneel inside, but certainly not to stand. The fabric is off-white and it has seen better days.

It reminds me of a miniature, worn-out version of the tents that my father and brother stayed in when they went hunting. Teams of servants would ride ahead of the hunting party to erect them before the noblemen and women arrived. The structures would be dressed in silks and banners, some with interiors as nice as rooms in the palace itself.

This tent is nothing like that.

And yet, it is so much better. Because Callum did this. He did this for me.

An unfamiliar rush of emotion surges through my body.

"Yes," I say softly. "I like it very much."

"Do you. . . do you want to go inside?" Again, that slight note of uncertainty in his tone. As if part of him expects me to say no.

My pulse hammers against my chest. I nod, crouch down, and crawl through the opening.

Red tartan rugs, furs, and cushions cover the ground—giving it a cozy feel, despite the cool air and the breath that plumes in front of my face. A candle Callum must have lit earlier flickers at one side, filling the space with warm orange light.

I kneel upright, and smile.

I'm about to turn around when the fabric rustles. Callum's thighs brush my hips as he kneels behind me and places a hand flat on my stomach. A lick of heat flares in the pit of my stomach as my back touches his chest.

"I wanted to do more." He runs his thumb along my torso, and I wish my shirt wasn't in the way of his touch. "We could only carry so much on horseback."

"It's perfect."

"I'm glad you like it."

He dips his mouth, and kisses the sensitive spot behind my ear, then peppers a trail of kisses on the back of my neck. I suppress a moan.

"Goddess," he says. "I've wanted to be alone with you like this for so long."

Gently, he tugs the hem of my shirt out of my breeches, and slides his hand beneath. His palm is rough and warm as it skims my torso. My gaze snaps down, transfixed, as he moves his hand lower and unfastens the button of my breeches.

My heart is hammering against my chest. It is almost deafening in my ears.

I want his hand there. I ache for it. There is heat between my legs, throbbing and wet, and it is almost unbearable.

And it is not as if he hasn't touched me there before.

Yet it feels different this time. Perhaps because it means something. It symbolizes that I am truly leaving the past behind. It solidifies the truth, and the choice I made so many nights ago.

I choose him.

Or perhaps it is because before, when we were in his bed, he was only willing to give to me. This time, he will take from me, too.

I have not done this before. What if I disappoint him?

Callum stills. He removes his hands from the fastening of my breeches, and flattens his palm on my bare torso.

"You don't need to fear me," he says, softly.

"I'm not afraid. I'm—" I exhale, realizing there is no use in trying to hide my emotions from him. "You can hear my heartbeat, can't you?"

"Aye." He lets out a breathy laugh. "I can."

"I'm sorry—"

"Turn around."

I shuffle, the furs soft beneath my knees, and face him. He shifts to accommodate me between his thighs. He looks so huge and strong in the small space, his head almost brushing the fabric ceiling of the tent. His expression is soft.

"Give me your hand," he says.

He brushes his lips against my knuckles, then presses my hand against his chest. His heartbeat thumps quickly, agitatedly, against my palm.

My eyes snap up to his. "You're afraid?"

"I told you, you're a fearsome creature."

When I narrow my eyes, he grins.

"No. I'm not afraid. I am. . ." He drags his teeth over his bottom lip. "I am excited. Excited that I have you alone. But I'm nervous, too. I'm nervous that I will not please you. I'm nervous you will not share your emotions with me, and I will push you too hard. I'm nervous that I will scare you away." He inclines his head at me. "Now it's your turn. Tell me what it is that you fear."

My pulse beats faster.

I am not used to sharing my emotions with anyone. I'm not used to people caring what I think, or what I want, or what I feel. Yet this evening, I have already shared more than I have before in my life.

Callum lets the silence extend, stroking my knuckles with his thumb, his heart thumping beneath my fingers. The air in the tent is hot. Too hot. Stifling.

I swallow.

"I am scared," I admit. "It is not because I fear you. I do not. It's just. . ." I glance away, not quite able to meet his eye. "I have not done this before. I do not know. . . how to do it. I do not know what to. . . what to expect, or what is expected from me. It may not. . ." My cheeks flame. "It may not be very good for you."

I expect him to laugh at me, but instead he raises my chin.

"I will not hide from you that I want you," he says. "I've wanted you since the moment I first set eyes on you. I told myself I took you from the Borderlands because I needed you for the Heart of the Moon, but I think even then, I knew the truth. I couldn't bear the thought of leaving you there. And I wanted you. Goddess, I wanted you. I've been like a lovesick pup since that moment. I think about you all the time. I want to make you smile, and make you happy, and to impress you." He lets out a half-laugh. "I don't usually make a habit of wearing breeches. I wore them because I thought you might like me in them."

His eyes darken. "And, aye, I want to lose myself in you, too. I want to feel your warmth and your heat. I want to take my pleasure from you."

His heart thumps quickly beneath my fingers, despite the stillness of his body.

"But I do not expect anything from you. Do not think that for a minute. And don't apologize, nor think you could ever disappoint me. We will only do what you want, Aurora. We will take this only as far as you wish to take it. There is no rush."

He smiles, and the pressure bearing down on me lifts. Yet the air in this tent does not feel any easier to breathe. It feels hot and thick and static.

"It's just you and me now. We have all the time in the world." He cups my face in his hand. "Tell me, what do you want, Princess? If you only want to lie down and go to sleep in my arms, I will still think myself the luckiest wolf in the Northlands."

Warmth swells inside me.

What do I want? I have asked myself this question many times since I came to the Kingdom of Wolves. It was a question I never dared ask myself before I left with Callum.

And for the first time, it seems, I have an answer.

I want him. This. Us.

Still, I am lost. Inexperienced. Out of my depth.

"I do not want to go to sleep," I tell him and a slow grins spreads across his face. "But... well... I do not know... specifically." My cheeks feel hot.

He inclines his head gently, as if he understands. "How about I tell you what I want? And you can tell me whether or not you find it agreeable."

I swallow, and incline my head.

"Good," he says. "I want you to take off your shirt so I can see you."

His eyes glint as he waits to see if I will do it.

I pull my hand away from his chest.

The smile dies from his lips as, slowly, I unfasten the buttons. His eyes track my every movement as I part the material, then shrug the shirt off my shoulders.

He makes a low sound in his throat, almost a growl. My breasts feel heavy, swollen, and my nipples harden at the approval that ripples from him in waves.

I expect him to touch me—I want him to touch me—but his arms remain at his sides. His biceps strain against his sleeves as if he's restraining himself.

"Good." He nods, and his voice is gruff. "Now, your breeches too. I want to see all of you."

My breathing quickens, but I shift back. I take off my boots. I touch the already-open fastening of my breeches. He inclines his head.

I pull down my breeches and underwear, and shuffle out of them.

The wolf flickers behind his eyes. He swallows, his jawline hardening.

"Come here," he says.

I move closer.

One of his hands cups my hip. His other moves to the back of my neck, his thumb stroking my cheek. "Now, I want you to kiss me."

I lean forward, and brush my lips against his. He groans softly, before claiming my mouth with his.

His hand slides into my hair, his tongue moving in deep hot strokes against mine. His kisses are dominant. Powerful. Hungry. It is as if whatever control he has been keeping over himself is slipping, and the beast inside him has been set free. And I want it. I crave it.

I match his wildness with my own, wrapping my arms around his neck, pulling his face closer. He groans, and my body melts into his. A jolt of pleasure surges through me as my nipples brush against his shirt. His hand moves lower down, cupping my bum and squeezing. I whimper.

He pulls back.

Despite my vulnerability, a thrill courses through me at the way he is looking at me. As though I am the only thing in the world. As though he wants to devour me.

He is holding back, his chest rising and falling deeply, his muscles tense.

I almost whimper.

I may be naked, but the alpha of Highfell is on his knees before me—waiting for me to give him permission.

"What do you want me to do next?" I ask, my voice breathy.

His jaw tightens. "I want you to lie down, and spread your legs for me."

I breathe in sharply at the impropriety of what he's asking me to do. A surge of heat floods me and makes it hard to think straight. My core throbs, aches.

I shuffle backward. I lie down on the furs and rugs, and rest my head on one of the cushions. All I can hear is my heart pounding in my ears.

Tentatively, I spread my legs.

A low sound scrapes against his throat as he curses under his breath.

He shifts closer, and pushes my knees further apart to spread me even wider for him. The wolf is dominant in his eyes as he stares at the place between my legs that aches and throbs with need. My cheeks flame, yet beyond the shame of letting him look at the most intimate part of me, I feel powerful.

He seems completely enthralled.

"Fuck. You're so beautiful." His eyes travel up my body. His eyelids seem heavy, and his breathing is fast. "Do you want to know what I want you to do for me next?"

I nod, breathless, sure that whatever it is, I will give it to him. I will give anything to keep him looking at me in this way. Anything that might ease this throbbing ache inside me.

The corner of his lip quirks. "I want you to come in my mouth, against my tongue, as I taste you."

I blush deeply, heat surging through my body.

"Do you think you can do that for me?" he asks.

"Yes," I whisper.

Chapter Fifty-Two

Callum smiles.

His rough hands slide down my inner thighs, holding me open. Keeping his gaze on mine, he dips his mouth to my most intimate place, and drags his tongue along my center. I gasp, my back arching from the pile of rugs and furs beneath me.

A low growl rumbles in Callum's chest. "Fuck." He groans against me, causing me to whimper. "This is all I've been able to think about since I had you in my bed. You have no idea how much I'm going to enjoy devouring you."

Then his mouth is on me—hot and wet. He feasts on me. His tongue slides up and down my core hungrily, greedily. As if he cannot get enough of me. He spreads me wider still and groans. I cry out, my fingers curling in the furs.

"Callum!" I gasp.

I grow more feral with each lick and suck and growl. I feel like a caged storm that needs to be set free. I rock against his mouth, desperate for more of this feeling. More of him.

A low, throaty sound escapes him and vibrates against my center. "That's it, Princess. Take your pleasure from me."

He slides his hands up my waist and holds me firmly against his mouth as I move my hips. When I cry out, he moves one hand up my chest and plays with my nipple as he continues to stroke my center with his tongue.

It is almost too much to bear. Merely the sight of his big shoulders between my spread legs, his mouth moving against me, his eyes primal, is almost enough to push me over the edge.

But then he teases my opening with his tongue, before sliding inside.

I cry out with the surprise of it. My back arches, and my head rolls back. "Goddess!"

And I am lost. I cannot think anymore. I am not a human. Not a princess. I do not know my name, or where I am. I am just this feeling. This pleasure.

I grab his wrist as he palms my breast, holding onto him, stopping myself from floating away completely.

He brings his other hand to my inner thigh. He rubs the wet, sensitive bundle of nerves with his thumb—moving in circles. The sensation of his tongue and his thumb, stimulating different parts of me at the same time, provokes sounds from me I have never made before—animalistic moans as I rock against him.

"Callum. . . I'm going to. . . I feel. . . Goddess!"

He groans, and release crashes through me. I cry out, loudly, my back arching, my body shuddering as ripples of pleasure consume me. Callum continues to lick and suck, as if determined to devour every last drop of me, until finally I still.

He kisses me once more between my legs, then crawls up my body—placing his forearms on either side of my head and caging me within them.

His lips are swollen and wet, and the wolf is behind his eyes as he looks down at me.

I'm breathing fast, and so is he. I'm not sure whether the pounding of my heart is due to the release that crashed over me. Or whether it is nervousness, anticipation, of what might come next.

I want to give him what he just gave me. I want him to come undone.

I pull his face down to mine, and I kiss him. He groans into my mouth, stroking my tongue in the same expert way he moved between my legs. Heat starts to pool again, more so when I realize his hard length is pushing against my thigh through the rough material of his kilt. I hook my ankles around his, melting into his solid body.

"Now, tell me what *you* want, Princess," he murmurs against my lips. "Tell me what you want, and I shall give it to you."

What do I want? I want *him*. All of him.

I push him gently, so that he is kneeling.

With shaking fingers, I undo the buttons of his shirt. I untuck it from his kilt, then slide it off his big shoulders. His breathing deepens as he watches me. He keeps his hands at his sides, as if waiting for permission to touch me more.

I swallow, and look down at his kilt. "I want you to take it off."

He cups my cheek and kisses me gently. "Okay."

He shifts back to unlace and pull off his boots—struggling in the confines of the small space. When it comes to taking off his kilt, he curses again as he tries to maneuver out of it and kicks one of the walls of the tent.

"This isn't very dignified," he says. I giggle, and his grin widens. "Give me a second. I fear I shall ruin the mood."

He ducks out of the tent—letting in a refreshing gust of cool night air through the flap—only to remerge a few seconds later, without any clothes on. My heart catches in my throat as he kneels in front of me again.

I look down at his sculpted torso and strong, muscular arms. How can a male be built this way? I drag my fingers down the ridges of his torso, and he takes a deep, shuddery breath.

I saw him naked once before, in the forest when he shifted from a wolf to a man. I didn't give myself permission to look openly, then. But I do now.

His length is hard. Thick. His arousal obvious.

My insides clench.

I do not know much about the anatomy of men, but I know this part of him will be inside me. And for that reason, it seems large. Larger than I was expecting. My heart beats a little faster, yet heat pools between my legs, and an ache begins to grow.

My fingers twitch. I start to move my hand lower, but he shifts forward and lays me down on the rugs—enveloping me in his searing body heat.

And how strange it is, to have a naked male on top of me. I run my hands over his shoulders, then trace my fingers down the muscles of his back.

"You're beautiful," I tell him.

"I knew you thought I was handsome."

I giggle and his eyes dance with mischief. He kisses me deeply, languidly, his mouth claiming mine and his hand sliding into my hair.

"I want. . ." I murmur against his lips.

"Tell me," he whispers. "Anything. It is yours."

"I want. . ." I take a shaky breath, unused to voicing my desires. "I want you to take your pleasure from me."

He looks down at me, his breath mingling with mine. "Are you sure?"

"Yes."

He takes a deep breath. "You must promise me that if I do something you don't like, if you want to stop, you will tell me."

"Yes." I know he will not do anything to harm me, and I know I will never want him to stop. I try to fight my blush. "Do you take. . . do you take the herbs?"

"Aye," he says, smiling. "No chance of making a pup this time."

I push against his chest, and start to turn around—remembering what I was told about how Wolves like to take their women. Callum gently grabs my arm and pulls me back. "Where are you going?"

"I thought. . . I thought that was how Wolves. . ." My cheeks flame. "I thought that was how you did it."

He smiles, though I am glad he doesn't laugh at me. "Sometimes," he says. "But I want to be face-to-face with you tonight."

Kissing me softly, he guides himself to my entrance.

He holds my gaze slowly as he pushes. He groans as he fills me.

There's a pinch of pain, and I tense. He feels impossibly big. I do not think he fits. My heart is beating fast.

He stills, resting his weight on his forearms on either side of my head. He's breathing hard, his biceps clenched. His expression is strained.

I wonder why he isn't moving, whether he expects me to do something—but then, as he waits, my body starts to adjust to him. He moves slowly, and the pain transcends into something else. Something unfamiliar. Something I want more of. Pressure, and friction, and the feeling of being completely filled.

"Oh," I say softly.

My body relaxes, then tenses again in an entirely different way. My breathing becomes steadier, then faster. I grip onto his shoulders, sinking my fingers into his muscle.

As if sensing the change in me, he pushes fully inside me. A growl builds in his throat as I cry out.

His hand slides into my hair, and he claims my mouth with his as he rolls his hips again. Moaning, I open myself fully for him, hooking my hands around his neck and pulling him closer.

He dips his mouth to my throat, where he kisses and sucks and nibbles.

"I've wanted this for so long." His voice is strained as he murmurs into my ear. "I've wanted *you* for so long."

I slide my hands down to his shoulders, feeling the tension in his muscles. His skin is hot and damp, and I feel the restraint rippling through him.

Even now, he is holding back. Afraid I will break. Afraid he will scare me away.

I grab his face. His jawline is taut and the wolf flickers in his eyes.

"I will not break," I whisper. "Take what you want from me. I want to give it to you."

"Rory—" His voice is strained.

"Take it."

I sink my teeth into his bottom lip—determined to provoke that primal side of him. Determined that he will take what he wants from me, what he needs.

He growls, and he plunges into me. Hard. I cry out.

"*Fuck.*" He curls his fist into the cushion by my head. "*Sorry.*"

"Take it," I growl.

I tilt my hips to take him deeper, desperate for more of him, and slide my hands down his back—urging him further inside.

He groans and I feel his submission. His shoulders relax beneath my fingertips; his expression changes from restrained to hungry. The wolf glows behind his eyes.

"I told you you were a demanding, fearsome creature," he whispers.

"You also told me you would give me what I want."

He thrusts into me, hard and deep. *Goddess!* He groans loudly.

I hook my legs around his waist, curling my ankles around his back, and he takes me deeper still. The change in pressure and friction provokes harsh sounds from the back of my throat. Feral sounds. Sound I did not know I was capable of. I grip onto his shoulders, my fingernails digging into his skin.

"So beautiful," he murmurs. "So beautiful."

Something within him calls to something wild within me. Delicious tension builds as he moves deeper, faster. And I cannot get enough. I kiss his neck. I sink my teeth into his shoulder. I grip him tighter.

Goddess! My head tilts back.

"Look at me, Princess," murmurs Callum.

I bring my eyes back to his. There is something like awe in his, flickering with the wolf that lingers there. He plunges deep inside me, and it pushes me over the edge. Release surges through me and I come completely undone beneath him. I cry out, gripping tightly onto him as my whole body shudders.

His rhythm becomes feverish. His shoulders tense and his cheeks redden. His face is strained for a moment. Then he groans, long and hard, his muscles spasming beneath my fingers as he spills into me. *"Fuck. Aurora. Fuck."*

When he's finally stilled, he crumples down on top of me, dipping his face into the nook between my neck and my shoulder. He's murmuring under his breath in a language I do not understand. I can feel his heartbeat thudding against my chest, beating as quickly and frantically as mine. His weight is almost too much for me to bear, but I cannot bear the thought of him being further away from me, either.

I run my hand over the back of his neck, holding him close.

After a moment, he slides his hand out of my hair, and props himself on his forearms. The feral look is gone from his expression. He looks relaxed. Soft. There's a playful glint in his eyes. He kisses my nose, then my mouth.

He looks down at me and a slow smile spreads across his face.

I return it, an unfamiliar feeling of elation bubbling inside me.

He laughs, and I laugh too. I do not know what is so funny, but we laugh until my cheeks ache, and tears spring into

Callum's eyes. And all the while, he looks at me as though I am the most wonderful thing he has set eyes upon.

"I think we should do that again sometime," I say, stroking his cheek.

"You shouldn't have said that, Princess." He brushes his lips against throat, then my jaw. "I fear we shall never make it to Highfell."

***

Callum wakes me twice in the night.

He takes pleasure from me languidly, sleepily—his body warm and comforting as he draws moans from my lips and groans softly in my ear. When we fall asleep, we are a tangle of limbs. His warmth prevents the need for me to cover myself in the furs and rugs laid on the ground.

I wake first thing in the morning. The sunlight creates streaks of cold light on the tent's surface. The trees whisper outside in the breeze.

My back is flush to Callum's chest, and his arm is slung possessively over my waist. He snores gently in my ear.

I want to stay where I am, but I need to relieve myself, so I try to disentangle myself from him.

He growls once, his eyes still closed.

"Get off me, you brute," I whisper, not bothering to suppress my smile as I remember the first time we were in this position—just after Callum had taken me from Sebastian's castle.

He grunts, and I wriggle free.

Not wanting to dress yet, I pull on Callum's big shirt, letting it hang down to my knees. I crawl out of the tent and relieve myself behind a bush nearby.

When I'm done, I wander onto the shore and look out at the rippling grey waters of the loch.

I shiver; the air is bitingly cold. The wind whips my hair, and the pebbles are cold and hard beneath my bare feet. The sky is grey, and rain might be coming.

Yet I smile.

The water laps the shore near my feet. All I can hear is my own breathing, and the gulls that swoop down to the water to catch fish.

I am happy.

I am safe.

I am *free*.

There's a crunch of pebbles behind me. I do not turn around. I can sense him. Smell him. He hooks an arm around my waist, and nuzzles the back of my neck.

"It's beautiful out here," I say, my breath misting in front of my face.

"Aye. Just wait until we get to Highfell." He nibbles my earlobe. "The mountains and lochs around here are small wee things in comparison."

He slips a hand beneath my shirt and runs his hand along my stomach. I'm aware of his hard length, pressing against my lower back.

"You seem to be missing your clothes," I say.

"Aye. Imagine my horror when I went to get dressed only to find my shirt was gone."

I giggle. "So that is why you came outside completely naked. You were looking for your shirt?"

"Oh, aye. Luckily, I have found the thief." He nips my ear with his teeth and a burst of heat surges through me.

"Aren't you cold?" I ask.

"No." He runs his hand down my stomach, then slides it between my legs. "Aren't you?"

He strokes me, and I moan, pressing my head back against his shoulder. His warmth wraps around me, and his fingers stoke a fire in my center. "No," I whimper.

He rubs slow excruciating circles on the most sensitive part of me, until I cry out with release, my knees buckling.

He throws me over his shoulder. His shirt rides up to my chest, exposing my most intimate parts to the elements.

I squeal. "Callum!"

He chuckles. "What? I'm giving the gulls something to look at." He taps my bum lightly and I squeal again.

While I'm laughing, my legs flailing over his shoulder, he carries me back to the tent.

***

When Callum is done with me, his spirits are higher than I think I've ever seen them. He announces that his appetite is simply too large for bread and cheese this morning, and he will hunt us something proper for breakfast.

After getting dressed, I sit on a rock and wait for him on the shore where we ate last night. I warm my hands by the fire we built before he left. I cannot fight the smile on my face.

I feel so different from the woman I was before I came to the Northlands. I am dirty and unbathed. I am wearing breeches. I can smell Callum on my skin. I am sore, and I do not know how that can be a good feeling, but somehow, it is.

I feel. . . full. Content. Excited for the future. Excited for Highfell.

You're free, the wind seems to whisper. *You're free*.

I hear the crunch of pebbles close by, and I turn—not expecting Callum back so soon.

My stomach drops and I jump to my feet.

Two men in kilts are walking along the shore, fifty meters or so away. One of them looks right at me, and I recognize him. It's Duncan, the male I met when I arrived at the castle. My blood turns to ice. They're James's men.

"Over there!" He points at me. "They're still here! She's over there!"

I turn, and I run.

Heavy footsteps pound after me.

I tear across the shore, then scramble up the rocks by our tent. I run as fast as I can over the sloping land, to the forest ahead where Callum went hunting. The shouts of the men behind me get closer.

"Callum!" I yell.

I run as fast as I can, bumping my shoulders against tree trunks as the forest gets deeper, darker. Thorns snag my shirt, and pine needles crunch beneath my boots.

"Callum!"

I trip over a fallen branch and go flying into the dirt. I scrape my hands and knees on stones and twigs that litter the floor.

Get up, the trees whisper. *Get up*.

I scramble to my feet, but it's too late. Five men enter the clearing.

No. This can't be happening.

I step warily back, and I hit something solid.

A strong arm hooks around my waist, and the familiar scent of the forest at night washes over me. My blood turns to ice. I buck against the male who holds me, but he merely tightens his grip.

He pushes a cloth over my mouth, and I smell something chemical that makes my eyelids droop.

No. No. No.

He dips his mouth to my ear. His tone is as dark and smooth as the shadows that surround us. "You should have run faster, little rabbit."

Then, black.

Chapter Fifty-Three

Drip. Drip. Drip.

I'm cold. There's something hard beneath me. The air smells like mildew. Somewhere, something is dripping.

"You should bathe her before you present her to him. She smells strongly of the Highfell wolf." A deep, unfamiliar male voice rumbles through my fuzzy mind and makes my muscles harden.

"He's territorial. It works in our favor." This voice is familiar. Bored. A dark, smooth caress on my senses.

I force my eyes open, but I remain perfectly still. I do not know what is happening. I do not know where I am. I'm like a rabbit in a trap, trying to avoid attention from predators.

I calm my pulse and take stock of my surroundings.

I'm lying on a cot in the corner of a small, dank dungeon cell. The stone walls are wet, and the air is thick. We're underground, I presume. Through the bars, two men lean against the opposite wall, torchlight dancing over their features as they talk.

One, I have never seen before. He is tall and broad-shouldered. His dreadlocks are tied back from his face to reveal bright brown eyes and a chiseled jaw. He is not dressed like a wolf. He wears black leather breeches and a white shirt, sleeves rolled up to expose tattoos inked on his dark skin.

The other is Blake. His dark clothes make him look at one with the shadows.

A jolt of hate surges through me—so powerful I almost cry out. The worst thing is, I feel betrayed. I shouldn't. I should have known Blake would turn on me. How naïve I have been.

I try to calm my breathing, afraid they will turn their attention to me.

I need to think. I need to get out of here.

"The Highfell wolf is secure, by the way," says the man.

My pulse accelerates. *Callum.*

"Good." Blake adjusts his cuffs. "Did he cause you any trouble?"

"A little. We handled it. He may cause you some trouble when all this is through, though."

"I imagine so. And what news from the continent?"

"My men looked. Couldn't find him."

"And the Snowlands?"

"Cold. Dark. They fear the night that spreads."

"Hm. Interesting."

"Is it?"

Blake shrugs. "Depends on your interests, I suppose."

"We have an eavesdropper, by the way."

My heart stills as I squeeze my eyes shut.

"Oh yes, I know," replies Blake. "She's been awake for a couple of minutes now."

My blood runs cold and I grit my teeth, trying not to shudder.

"I'll leave you to it," says the man. "See you back at the castle once this is all through?"

"Yes. Be careful with him, Jack. I need him alive."

"Right. I'll do my best."

There's the sound of a door opening and shutting. Jack's footsteps fade into nothing.

For a moment, the air is thick with silence.

"There's no use pretending to be asleep, little rabbit." Blake's voice is like silk. "I can hear your heartbeat."

He walks to the barred wall of my cell, his footsteps echoing in the cavernous dark. I open my eyes to glare at him.

"Where's Callum?" My voice is hoarse. I'm not sure if it's the aftermath of whatever Blake drugged me with, or from screaming in the forest.

"The rabbit wakes up in a cage, and her first thought is of the wolf who captured her." He clucks his tongue, eyes dancing in the firelight.

"You are my captor, you idiotic man."

A dimple punctures his cheek. "I suppose I am. Callum is not here, but he is safe. You will be too, if you play along."

I push myself upright. My head pounds, and I put a hand on my forehead, wincing. Feeling Blake assessing my weakness, I quickly force my arms to my sides, and slide my legs off the cot. I straighten my back.

"Play along with what?"

"You'll find out soon enough."

If I felt stronger, I would strangle him through the bars. Blake smirks as though he knows it. It stokes a fire within me so fierce I fear I will combust. If it weren't for the bitingly cold air, perhaps I would.

"My orders are to take you to the Wolf King, now you are awake," he says.

I calm my breathing. I need to be smart. I need to find out where I am, and what his intentions are with me, if I am to escape.

I swallow. "Where are we?"

"An abandoned manor house, close to the Borderlands."

My stomach drops. "Is Sebastian coming for me?"

"Yes."

The temperature in the cell seems to drop even further. "You truly are a snake, you know."

"Oh, come now. It's not so bad. I could have been worse to you."

"You drugged me! You captured Callum! You let us go, then you came after us anyway! You locked me in a cell, and now you're handing me back to Sebastian! You. . . You acted as if you were helping me and forfeited my life anyway! How could you possibly have been worse?"

I trusted you, I don't say. But the words spread through my body like poison.

He leans against the bars, dangling his arms in the gaps between. His gaze lazily travels to some handcuffs hanging from the ceiling in the center of the cell. "I could have bound you in chains."

A feral sound escapes my throat and Blake laughs.

"You're not even a snake," I spit. "You're a coward. I know why you're doing this, you know? You're not as mysterious as you like to think."

"Oh, no? Pray, tell me—why am I doing this?" His eyes glint in the darkness.

"You weren't born into the Kingdom of Wolves, were you? That must be lonely, to be a wolf, but be born among men. How hard it must have been for you. And how pathetic, for you to want so desperately to belong to them that you lie, and scheme, and play with people's lives. Though I suppose handing me to James will gain you the favor you desire."

Blake clucks his tongue. The gesture is almost teasing, but something cold flickers across his face.

"Come now, you're smarter than that. Do you truly think I want to belong to the Wolves? My father was a wolf, and I killed him." He steps back, unbuttons his sleeve, and rolls it up to reveal the jagged white scar on his forearm. "A wolf bit me and activated this curse, and I killed him too. And the wolf gene that has always been a part of me... well... it condemned me to the darkness from the moment I was born."

He smiles coolly. "No, darling, I do not want to belong to the Wolves. I want to rule them."

Darkness emanates from him, twisting with the shadows. For a moment, words evade me.

Then I laugh, shaking my head. "You wish to be the Wolf King?"

"Is that truly so amusing?"

"Amusing? No. Deranged, perhaps."

"Perhaps." He shrugs, pulling his sleeve back down, seemingly unaffected by my derision. "Perhaps not."

"What if I tell James what you've just told me?"

"You won't."

"How can you be so sure?"

"Because if something were to happen to me, what do you think would become of Callum?" He fastens the silver button on his cuff. "What will become of you?"

My soul hardens. Every bone in my body turns to ice. My muscles stiffen, and my fingers dig into the thin mattress that sits on the cot.

Blake pulls a key from the pocket of his breeches, and turns it in the lock. The door screeches open.

He holds out his arm for me to take. "Come. James is expecting us."

My laugh sounds bitter and twisted. "Why on earth would I come with you?"

"Play along with my game, and you might survive. You may even avoid being sent back to the Southlands."

I grit my teeth. "How does giving me to James help you to get what you want?"

He gestures with his head. "Come and find out."

When I make no sign of movement, he exhales. His breath plumes in front of his face.

"When I present you to the king, you will be presented with a choice," he says. "Choose correctly, and you will be safe. You have my word."

"Your word means very little to me, Blake."

He shrugs. "Of course, I could come in there and throw you over my shoulder. I could carry you kicking and screaming to the Wolf King. Is that truly how you wish to present yourself to him when so much is at stake?"

He holds out his hand. I glare at it, then him.

I know he is serious. If he came into this cell, I could hit him and try to run free. But I felt the strength in his body when we danced. I recall Callum telling me that Blake is stronger, more competent, than he seems. Perhaps it would give me some satisfaction, to inflict even the smallest bit of damage onto this snake. But he will win, in the end. And then what?

No. I will not fight him. Not yet. I will bide my time. I will be smart. I will find out what the Wolf King has to say.

Perhaps I can make my own bargain. Perhaps I can play my own game.

I take a deep breath and I rise. I brush some mud from my breeches, watching as it scatters across the stone floor. My legs are shaking, but I raise my head as I cross the cell, ignoring Blake's outstretched arm.

"I hate you," I tell him through gritted teeth as I walk past him into the gloomy corridor.

"Oh, darling, I know." The door to the cell swings shut, and he falls into step beside me.

We walk up some stone steps. They're damp and they glisten in the torchlight. At the top, Blake unlocks another door, then leads me down a tired walkway, the walls lined with fading portraits. There's a murmur of voices in one of the rooms that we pass, and I wonder how many men James has brought with him. If there are not too many, perhaps I can escape them.

I shiver, wishing I had my cloak as we head up a stairway and toward a door at the end of the landing.

Blake taps his knuckles against it, and my stomach clenches when he pushes it open. He stands back to let me enter first.

I'm hit first by a wave of warmth from the fire in the hearth. We appear to be in some kind of drawing room. There is a worn rug on the floorboards, a writing desk by one wall, and a few battered leather armchairs collected around the fireplace. James sits in one of them.

His presence seems to fill the entire room.

It is not just his size, it is the power that radiates from his eyes when they land on mine.

His brown shoulder-length hair is wild, and he is dressed in his red kilt, slightly different to Callum's. The sleeves of his cream shirt are rolled up to his elbows and I notice one of the tattoos on his forearms is a flower—a contrast to his otherwise hard demeanor.

I grit my teeth, and hold my head high. I won't cower before him.

He scratches his jaw, then smiles. "Take a seat."

I sit in the armchair opposite him. Blake crosses the room and leans by the wall beside the window.

"I apologize for how I got you here, Princess." I flinch at him calling me that—even though it is my title. It is what Callum calls me, and it sounds wrong coming from his mouth. "You shouldn't have run from me."

I do not reply. What does he expect me to say?

"I have sent word to Sebastian. He is on his way."

"He won't give you the Heart of the Moon, you know?" I say.

James runs a hand over his mouth. "No. I doubt he will."

I try to remain calm, even though I feel as if there's a tornado in my chest. "So what is the point in all this? Why give me back to him? Why betray your brother?"

His eyebrows raise. "You think *I'm* the one betraying my brother? He turned his back on his people when he stole you from me."

"I am not an object to be stolen. And you haven't answered my question."

He shifts back in his armchair, the leather squeaking beneath him.

"I don't give a shit about the Heart of the Moon. Men win wars, not goddess-blessed relics. If Sebastian brings it, then great. If not, no harm done. What I care about is Sebastian. I want to hurt him. I can use you to do that."

I wish he could not hear my pulse as I stiffen. "You're going to hurt me?"

"Did Callum tell you what happened to our mother?" asks James.

"He said she ran away."

"Aye. She did. I never had the heart to tell him what happened next."

Despite the blazing heat coming from the fire, my blood runs cold. "What?"

"Sebastian got her. I do not know what she endured in the weeks before, but I know what happened on the night of the full moon. My father received confirmation a few days after when a fur coat arrived on our doorstep."

A wave of nausea rolls through me so strongly that I grip the arms of the chair. I know that Sebastian is a monster, but finding out that he tortured Callum's mother is almost too much to bear. What's more, James knew this, and let Callum travel to King's City to look for her anyway.

"You never told Callum." My voice is quiet, almost inaudible.

"I wanted to spare the lad." He grits his teeth, his jaw hardening.

I wonder if he really believes this, or whether keeping this information from Callum was part of his ploy to keep hold of the throne.

"I have done more for him than he will ever appreciate," says James. "And this is how he repays me? By taking you away?"

My pulse accelerates. "Sebastian does not care about me, you know? If you hurt me, it will mean nothing to him."

He stares at me long and hard.

"Perhaps. Perhaps not. So here is where I offer you a choice. The first option is that we go ahead with the trade. Sebastian will come for you, and I will give you to him. He will bring his men, and I will bring mine. And when he gives me whatever piece-of-shit rock he thinks I'm going to believe is the Heart of the Moon, and when I've handed you over, war will break out. I will do whatever it takes to kill him. And perhaps he'll get away with you, or perhaps you'll get caught in the crossfire. Either way, I do not think your chances of survival are very high."

"So, what is the other option?"

"The other option is that I take something from him. Something that will humiliate him. Something that will send a message to all of the Southlands." He leans forward in chair, resting his elbow on the arm. "You're a bonny lass, Aurora. And it's about time I found myself a queen. The other option is you marry me."

Chapter Fifty-Four

It is like I am underwater. The room swims around me. The fire in the hearth, the battered armchairs, and James's face pulse in and out of focus.

He wants me to marry him?

Fire erupts from the pits of my soul. It surges through my body and spills out of my mouth before I can even weigh up my options.

"No," I say.

My pulse calms. The edges of the wooden fireplace, the pattern of the sun on the worn rug, the tattered leather beneath my fingertips, all come back into focus.

James shifts and the chair squeaks beneath his large frame. His jaw hardens, just like Callum's does when he is displeased.

"No?" he says.

"No."

Blake watches from the window and there's a calculated look of disinterest on his face.

"I offer my protection, and the most coveted position for a woman among the Kingdom of Wolves, and you turn me down?" James's voice is soft, but there's a note of anger rippling through it.

"You offer me protection from a danger of your own devising! You know that Callum and I are. . ." I trail off, not sure how to end that sentence.

"You and Callum are what? Married? No. Does your union with him offer any political advantage? No. You've gone off and lived your wee fantasy for a while, but it's time to come back to the real world now, Aurora. Blake told me you were smart. Do not disappoint me."

I grit my teeth, trying to swallow the rising storm. Of course Blake had something to do with this.

I glare at James. "Callum is your brother."

And I think that I am falling in love with him.

"Aye. And he needs to come back and live in the real world, too." He shakes his head, his brown hair brushing his broad shoulders. "Callum cannot offer you anything. I am the king, and I am offering to make you my queen. Do not be a fool, Aurora."

My breathing is fast. Waves of venom ripple through me, tainted by fear. I am like a cornered viper, a wall behind my back and a cage in front of me. This cannot be my fate. I cannot have escaped one marriage, only to be forced into another.

"What do you think Sebastian will do to you when he realizes my brother has had you first?" says James. "It doesn't please me, either. I am willing to overlook it."

My pulse accelerates again. Not only at the thought of what Sebastian might do to me, but also at the thought of what James will expect from his wife if I were to accept his offer. If I marry him, I will have to submit my body to him too.

No. I will not do it.

"I will not marry you. Not now. Not ever."

James's face darkens. "I am the Wolf King."

"You are the Wolf King because Callum allowed you to be."

A flash of pain bursts into my cheek and my head is snapped to the side as James backhands me. My mouth fills with the metallic taste of blood, which sprays across the rug. Cold adrenaline floods my body. The backs of my eyes burn.

I blink hard.

I force my gaze back to James, my cheek burning and strands of hair hanging in front of my eyes. "I will never marry you."

He's settling back in his chair, his face like stone.

Over his shoulder, I notice Blake watching. His expression is nonchalant. Bored, even. I catch a flash of darkness behind his eyes. When he sees me looking, he leans back against the window ledge and moves his gaze to the mountains outside.

I feel another burst of hatred so strong that I fear I will combust.

James whistles, and the door opens behind me.

"Put the princess back in her cell," he says to the two men who enter the room. "And make sure she is not comfortable. She needs some time to reconsider her choice, and to be reminded of my mercy."

My arms are grabbed, and I am pulled to my feet.

"I have made my choice," I hiss, the taste of blood strong. "I will never choose you."

James's gaze moves back to me. "You have until sundown. At which point, I will either ride with you to a chapel just north of here, or I will ride with you to meet with Sebastian. Don't be a fool."

He clicks his fingers in dismissal, turning his gaze to the roaring fire. I struggle against the men to no avail as I'm dragged out into the corridor.

"Blake," says James. "Make sure she makes the right choice. Do whatever is necessary."

"As you wish, Your Majesty." Blake's voice is smooth and calm amid the chaos.

He bows before following us out of the room.

***

My hands are bound above my head. The metal handcuffs that hang from the ceiling bite into my wrists. I'm forced to balance on my tiptoes and the muscles in my arms are screaming.

I'm shivering violently. The damp air seeps through my shirt, and into my bones. Only my cheek is warm, burning, where James hit me. My shaky breaths plume in front of my face, and I stare longingly at the flaming torch through the bars of my cell.

I do not know how long I've been here—alone in the darkness. My stomach growls. It feels like hours since I last ate.

Blake was supposed to make me change my mind, but he did not follow us down into the cell when they strung me up here. That snake has yet to make an appearance. I presume he thinks by leaving me here, in pain and in a place devoid of hope, I will change my mind on my own.

The burst of anger that provokes gives me something tangible to hold on to.

I do not think my story will end happily. Not any longer. But it *will* end on my own terms. I won't be forced into this marriage. I will not bed James.

James will take me to the front line to hand me to Sebastian. And when war breaks out, I will run.

I would rather take my chances. I would rather run wild and free with the wind in my hair, and the grass beneath my feet, than spend tonight as the wife of the brother of the male I think I am in love with. Even if it ends in bloodshed.

And I will not go back to Sebastian.

Footsteps echo in the darkness. I jerk my head upright as Blake walks to the cell door. He's carrying a small flask. His dark clothing is pristine, but his hair is messy like it was the night of the storm. I wonder if he's stressed for some reason. Perhaps he doesn't want to torture me on James's behalf.

"Hello, little rabbit."

My insides harden. I am trapped, vulnerable. Yet I do not want him to see any weakness from me. I turn my head away from him, careful to keep my balance. "I have made my choice."

I keep the corner of my eye on him, though. It is unwise to look away from a predator.

He opens the door to my cell and walks inside.

"Are you afraid?" he asks.

"No," I lie.

He leans back against the barred wall, slipping his arms through the gaps. The air in the cell feels thick, unbreathable. His presence fills the small space, somehow. He tilts his head to the side, the movement almost catlike, as he watches me.

My arms ache. I wobble, off-balance, under his scrutiny.

"Quite the mess you've gotten yourself into," he says.

"*You* got me into this mess. Not me."

"I disagree."

He takes a sip from his flask, and my eyes snap to his throat as he swallows—suddenly aware of how bone-dry my mouth is. He puts the stopper back in, then threads his arm back through the bars of the cell.

"The way I see it," he says, "you could be bathing right now in front of a warm fire. You could have eaten a hearty meal. You could be putting on a pretty dress, and preparing to ride north. Yet here you are."

He looks around the dank cell with distaste.

"Bound and chained. Vulnerable. *Defenseless*." He makes a *tsk*ing sound. "That was your choice, was it not?" His expression darkens. "I've been ordered to make you change your mind."

Cold dread spreads through my body.

I recall the hand-drawn diagrams I found in Blake's medicine books, and the depictions of torture that seemed like they came from experience. His eyes were cold when he told me what he'd done to his father. The Wolves in this kingdom all seem to fear him.

"What are you going to do to me?" I ask—my voice sounds small. I wish it didn't.

The corner of his mouth lifts. "Darling, I'm not going to torture you. You have nothing I need. I'm merely going to implore you to see reason."

I relax slightly, but the tension in the room is thick. "I won't marry him."

"Why not?"

"I will not be a pawn in another game between men."

"You wouldn't be a pawn. You'd be a queen. Is she not the most powerful piece on the board?" His voice is a gentle, seductive caress—as dark as the night sky.

"How does this help you get what you want?"

"Who says that it helps me?" He cocks his head to the side. "Listen, I know what you're thinking. You think that during the fight that breaks out, you'll be able to slip away. You won't. Have you ever seen the front line of a battle? It is not a place many trained warriors walk away from. Let alone little rabbits who have strayed far from their burrows. Even if you *do* manage to break free, James or Sebastian will kill you. You smell of wolf." Blake's nose curls. "Sebastian will not let you live for that. And James would gladly kill you to take something from Sebastian."

He has an ulterior motive, I remind myself. I cannot trust anything he says. "You're telling me this to help me, are you? You don't need me to marry James? The marriage was your idea, was it not?"

He shrugs. "Yes. That was my idea. But whether or not you accept him matters little to me. My game is already in motion."

"What is your game?"

"Play with me, and find out."

I calm my breathing, wondering if I can implore *him* to listen to reason. "If it doesn't matter to you, why not let me go?"

Blake laughs. "I'm not your knight in shining armor, Aurora. I am not here to rescue you. I *have* given you a way out. It's your choice whether or not you take it."

"A way out? You will have me. . . submit myself, my body and soul, to a man I do not want?"

A muscle feathers in his jaw, though his posture remains relaxed against the barred wall of the cell. "He will not harm you."

"Like he didn't harm me upstairs, just hours ago?"

Blake's eyes move to my cheek. "I didn't relish that, believe it or not."

"I don't believe a word you say. Has anything you've told me actually been true?"

"I deceive, often. But I rarely lie. I can recall being untruthful to you only once."

"When?"

He shifts, crossing his ankles as he leans further back. The torchlight on the wall outside the cell flickers across his features. He seems pensive.

"When we first met, I said I recognized you from the palace. I didn't. I hadn't seen you before in my life. I was only in the King's Guard for a couple of years, and I didn't spend much time in the palace. Though I knew from stories that your mother had red hair." He shrugs. "Your identity was an educated guess."

My eyebrows lift. Of all the things he'd said to me that could have been lies, this was the least expected. Partially because I thought he looked familiar when I first set eyes upon him.

"Accept James's offer," he says. "You may not believe me, but I would rather you survive this."

"I will find my own way to survive."

"Very well." He looks at me curiously. "I really wasn't sure which way this would go, you know? I didn't know whether you'd accept his proposal or not. Usually I can figure people out, but not you. On the one hand, you're smart. You've endured a lot, and you know how to survive. Yet you're also mind-numbingly stubborn, proud, and ill-tempered. It has made the outcome of all this harder to predict."

I narrow my eyes. "I'm so sorry to disappoint."

"Oh, darling, I'm not disappointed." He removes the stopped of his flask, and takes another sip. I swallow, my throat aching. "Thirsty?"

"No."

He walks toward me, and my muscles harden as he stops inches away from me.

"Don't be stubborn." He brings the flask to my lips. "Here."

I jerk my head away, wobbling on my tiptoes. I try to get purchase on the chains above my handcuffs, regaining my balance.

"Come, now, what are you—"

I grab the chains and lift my body. I kick wildly at Blake. A surprised laugh escapes his lips as he grabs my legs. I swing and grapple with him. Ice-cold water from his flask spills down both of our chests.

"Stop it!" Blake dodges my foot. "What are you doing? I'm trying to help you!"

The muscles in my arms are taut and screaming. My fingers curl around the chains, even as the handcuffs bite into my skin. I jerk against him, determined to land a kick on him at least once. Preferably between his legs.

He drops the flask as I rear up again, and he grabs me. His fingers tighten beneath my thighs, and he jerks me toward him. My core slams against his hard torso, and my legs wrap around his waist. The laughter dies from his expression.

His face is inches from mine. We're breathing fast. His muscles are taut.

The air in the cell is thick and silent.

And an emotion stronger and uglier than hate surges through my body. It is consuming. Unbearable. Dark and powerful and unfamiliar. I want to tear inside of myself and rip it out.

Blake's jaw hardens. There is no humor, no amusement, in his eyes. Only darkness.

He smells like night, like the most dangerous part of the forest, like dark forbidden places. His warm breath mingles with mine.

His gaze dips to my mouth and he swallows.

"If you kiss me, I will bite off your tongue," I whisper.

He staggers back, dropping my legs, and I grip onto the chains to keep my balance. Something like horror or disgust twists across his face.

Without another word, he turns on his heel. He locks the cell door, then disappears out of the dungeons. He doesn't give me a backward glance.

My shirt is now soaking and I shiver violently. My heartbeat rages. The memory of his grip lingers on my thighs.

I hate him.

I hate him. I hate him. I hate him.

It's all I can think about for hours. My hatred is so strong that it dulls the pain. It stops my body from completely sagging, and keeps me from freezing. And it urges me to survive this, to beat him. I start to form a plan that might get me out of this mess.

When one of the men who brought me down here earlier walks to the cell door, I lift my head to meet his cold stare.

I will not die tonight.

"It's sundown," he says. "I'm to take you to the Wolf King. He awaits your decision."

Chapter Fifty-Five

I am taken to a room on the ground floor of the manor.

It is dark and sparsely furnished. In one corner, there is a bucket filled with water. A white dress is draped over one of the tattered armchairs.

The hearth is unlit and the air is stale and bitingly cold.

"You're to bathe, then dress," says my guard. His voice is gruff and devoid of warmth.

He has a dark beard, severe eyes, and wears the same green kilt that Robert and Magnus wear.

I swallow, calming my racing pulse.

I will get out of this. I will survive.

I survived my mother's illness, and the beatings from the High Priest. I came with Callum to the Northlands in search of my freedom.

I will find it.

But I must pick my moment. I must play this game, and accept my role in it. Until the opportune moment comes for me to make a move.

I nod. "Very well. Wait outside, please."

"Bathe. Now."

Does he really expect me to undress in front of him?

"Are you aware of the choice your king has presented to me?" I ask.

"Aye."

I remember what Blake said to his friend when I awoke in the cell.

He's territorial. It works in our favor. Was he talking about James?

"Then you know he has offered me a betrothal." I raise my chin. "Do you think he will be pleased to find out you have watched his potential future wife undress?"

He clenches his jaw and glares at me. "You have five minutes. And if I can smell the Highfell Wolf on you when I come back, I'll bathe you again myself."

He turns on his heel and walks out of the room, slamming the door behind him.

I release a breath and it plumes in front of me in the darkness.

I rub my sore and aching wrists. The skin is red and raw from the handcuffs.

Untangling the ball of nerves in the pit of my stomach, I scour my surroundings for anything that might be of use. The room is decaying and barren. There is no poker by the fire, no weapons in sight. One of the armchairs is covered with a tattered sheet. There's a layer of dust on the floorboards.

I walk to the window.

Even if it were not fastened shut with bars across it, I would not be able to escape through it.

Outside, against a backdrop of shadowy mountains, Wolves are gathering with their horses. There must be about one hundred of them. Their voices seep through the thin glass, low and excitable. Men preparing for war.

The night sky above them is lit by the moon. Although not full, it is brighter than usual. It is as if the Moon Goddess herself has come forth to watch the events of this evening unfold. It is a good job she is locked away in Night's prison, because surely her favor would fall upon the Wolf King—not the princess of a kingdom that worships the Sun.

I turn away from the freedom that taunts me, and walk to the bucket in the corner. I strip off my damp shirt and breeches.

The water is ice-cold, but the anger burning in my soul keeps me from shuddering as I lather up the soap and wash myself. As I do, I'm aware that I'm washing away all trace of Callum's touch. It fills me with a profound sadness.

How could only a day have passed since I was in his arms, thinking we could be free together? How could I have been so naïve to think I would have a happy ending?

I recall Blake's touch as we grappled in the cell, his grip on my thighs, his mouth close to mine.

I scrub myself harder.

When I'm clean, I shiver as I pat myself dry with the towel by the bucket. I pull on the dress that has been laid out for me.

My muscles harden as I realize it is the long-sleeved white dress I was going to wear to meet the Wolf King for the first time. The one Blake said made me look like a doll. Did he bring this here for me to wear?

It serves both of James's purposes, I suppose. It is the right color for a wedding gown, should I accept his proposal. But it also signals an innocence I no longer possess, should he need to sell me back to Sebastian.

I take a deep breath, and taste dust and decay on the air. I smooth down the front of the dress, then run my fingers through my tangled red hair. I straighten my posture.

I know what I must do.

The door opens, and the guard returns. He reaches for me, but I step back.

"I will not run," I say, meeting his hard glare. "I am ready to meet with your king."

He nods. "Fine."

He leads me out of the room.

We exit the manor through a cold entrance hall, and step out onto the grounds outside where the Wolves are gathering. The wind whips my hair, and ruffles my dress, yet I am not cold. I am too fired up with adrenaline for that.

We weave through the crowd. Swords and daggers glint in the moonlight. My boots sink into the mud. The air smells like horses and male sweat, sweetened by the heather that grows in the surrounding mountains.

A little way ahead of them stands James with a large white horse. Its mane is the color of moonlight. He's looking away from his men, up at the sky.

Not far from him, I spot Blake.

He's dressed all in black, and stands still among the chaos. The wind ruffles his dark hair. His expression is unreadable.

A flash of anger surges through me. I walk to him, and tilt my head.

There is no smirk on his lips. He emanates darkness.

"You will get what is coming to you, Blake." My breath plumes, twisting in the air between us. "Everything that you have, everything that you are, is built on lies and pretense and falsehoods. One day, you will make a wrong move, and it will all crumble around you. One day, you will be your own undoing. I only wish I could be there to see you fall."

He brushes past me and weaves through the crowd toward the manor without so much as a word.

A tornado of rage whirls inside my chest. That is the last interaction we are to have? Does he not have anything to say to me? Is he even coming with us?

"Keep going." The guard pushes me, and I stumble forward toward the Wolf King.

James turns.

All thoughts of Blake dissipate. I gather myself, and stare at the more pressing threat before me. He's dressed for battle with a sword and a dagger on his belt. He's an imposing figure, standing in front of a backdrop of shadowy mountains with the wind stirring his shoulder-length hair.

He arches an eyebrow. "Well?"

I brace myself. "I have not changed my mind. I will not marry you. But I have another option—"

"No. If you will not accept my gracious offer, there is only one other option available." Before I can step back, he scoops me up and hoists me onto the horse.

Panic fizzes inside my chest. "Listen—"

"Quiet." His voice is hard and commanding as he mounts behind me. He hooks an arm around my waist, and my skin crawls.

"Get off me!" I elbow him in the side.

"No." He jerks me closer.

He looks over his shoulder.

"Prepare yourselves, lads," he shouts—and silence falls among the Wolves behind us.

Even I still.

"For centuries, they've stolen our lands," growls James. "They've slaughtered our brothers. They've taken our women. How many of us have lost someone to that Borderlands cunt, Sebastian? He is in our grasp tonight. His woman is in my grasp tonight."

Some of the Wolves jeer and my muscles stiffen.

"And tonight, we take what is ours by right. Brothers, look up at the sky. Look at how the Moon shines for us. Look at how *Ghealach* lights our way and bestows her favor. It is a sign the Borderlands will fall. It is a sign the humans will bleed, and the Kingdom of Wolves will be triumphant. So join me, brothers. Tonight, we take back what is ours! Tonight, we ride to war!" A grin spreads across his face. "Let's go kill some Southerners, shall we?"

Cheers resound through the night, sending chills down my spine.

James jerks the reins of the horse.

Then we're riding through the darkness, the thunder of hooves filling the air.

***

Do not struggle. Gain his trust. Propose your plan.

I repeat the words like a mantra as I grip onto the saddle so tightly my knuckles turn white.

The moon shines bright. It bathes the landscape in a ghostly glow as it blurs past us—lighting up peaks and lochs and wild swaying grass. The streams that flow down the mountains look like molten silver. They remind me of chains and shackles.

I saw this landscape as freedom once. Now it taunts me with what could have been.

I'm running out of time.

"I can help you," I say.

"Quiet." His voice is harsh.

His arm is tight around my waist. His hold is not gentle and protective like Callum's. It is hard and unrelenting. It is the hold of a jailer. A monster. A king.

"I know what you want, and I am offering—"

"I offered you the world, and you threw it in my face. There'll be no more discussion on the matter."

"Are you truly so stubborn?"

"Are you?" he bites back.

The hint of frustration in his tone gives me hope. There must be something behind his hard demeanor.

"I know your enemy better than you do," I implore. "Will you truly not listen to what I have to say? By sunrise, there will not be another chance."

He doesn't ask me to voice my offer, but he doesn't shut me up, either.

"No one needs to die," I say.

"Sebastian needs to die."

"I have no love for Sebastian. I did not want to marry him. I left the Borderlands with Callum to escape him. And I like him even less now I know what he did to your mother."

A growl builds low in his chest.

"Yes. He should die. But your men do not need to die," I say. "You don't need to die. And neither do I. Take me to Sebastian as planned. Hold back your men. Let me go with him. Give me a weapon. Something small. I can get close to him without his guard being raised. If you wish him dead, then I shall kill him myself. You will send some men to retrieve me when it is done, and you will bring me back to Callum."

He lets out a throaty, bitter laugh. "Even if I believed you had it in you to kill him—which I don't—why should I deprive myself of the pleasure of doing it myself?"

"Because lives will be lost if you choose to attack. The lives of your men."

He swallows, and I wonder if he is considering it. But then his grip on the reins tightens. "I will not squander this opportunity. I will be killing Sebastian this night. That's the end of the discussion. You're lucky I do not execute you myself."

"I love him," I say, softly. "I cannot marry you, because I love Callum."

The admission surprises me as it escapes my lips. It is as if it were trapped somewhere deep within my soul. And as it gains freedom, wisping away with a plume of my breath, some of the weight bearing down on my chest lifts.

It is true, I realize. I love him.

I may not know much about love. I may have guarded my heart and kept my emotions locked within me for many years now. But somehow Callum got inside me, and made me feel free. And somewhere along the way, I fell in love with him.

I may never see him again. I may die tonight.

But I die knowing that truth, and knowing the taste of freedom it gave me.

In the distance, there are dots of light puncturing the shadows.

Sebastian's men.

My heart sinks.

James pulls the reins abruptly, and the horse halts. I inhale sharply, wondering why we've stopped.

He whistles, then dismounts and strides over to someone who is on horseback. My eyebrows raise when I realize it is a female soldier. She hands something to him, a strap of some kind, and he walks back toward me.

"Off the horse," he says.

Pulse racing, I slide down. My legs are shaky when my feet hit the earth.

The rest of his men linger on the grassy land behind, waiting for their king's orders to ride onward.

James pulls a knife out of his belt, and I step away—my back hitting the horse's body. The sharp blade glints in the moonlight with the same dangerous intent that glitters in his eyes.

His jaw is clenched, and every muscle in his body is taut as he steps toward me.

He looks angry. Furious. A monster of a man.

A king of Wolves.

My breathing quickens.

He crouches by my feet, pressing one knee into the muddy earth. He hoists up my skirt.

Cold terror seeps through my bones, freezing me in place even though my mind is screaming at me to run, to fight, to do anything but stand here—letting him do whatever he wants with me.

He slips a holster around my thigh and tightens it, before sliding in the knife. The cold weight of it presses against my skin. He releases me, letting the fabric of my skirt cover me once more.

His eyes snap up to mine. They're the same shape as Callum's but darker, and sterner.

"I do this for my brother, not for you. At least I can say I gave you a chance. My men will still attack. If by some means Sebastian gets away with you, if you kill him, I will allow you back into my kingdom."

I swallow, then nod. A small knife is not much against an army. But it is better than nothing. And if I get the chance, I will gladly sink it into Sebastian's heart.

"Thank you," I say.

He inclines his head, then rises to his full height. "Back on the horse."

He hoists me up, then mounts behind me.

We ride onward.

***

It is not long before we stop at the edge of the valley.

The moon bathes the land below in white light, washing the color from the grass, and turning the heather silver. Up here, we are concealed by tall trees that spill down the mountainside—enveloped by shadows and the scent of pine.

I spot torchlight in the valley below. Borderlands men await.

James sends one of his men down there to check Sebastian is among them, and to confirm they have the Heart of the Moon—fake or otherwise.

"How do you know they won't just slaughter you when you ride down?" I say.

"Because I know Sebastian. And I have the daughter of their king."

"I think you overestimate my value."

"Let's hope not." His voice is curt—almost a warning—and signals the end of our conversation.

The rider comes back ten minutes later, and nods at James before re-joining the army.

Nerves twist in my stomach.

"What if he's brought the real Heart of the Moon with him?" I ask.

I hear the menacing smile in James's voice. "Then we shift, and it will turn out to be a very quick battle indeed."

He looks over his shoulder at his men.

"I want ten of you to ride down with me for the exchange. The rest, wait on my signal."

"What's the signal?" calls a male from within the trees.

"Southern screams," says James.

The soldiers laugh and jeer.

"Let's get you back to your betrothed, shall we?" says James.

He digs his heels into the horse and my stomach drops.

We descend into the valley where Sebastian awaits.

Chapter Fifty-Six

Want is a strange thing.

If you feed it, it gets hungrier and it grows. You find yourself wanting more and more and more—your appetite never quite sated. If you starve it, it fades away. It shrivels, and dies, until it's nothing at all.

When I was a young, I wanted things. I wanted to be lady of a grand house, or even a queen. I wanted a husband who loved me. I wanted to help my people.

After my mother died, I just wanted to endure.

Then, one day, I wanted nothing at all.

I lived like that for a long time. My life was passive, meandering, meaningless.

But I am not an empty husk anymore.

I want to get through this. I want to escape. I want the life in Highfell that Callum promised. I want freedom. I want vengeance.

I *want*.

"You will pay for this," I whisper.

"I doubt that very much, Princess," growls James in response.

Princess. The title sounds foul on his tongue.

I look into the endless sky as we ride into the valley. If the stories are true, the Moon herself is a prisoner—sentenced by the Sun, and shackled by Night.

We are not so different, you and I. I send the thought to her on the winds that whip my hair and stir the trees. *Give me strength. Give me courage. Let me prevail.*

And then, there is no more time for prayers.

Sebastian is waiting. He's like a dark specter in the swaying grass and he's flanked by ten of his men. The moonlight paints his skin a sickly white, and reflects off the threads of grey in his dark hair, which is tied at the nape of his neck.

A man on one side of him is holding a box. On his other side is a large man with scars all over his face and neck.

Behind him, there is an army that vastly outnumbers the Northlands Wolves, their silver star sigils glinting in the ghostly light.

James pulls on the reins and we halt. Silence sweeps over the valley. Even the wind stops whispering.

He dismounts from the horse and I take a shuddery breath. Before James can grab me, I jump down myself. I land hard on the grass, the force of the impact juddering up my ankle, but I do not show it on my face.

Whatever my fate, I will face it on my own terms.

I turn away from the Wolf King, and straighten.

Sebastian's lips twist into a thin smile that doesn't meet his eyes.

"My sweet betrothed." His voice is as cold as the Northlands air. "Are you well?"

Nausea rolls through me. The knife James gave me burns into my outer thigh. I make a silent vow that I will use it when I get the chance. I raise my chin. "Yes."

"Thank goodness. I was so worried. Have they defiled you?"

For a moment, I wonder what would happen if I said yes.

I wonder what would happen if I told him, in front of all his men, that just twelve hours ago, I took my pleasure from the brother of the Wolf King. That he spilled inside me, and made me cry out with release. That he held me in his arms, and was going to take me to his home. That I love him. I choose him. I *want* him.

My heartbeat resounds in my ears, daring me to do it.

"No." James's voice is low and gruff behind me.

Sebastian doesn't acknowledge the Wolf King. It is as if he is beneath him. Instead, he looks at the man with scars who stands beside him.

James tenses ever so slightly. I remember what he said about Sebastian having Wolves working for him. With his wild, pale hair, muscles, and scars, I wonder if this male is one of them.

He steps closer, his shadow swallowing me, and sniffs me.

Do it, I will him. *Tell them. Tell Sebastian I cannot be his virgin bride.*

The corner of the male's lip twitches—just for a moment. I almost wonder if I imagined it. He nods.

"The lass retains her innocence," he says.

I frown, wondering why he lied while simultaneously cursing him for it.

"A trade can be made," says James.

Sebastian flicks his wrist.

The man with the box approaches.

"Duncan," says James.

The blond male dismounts and grabs the box. My heart stops, and the wind seems to hold her breath as Duncan opens it.

His eyebrows raise, and he shows the contents to James. There's a white rock within it that seems to absorb the moonlight.

Is it the Heart of the Moon? Or a replica?

I wonder if I will ever know.

James nods, then pushes me forward. I stumble the few paces away from the Northlands Wolves, the long grass snagging on my skirts.

And then I am on the Borderlands side of this war. Sebastian, my betrothed and my new captor, at my side.

Sebastian does not acknowledge me. Nor does he show any indication that he means to leave. James stands just as still.

A strange energy hangs over the valley—taut and dangerous.

"We finally meet," says Sebastian. "*Your Highness.*" His smile is mocking.

"Aye, so we do." James's voice is quiet, yet filled with menace. "And what an honor it is when usually you have your men do your dirty work for you."

"Oh, I thought I'd make an exception for this."

My muscles clench. At the sides of the valley, James's men are readying to charge. Behind me, the air is thick. Violence whispers through the trees. I can smell the promise of war in the scent of male sweat and silver and steel.

"You're a fine specimen, you know," says Sebastian. "You'd do well in our fighting rings."

The wolf flickers in Duncan's eyes at the insult to his king. One of the horses drags her hoof across the earth. Sebastian's men put their hands on their swords.

James merely smiles. "Is that so?"

"Oh yes," says Sebastian.

My gaze flits across the landscape, as skittish as a rabbit among Wolves. I cannot find a route to escape. Blake was right. When the battle begins, I will be consumed within its jaws. Did I make the wrong choice?

No. I could not marry James.

I made my decision, and I will live—or die—by it.

I turn my insides to stone, to steel.

"Better than your mother, at least," says Sebastian.

James's expression darkens.

"No. She was not made for the fighting ring." Sebastian lowers his voice. "Although we got our entertainment from her in other ways."

The valley holds its breath. Hate rises within me, sharp and bitter. I feel sick. How could I ever have agreed to wed this monster?

James lunges at him, only to stagger back with a grunt. His eyes widen. An arrow protrudes from his shoulder. I spin around and an archer on horseback behind me smiles.

The ground shakes as Wolves spill down the hillside to defend their king.

"Put her in the carriage," says Sebastian, flicking a dismissive wrist at me. "Let me finish off this savage."

Panic rises and roils over me in waves. I barely register the man who grabs my arm and pulls me back. Nor James, as he breaks the arrow with a grimace that turns into a smile promising violence.

"You're a dead man, Sebastian." James throws the arrow aside.

"I don't think so."

The valley is loud with the sound of thundering hooves. I'm dragged through the men that are getting ready to fight.

My pulse races.

No.

The wind rages around me, stirring my skirts and stinging my skin. It whispers to me. It stirs the wildness within.

I'm not going to die.

I rip myself out of the man's grip. Something thrums in the air. An energy. Or a song. It flows through my body and pulses through my soul.

Goddess, help me.

I will not be a prisoner again.

The clouds block the moon, and the valley plunges into darkness. I am blind to the surrounding danger, yet I do not fear it. The shadows seem to curl around me. They protect me.

There's a murmur of voices, a skidding of hooves.

Confusion rings in the air.

A soft light draws my eye. Within the box Duncan holds, the white stone glows. I hear a voice on the breeze, soft and female. It is a song, ancient and in a language I do not know. Yet in my heart, I know the tune.

Freedom, it sings.

As if in answer to the song, or perhaps it is in answer to my prayer, the Moon pushes from behind the clouds and floods the valley. It brightens, as blinding as the darkness. Ahead of me, Sebastian's eyebrows knit together, a flash of confusion on his face.

James's eyes widen in surprise, then triumph. His muscles jerk. The crack of bones resounds in the night. And when he lunges forward again, he is not a man.

He is a wolf with brown fur and rippling muscles and sharp teeth. There are markings on his forelegs where his tattoos are inked when he is a man.

The male beside Sebastian shifts and meets James in mid-air, and the two hurtle to the ground, gnashing their jaws. The Borderlands army charges past me, knocking me between them. The rest of James's men have shifted, and an army of bloodthirsty Wolves charge at them.

Sebastian rears back, grabs my arm, and drags me away from the screams.

I let him.

Not because I am scared by the violence. But because the violence has fed something wild and hungry inside me. And now it wants more.

I will do this for Callum. For Callum's mother and all the others Sebastian has harmed.

And I will do it for me.

I will do it for the future I never dared to hope for.

The knife is heavy at my thigh as Sebastian hurls me into a horse-drawn carriage.

"Ride!" he hisses at the driver, before throwing himself in after me.

Chapter Fifty-Seven

The carriage hurtles across the landscape.

We're followed by the sound of howling Wolves, and the roars of battle.

Sebastian settles on the bench in front of me and smooths down his breeches and dark tunic. He's the picture of calm despite what is happening. His sword and daggers hang in his belt—deadly but unused as he leaves his army to fight for him.

He smiles.

"My sweet betrothed, it is time we had a chat, don't you think?"

I straighten and smooth down my dress. I force myself to smile back sweetly, even though violence coats my tongue. "Yes, it is."

"Did you spread your legs for him?" asks Sebastian—as though discussing the weather. "Their *king.*"

"Didn't your wolf confirm I didn't?"

He shrugs. "If he had voiced the truth, I'd have killed you both on the spot. I can't marry you if my people know you've fucked a wolf. And if I can't marry you, you are of no use to me. But I don't believe you've been with those savages for this long, and not been touched by at least one of them. Let us be honest with one another, shall we? Was it their king that you fucked?" He arches an eyebrow. "Or was it the one from my kennels? The one you ran away with?"

My insides harden. He makes a tutting noise, his expression cold.

"Or did you think I didn't know about that?" He smiles, his eyes dark. "You were seen, you know? Running away with him. Which one was it? Or did you open your legs for both of them? No matter. I'll have them both killed before long. And before tonight is through, you'll have my heir inside you and everyone will know you are mine alone."

My blood runs cold, but I refuse to look away. The knife is heavy against my thigh, but I do not know how to reach for it without alerting Sebastian to its existence.

"Yes," Sebastian continues. "Soon, this will all be just a bad memory. And you will learn to conduct yourself better in future as my wife, and lady of the Borderlands. Otherwise you may find yourself meeting the same fate as your mother."

My insides turn to ice. "My mother died of illness."

"No. She was murdered." He laughs coldly. "Oh, didn't you know?"

A battle rages inside me, as vicious as the one I can hear in the distance. The demand for answers fights the demand for blood. "What are you talking about?"

"Your father arranged it. A very. . . particular. . . poison." The bright moonlight that streams through the carriage windows highlights the glee in his expression, and I know he is telling the truth.

I feel as if the world is shattering around me. My father was never kind to my mother. He viewed her as a possession rather than a person—just as he views me. The thought that he killed her makes me feel as if I've swallowed the Northland winds that rattle the carriage. They rage in my chest, and I can barely contain them.

For so many years I desired his approval. I stayed silent and obedient for him. I intended to give him information about the Wolves. I agreed to marry the monster that sits before me.

My mother told me that we always have a choice. But my whole life I have let others control my fate.

Tonight, that changes.

Adrenaline pumps through my body as we rattle along the wild terrain. I embrace it, and let it feed the violent beast that is stirring within me.

"I cannot believe you didn't know," says Sebastian.

If Callum was in this situation, I have no doubt he would end Sebastian in an instant. He would lurch forward and strangle him, sinking a dagger into his heart with ease.

I do not have his strength. Not physically.

I find myself wondering what Blake would do if faced with a larger opponent. He would find another way to defeat him—using his wit and his silken words and his aura of shadows. He somehow rose high in the Kingdom of Wolves, became an alpha, and whispered into the ear of the Wolf King—all while being an outsider.

I'm playing a game, little rabbit. And part of you wants to play too—just to see if you can beat me.

I slip on the mask I wore for many years—the mask of a dutiful princess, an obedient woman, a prize to be won—and I hope it hides the darkness that rises within.

"I am glad you saved me." My voice is sweet as sugar and it makes me feel sick. "I was so afraid."

Sebastian's eyes flit to mine and narrow.

"I was kidnapped, but no one touched me. They said I had to be kept pure so they could trade me for that rock you gave them. And I wouldn't have let them touch me, anyway. I would never let a *wolf* touch me."

I put all my disgust at the man before me into the word.

"Is that so?" says Sebastian. "You didn't let that beastly wolf from the kennels touch you?"

My insides scream. Wildness rattles against a cage in my chest. The thought that a monster such as Sebastian could call Callum beastly sets my insides aflame.

I let my mask cover my rage.

"I would never let him touch me," I say. I lean forward and put my hand on his leg, inwardly flinching at the contact. "Let me prove it to you."

His eyes darken, and something cold and hungry flashes behind them. Whatever beast resides beneath his skin stirs. I see it. I want to cower away from it. A wave of lust ripples from him, and my aura seems to curl in on itself, trying to get away.

I force myself to rise. I close the small space between us, and straddle his lap—my dress rising up my legs, and revulsion rising up my throat.

I will him to keep his eyes on mine, so he does not notice the now-exposed blade strapped to my thigh.

"We are to be man and wife soon," I say softly, sweetly.

His gaze drags down my neck, my collarbone, my breasts—leaving a trail of cold in its wake. He licks his lips. My heartbeat pounds in my ears so hard that if he were a wolf, he would know my deception.

"Sebastian," I whisper.

I remember being in Callum's chambers, a silver letter opener in my hand, his hand rough and warm around mine.

Go for the throat, he told me.

In a sudden movement, I grab the knife. Before I can sink it through his pale flesh, he grabs my wrist. His other hand curls up into my hair, gripping tight.

I shriek—releasing the wildness in my soul—as I struggle against him. I try to push the blade against his neck. My scalp screams as Sebastian pulls my hair, and his fingers tighten around my wrist painfully.

He laughs. The sound is cold and dark, and his eyes flash with danger.

"Grew some teeth while you were with the Wolves, did you?" He bares my throat to him. He bends my wrist, hard, and the knife flies from my hand. "Not to worry. I've tamed many wild creatures in my time. I don't like to be teased, Aurora. Especially not by little sluts like you. How about you show me what else you learned while you were being a whore to that Highfell beast?"

"*Fuck you*," I hiss.

"Get on your knees."

Fear and bile roll over me. The carriage blurs. I'm cold. Frozen.

"I said, get on your—"

Something hurtles into the side of the carriage, and the two of us are flung across the space. My shoulder slams painfully into the side as Sebastian's body crashes into mine. For a moment, we're a tangle of limbs and shattered glass and splintered wood. My head bashes against the ceiling, then the walls, as the carriage rolls.

It shudders to a halt on its side.

Everything is still.

I fight the adrenaline that's making everything seem far away. I taste blood. My shoulder is crushed against one of the windows, and the carriage door is now above us. Long grass and jagged rocks splinter the glass. Sebastian stirs beside me, and there's a crunching sound.

The knife has pierced the wood on the other side of his body. It glints in the moonlight that streams down. My pulse rages.

I lurch for it, shoving my knee into his crotch. He hisses, his eyelids flickering open.

Go for the throat.

In a swift movement, I slide the blade across Sebastian's neck.

His eyes widen. He reaches for the wound as hot, red blood spills between his fingers.

"That is what I learned while being the whore to the Highfell Beast," I snarl.

I expect to see horror on his face. Instead, his lips curve into a smile that mimics the slit across his throat.

"You... stupid... bitch..." he rasps as I lean over him. "Now you'll... never know... the truth. Night... is ... spreading. It will... take you all."

A manic laugh bubbles from his lips with his last breath.

And then his body is still. Empty. Nothing but a grotesque and bloody statue of the monster he once was.

Disbelief crashes over me. I killed him. He's really dead.

Shaking, I shove the door above me, and it flings open. I pull myself out of it, wood splintering my skin. Glass sprinkles off my dress when I stand. I think I am in shock, because everything feels far away. Cold adrenaline pumps through me, even though the danger has passed.

I stagger over the grass, almost tripping over the dismembered wheel of the carriage.

I'm in a clearing. The horses are gone. The man who was driving lies dead on the hill we rolled down. I'm alone.

The moon shines down on me, and the air has never tasted so sweet. It tastes like freedom. It tastes like a future I never dared to imagine. It tastes like hope.

I have just killed someone, and I'm sure I will feel something about that later. And yet, right now, I smile.

Until a growl rumbles through the night behind me.

I spin around.

A large brown wolf with markings on his legs stalks toward me, his muscles rippling with each thud of his paws. He bares his teeth.

I sigh, realizing what caused the carriage to roll over.

"James?" I say softly, soothingly. "It's okay. It's over. I killed him."

His eyes flash with menace. I step back, frowning.

"James, what are you doing? You said. . ."

I sense the danger that emanates from him.

He is bigger, even, than Callum. The ground rumbles with every step he takes.

I do not know if he is angry I have robbed him of his kill, whether he wants to take something from Sebastian even after his death, or whether the wolf within him has taken over and just wants blood.

But his eyes promise death.

I release a half-laugh, almost manic, as hysteria bubbles inside me. I shake my head.

"No. You can't do this. This cannot be the end." My hand curls around the hilt of the bloody knife. "It can't be."

He growls, and I feel it vibrating through my soul.

"*No*."

Yes, he seems to say.

I turn.

I run.

James crashes on top of me and the knife flies out of my grip. I scream as his teeth sink into my waist. He rolls me over, and hot blood pours from my body and paints his mouth crimson.

And I'm on fire. There is nothing but pain. Violence.

He snarls. He opens his jaw, exposing his sharp teeth.

I try to push him off me, but my body is heavy. So heavy. The life is draining out of me.

My vision blurs and I think of my mother. I wonder if I'll see her again in the afterlife.

James is ripped from my body.

I blink as cold air bites into me. I can breathe again, but it hurts. Goddess, it hurts. A wolf snarls. I force my head to the side so I can see.

A large wolf, almost as big as James, is facing his king. His fur is tawny, and I catch the glint of forest-green in his eyes as the moon hits them.

"*Callum*," I rasp.

The two Wolves growl as they circle one another.

Callum attacks.

He is as fierce, and feral, and vicious as I knew he could be. He tears into his brother's throat, hurling him across the clearing as though he is a stuffed toy. James skids to a halt, unearthing grass and creating tracks in the mud.

The two launch through the air. They're a blur of muscle and teeth. I cannot tell who is winning. I can barely see anything at all. Dots dance in front of my eyes and blood pools around me.

James slams Callum to the ground and sinks his teeth into Callum's neck. Callum whimpers and the sound punctures my heart.

No.

The wind stirs around me.

No.

My body is weak, but I push myself up. I grip my side, and I force myself to stand. My legs tremble.

I move toward them and every step feels like I am pushing through syrup. My skin is clammy, and my hair sticks to my face. Blood pumps hot through my fingers.

I can't let him kill Callum. My knees buckle and I fall, hard.

My eyes burn and Callum whines again.

I extend my arm, knowing I cannot reach him. *Goddess, please.*

There's a flash of black fur.

The moon disappears behind the rolling Northlands clouds, plunging the land into darkness. When the black wolf crashes into James, the two of them shift into men and hurtle across the grass.

Callum shifts back too, and stumbles to his feet, his neck already healing. He turns to Blake, who has his hand curled around James's neck. The scars on his muscular back are vivid even in the darkness.

"Get her out of here!" roars Blake. "Now!"

Callum bolts toward me.

He gathers me in his arms. I melt against his chest as I feel his warmth and smell his familiar scent.

I am going to die. But I am glad he is here with me.

Holding me closely, delicately, Callum looks at Blake once more. Confused. Or perhaps he is conflicted about leaving his savior alone with his physically stronger brother.

"Now!" roars Blake.

Callum turns, and he runs.

Chapter Fifty-Eight

The air is thick with the scent of pine and darkness.

Somewhere, an animal is whimpering.

I push through the undergrowth toward it. Thorns snag my clothes, and brambles squish beneath my bare feet. I emerge into a moonlit clearing.

A wolf the color of moonlight lies in the center, but blood tarnishes her fur. She is injured. Her foot is caught in a trap.

She snarls as I approach, but I cannot leave her to die.

"Shh," I whisper. "It's going to be okay."

I prize open the jaws of the trap, my fingers bleeding and slipping on the harsh metal teeth.

The wolf cries. She stumbles free, turning to face me.

For a moment, we stare at one another.

"Don't go," I say. "I need you."

She turns. She flees.

"No!"

I'm plunged into darkness.

"Come back!"

The wind no longer whispers through the trees, and the moon is snuffed out. Shadows creep through the undergrowth, and slither through the grass like snakes.

"Don't leave me!" I scream. "Please!"

I am lost.

I am empty.

I am alone.

The darkness swallows me.

But I hear a voice in the distance.

"Stay with me."

***

"Stay with me, Princess. Please."

Pain crashes through me. I force my eyelids to open but they are heavy.

Everything is blurry. There's something soft beneath me. I scrunch my fingers and feel wet grass.

Callum's face comes into focus.

His eyes are panicked and covered in a watery film. His dirty-blond hair is tangled, and there is blood on his neck and chest.

He's leaning over me, and his hand is pressed into my side.

"Oh, Goddess." His voice breaks. "I'm so sorry, Aurora. I'm so sorry. I never should have left you."

"You're here." My words are weak and they're carried away on the breeze.

"I'm here." A tear rolls down his face. I want to reach for him, to brush it away, but he is too far away. My body is too heavy. He touches my cheek. "I'm here."

I smile.

He makes a sound in his throat, a sob. "You're going to be okay."

And I know then that he thinks I'm going to die.

There's something important I want to tell him, but my brain is fuzzy. I cannot find the words.

My eyelids flicker. The world dulls.

"Stay with me, Princess. You have to fight this. Please—"

Callum stiffens and looks over his shoulder. A second later, someone crashes to their knees beside him.

"Move aside." A sharp male voice cuts through the darkness.

Callum keeps his hand on the bite, but shifts slightly. He takes one of my hands, and his fingers curl tightly around mine as if he can stop me from falling away.

"Can you save her?" Callum's voice is small. Afraid.

Even though I'm so far away right now, I know that his voice should not sound that way. He is strong and certain—a warrior. He does not fear anything.

"I don't know." Blake's face swims into focus.

He is a monstrous vision. His neck and chest are crimson with blood, and there's mud caked in his hair. His expression is serious, and that, too, seems wrong.

Where is the mockery? Where is the smirk on his lips?

I close my eyes.

He taps my cheek. "Look at me."

My eyelids are seared shut. I do not want to look at him, anyway.

"I should have known you were too weak," says Blake. "Or perhaps it is not weakness, perhaps you are simply too ashamed to face me. Do you remember when you slapped me, little rabbit? Back in my chambers? I was on my knees before you. Do you know what I think? I think you were angry with me because you were imagining riding my face. And you liked it."

My eyes flicker open. Shock and irritation ripple through me.

"What the fuck—" snarls Callum.

"Quiet," snaps Blake. "Do you remember when I betrayed you, little rabbit? Had you strung up in the dungeons?"

Callum's growl vibrates through me, but I keep my eyes fixed on Blake's. The stars shimmer in and out of focus above him.

"I used you to get what I wanted. I made you a pawn in my games. I took you away from Callum, and had him locked up, too. I enjoyed seeing you like that, you know? Bound and chained. Defenseless. *Helpless.* I could have done all manner of things to you. All manner of perverse things. Would you have liked that, Aurora?"

Anger flares inside me, hot and wild and putrid. It pushes up my throat like a venomous snake, and a hiss escapes my lips. It hurts. Goddess, it hurts.

I whimper, and my eyelids flicker shut.

"Gods, Aurora!" Blake slams his hand into the ground by my head. I don't even flinch. "Get angry! Get angry with me!"

"That's enough, Blake!" says Callum. "I don't know what you're doing, but find another way. Get some herbs. Stitch her up. Just do it. Fix her!" The plea in his voice breaks my heart.

"She's been bitten, Callum! The only way she survives this is if she stops suppressing it!"

"Suppressing what?"

"Her wolf!" Blake's exasperated voice cuts through the darkness that is settling over me.

Callum falls silent for a moment. "What the fuck are you talking about? She's not a wolf."

"Of course she is, you fool. She's a half-wolf, like me. And James's bite will either force her wolf to fight back, or it'll dominate it and kill her." He slaps my cheek again. "Look at me. I'm not finished with you yet."

I roll my head away, unable to make sense of anything they're saying.

"Aurora! Damn it!" snaps Blake.

He grabs my chin.

Life is spilling out of me. I can feel my soul leaving my body, turning me back into the husk I was for so many years. Darkness fills my chest, and I'm cold. So cold.

Even Callum's hand around mine offers no warmth anymore.

My cheeks are wet, and I wonder if I'm crying, or whether it's blood.

Frantic male voices fill the air but they don't make sense.

"Just do it," Callum snarls.

"Fuck. It's not. . . it's not medicine. It's something I read."

"She's not—"

"*She is a wolf!*"

I try to focus on the men kneeling beside me. I try to focus on what they're talking about. It's something to do with me. Something important.

"What is it?" says Callum, his voice dark.

"I think I can share my. . . life force with her. If she's a wolf."

"I should do it," says Callum.

"No. It has to be. . . I. . . I don't have time to teach you. Just. . . get out of the way."

"Blake—" Callum's voice is low. Warning.

"Get out of the way!" Blake's voice is all wrong. Angry. Feral. Forceful.

He shifts over me and I can almost feel his warmth.

He rests his forearm on one side of my face, putting his hand on my cheek as I try to roll my head away. He pushes his forehead against mine, and he whispers something in a language I do not know. I cannot tell if it's a chant, or a prayer, or a plea. All I know is my pulse is slow, and the air is cold, and my body is draining of life.

And I'm tired. So tired.

If I had the strength to pray, I'd tell the Goddess I'll choose to live differently, if I survive this. I'll live my life fully. I'll dare to hope and dream and *want*. I'll stand up for myself and for others. I'll learn to fight. I'll make my own stories, rather than be the side character in the stories of kings. I'll never be shackled again.

And I'll love. I'll love wholly and unreservedly. I'll love until I am bursting with it.

My breathing slows. The night swims around me, dark and full of shadow. My soul aches. My eyelids close. Someone is shouting. Someone is whispering.

Everything is cold.

And then, silence.

I'm back in that forest, in the cavernous dark.

The branches don't whisper, and the undergrowth is still. There is nothing but thick unrelenting darkness.

And I don't want this.

I want to live.

A wisp of light flits toward me.

I frown as I reach for it.

My eyes jolt open at the same time as Blake's. His lips part, and he exhales.

"Yes." The muscles in his forearm clench. "That's it. Take it."

I grab onto it, whatever it is, and I feel. . . *life*.

It is dark, and smoky, and warm. I pull it toward me, and Blake slips. A low sound scrapes against his throat as he prevents himself from crushing me.

"That's it." He swallows. "Take it."

The scent of the night fills my lungs. I smell dark forests, and musty parchment, and flickering candlelight.

I breathe it in. I pull it closer. Blake's arm shudders, and his fist curls into the earth.

The sound of dripping water echoes in my ears. I taste mildew on the back of my tongue. Thunder rumbles, or perhaps it is the sound building in Blake's chest.

I need it. I want it.

My fingers sink into the wet earth, and I pull harder.

My back arches as the wind builds around us.

I see a glint of silver. A surgical knife. I see shackles, and chains and blood. There is so much blood. Someone, somewhere is screaming. Is it me? Is it someone else?

I don't care. I just want more.

Images flicker before me. There's a woman shouting. A rabbit runs across a dark room. There's the cracking of a whip. The taste of lightning. A thousand stars light an endless sky.

I smell poison, blood, and darkness.

"*Fuck, Aurora.*" Blake is breathing hard, and his eyes are bright.

And I'm walking through a forest.

Or perhaps I am in the church in the King's City. Only, branches have burst through the stained-glass windows. Vines curl around the stone columns, and weeds break the mosaiced floor. It is dark, as if someone has blocked out the sun.

A low growl rumbles through the space and shakes the altar. It is coming from the dark mouth of the crypt, where shadows trickle out like smoke.

My footsteps echo as I walk toward it.

Eyes glint in the darkness.

There is something down there, and it snarls.

"There you are," whispers Blake.

My gaze latches onto his. The sky is vast behind him. The wind ruffles his hair.

More.

Blake hisses through his teeth, and his body shudders. I feel him trying to retreat, and I hook my arm around his neck and pull him down. He makes a low sound in his throat, his muscles tensing beneath my fingers.

"That's enough." Callum's panicked voice sounds far away.

Blake presses his forehead against mine. The wolf is in his eyes.

"That's enough!"

Blake is ripped away from me. I exhale, and my breath twists into the Northlands sky. I am soft. Weightless. I tip my head back into the grass. I feel weak, but whole. Blood no longer pumps out of my body. The pain has faded. I touch my side with a heavy hand, and it's sore but there is no wound.

Callum's face crashes into focus.

"Callum?" I whisper.

"I'm here." He smiles softly, and a tear rolls down his muddy cheek. "I'm here. You're going to be okay."

He scoops me into his arms, and holds me against his chest. I sigh again, his warmth cocooning me.

I'm going to be okay.

"My castle's a few miles from here." Blake's voice sounds odd. He clears his throat. "We'll go there."

Callum looks over my shoulder, and nods. His gaze drops, and his expression darkens. "Get a hold of yourself."

Blake's expression hardens.

"Fuck off, Callum." He stalks across the shadowy landscape. "You've got no fucking idea. . ." His voice is swallowed by the wind.

Callum exhales, then pulls me closer.

"Let's get you somewhere warm," he says, before heading after Blake. "You're safe now."

Chapter Fifty-Nine

I'm warm. Comfortable. There is something soft beneath me. I smell woodsmoke and books.

Male voices drift into my consciousness, but I keep my eyes shut, savoring the safety that cocoons me.

"How did you get away from my brother, anyway?" Callum's voice is quiet, as if he doesn't want to wake me.

"I've been ingesting small doses of wolfsbane for years," says Blake—nonchalant. "If a wolf takes a bite out of me, it ends worse for them."

Callum chuckles. "You're a diabolical wee shite, you know that?"

A smoky wave of amusement washes through me, though I'm not sure where it originates from. It is strange, I suppose, hearing them talk to one another almost as though they are friends.

"So they say," says Blake.

"But you didn't kill him."

"No. It just weakened him enough to knock him out."

"Can I ask you something?" There's no response, and I presume Blake must have shrugged because Callum continues. "The scars on your back. How did you get them?"

"The same way as your pet, I presume."

There's a shift in the air. "How do you know about—"

"Calm down. I saw her in the bath that time, remember?" I hear flames crackling in a hearth, and the wind rattles a window. "It's an old Southlands tradition. If they suspect you have wolf genes, they try to beat the wolf into submission."

Something Blake said earlier ebbs into my mind, but I'm fuzzy with sleep and I can't quite grasp it.

"They did that to her?" Callum's voice is filled with horror.

"It seems like it."

A dark lull spreads through the room, and, whatever they're talking about, I'm not ready to face it yet.

"What about the scars on your front? The one near you hip. . . it looked. . . nasty."

"You know, it's not particularly polite to ask a man about his body," says Blake. "What next? Shall we compare cock size?"

"It's not the size of your cock that concerns me." Callum's tone is pointed, like a sharpened blade.

"Oh, relax. I have no interest in your pet."

"That's not the way it seemed. She was dying, Blake. Is that what does it for you? They say you have dark tastes—"

A ripple of exasperation, of irritation, surges through me and I frown as I push it back. I do not know why I feel this way. I'm warm, and safe, and comfortable.

"Oh yes, you've figured it all out. My origin story. That's why I became a healer. Sick people turn me on so much." Blake's tone is dripping with sarcasm. "I don't know why they say those things about me. If I wanted Aurora, you'd know about it."

"Hm. Can I ask you something else?"

Blake exhales. "What?"

"My father let you into his inner circle because you healed him."

"Yes."

"You were the one who made him sick in the first place, right? I've thought about it a lot over the past couple of years. I can't think of how else it could have happened."

"What? Poison a king just so I could heal him and gain his favor? Does that sound like something I'd do?"

There's a weighted silence, but then Callum huffs a laugh. "Aye. I thought as much. You really are a piece of work, Blake."

"Thank you." I hear the smile in his voice. I *feel* it.

"It's not a compliment," replies Callum—and yet, I think that it is.

"Your pet is awake, by the way," says Blake.

Footsteps thud across the room. I open my eyes as Callum crashes to his knees beside the bed. "Rory! Goddess, are you alright?"

His eyes are brimming with wonder, and concern, and relief. No one has ever looked at me like that before, and I smile.

I'm not sure how to answer his question, though. Am I alright? I was captured. I killed a man. I almost died. I *should* have died.

And yet I feel *alive*.

My side throbs a little, but other than that, I feel *good*.

I touch his cheek. "I'm alright." My voice sounds raw and I clear my throat. "Are you?"

A wide smile spreads across his face. "Aye. I'm alright."

I groan as I push myself into a sitting position, resting my head against a wooden headboard. One of his hands moves across my lap, his thumb softly stroking my hip. "Goddess, I was worried about you."

I try to piece together what happened but my memories are distorted. "Where are we?"

The bedchamber is modest. There's a fire crackling in the hearth. The mantelpiece creaks beneath books, small trinkets, and a decanter of whisky. The bed I'm in is small, but comfortable. Night seeps through the window behind me. I'm not sure if I've been asleep for a couple of hours, or an entire day.

Blake sits in one of two armchairs by the door, his legs stretched out and crossed at the ankles.

Both men are now dressed, though Callum's white shirt is ill fitting and it strains against his broad shoulders. Blake has clearly bathed, his face is no longer covered in blood and his hair is wet, while Callum has dirt smeared across his cheek and smells like perspiration.

"We're at Blake's castle," says Callum. "Safe for now."

"How long have I been asleep?"

"Just a few hours."

"You were captured," I say.

"Aye." A flicker of shame crosses his face. "I was. But one of Blake's men set me free. I came as fast as I could." His jaw hardens. "I'm sorry I was too late to spare you from it all. Can you remember? Can you tell me what happened?"

I take a deep breath as I try to sort it all out in my mind. Then I spill everything that took place since I was taken from Callum. When I tell him the choice James gave me, a low growl rumbles in Callum's chest and the wolf flashes behind his eyes. His fist curls into the sheets by my thigh.

"James asked you to marry him?"

"Yes. And Blake persuaded him to present me with that choice."

Callum's head whips around, and Blake raises his hands—though a smile plays on his lips.

"Tattletale." A strange ripple of amusement passes through me, even though I am far from pleased by his response. "I was *trying* to save her life. It's not my fault she was too stubborn to see that."

The lie just slips off his tongue—and I *know* it's a lie. Why do I want to laugh? This isn't funny.

When Callum turns his attention back to me, Blake winks.

I ignore him, and continue with my story. When I get to the part about the Heart of the Moon, and how the Wolves all shifted, I feel Blake's attention on me once more. Callum looks over his shoulder again.

"Sebastian really gave up the Heart of the Moon?"

"Apparently," says Blake. "Perhaps he didn't know what is was."

He doesn't believe that. Neither do I. But what other explanation could there be? The thought that the Moon Goddess answered my prayer is too ridiculous to voice out loud.

"Then what happened?" asks Callum.

I tell him about the carriage ride and my blood turns cold. I reveal the moment when I slid my blade across Sebastian's throat, unsure of what Callum will think of me now I am a killer.

I expect judgement, or perhaps horror. Instead, a proud smile spreads across his lips. I feel dark satisfaction rise within me, too. Though the emotion feels like it belongs to someone else, and it tastes like the outdoors at night.

When I get to the part where James attacked me, Callum stills.

"He's a dead man." Callum's eyes flash. "He's a fucking dead man. I allowed him to be king. I've stood by him for all these years. And this is how he repays me? He tries to take what is dearest to me. He tries to make you *his*. He *hurts you*. No. I will make him wish he hadn't laid a finger on you. I had no designs on the throne, I didn't want to rule, but that all changes tonight. If he wants a war, I shall give him one. I shall gather the outlying clans. I shall *end* him. And I shall take the throne for myself."

A surge of triumph floods through me, so strong I gasp. A strange, smoky darkness twists inside my chest—unwelcome, but familiar. A laugh spills from my lips, though I'm not sure where it's coming from.

Callum's brow furrows. "Princess? What is it?"

"I. . . I frown. "I don't know. Sorry. I. . . what were you—?"

Blake is watching me. And I. . . I *feel* it. I feel his amusement as strongly as I feel my own confusion.

I recall the moment when I was dying. He offered me something and I took it. I *felt* him then, too. Dark, and smoky, and scented like the forest. He filled me. He was inside me. He gave me light. And I saw things. Felt things. Flickers of memories that weren't mine.

Dread seeps through my bones.

"What have you done?" My words are quiet and filled with horror.

Callum's eyebrows knit together as he turns to look at Blake.

"Ah, yes, about that. . ." Blake straightens the cuffs of his black shirt. "I shared my life force with you to save you. Only, it appears there may be a slight. . . consequence. . ."

"What consequence?" I hiss.

Blake runs a hand over his jaw. "It seems to have created a. . . bond. . . of sorts, between us."

He shrugs as though his words are meaningless but they slam into me so forcefully I physically jerk back.

"What do you mean?"

"I can feel what you feel. You can feel what I feel. It's not a big deal."

"*Not a big deal?*"

My blood turns cold, while Callum's entire body hardens.

Before I can do it myself, Callum crosses the room, grabs Blake by his collar, and slams him into the closed door. "You piece of—"

Pain surges through me and I cry out.

Blake arches an eyebrow.

"Did you not hear what I just said?" he asks. "If you hurt me, you hurt her. If you kill me, she dies. And if your brother gets hold of me—then any pain he inflicts upon me will also be inflicted upon Aurora, too. So, if I were you, I'd focus your aggression on him. Because I stuck my neck out for the both of you, and you'd better believe James is going to come after me for it."

Callum relaxes his hold on Blake's neck, though his shoulders are still hard.

Blake sighs. "Do you think I wanted this? I'm a private person, in case you hadn't noticed."

The two stare at one another for a long moment, before Callum lets him go. "You'd better find a way to break this. . . connection."

Though Blake is acting sincere, I can taste the smoky amusement on the back of my tongue. "Believe me, this pains me more than it does you," says Blake.

He smirks.

"I hate you," I say.

"Oh, believe me, I know."

Blake smooths down his shirt as Callum comes to sit down on the bed beside me, his jaw tense.

"In the meantime, you're both welcome to stay at my castle," says Blake. "I'll help you recruit the outlying clans before you challenge James for the throne. You won't be able to take the throne without their support."

"You'll help?" Callum's eyebrows raise in surprise.

I watch Blake. Even if I couldn't *feel* the dark waves of smugness coming off him, I'd know he was plotting something.

"What's in this for you, Blake?" I ask.

"I'd prefer Callum as king. And I'm better at politics than he is. He doesn't know how to play the game."

The ghosts of our previous conversations curl around us. For a moment, I wish I could read his thoughts as well as his feelings.

He turns and opens the door. "I'll see if any word has come back from my scouts. James is probably licking his wounds right now, but it doesn't hurt to be vigilant. We'll start recruiting the outlying clans tomorrow."

"Aye. Okay. You're an obnoxious prick, Blake. But you saved Rory. I'm thankful for that."

Blake glances at me, and a strange feeling I cannot quite place washes over me. He shrugs, and strides out into the hallway.

Callum sighs. "Budge over," he says, knocking me gently with his hip.

He slides his legs onto the bed beside me, pulling me into his arms. "I'm sorry I left you. I won't do it again."

I breathe him in, and soften against his solid body. "I don't want to be powerless again. I want to learn to fight. To defend myself."

"Aye?" I hear pride in his voice again. "You did a good job, as far as I'm concerned. But I shall teach you."

"Good."

I stiffen as I remember the conversation Callum and Blake had while I was dying.

"Am I a wolf?"

"It. . . er. . . it seems that may be the case." He chews his bottom lip. "Blake thinks your mother was a wolf. The way she died. . . he thinks she was poisoned with wolfsbane. He thinks *you* were poisoned with it, too, for a while."

My soul freezes and ice spreads through my veins. "Sebastian said my father murdered her."

Callum exhales, his expression gentle. "Aye. That was the conclusion Blake came to, too. I'm sorry, Princess."

I shake my head, trying to process it all. Until fear dowses the anger. "What does that mean? Will I shift at the next full moon?"

"I don't know, Princess. James's bite could have activated the wolf inside you. What Blake did might have stopped it. I don't know. If you do shift, I'll be right there beside you." His arm tightens around my shoulder. "There's nothing to fear. I swear it."

My head sinks into the crook of his shoulder, and he pulls me down onto the mattress, stroking my hair. I sigh.

"You're going to challenge James for the throne?" I ask.

He hesitates. "I know I said I'd take you to Highfell—"

"No," I say, my muscles hardening. "Let's take his throne. I have just as much cause for revenge as you. I want to make him pay."

Callum grins, then brushes his lips against mine. "My wild and fearsome creature," he mumbles against my mouth.

"My wolf," I say as I kiss him back.

***

Something wakes me. Perhaps it is the dull throbbing in my side where James bit me. Or perhaps it is Callum's absence. I feel it instantly. There is a lack of warmth. Of comfort. Of safety. Instead, a darker aura pulses against my senses.

I jerk upright in the covers. Wincing, I press the spot where James bit me.

The room is dark, though the dying embers glow red in the hearth, and a couple of candles flicker on the mantelpiece.

Blake freezes beside the bed, halfway through the motion of placing something on my bedside table.

"I didn't mean to wake you," he says.

"What are you doing here?"

"Tea." He places a chipped cup on the bedside table. "For the pain."

I eye him warily as he straightens. I try to sense the joke, the deceit, but I feel only sincerity. I take the cup and bring it to my lips, smelling willow bark.

"I can feel it, you know," he says. "The pain."

I place the cup back down. "Good."

"Are you truly so stubborn?"

When I merely stare at him, he sighs.

"Very well. I've experienced worse."

He steps back and leans against the fireplace.

"Callum is getting his people out of Castle Madadh-allaidh," he says. "He's worried James will know we're planning something and go after Fiona and Ryan."

"Why did you do it?"

He picks up the decanter on the fireplace, and pours a dram of whisky. "Save you?"

"Yes. No. All of it. How does helping Callum get you what you want? Why capture me and plot against Callum only to save us both? It doesn't make sense." My brow furrows. "You planned all this, didn't you?" I say.

I stretch my mind back to earlier. I'd felt Blake's triumph when Callum said he was going to take the throne.

"You wanted Callum to challenge James all along, didn't you?" I say. "Is that why you wanted James to propose to me? He was going to send me back to Sebastian, anyway. That would have been enough to make Callum fight."

Blake shrugs, swirling his glass. "If James had sent you back to Sebastian, Callum would have torn the world apart to get you back. But he would have understood, deep down, why James had done it. If he'd married you, though. . . If James had taken what Callum believed to be his. . . no, Callum would never forgive him for that."

I shake my head. "Why? Why do you want Callum to be the next Wolf King? And why would you. . . bond our lives together like this? How does this get you what you want?"

My soul hardens, and I feel the shadowy caress of his darkness twisting around it as something occurs to me. Back in the dungeons, Blake told me he wanted to rule the Wolves.

"Because now Callum can't kill you," I whisper in horror. "You'll gather support among the outlying clans while you're pretending to support Callum. And once Callum gets rid of James for you—once he takes the throne—you'll challenge him. Callum will forfeit. He'll have to. Because you bonded our lives together. He can't hurt you without hurting me. That's what this is, isn't it? That's what this has all been about."

And despite the outrage that rises like bile within me, triumph ripples through me too. Because now I know his game, I can play to beat him.

Blake's eyes glint in the dying embers, and I know he feels the challenge that radiates from me. I know he *welcomes* it.

He raises his glass, and a slow smile spreads across his lips.

"Long live the king," he says.

Author Note

Thank you so much for taking a chance on this book and coming on this journey with Aurora, Callum, and Blake. I can't wait for you to see what is in store for them in book 2!

Make sure you're following me on Instagram (@LaurenPalphreyman), Facebook (@LEPalphreyman) or TikTok (@LEPalphreyman) for updates and teasers! You can also visit my website www.LaurenPalphreyman.com to find out more.

Lastly, If you enjoyed this book, I would be forever grateful if you'd consider leaving a rating or review on Amazon or Goodreads. Reviews are really helpful to authors as they help get books out in front of new readers!

Hope to see you again for book 2!

Love,

Lauren

Acknowledgements

Thank you to everyone who read The Wolf King in its early stages. Your encouragement kept me going, and your feedback helped shape the story.

Thank you to Rachel Rowlands for all your hard work on the copy edits.

Thank you to Damonza.com for the amazing cover. I love it.

Thank you to Jamie for listening to my constant chatter about hot alpha werewolves!

And lastly, thank you to you. Thank you for taking a chance on this book and coming on this journey with Aurora, Callum, and Blake. I can't wait for you to see what is in store for them in book 2! Make sure you're following me on Instagram (@LaurenPalphreyman), Facebook (@LEPalphreyman) or TikTok (@LEPalphreyman) for updates and teasers!

You can also visit my website www.LaurenPalphreyman.com to find out more.

About the Author

Lauren Palphreyman is an author based in London. She writes books full of romance and fantasy. Her serial fiction has garnered over 70 million views. Her other books, Cupid's Match, and Devils Inc., are out now.

Connect with Lauren by following her on Instagram (@LaurenPalphreyman), TikTok (@LEPalphreyman), or Facebook (@LEPalphreyman). Or visit her website: www.LaurenPalphreyman.com.

Also by Lauren Palphreyman

Devils Inc.

The awkward moment when you exchange your soul for free Wi-Fi. . .

When Rachel accidentally signs away her soul to the Devil, she must join forces with a snarky Angel and a morally grey Bad Omen to stop the Apocalypse. Perfect for fans of Good Omens, Lucifer, and Supernatural.

Cupid's Match

He's mythologically hot, a little bit wicked, almost 100% immortal. And he'll hit you right in the heart . . .

Mythological mayhem ensues when Cupid comes to Lila's high school looking for his match. Perfect for fans of The Vampire Diaries